THE
SCOURGE
OF
GOD

THE
SCOURGE
OF
GOD

WILLIAM DIETRICH

HarperCollins*Publishers*

HarperCollins books may be purchased for educational, business, or sales promotional use. For information, please write: Special Markets Department, HarperCollins Publishers Inc., 10 East 53rd Street, New York, NY 10022.

FIRST EDITION

Designed by Joseph Rutt
Map by Paul J. Pugliese

Printed on acid-free paper

Library of Congress Cataloging-in-Publication Data
Dietrich, William.
The scourge of God / William Dietrich.—1st ed.
p.   cm
ISBN 0-06-073499-X
1. Rome—History—Germanic Invasions, 3rd–6th centuries—Fiction.
2. Attila, d. 453—Fiction. 3. Huns—Fiction. I. Title.

PS3554.I367S35 2005
813'.54—dc22   2004059656

05 06 07 08 09 ❖/RRD 10 9 8 7 6 5 4 3 2 1

To my mother, and in memory of my father.
They gave me a children's book recounting the Battle of Châlons
and sparked a lifelong curiosity.

DRAMATIS PERSONAE

ROMANS AND FRIENDS

Jonas Alabanda: A young Roman envoy and scribe
Ilana: A captive Roman maiden
Zerco: A dwarf jester who befriends Jonas
Julia: Zerco's wife
Aetius: A Roman general
Valentinian III: Emperor of the Western Roman Empire
Galla Placidia: Valentinian's mother
Honoria: Valentinian's sister
Hyacinth: Honoria's eunuch
Theodosius II: Emperor of the Eastern Roman Empire
Chrysaphius: His eunuch minister
Maximinus: Ambassador to Attila
Bigilas: A translator and conspirator
Rusticius: A translator
Anianus: Bishop and (when it suits him) hermit

THE HUNS

Attila: King of the Huns
Skilla: A Hun warrior who loves Ilana
Edeco: Uncle of Skilla and warlord of Attila

Suecca: Edeco's wife
Eudoxius: A Greek doctor who is an envoy of Attila
Hereka: Attila's first wife
Ellac, Danziq, and Ernak: Attila's sons
Onegesh: A Roman-born lieutenant of Attila

THE GERMANS
Guernna: A captive like Ilana
Theodoric: King of the Visigoths
Berta: Theodoric's daughter
Gaiseric: King of the Vandals
Sangibanus: King of the Alans
Anthus: King of the Franks

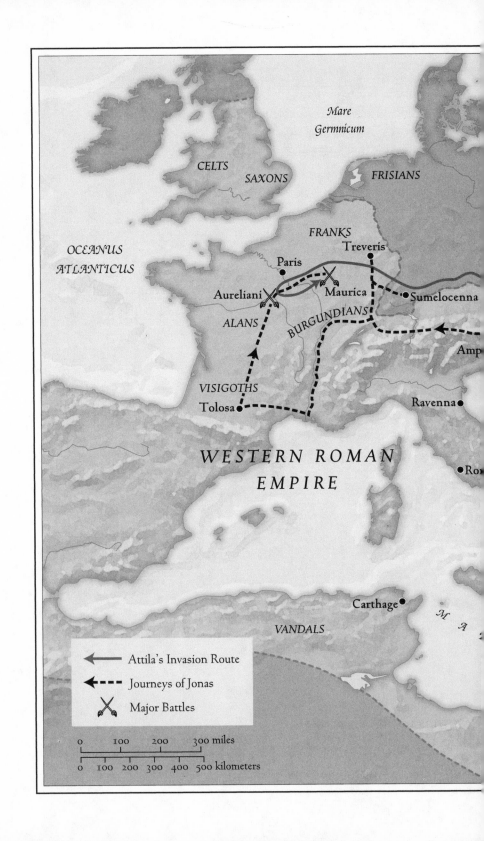

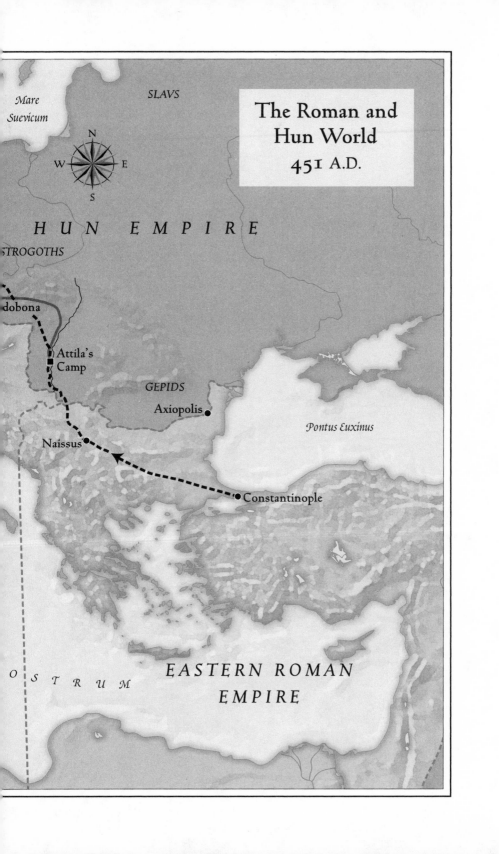

SLAVS

The Roman and
Hun World
451 A.D.

N
W   E
S

HUN   EMPIRE

STROGOTHS

dobona

■ Attila's
  Camp

GEPIDS

Axiopolis

Pontus Euxinus

Naissus

Constantinople

O S T R U M

EASTERN ROMAN
EMPIRE

THE
SCOURGE
OF
GOD

INTRODUCTION

Three hundred and seventy-six years after the birth of Our Savior, the world was still one. Our Roman Empire endured as it had endured for a thousand years, extending from the cold moors of Britannia to the blistering sands of Arabia, and from the headwaters of the Euphrates River to the Atlantic surf of North Africa. Rome's boundaries had been tested countless times by Celt and German, Persian and Scythian. Yet with blood and iron, guile and gold, all invaders had been turned back. It had always been so, and in 376 it seemed it must always be so.

How I wish I had lived in such security!

But I, Jonas Alabanda—historian, diplomat, and reluctant soldier— can only imagine the old Empire's venerable stability the way a sailor's audience imagines a faraway and misty shore. My fate has been to exist in harder times, meeting the great and living more desperately because of it. This book is my story and those I had the fortune and misfortune to observe, but its roots are older. In that year 376, more than half a century before I was born, came the first rumor of the storm that forever changed everything.

In that year, historians recount, came the first rumor of the Huns.

Understand that I am by origin an Easterner, fluent in Greek, conversant with philosophy, and used to the dazzling sun. My home is Constantinople, the city that Constantine the Great founded on the Bosporus in order to ease the administration of our Empire by creating a second capital. At that junction of Europe and Asia, where the Black Sea and Mediterranean join, rose Nova Roma, the strategic site of ancient Byzantium. This division gave Rome two emperors, two Senates, and two cultures: the Latin West and Greek East. But Rome's armies still marched in support of both halves and the Empire's laws were coordinated and unified. The Mediterranean remained a Roman lake; and Roman architecture, coinage, forums, fortresses, and churches could be found from the Nile to the Thames. Christianity eclipsed all other religions, and Latin all other tongues. The world had never before known such a long period of relative peace, stability, and unity.

It never would again.

The Danube is Europe's greatest river, rising at the foot of the Alps and running eastward nearly eighteen hundred miles before emptying into the Black Sea. In 376 its length marked much of the Empire's northern border. That summer, Roman garrisons at posts along the river began to hear reports of war, upheaval, and migration among the barbarian nations. Some new terror unlike any the world had ever seen was putting entire peoples to flight, stories went, each tribe colliding with the one to its west. Fugitives described an ugly, swarthy, stinking people who wore animal skins until they rotted off their backs, who were immune to hunger and thirst but drank the blood of their horses, and who ate raw meat tenderized beneath their saddles. These new invaders arrived as silently as the wind, killed with powerful bows from an unprecedented distance, massacred with swords any who still resisted, and then galloped away before cohesive retaliation could form. They disdained proper shelter, burning all they encountered and living much of the time under the sky. Their cities consisted of felt tents, their highways the trackless steppes. They rolled across the grasslands in sturdy wagons heaped with booty and trailed by slaves, and their tongue was harsh and guttural.

They called themselves the Huns.

Surely this news was exaggerated, our sentries assured each other. Surely fact had become confused by rumor. Rome had long experience

with barbarians and knew that, while individually courageous, such warriors were poor tacticians and worse strategists. Fearsome as enemies,
they were valuable as allies. Had not the terrible Germans become, over
the centuries, a bulwark of the Roman army in the West? Had not the
wild Celts been civilized? Couriers reported to Rome and Constantinople that something unusual seemed to be happening in the lands beyond
the Danube, but its danger was still unclear.

Then rumor turned into a flood of refugees.

A quarter million people from a Germanic nation known as the
Goths appeared on the north bank of the river, seeking asylum from the
marauding Huns. With no way to stop such a migration short of war,
my ancestors reluctantly gave the Goths permission to cross to the
southern shore. Perhaps these newcomers, like so many tribes before
them, could be safely settled and become "federates" of the Empire like
the unruly but calculating Franks: an allied bulwark against the mysterious steppe people.

It was an unrealistic hope, born of expediency. The Goths were
proud and unconquered. We civilized peoples seemed pampered, vacil-
lating, and weak. Romans and Goths soon quarreled. Refugees were sold
dog meat and stole cattle in return. They became plunderers and then
outright invaders. So on August 9, A.D. 378, the Eastern Roman Emperor Valens fought the Goths outside the city of Hadrianopolis, just
one hundred and fifty miles from Constantinople itself. The numbers
were evenly matched and we Romans were confident of victory. But our
cavalry fled; our infantry panicked; and, surrounded by Gothic horsemen, our soldiers were packed so tightly together that they could not
raise arms and shields to fight effectively. Valens and his army were destroyed in the worst Roman military disaster since Hannibal had annihilated the Romans at Cannae, almost six centuries before.

An ominous precedent had been set: The Roman army could be
beaten by barbarians. In fact, the Romans could be beaten by barbarians
who were fleeing even *more* fearsome barbarians.

Worse was soon to come.

The Goths began a pillaging migration across the Empire that would
not stop for decades. Meanwhile, the Huns ravaged the Danube River

valley; and, far to the east, they pillaged Armenia, Cappadocia, and Syria. Whole barbarian nations were uprooted, and some of these migrating tribes stacked up on the Rhine. When that river froze solid on the last day of 406, Vandals, Alans, Suevi, and Burgundians swarmed across to fall on Gaul. The barbarians swept south, burning, killing, looting, and raping in an orgy of violence that produced the horrid and fascinating tales my generation was weaned on. A Roman woman was discovered to have cooked and eaten her four children, one by one, explaining to authorities that she hoped each sacrifice would save the others. Her neighbors stoned her to death.

The invaders crossed the Pyrenees to Hispania, and then Gibraltar to Africa. Saint Augustine died while his North African home city of Hippo was under siege. Britannia was cut off, lost to the Empire. The Goths, still seeking a homeland, swept into Italy and in 410 shocked the world by sacking Rome itself. Although they withdrew after just three days of pillage, the sacred city's sense of inviolability had been shattered.

The barbarians began to settle on—and rule—large tracts of our Western Empire. Unable to defeat the invaders, the increasingly desperate Western emperors sought to buy them off, to confine them in specific territories, and to play one barbarian nation against another. The imperial court, unable to guarantee its own safety in Rome, moved first to Milan and then to Ravenna, a Roman navy base on the marshes of the Adriatic Sea. The Visigoths meanwhile occupied southwestern Gaul and Hispania, the Burgundians eastern Gaul, the Alans the valley of the Loire, and the Vandals North Africa. Christian heresies competed as barbarian religion merged with that of the Messiah, leaving a thicket of beliefs. Roads fell into disrepair, crime increased, taxes went unpaid, some of the brightest minds withdrew to monasteries . . . and yet life, under a loose confederation of Roman and barbarian leadership, went on. Constantinople and the East still thrived. New palaces and churches were built in Ravenna. Roman garrisons still soldiered because there was no alternative. How could there be no Rome? The slow collapse of civilization was as unimaginable as it was inescapable.

And still the power of the Hun grew.

What had been mysterious rumor in the fourth century became grim and terrifying reality in the fifth. As the Huns rode into Europe and occupied what came to be called Hunuguri, they melded the barbarian tribes they overcame into a new and ominous empire. Ignorant of industry and disdainful of technology, they relied on enslaved nations, the plunder of raids, extorted tribute, and mercenary pay to sustain their society. Rome, wheezing and in decline, occasionally hired the Huns to subdue other tribes in its territories, trying to buy itself time. The Huns used such pay to attract more allies and increase their power. In 443 and 447, they initiated disastrous raids in the Empire's eastern half that wiped more than one hundred Balkan cities off the map. While the stupendous new triple wall of Constantinople continued to deter assault, we Byzantines found it necessary to pay off the Huns to guarantee a humiliating and precarious truce.

By the middle of the fifth century when I reached adulthood, the Hun empire stretched from Germania's Elbe River to the Caspian Sea and from the Danube northward to the Baltic. Its leader, headquartered in Hunuguri, had become the most powerful monarch in Europe. He could with a word gather a hundred thousand of the most fearsome warriors the world had ever known. He could enlist a hundred thousand more from his conquered tribes. His word was law, he had never known defeat, and his wives and sons trembled in his presence.

His name was Attila.

What follows is his true story and my own, told through the eyes of those I knew well and, where I played a role, my own. I set this down so my children can understand how I come to be writing this in such strange times, on such a tiny island, so far from where I was born, with such an extraordinary wife.

PART ONE

THE EMBASSY
TO ATTILA

I

BROTHER AND SISTER

RAVENNA, A.D. 449

"M" y sister is a wicked woman, bishop, and we are here to save her from herself," the emperor of the Western Roman Empire said.

His name was Valentinian III, and his character was unfortunate evidence of dynastic decay. He was of only middling intelligence, without martial courage and with little interest in governance. Valentinian preferred to spend his time in sport, pleasure, and the company of magicians, courtesans, and whichever senatorial wives he could seduce in order to gain the greater pleasure of humiliating their husbands. He knew his talents did not match those of his ancestors, and his private admission of inferiority produced feelings of resentment and fear. Jealous and spiteful men and women, he believed, were always conspiring against him. So he'd brought the prelate for tonight's execution because he needed the church's approval. Valentinian relied on the beliefs of others in order to believe in himself.

It was important for his sister, Honoria, to recognize that she had no champions in either the secular world or the religious, the emperor had persuaded the bishop. She was rutting with a steward like a base kitchen trollop, and this little surprise was really a gift. "I am saving my sister from a trial as traitor in this world and from damnation in the next."

"No child is beyond salvation, Caesar," Bishop Milo assured. He shared complicity in this rude surprise because he and the girl's wily mother, Galla Placidia, needed money to complete a new church in Ravenna that would help guarantee their own ascent into heaven. Placidia was as embarrassed by her daughter's indiscretion as Valentinian was afraid of it; and support of the emperor's decision would be repaid by a generous donation to the Church from the imperial treasury. God, the bishop believed, worked in mysterious ways. Placidia simply assumed that God's wishes and her own were the same.

The emperor was supposed to be in musty and decaying Rome, conferring with the Senate, receiving ambassadors, and participating in hunts and social gatherings. Instead, he had galloped out four nights ago unannounced, accompanied by a dozen soldiers handpicked by his chamberlain, Heraclius. They would strike at Honoria before her plans ripened. It was the chamberlain's spies who had brought word that the emperor's sister was not just sleeping with her palace steward—a reckless fool named Eugenius—but also was plotting with him to murder her brother and seize power. Was the story true? It was no secret that Honoria considered her brother indolent and stupid and that she believed she could run imperial affairs more ably than he could, on the model of their vigorous mother. Now, the story went, she intended to put her lover on the throne with herself as augusta, or queen. It was all rumor, of course, but rumor that smacked of the truth: The vain Honoria had never liked her sibling. If Valentinian could catch them in bed together it would certainly prove immorality, and perhaps treason as well. In any event, it would be excuse enough to marry her off and be rid of her.

The emperor excused his own romantic conquests as casually as he condemned those of his sister. He was a man and she was a woman and thus her lustfulness, in the eyes of man and God, was more offensive than his.

Valentinian's entourage had crossed the mountainous spine of Italy and now approached the palaces of Ravenna in the dark, pounding down the long causeway to this marshy refuge. While easy to defend from barbarian attack, the new capital always struck Valentinian as a dreamlike place, divorced from the land and yet not quite of the sea. It floated separately from industry or agriculture, and the bureaucracy that had taken refuge there had only a tenuous grip on reality. The water was so shallow and the mud so deep that the wit Apollinaris had claimed the laws of nature were repealed in Ravenna, "where walls fall flat and waters stand, towers float and ships are seated." The one advantage of the new city was that it was nominally safe, and that was no small thing in today's world. Treacheries were everywhere.

The life of the great was a risky one, Valentinian knew. Julius Caesar himself had been assassinated, almost five hundred years before. The gruesome endings of emperors since was a list almost too long to memorize: Claudius poisoned; Nero and Otho both suicides; Caracalla, the murderer of his brother, who was assassinated in turn; Constantine's half brothers and nephews virtually wiped out; Gratian murdered; Valentinian II found mysteriously hanged. Emperors had died in battle, of disease, debauchery, and even of the fumes from newly applied plaster, but most of all from the plottings of those closest. It would have been a shock if his cunning sister had *not* conspired against him. The emperor was more than ready to hear his chamberlain's whisperings of a plot, because he had expected no less since being elevated to the purple at the age of five. He had reached his present age of thirty only by fearful caution, constant suspicion, and necessary ruthlessness. An emperor struck, or was struck down. His astrologers confirmed his fears, leaving him satisfied and them rewarded.

So now the emperor's party dismounted in the shadow of the gate, not wanting the clatter of horses to give warning. They drew long swords but held them tight to their legs to minimize their glint in the night. Cloaked and hooded, they moved toward Honoria's palace like wraiths; Ravenna's streets dark, its canals gleaming dully, and a half-moon teasing behind a moving veil of cloud. As a town of government instead of commerce, the capital always seemed desultory and half deserted.

The emperor's face startled sentries.

"Caesar! We didn't expect—"

"Get out of the way."

Honoria's palace was quiet, the tapestries and curtains bleached of color by the night and the oil lamps guttering. Domes and vaults bore tile mosaics of saints who looked serenely down at the sins below, the air languid with incense and perfume. The emperor's entourage strode down dark marble hallways too swiftly for any challenge; and Honoria's chamber guardian, a huge Nubian named Goar, went down with a grunt from a crossbow bolt fired from twenty paces before he even understood who was approaching. He struck the marble with a meaty thud. A wine boy who startled awake, and who might have cried warning, had his neck snapped like a chicken's. Then the soldiers burst into the princess's quarters, knocking aside tables of honeyed sweets, kicking a cushion into the shallow pool of the bath, and butting open the door of her sleeping chamber.

The couple jerked awake, clutching and crying out behind the gauze of the curtains as a dozen dark shapes surrounded their vast bed. Was this assassination?

"Light," Valentinian ordered.

His men had brought torches, and they turned the scene bright and lurid. The steward, Eugenius, slid away on his backside until he bumped against the headboard, his hands seeking to cover himself. He had the look of a man who has stumbled off a cliff and, in one last moment of crystalline dread, knows there is nothing he can do to save himself. Honoria was crawling toward the other side of the bed, naked except for the silken sheet draped over her, her hip bewitching even in her terror, clawing as if distance from her commoner lover would provide some kind of deniability.

"So it is true," the emperor breathed.

"How dare you break into my bedchamber!"

"We have come to save you, child," the bishop said.

The exposure of his sister strangely excited Valentinian. He'd been insulted by her mockery, but now who looked the fool? She was on humiliating display for a dozen men, her sins apparent to all, her shoulder bare, her hair undone, her breasts dragging on the sheet. The situation gave him heady satisfaction. He glanced back. Goar's prostrate form was just visible in the entry, blood pooling on the marble like a little lake. It was his sister's vanity and ambition that had doomed those around her.

As she had doomed herself! The emperor spied a golden cord holding the drapery around the bed and yanked, pulling it free. The diaphanous shelter dropped to the floor, exposing the couple even more, and then he stepped forward and began flailing with the cord at Honoria's hips and buttocks as she flinched under the sheet, his breath quick and anxious.

"You're rutting with a servant and plotting to elevate him above me!"

She writhed and howled with outrage, pulling the covering away from poor Eugenius in order to wrap herself. "Damn you! I'll tell Mother!"

"Mother told *me* when and where I'd find you!" He took satisfaction in the way that betrayal stung. They had always competed for Placidia's affection. He whipped and whipped, humiliating more than injuring her, until finally he was out of breath and had to stop, panting. Both he and his sister were flushed.

The soldiers dragged the steward out of bed and wrenched his arms behind his back, forcing him to his knees. His manhood was shrunken, and he'd not had time to muster a defense. He looked in beseeching horror toward the princess as if she could save him, but all she had were dreams, not power. She was a woman! And now, in gambling for her affections, Eugenius had doomed himself.

Valentinian turned to study the would-be emperor of Ravenna and Rome. Honoria's lover was handsome, yes, and no doubt intelligent to have risen to palace steward, but a fool to try to climb above his station. Lust had bred opportunity and ambition had encouraged pride, but in the end hers was a pathetic infatuation. "Look at him," Valentinian mocked, "the next Caesar." His gaze shifted downward. "We should cut it off."

Eugenius's voice broke. "Don't harm Honoria. It was I who—"

"Harm Honoria?" Valentinian's laugh was contemptuous. "She's royalty, steward, her bloodline purple, and has no need of a plea from you. She deserves a spanking but will come to no real harm because she's incapable of giving it. See how helpless she is?"

"She never thought of betraying you—"

"Silence!" He slashed with the cord again, this time across the steward's mouth. "Stop worrying about my slut of a sister and start pleading for yourself! Do you think I don't know what you two were planning?"

"Valentinian, stop!" Honoria begged. "It's not what you think. It's not what you've been told. Your advisers and magicians have made you insane."

"Have they? Yet what I expected to find I found—is that not right, bishop?"

"Yours is a brother's duty," Milo said.

"As is this," the emperor said. "Do it."

A big tribune knotted a scarf around Eugenius's neck.

"Please," the woman groaned. "I love him."

"That's why it is necessary."

The tribune pulled, his forearms bulging. Eugenius began to kick, struggling uselessly against the men who held him. Honoria began screaming. His face purpled, his tongue erupted in a vain search for breath, his eyes bulged, his muscles shuddered. Then his look glazed, he slumped; and after several long minutes that made sure he was dead, his body was allowed to fall to the floor.

Honoria was sobbing.

"You have been brought back to God," the bishop soothed.

"Damn all of you to Hell."

The soldiers laughed.

"Sister, I bring you good news," Valentinian said. "Your days of spinsterhood are over. Since you've been unable to find a proper suitor yourself, I've arranged for your marriage to Flavius Bassus Herculanus in Rome."

"Herculanus! He's fat and old! I'll never marry him!" It was as hideous a fate as she could imagine.

"You'll rot in Ravenna until you do."

Honoria refused to marry and Valentinian held to his word to confine her, despite her begging. Her pleas to her mother were ignored. What torture to be locked in her palace! What humiliation to gain release only by marrying a decrepit aristocrat! Her lover's death had killed a part of *her*, she believed; her brother had strangled not just Eugenius but her own pride, her belief in family, and any loyalty to Valentinian. He had strangled her heart! So, early in the following year, when the nights were long and Honoria had entirely despaired of her future, she sent for her eunuch.

Hyacinth had been castrated as a child, placed in a hot bath where his testicles were crushed. It had been cruel, of course, and yet the mutilation that had denied him marriage and fatherhood had allowed him to win a position of trust in the imperial household. The eunuch had often mused on his fate, sometimes relieved that he had been exempted from the physical passions of those around him. If he felt less like a man because he'd been gelded, he suffered less, too, he believed. The pain of emasculation was a distant memory, and his privileged position a daily satisfaction. He could not be perceived as a threat like Eugenius. As a result, eunuchs often lived far longer than those they served.

Hyacinth had become not just Honoria's servant but also her friend and confidant. In the days after Eugenius's execution, his arms had comforted her as she had sobbed uncontrollably, his beardless cheek against hers, murmuring agreement as she stoked the flames of hatred for her brother. The emperor was a beast, his heart a stone, and the prospect of the princess's marriage to an aging senator in tired Rome was as appalling to the eunuch as it was to his mistress.

Now she had summoned him in the night. "Hyacinth, I am sending you away."

He blanched. He could no more survive in the outside world than a domestic pet. "Please, my lady. Yours is the only kindness I have known."

"And sometimes your kindness seems the only that I have. Even my mother, who aspires to sainthood, ignores me until I submit. So we are both prisoners here, dear eunuch, are we not?"

"Until you marry Herculanus."

"And is that not a prison of another sort?"

He sighed. "Perhaps the marriage is a fate you must accept."

Honoria shook her head. She was very beautiful and enjoyed the pleasures of the bed too much to throw her life away on an old patriarch. The reputation of Herculanus was of a man stern, humorless, and cold.

Valentinian's plan to marry her off would snuff out her own life as effectively as he had snuffed out Eugenius's. "Hyacinth, do you recall how my mother, Galla Placidia, was taken by the Visigoths after the sack of Rome and married to their chieftain, Athaulf?"

"Before I was born, princess."

"When Athaulf died, Mother returned to Rome, but in the meantime she had helped civilize the Visigoths. She said once that her few years with them were not too terrible, and I think she has some spicy memories of her first husband. The barbarian men are strong, you know, stronger than the breed we now have in Italy."

"Your mother had many strange travels and adventures before assuring the elevation of your brother."

"She is a woman of the world who sailed with armies, married two men, and looked beyond the palace walls as she now looks to Heaven. She always urged me to do the same."

"All revere the augusta."

Honoria gripped her eunuch's shoulders, her gaze intense. "This is why we must follow her brave example, Hyacinth. There is a barbarian even stronger than the leader of the Visigoths. He is a barbarian stronger than my brother—a barbarian who is the strongest man in the world. You know of whom I speak?"

Now the eunuch felt the slow dawning of dread. "You mean the king of the Huns." Hyacinth's voice was a whisper, as if they were speaking of Satan. The entire world feared Attila and prayed that his plundering eye would fall on some other part of the Empire. Reports said that he looked like a monkey, bathed in blood, and killed anyone who dared stand up to him—except for his wives. He enjoyed, they said, hundreds of wives, each as lovely as he was grotesque.

"I want you to go to Attila, Hyacinth." Honoria's eyes gleamed. Strong women relied not just on their wits but also on their alliances with strong men. The Huns had the most terrifying army in the world, and mere word from their leader would make her brother quail. If Attila asked for her, Valentinian would have to let her go. If Attila forbade her marriage to Herculanus, Valentinian would have to accede. Wouldn't he?

"Go to Attila!" Hyacinth gasped. "My lady, I scarcely go from one end of Ravenna to the other. I'm not a traveler. Nor an ambassador. I'm not even a man."

"I'll give you men as escort. No one will miss *you*. I want you to find your courage and find *him*, because both of our futures depend on it. I want you to explain what has happened to me. Carry my signet ring to him as proof of what you say. Hyacinth, my dearest slave, I want you to ask Attila the Hun to rescue me."

II

THE MAIDEN
OF AXIOPOLIS

"Father, what have you done?"

Seven hundred miles east of Ravenna, where the valley of the Danube broadens as that great river nears the Black Sea, the Hun were finally inside a small Roman colonial city called Axiopolis. Like all such Roman cities, it had initially been laid out in the neat grid pattern originating with the legionary camp, its forums, temples, and governing houses placed like board pieces in their logic. Like all such cities, it had been walled in the third century, when wars of unrest grew. Like all such cities, its pagan temples had become churches in the fourth, after Constantine's conversion to Christianity. And like all such cities it had trembled with unease at each sacking of brethren settlements up the Danube.

Now the Huns were here. Their entry was like the advent of a storm: the sound a rising wail of terror that spread outward from the gates in a siren wave. With the sound came the false dawn of fire, orange and pulsing. In her family's dining room Ilana tried to shut out what she had dreaded so long to hear: oaths and cries, the clatter of unshod horses on stone paving, the desperate grunts and clangs of futile resistance, and the low hiss and rumble of fire. She glimpsed from the corner of her eye the birdlike flash of an arrow winging down the street, having missed its mark and now on its way to another target at random, a hum-ming hornet in stygian gloom. Her neighbors were running as if from the gates of Hell. The apocalypse had finally come.

"I think I have saved us, Ilana," Simon Publius said, his voice's quaver betraying his doubt. The plump merchant had developed a thousand-year-old face in recent weeks, his jowls sagging, his sleep-robbed eyes hollow, his pink skin sweaty and mottled like rancid meat. Now he had bet his family's survival on treason.

"You opened the gates to them, didn't you?"

"They would have broken through anyway."

The street was filling with horsemen shouting in a harsh, ugly tongue. Strangely, she could make out the particular noise of swords cut-ting through the air that sounds like rending fabric and then a deeper thunk when they struck. It was as if all her senses were heightened and she could hear every cry, every whisper, and every prayer. "But we were going to wait for the legions."

"As Marcianopolis waited? Then there would be no mercy, daughter. I have Edeco's promise that by aiding him, some of us will be spared."

There was a shriek and then a gabble of hopeless pleading, making clear that not everyone would be spared. She peeked out. The dark below was filled with fleeing and thrashing forms and the occasional moonlike appearance of a human face, mouth agape in the glare of a torch before it was sucked away. Ilana felt numb. She'd been afraid for so long that it seemed an eternity of fear: frightened for years, really, as hor-rid tales filtered down the river. Then the paralyzing dread when the Huns and their allies finally appeared under a plume of smokelike dust, just two weeks ago. They had surrounded Axiopolis at a gallop and threatened annihilation if the city did not surrender.

No such surrender had come, despite the pleas and urging of some. The inhabitants had the pride of Moesia and the fire of Thrace in their veins, and most wanted to fight. There had been brave Roman resis-tance since: fierce stands; moments of encouraging heroism; and even small, momentary victories. But there had also been a growing hope-lessness as the dead and wounded were carried down off the walls, each day seeming grimmer, each night longer, each rumor wilder, each heartbroken widow and orphaned child adding to the city's fatalism. Incense curled in the churches, prayers echoed up to heaven, priests paraded on the walls, messengers tried to creep away to summon help, and yet no relief arrived. The modest stone walls began to come apart like crumbling cheese. The roofs were pockmarked with fire. Outside, crops were burned and boats destroyed. Inside, doughty old men who had been given spears were picked off the walls because they stood too long, trying to see enemies with aging eyes. So Ilana's mind had taken refuge in dull despair, welcoming an end instead of fearing it. What was so good about this life anyway? She only hoped death would not hurt too much. But now her father, the city's most prominent merchant, had betrayed them.

"They would have killed us all, once they stormed the walls," he said. "This way . . ."

"They're cavalry," she replied numbly. "They lack skill . . ."

"Their mercenaries know sieges and siege engines. I had to do *something*, child."

Child? How long ago *that* seemed! Child? Her great love, Tasio, the man she was to marry, had died on day three, shot through the eye with a Hun arrow and succumbing after four long hours of screaming agony. She had never dreamed the body could leak so much blood so ceaselessly. *Child?* That was a word for blessed ignorance, creatures that still had hope, innocents who might someday have children of their own. Now . . .

"I've hidden some coin. They have promised safe passage. We'll go to Constantinople and find new lives there. Your aunts, the servants . . . his spies promised all of us could go. More will be spared, too, I'm sure. I've saved many lives this night."

She wanted to believe him. She longed to believe in an elder, and in the future. But now there was only an endless furious *now*, that storm wind of screaming, the pattering hail of arrows, and the pitiless grunts of warriors taking what they wished. "Father . . ."

"Come." He jerked her into reluctant action. "We've to meet the chieftain by the Church of Saint Paul. God will protect us, child."

The streets were a surf of churning humanity that their own frightened little group breasted by pushing like a phalanx past groaning bodies, smashed doorways, and lurid flames. They clutched useless things: an ancestral bust, an old wedding chest, a sheaf of accounts from a business now destroyed, a frightened dog. The sacking was anarchic, one home invaded and another passed by, one group of refugees slain and another ignored as its members huddled in the shadows. Here a pagan claimed that Jupiter had saved him, there a Christian rejoiced that Jesus had saved her, and yet people of all faiths were equally butchered. Everything had become random chance, death and life as whimsical as a butterfly's wing. The Huns galloped into sacristies and kitchens without fear of resistance, shooting arrows as if at timid game, and contemptuous of anyone slow enough to be trampled under. The only mercy was that night made impossible the identification of her friends, relatives, shopkeepers, and teachers. Death had become anonymous. The city was being snuffed without names being called out.

When Ilana and her father arrived in the forum, the church was being crammed with citizens seeking miracles from a God who seemed to have forsaken them. A cluster of Huns watched the Romans run inside the sanctuary without interfering, instead conferring on horseback with each other as if commenting on a parade. Occasionally they'd send messengers galloping down the streets with orders, suggesting there was more discipline to the sacking than the young woman had assumed. The fires were growing brighter.

"Edeco!" Simon Publius called, hoarse from the night's shouting. "I bring you my family for protection as we agreed! We are grateful for your mercy. This slaughter is not at all necessary—we will give up whatever you require . . ."

A lieutenant, looking of Greek origin, translated. The Hun chieftain, identifiable by his fine captured Roman lorica, peered down, his features shadowed, his face scarred, his beard thin. "Who are you?"

"The merchant Publius! The one who sent word and opened the gates as your emissary demanded! Of course, we have not seen each other yet. It is I, your ally who asks only to be allowed to go downriver! We'll take ship far away from this place."

The Hun considered as if this were a new idea. His eye fell on Ilana. "Who is she?"

Simon winced as if struck. "My daughter. A harmless girl."

"She is pretty." The young woman had a high and noble carriage, her hair a dark cataract of curls, her eyes almond shaped, her cheekbones high, her ears as fine as alabaster. About to be wed, until the siege came.

"There are many beautiful women in our city. Many, many."

Edeco belched. "Really? The ones I've taken look like cows." His men laughed.

The old merchant sidled in front of his daughter, blocking her as much as possible from view. "If you could give us escort to the river, we'll find a boat."

The chieftain considered a moment, then looked toward the church at the end of the forum. The shadows within seethed with the pack of refugees. More people were pushing to get inside. He spoke something in Hunnish to one of his men, and several trotted their horses to the entrance, as if considering attacking it. The Romans trying to gain entry scattered like mice. Those already inside swung the great oaken doors shut and locked them. The barbarians let them.

"God will reward your mercy, Edeco," Simon tried.

The Hun smirked. "You've talked to him?" He called to his men across the paving, and they dismounted to begin piling furniture and debris against the church doors. The members of Simon's small party began to gasp and murmur in alarm.

"He talks to all who listen," Publius assured earnestly. "Do not turn your ear away."

Edeco had watched enemies pray in desperation to a hundred gods. All had been conquered. Romans and Huns watched the work in silence for a while, the Roman party not daring to move without permission, waiting in suspense for what must come. People in the church, packed too tightly, began to shout and plead as they realized that, having locked themselves in, they couldn't get out.

Edeco finally turned back to the merchant. "I have decided. You can go with the cows, the ugly ones. Your daughter and the pretty ones stay with us."

"No! That was not our agreement. You said—"

"You dare to tell me what *I* said?" His face, swarthy and slanted and puckered with those scars, darkened.

Publius blanched. "No, no, but Ilana must stay with her father. Surely you understand that." His face had a sick sheen and his hands were trembling. "She's my only daughter."

Torches were hurled onto the barricades blocking the church doors and held against the eaves. The wood under the tile, dry and cracked, gulped the flames with greed. They ran in rippling waves toward the peak, and the shouts inside began to turn to screams.

"No. She is pretty."

"For God's sake . . ."

Ilana touched his sleeve in warning, realizing what must happen. "Father, it's all right."

"It is *not* all right, and I'm not about to abandon you to these savages. Are you devils?" he suddenly cried. "Why are you frying people who have turned to God?"

Edeco was irritated at the man's intransigence. "Give her to me, Roman."

"No! No. I mean . . . please . . ." He held up his hand in supplication.

Edeco's sword was out of its scabbard in an instant and whickered to take the hand off. The severed palm flew, bounced, and then skittered against the base of a fountain, its fingers still twitching. It happened too quickly to even elicit a scream. Publius staggered, more shocked than pained, uncertain how to bring things back under control. He looked at his own severed wrist in wonder. Then an arrow hit his breast. And another and another—a score of them thunking into his torso and limbs while he stared in disbelief—and the mounted warriors laughed, drawing and firing almost faster than the eye could see. He sat down heavily, as spiny as an urchin.

"Kill them all," Edeco ordered.

"Not the girl," a young Hun said. He leaned to scoop her up and throw her shrieking across the front of his saddle.

"Let me go to my father!"

He bound her hands. "Do you want to end like them?" he asked in Hunnish.

The rest of Simon's party were shot down as they made for the corners of the forum. Any wounded were chopped as they begged. The conflagration at the church had become so fierce that its roaring finally drowned out the screams of the dying inside, and their souls seemed to waft upward with the heat, the illumination joining an eastern sky that was now lightening. As lines of stunned captives began to appear from other parts of the city, looped with line like a train of donkeys, the church's walls caved in.

Ilana was sobbing, so choked with sorrow that she could scarcely breathe, her body splayed across the horse's shoulders and the Hun's muscled thighs, her hair hanging down in a curtain, exposing the nape of her neck. So why wouldn't he kill her, too? The nightmare seemed to have no end, and her father's treachery had been useless. Everything of her old life had been burnt and yet she, cruelly, was still alive.

"Stop crying," the young Hun ordered in words she could not understand. "I have saved you."

She envied the dead.

Edeco led them out of the city he had destroyed, its memories a column of smoke. The besieged always opened the gates in the end, he knew. Someone always hoped, vainly and against all history and reason, that there was a chance he might be spared if he treated with an invader. The Huns counted on it. He turned to the lieutenant who carried the trussed Ilana, a warrior named Skilla. "Attila would have enjoyed this night, nephew."

"As I'll enjoy the coming one." His right hand was on the captive's waist, pinning her as she squirmed. Her thrashings made Skilla want to take her right there. What a fetching rump she had.

"No." His uncle shook his head. "That one is too fine. We carry her back to Attila, for judgment to be made there."

"But I like her."

"She is Attila's to assign. Yours to ask for."

The younger man sighed and looked back. He had ridden before he had walked; fought since he was a toddler; hunted, pursued, and killed.

Still, this was his first sacking, and he wasn't used to the slaughter. "The ones in the church . . ."

"Would make pups to rebuild the walls." Edeco sniffed the smoke, roiling to blot out the rising sun. "This is a good thing, Skilla. Already the land breathes free."

III

PLOTTING AN
ASSASSINATION
CONSTANTINOPLE, A.D. 450

It was easier to buy a Hun than kill him, and easiest to buy those Huns who knew there are things worth a coin.

At least that was the theory of Chrysaphius, chief minister to the emperor of the Eastern Roman Empire, Theodosius II. Chrysaphius had been urging his emperor to pay tribute to the Huns for a decade now, because the thousands of pounds of gold sent north had forestalled a final assault on Constantinople. However humiliating, submitting to extortion was cheaper than war. The government pretended its payments were for a barbarian ally, similar to what the Western emperors sent the Franks, but this fiction for the masses fooled no one in authority. Now Attila's demands were rising, the treasury was strained, the Byzantine army was preoccupied with Persia, voices in court were muttering against the minister's craven appeasement, and somehow the tribute had to end. Accordingly, Chrysaphius wanted to buy one Hun in particular, for a very specific purpose. He sent his minion Bigilas to begin to do it.

"Show this Edeco our great Nova Roma, translator," the minister had said while dissecting a Galatian pear with a silver knife. "Show him our wealth and our walls and our power, and then bring our unwashed guest to my palace and show him me."

Several months after the sack of Axiopolis, the Hun general Edeco had been sent south to Constantinople to press Attila's demands that the terms of the Treaty of Anatolius, negotiated two years before, be fulfilled. The Byzantines were slow to pay all the gold they had promised, and the swelling Hun armies had a tireless appetite for the metal. Chrysaphius hoped to turn this new barbarian envoy from tormentor to ally.

The meeting did not begin auspiciously. Bigilas had to go to meet the Hun delegation outside the city by the Golden Gate, since the barbarians refused to venture inside without a guide. The translator found himself squinting up at the man he had been instructed to impress. Though Bigilas arrived with bodyguard, personal chamberlain, and a slave to hold his parasol, he was on foot and the Huns were mounted; and the warriors had maneuvered their beasts so their backs were to the sun that shone in the Roman's eyes. Yet Bigilas dared not complain. The haughty barbarian was not just key to his master's hopes but dangerous if offended. If Edeco didn't return to Attila with satisfying answers, war might resume.

For his part, Edeco considered this mission between campaigns as an opportunity for easy profit, regardless of treaty gabble. The Romans always tried to soothe the Huns with gifts, and so this visit was a reward to Edeco for the capture of Axiopolis and an opportunity to examine the capital's more intimidating defenses. Someday, the Hun hoped, he would do to Constantinople what he had done to Ilana's city.

As Bigilas expected, Edeco was dusty from the long journey but far from ragged. The rabbit skins that his people had first appeared in had long been supplanted by bear, fox, and sable; and crude leather jerkins had been tossed aside for captured mail and padded tunics. Silks and linens that would adorn a Roman girl's breast were apt to peek from behind a lorica because the Huns had a childlike fascination with finery and no knowledge of proper fashion. Nor were they at all self-conscious. It was the People of the Dawn who decided how lords should dress, and everyone else knelt before them.

Like all the Huns, Edeco looked as comfortable on horseback as a Roman at ease in a chair. He was short but powerful, with a long sword hanging from his waist, a short bow strapped to his saddle, and a quiver full of arrows on his back. Also, like all the Huns, he was ugly—at least to Roman eyes. His skin had the bronze cast of the East and the rugged-ness of leather, and his cheeks were corrugated with ritual scars. Many Romans believed the common story that the Huns cut their boys at birth to teach them to endure pain before letting them suckle, but Bigilas knew the puckering was more likely the result of self-mutilation from mourning a close relative. Most adult Hun men, and many women, had such scars.

Edeco's manner exuded menace, like a low criminal; and his expres-sion seemed fixed in a permanent scowl, given emphasis by a thin mus-tache that curled downward. Yet he was a calculating brute, the translator guessed, who killed and stole with predatory intelligence. That meant he could be reasoned with. Or so master Chrysaphius hoped.

The Hun was not looking at Bigilas, who he knew was a bureaucrat of minor status, but at the triple walls of Constantinople that stretched four miles from the Sea of Marmara to the harbor known as the Golden Horn. His was a soldier's gaze, trying to guess a way through or around the barrier. The height of the walls, one hundred feet, astounded him.

"The minister Chrysaphius invites you to supper," Bigilas said now in the guttural tongue the Hun spoke. Compared to Greek or Latin, it sounded like the grunting of animals.

The fortifications were the thickest Edeco had ever seen.

"You will have to leave your horse outside the city," the translator added.

This, at least, got a response. The Hun peered down. "I will ride to the palace."

"No one rides in Constantinople except the emperor," Bigilas in-sisted. "It's too crowded. It would frighten your horse." The Huns lived on horseback, he knew. They fought there, parleyed there, ate there, sometimes slept there, and for all he knew they made love there. They'd ride a hundred paces if it would save them a walk, and fitted their mounts so easily that they seemed a single beast. They also had to be manipulated like petulant children. "If you'd prefer, I can call a litter."

"A litter?"

"A couch, carried by slaves. You can ride that way."

Edeco sneered. "Like a baby or a woman?"

"It is three miles to the palace." He looked deliberately at the Hun's bandy legs.

The Hun scowled. "What did you do to get here?"

"I walked. Even our senators and generals walk, ambassador. It will make it easier for me to show you the glories of our capital."

The Hun shook his head. "Why live where you can't ride?" But he slid off his pony anyway, not as surprised as he pretended. Previous envoys had warned him that if he allowed it, his horse would be stabled outside the city in a box just like the Romans lived in, a confinement that would make the pony fat and weak. These were an insect people, and they swarmed in their cities like maggots. The trick was to get your presents and get out.

Bigilas was pleased the Hun was not making an issue of his horse. It was an unexpected characteristic of these slaughterers that they would actually negotiate. He had begun to learn their tongue when taken captive in Attila's raid of seven years before, and after being ransomed he had learned more when his skill won him jobs as a trader. His ability to translate had brought him to the attention of the imperial government and eventually to Chrysaphius himself. Bigilas knew the Huns without liking them, which was just the quality the chief minister wanted.

The translator watched the Hun give his reins, bow, and quiver to an attendant he called Skilla. Edeco instructed the young man and another ranking Hun, a Roman-born lieutenant and turncoat named Onegesh, to wait outside the walls. If he did not return when expected, they were to report to Attila. "Do not let them box my horse and do not let them box you. It will cost you strength."

"But we've arranged a villa and stables," Bigilas said.

"Our roof is the stars," the young man replied just a little too proudly. Skilla, like his uncle Edeco, was looking at the triple walls of Constantinople with a mixture of contempt and envy. "We will camp at the river and await you there."

Chrysaphius wouldn't like the Huns keeping to themselves, outside Roman control, but what could Bigilas do? "Do you want food?"

"We will get what we need."

What did that mean? Were they going to poach from farms, steal from pilgrims? Well, let them sleep in the dirt. "Come then," he said to Edeco. "Chrysaphius is waiting." As they walked to the great gate he looked back at the two Huns left behind. They appeared to be counting the towers.

The new capital of the Eastern Roman Empire was a triangle, the apex that jutted into the water containing the imperial palaces, Hippodrome, and the church of Hagia Sophia. The triangle's base, to the west, was the four-mile-long triple wall. The two watery sides of the triangle were also walled and lined with artificial harbors crowded with shipping. All of the world's commerce now seemed to pass through this funnel; and the Eastern emperors had imported statues, art, marbles, and mosaics to give their new city instant respectability. There were probably as many Romans in Constantinople as there were Huns in the entire world, Bigilas knew; and yet it was the city that paid tribute to the barbarian, not the other way around. It was an intolerable situation that must come to an end.

The Golden Gate was a triple archway, the arch in the center being the highest and broadest; and its wood-and-iron doors were reinforced with a relief of enormous brass elephants polished to a golden sheen. The portal passed through all three walls in a tunnel that would be a corridor of massacre for any army that broke through: Its ceiling was peppered with kill holes through which arrows could be shot or hot oil poured. Moreover, the third and innermost wall was the highest so that each barrier overlooked the one in front, giving the appearance of a forbidding mountain range.

Edeco stopped just short of the outer entrance, peering up at statues of emperor, victory, and fortune. There was Latin lettering above. "What does it say?"

Bigilas read aloud: "'Theodosius adorns this place, after the doom of the usurper. He who constructed the Golden Gate brings in the Golden Age.'"

The barbarian was silent a moment. Then, "What does it mean?"

"That our emperor is a god and that this is the new center of the world."

"I thought you Romans only had one god, now."

"I suppose." The translator frowned. "The divinity of the emperor is still under theological debate."

The Hun grunted, and they passed through the darkness of the triple walls to the bright sunlight on the inside. Edeco stopped again. "Where is your city?"

Bigilas smiled. Here the immensity of Constantinople first struck the barbarians. "The central city remains behind the original walls of Constantine." He pointed at a wall nearly a mile ahead. "This new area, walled by Theodosius, is reserved for cisterns, gardens, monasteries, churches, and farmers' markets. The Lycus River flows under our walls and we have enough water and food to resist an invader forever. Constantinople can never be starved or conquered, Edeco, it can only be befriended."

The Hun said nothing for a while, his gaze rotating. Then, "I come as a friend. For presents."

"The chief minister has presents for you, my friend."

At the smaller, older, single-width wall of Constantine there was a marketplace before the Gate of Saturninus where Edeco eyed the goods with a predator's appetite. Nova Roma had become the world's new crossroads and every product, every pleasure, every smell, and every taste could be found here. His wives would quiver like excited geese to see booty such as this. Someday he would carry it back to them, spattered with the blood of the merchants who had owned it. The thought pleased him.

The pair went through the gate and entered the urban hub of the Eastern Empire, a raw, bustling capital of gilded churches, ostentatious palaces, crowded tenements, and teeming streets. Edeco suddenly felt shrunken and entirely too anonymous. If the Hun evoked fear outside the walls, he elicited only curious glances inside them. To Constantinople came all the peoples of the world: black Africans, blond Germans, dusky Syrians, shrouded Berbers, migratory Jews, glowering Goths, copper-hued Iberians, industrious Greeks, proud Arabs, clamoring Egyptians, and bumpkin Illyrians and Dacians. They pushed, threaded, and jostled one another, crying out bargains, negotiating prices, shouting for passageway, and promising pleasure. The Hun felt caught in a vast river he did not control. There was a heady stench of spice, perfume, sweat, charcoal smoke, food, and sewage and a cacophony of tongues. It made him want to vomit. Bigilas was gesturing to it all with pride.

The road they followed was stone, that Roman custom that Edeco believed was hard on feet and harder on hooves. The middle was open to the sky but on either side was a marble portico that offered shade and shelter and was just as crowded as the lane's center. The tops of the pillars were carved into fronds and leaves, as if to mimic trees. The Romans used rock instead of wood and then tried to make the rock look like wood! In the shadows beyond the portico was an endless line of shops tunneling into buildings so high that they made the street a canyon. The Hun could not keep himself from scanning the eaves, wary of ambush, and yet these Romans thronged without any apparent feeling of entrapment. In fact, they seemed to take comfort in this closeness. It was an unnatural way to live and it had made the Romans strange: loud, over-dressed, the painted women either too veiled or too exposed, the men too rich or too beggared, gamblers and whores beside monks and nuns, all of them clutching and calling and complaining with gusto. It was an ant's nest, Edeco thought, and when it all finally burned it would be a blessing to the earth.

Bigilas chattered like a girl as they pushed ahead through the confusion, saying this marble was from Troad and their street was called the Mese and that forum was called Arcadius, as if Edeco cared. The Hun was instead tabulating the wealth on display: the stalls of gold jewelry, the small hillocks of carpets, the linens from Egypt, the woolens from Anatolia, the jars of wine, the fine boots, and the metallic luster of aristocratic weapons. There were cups and bowls, bedding and pots, copper and iron, ebony and ivory, and fine carved chests to put it all away. How did the maggots make such things?

Periodically the Mese opened to wider places that Bigilas called forums. Many had statues of frozen men, for what purpose Edeco didn't know. Tall columns jutted to the sky but held nothing up. One was topped by a frozen man called Constantine. This was the emperor who had founded the city, Bigilas explained.

The Hun was more intrigued by a monumental four-sided arch at an intersection called the Anemodoulion. At its top was a weathervane, and the Hun watched in amazement as its eagle pointed this way and that. What foolishness! Only Romans needed a toy to tell them which way the wind blew.

Bigilas also pointed out the arches of what he called an aqueduct. Why, Edeco wondered, did the Romans build rivers instead of simply living by one? The Earth Mother gave people everything they really needed, and yet the Romans toiled their whole lives to duplicate what was free.

As they advanced toward the apex of the peninsula, the houses, palaces, and monuments grew grander and the noise even worse. The clanging from the copper factories was like the heavy hail of the steppe, and the whine of the marble saws was almost unbearable. Only the gates of the Hippodrome were more appealing, giving a glimpse of open sand surrounded by a huge oval enclosure made of steps that went up to the sky. "What is this?"

"The place of chariot races and games," Bigilas replied. "When they compete there are eighty thousand people here. Have you seen the scarves and ribbons? Those are our factions, the Greens the common folk and the Blues the nobles. There's a great rivalry, betting, and sometimes riots and fights."

"For what?"

"For who wins the game."

So they spent their energies on pretend war instead of the real thing. And with that they came to the palace of Chrysaphius.

The chief minister of the Eastern Roman Empire lived, in the manner of all beings in such exalted positions, on his wits, watchfulness, and ruthless calculation. Like so many in this new era of Roman government,

Chrysaphius was a eunuch. It was his early service to, and access to, the emperor's beautiful wife, Aelia—made possible because of his castration—that had started his own precipitous rise. He was now, by some accounts, more powerful than the emperor himself. And why not? Having observed the cunning of women his entire life, the minister had long concluded that the absence of balls did nothing to subtract from courage and everything to improve clarity of mind. The emperor Theodosius was normally equipped but was a hapless general and clumsy negotiator who had been dominated his entire life by his older sister, a woman so aware of the proper ranking of things that she had foresworn sex and devoted her life to religious chastity. Such purity made her as formidable and revered as it made her prickly and vindictive. What a contrast the dangerous Pulcheria was to the dim and lustful sister of the emperor of the West, a girl named Honoria, reportedly so stupid that she had been caught in bed with her palace steward! If only Pulcheria would exhibit such weakness. But, no, she seemed as immune to such feelings as Chrysaphius himself, which made her dangerous.

Pulcheria had first gotten rid of lovely Aelia by accusing her brother's wife of adultery, driving her in humiliation to Judea. Chrysaphius had barely escaped being caught up in that scandal himself, since Aelia had been his patroness. Yet his skill at negotiation had made him so indispensable, and his emasculation had made him so immune to sexual chicanery, that even Pulcheria could not dislodge him. Nor could the minister, in turn, persuade the emperor that his sister's public holiness was only a mask for private spitefulness. Now she was Chrysaphius's most implacable enemy. The minister's own greed and treacheries had made him many foes, and he knew his unsexing added to his unpopularity. He needed a dramatic achievement to fortify himself against Pulcheria.

This was why the oafish barbarian Edeco was now rudely stuffing himself at Chrysaphius's table.

So far, the political seduction had gone as planned. Bigilas had met the Hun outside the city walls and had escorted him through Constantinople, the translator confirming that he had dazzled the tribesman with the glories of Roman architecture, the richness of Byzantine mar-

kets, and the density and vigor of the population. The futility of assault-
ing Nova Roma should be evident by now. Edeco had then come into
Chrysaphius's palace, gaping like a peasant at its marbles, brocades,
tapestries, carpets, pools, fountains, and carved cedar doors. Sunlit court-
yards were filled like a meadow with flowers; bedchambers were seas of
silks and linens; and side tables groaned under mountains of fruit, bread,
honey, meat, and gleaming olives.

The Hun had grazed like a bull from room to room.

Chrysaphius had tried to get two of his tittering slave girls to coax
the barbarian into one of his baths, a divertissement that would have
made the creature more bearable at close range, but the Hun had suspiciously refused.

"They fear water spirits," the translator had whispered in explanation.

Chrysaphius groaned. "How can they stand to reproduce themselves?"

Bigilas had finally persuaded Edeco to shed his furs and armor for a
robe of Egyptian cotton that was laced with golden thread, edged with
ermine, and spotted with precious gems, a freshening that was like
throwing silk on a musty bear. The Hun's hands were still as rough as a
carpenter's and his hair suited to a witch, but the unfamiliar and per-
fumed clothes made him fit a little more naturally into the *triclinium* that
overlooked the Sea of Marmara. Lamps and candles lent a glittery haze, a
cool breeze came off the water, and constant refilling of the Hun's wine
goblet seemed to have put him in an agreeable mood. It was time for the
proposition.

The Huns were dangerous but greedy, Chrysaphius believed. They
were little more than horse-borne pirates, who had no use for cities and
yet had an insatiable hunger for their products. They hated the Romans
because they envied them, and they were as corruptible as children lured
by a bowl of sweets. For more than a decade the chief minister had
avoided a final showdown with Attila by buying the madman off, wincing as the demand for annual tribute had risen from the three hundred
and fifty pounds of gold demanded by Attila's father to the seven hundred insisted on by Attila's brother to the more than two thousand de-

manded by Attila himself. It was more than one hundred and fifty thousand solidi per year! To pay the six thousand pounds demanded to end the war of 447, the city's merchants and senators had had to melt their wives' jewelry. There had been suicides amid the despair. More important, there was barely enough money left to pay for Chrysaphius's luxuries! It was Attila who had turned the Huns from a confederation of annoying raiders to a rapacious empire, and it was Attila who had changed reasonable tribute to outrageous extortion. Eliminate Attila, and their cohesion would collapse. A single knife thrust or draft of poison, and the Eastern Empire's most intractable problem would be solved.

The eunuch smiled benevolently at the Hun and spoke, using Bigilas to translate. "Do you enjoy our epicurean delicacies, Edeco?"

"The what?" The man's mouth was disgustingly full.

"The food, my friend."

"It's good." He took another handful.

"The finest cooks in the world come to Constantinople. They compete with one another in the inventiveness of their recipes. They continuously astonish the palate."

"You are a good host, Chrysaphius," the Hun said agreeably. "I will tell this to Attila."

"How flattering." The minister sipped from his cup. "Do you know, Edeco, that a man of your standing and talents could eat like this every day?"

Here the barbarian finally paused. "Every day?"

"If you lived here with us."

"But I live with Attila."

"Yes, I know, but have you ever thought of living in Constantinople?"

The Hun snorted. "Where would I keep my horses?"

Chrysaphius smiled. "What need have we of horses? We have nowhere we need to go. The entire world comes to us, and brings the best of its goods with it. The brightest wits and best artists and the holiest priests all come to Nova Roma. The Empire's most beautiful women are here, as you can see from my own slaves and bath girls. Why do you need a horse?"

Edeco, realizing that some kind of offer was being prepared, shifted more upright on his dining couch as if to focus his half-drunken attention. "I'm not a Roman."

"But you could be."

The barbarian glanced around warily, as if everything might be taken away from him in an instant. "I have no house here."

"But you could have, general. A man of your military experience would be invaluable to our armies. A man of your station could have a palace exactly like this one. A man like you who gave his services to the emperor could be first among our nobles. Our palaces, our games, our goods, and our women could all be yours."

The Hun's eyes narrowed. "You mean if I leave my people and join you."

"I mean if you are willing to save *your* people as well as *ours*, Edeco. If you take your rightful place in history."

"My place is by Attila."

"So far. But must we next meet across the battlefield? We both know that is what Attila wants. Your ruler is insatiable. No victory satisfies him. No amount of tribute is ever enough. No loyalist is above his suspicion. While he is alive, no Hun and no Roman is safe. If he's not stopped, he will destroy us all."

Edeco had stopped eating, looking dubious. "What is it you want?"

Chrysaphius put his slim, soft hand over the Hun's hard one, grasping it warmly. "I want you to kill Attila, my friend."

"Kill him! I would be flayed alive."

"Not if it was done in secret, away from his guards, in quiet parley with Roman ambassadors with you as the key Hun negotiator. He would die, you would leave the discussion chamber, and chaos would erupt only later when his death was discovered. By the time the Huns decide who among them is in charge and who might be guilty, you could be back here, a hero to the world. You could have a house like this one and women like these and gold enough to strain your back."

He made no effort to hide his look of avarice. "How much gold?"

The minister smiled. "Fifty pounds."

The Hun sucked in his breath.

"That is simply an initial payment. We will give you enough gold to make you one of this city's richest men, Edeco. Enough honor to let you live in peace and luxury the rest of your days. You are one of the few trusted enough by Attila to be alone with him. You can do what no other man dares."

The Hun wet his lips. "Fifty pounds? And more?"

"Would not Attila kill *you* for the same prize?"

Edeco shrugged, as if to concede the point. "Where is this gold?"

Chrysaphius snapped his fingers. A male slave, a tall German, came in bearing a heavy chest, its weight displaying the man's powerful musculature. He set it down with a thump and flipped back the lid, revealing a yellow hoard. The minister let the Hun take a good long look at the coins and then, with his nod, the lid snapped shut. "This is your opportunity, Edeco, to live like me."

The Hun slowly shook his head. "If I ride back with that on my saddle Attila will know in an instant what I've promised. I'll be crucified on the Hunuguri Plain."

"I know this. So here is my plan. Let's pretend we could not reach agreement. Let me send a Roman ambassador back with you to Attila. Let me send Bigilas here as translator. You will receive enough gifts now that Attila will suspect nothing. Such talks take time, as you well know. You will become close to the tyrant once more. And to guarantee the Roman word, you will suggest that Bigilas slip away and bring back his son as a hostage for Roman honesty. He will not just fetch his boy but your gold. When you see it, and know my word is true, strike. Then come back here and live as a Roman."

The Hun considered. "It is risky."

"All reward requires risk."

He looked around. "And I can have a house like this one?"

"You can have *this* house, if you like."

He laughed. "If I get this house, I will make a pasture for my horses!"

Edeco slept in the palace of Chrysaphius two nights while the Roman embassy was organized and then purposely rode in a litter, like a woman, back out of the city. How wormlike to be carried! It was his joke

for his Hun companions. Skilla and Onegesh had ignored the villa prepared for them outside the city walls and camped beside it. Now Edeco
brought presents to share with them: rich brocades, intricately carved
boxes, jars of spice and perfume, jeweled daggers, and coins of gold. The
gifts would help buy each a personal retinue of followers back home.

"What did the Romans say?" Onegesh asked.

"Nothing," Edeco replied. "They want us to take an embassy to Attila and conclude negotiations there."

Onegesh frowned. "He won't be happy that we haven't ended this in
Constantinople. Or that we don't bring back the tribute. He'll think the
Romans are stalling."

"The Romans are bringing more gifts. And I am bringing something
even better."

"What is that?"

Edeco winked at Skilla, the nephew and lieutenant who had been included in this mission in order to learn. "An assassination plot."

"What?"

"They want me to kill our king. The girl man actually thinks I'd try
it! As if I'd get a hundred paces before being boiled alive! Attila will be
very amused by this and then very angry, and will use his outrage to
squeeze even more gold out of them."

Onegesh smiled. "How much are they paying you?"

"Fifty pounds of gold, to start."

"Fifty pounds! A big haul, for one man. Perhaps you should whet
your assassin's knife, Edeco."

"Bah. I'll make more with Attila and live to enjoy it."

"Why do the Romans think you would betray your king?" Skilla
asked.

"Because they would betray theirs. They are maggots who believe in
nothing but comfort. When the time comes, they will squish like bugs."

The turncoat Roman looked out at the high walls, not certain it
would be quite so easy. "And the fifty pounds of gold?"

"It is to be brought later, so Attila will not be suspicious. We will wait
until it comes, melt it over a fire, and pour it down the Romans' lying
throats. Then we'll send it back, in its new human sacks, to Chrysaphius."

IV

A ROMAN EMBASSY

And so this story comes to me. I could hardly believe my good fortune at being chosen to accompany the latest imperial embassy to the court of Attila, king of the Huns, in the distant land of Hunuguri. A life that had seemed over just one day before had been resurrected!

At the callow age of twenty-two, I was certain that I had already experienced all the bitter disappointment that existence allows. My skill at letters and languages seemed to offer no useful future when our family business was faced with ruin after the loss of a trio of wine ships on the rocks of Cyprus. What good are the skills of a trader and scribe when there's no capital to trade? My dull and stolid brother had won a coveted posting to the army for its Persian campaign, while my own boredom with martial skills robbed me of similar opportunity. Worst of all, the young woman I had given my heart to, lovely Olivia, had rejected me with vague excuses that, reduced to their essence, meant my own prospects were too poor—and her own charms too abundant—to tie herself to a future as uncertain as mine. What had happened to undying love and sweet exchange of feelings? Disposed of like stripped kitchen bones, it seemed. Discarded like an old sandal. I wasn't just crushed, I was baffled. I'd been flattered by relatives and teachers that I was handsome, strong, bright, and well-spoken. Apparently such attributes don't matter to women, compared to career prospects and accumulated riches.

When I saw Olivia in the company of my rival Decio—a youth so shallow that you could not float a feather in his depth of character and so undeservedly rich that he could not waste his fortune as fast as his family made it—I felt the wounds of unfair fate might be truly mortal. Certainly I brooded about various means of suicide, revenge, or martyrdom to make Olivia and the world regret their ill-treatment of me. I polished my self-pity until it glowed like an idol.

Then my father summoned me with better news.

"Your curious preoccupation with languages has finally borne fruit," he told me, not bothering to conceal his relief and surprise. I had taken to learning the way my brother had taken to athletics, and so spoke Greek, Latin, German, and—with the help of a former Hun captive named Rusticius who had enrolled in the same school—some Hunnish. I enjoyed the strange, gravelly sound of the hard consonants and frequent vowels of that tongue, even though there had been little opportunity to put the language into practice. The Huns did not trade, travel casually, or write; and all I knew of them was exotic rumor. They were like a great and mysterious shadow somewhere beyond our walls, many Byzantines whispering that Attila might be the Antichrist of prophecy.

My father had never seen a practical value in learning barbarian jargon, of course; and, in truth, Olivia's Tutiline family had been put off by it as well. She viewed my interest in obscure scholarly pursuits as somewhat peculiar, and despite my infatuation I'd been frustrated that she seemed bored by my fascination with the campaigns of Xenophon, my meticulous record of seasonal bird migrations, or my attempts to reconcile the movement of the stars with politics and destiny. "Jonas, you think about such silly things!" But now, unexpectedly, my aptitudes might pay off.

"There's an embassy going to parley with Attila and the scholar they selected as scribe has taken sick," my father explained. "Your acquaintance Rusticius heard of your unemployment and got word to an aide of Chrysaphius. You'll never be the soldier your brother is, but we all know you're good with letters. They need a scribe and historian willing to be away for some months, and have nominated you. I have negotiated some pay in advance, enough to lease a ship and resuscitate our business."

"You're spending my pay already?"

"There's nothing to buy in Hunuguri, Jonas, let me assure you, but much to see and learn. Rejoice at this opportunity, and put your mind to practical matters for a change. If you perform your duties and keep your head attached to your shoulders, you may catch the eye of the emperor or his chief minister. This could be the making of you, boy."

The thought of travel on a state mission was exciting. And the Huns were intriguing, if intimidating. "What am I to do?"

"Write what you observe and stay out of the way."

My family had emigrated from our home city of Ephesus to the new city of Constantinople a hundred years ago. Through trade, marriage, and government service, my ancestors had scrabbled their way into the city's upper classes. Capricious fortune, however, always prevented our entry into the highest ranks; the Cyprus storm being just the latest example. Now I had opportunity. I would be an aide to the respected Senator Maximinus, the ambassador, and would ride with three Huns and two translators: Rusticius and a man I'd never heard of named Bigilas. We seven men and our train of slaves and bodyguards would journey to the barbarian lands beyond the Danube and meet the notorious Attila. The thought immediately occurred to me that this would provide stories enough to impress any pretty girl. The haughty Olivia would burn with regret at her rejection of me, and other damsels would seek my attention! Yesterday my future seemed bleak. Today I was responsible for helping keep the world's peace. That evening I prayed to the saints at the Alcove of Mary for my good luck.

Two days later I joined the party outside the city walls, riding my gray mare, Diana, and feeling dashingly equipped, thanks to the anxious and hurried investment of my father. My sword was forged in Syria, my tightly woven wool cape came from Bithynia, my saddlebags were of Anatolian manufacture, my paper was Egyptian, and my ink and pens were the finest in Constantinople. Perhaps I would see great events, he told me, and write a book. I realized he had pride in me, and I basked in unaccustomed approval. "Get us a good ship," I told him grandly. "I believe our luck has changed, Father."

How little we understand.

Our route would take us west and north more than five hundred miles, through the Pass of Succi and down the course of the Margus to the Danube, then uncounted miles beyond to find Attila. It was a reverse of the path the Huns had followed in their great raids in 441 and 443, and I was well aware that the territory I was about to traverse was a ruin. That invasion and another, farther east in 447, had devastated Thrace and Moesia and destroyed such cities as Viminacium, Singidunum, Sirmium, Ratiaria, Sardica, Philippopolis, Arcadiopolis, and Marcianopolis. Smaller raids had followed, with poor Axiopolis falling just months ago.

Yet each winter the barbarians retreated like the tide to their grasslands. Constantinople still stood, Attila had refrained from further attacks after the promise of more tribute, and there was hope for recovery if war could permanently be averted. And why not? There simply was little left in the outlying provinces to easily plunder, and Hun losses had been as heavy as Roman. This embassy might put an end to the insanity of war.

I reported to a villa outside the city walls where the party was being assembled, the Romans sleeping indoors and the Huns outside, like livestock. At first I wondered if this was deliberate insult or clumsy oversight, but the Hun ambassadors, Rusticius explained when he greeted me, had disdained to stay within the walls. "They believe them corrupting. They're camped by the river, which they won't wash in because of their fear of water."

This was my first exposure to their odd beliefs. I peered around the villa corner to get a glimpse of them, but all I saw was the smoke of a cooking fire. The distance was disconcerting. "It seems an odd way to begin a partnership," I said.

"You and I will be sleeping on the ground with them soon enough."

I suppose their invisibility was fitting. I'd hoped for some immediate panoply that would give me recognition among my peers in the city, but there had been no announcement of our embassy. This mission, it seemed, was a quiet one. Chrysaphius was unpopular for the payments to Attila, and no doubt he didn't want to call attention to further negotiation. Better to wait until we could announce some kind of success.

So I went inside the villa to meet our ambassador. Maximinus, the emperor's representative, was examining lists of supplies in the courtyard, his head exposed to the sun and bright birds darting among the climbing roses. He was one of those physically blessed men who would rise by appearance even had he lacked ability. His thick white hair and beard, piercing black eyes, high cheekbones, and Grecian nose gave him the look of a marble bust come to life. He combined this handsomeness with the care, caution, and slow gravity of the diplomat, his voice deep and sonorous. When he was a thousand miles from Constantinople it would be his bearing alone that would convey the might of the Eastern Roman Empire, he knew; and he told me once that an effective diplomat was also an effective actor. Yet Maximinus had the reputation of being able as well as dignified and intelligent as well as connected. His greeting was gracious, without presuming friendliness or warmth. "Ah, yes, Jonas Alabanda. So you are to be our new historian."

"Secretary, at least." I gave a modest bow. "I make no pretense at being a Livy or Thucydides." My father had coached me not to put on airs.

"Sensible modesty. Good history is as much judgment as fact, and you're too young to make judgments. Still, the success of a mission often hinges as much on how it is reported as what it accomplishes. I trust you intend to be fair?"

"My loyalty is to you and to the emperor, ambassador. My own fortune depends on our success."

Maximinus smiled. "A good answer. Maybe you have a talent for diplomacy yourself. We'll see. Certainly we have a difficult task and need to support one another as much as we can. These are perilous times."

"Not too perilous, I hope." It was an attempt at a small joke.

"You've lived your life inside the walls of Constantinople. Now you're about to experience the world outside them. You will see things that will shock you. The Huns are brave, gracious, cruel, and unpredictable—as clever as foxes and as wild as wolves. And the omens of recent years have not been good, as you know."

"Omens?"

"Remember the killing winter of seven years ago? The floods six years past, the riots in the city just five years back, the plague a mere four, and the earthquakes just three? God has been trying to tell us something. But what?"

"It has not been a lucky time." Like everyone, I had heard the speculation from priests and prophets that this wretched string of woes foretold the biblical end of time. Many believed that the Armageddon the Church constantly expected was at last on the horizon and that the Huns represented the Gog and Magog of religious lore. While my hardheaded father derided such fears as superstitious nonsense—"The more ordinary a man, the more certain that his time must be the culmination of history"—the constant assaults on the Empire had given Constantinople an atmosphere of foreboding. One couldn't help but be affected.

"All that misfortune is combined with Attila's victories, crippling tribute payments, the loss of Carthage to the Vandals, the failure of the Sicilian expedition to get it back, the quarrels with Persia, and the refusal of the Western Empire to come to our aid. While Marcianopolis was burning, the celebrated general Flavius Aetius preferred to sit in Rome, leaving Moesia to her fate. So much for the promises of Valentinian, emperor of the West!"

"But the earthquake damage has been repaired," I pointed out with the optimism of youth. "The Huns have retreated. . . ."

"The Huns know our weaknesses better than any nation, which is why you and I can never afford to be weak. Do you understand what I'm saying, Jonas?"

I swallowed and stood straighter. "We represent our people."

"Exactly! We come not with strength but with the wit to manipulate a people simpler than ourselves. I'm told Attila is a great believer in prophecy, astrology, omens, and magic. He claims to have found the great sword of the god of war. He thinks he is invincible until someone convinces him otherwise. Our job, with no weapons and no tools, is to do that convincing."

"But how?"

"By reminding him how long Rome and Nova Roma have prevailed. By reciting how many chieftains have been smashed, like waves, upon the rocks of Rome. It will not be easy. I hear he is aware of the vision of Romulus, and that is just the kind of thing to give barbarians courage."

"I don't think I recall the vision of Romulus." I was less familiar with the legends of the West.

"Pagan nonsense. Still, I suspect Attila is crafty enough to use it to his advantage. The legend is that Romulus, the founder of Rome, had a dream in which he saw twelve vultures over the city. Soothsayers have long contended that each bird represents a century and that Rome will come to an end at the end of the last one."

"Twelve hundred years? But——"

"Precisely. If our historians have counted correctly from the city's founding, the prophecy calls for Rome's end in just three years' time."

It was a strange party that set out to reach Attila. Maximinus I have already described. Rusticius was more acquaintance than friend, but an earnest and well-meaning fellow who greeted me warmly. He was in his thirties, widowed by the plague, and, like me, viewed this mission as rare opportunity for advancement. He'd been captured by the Huns while on a trade mission from his native Italy and ransomed by a relative in Constantinople. At school, he had shared tales of his life in the West. Since we were natural allies and I felt somewhat in his debt, we immediately decided to share a tent. Though not particularly quick nor a leader, Rusticius was consistently good-humored and accepted new situations with equanimity. "Had I not been captured I would not know Hunnish, and had I not known Hunnish, I would not know you or be on this embassy," he reasoned. "So who but God is to say what is good and what is bad?"

He would become my closest friend on this expedition, humble and steady.

The other translator was unknown to me and somewhat aloof: not from shyness but from self-importance, I judged. He was an older, shorter, and rather oily Roman named Bigilas, quick to talk and slow to listen, whose manner had the false sincerity of a rug merchant. This fellow, who had been a captive and done some bartering with the Huns, carried himself with an odd presumption of rank. Didn't he know his place in the world? He even pretended to some secret familiarity with the Hun leader, Edeco, and talked to him like a comrade. Why the Hun tolerated this self-importance, I didn't know, but the barbarian made no move to put Bigilas in his place. I found his cultivation of mystery irritating, and he in turn ignored me unless to give unsolicited advice about what I should wear or eat. I decided he was one of those people who think constantly of themselves and have no empathy for others, and I took mean satisfaction in noticing he had fondness for the grape. This man, I thought early on as I watched him drink, is trouble.

The Huns, when I finally met them, were simply arrogant. They made it clear that in their world a man's worth was measured by his skill at war and that any Hun had ten times the skill of a Roman. Edeco was proud, crude, and condescending. "In the time it takes Romans to pack a mule, a horse and donkey could produce a new one," he growled the morning we left.

Onegesh was more urbane, given his background, but left no doubt that he felt he had improved himself by trading the Roman world for this new barbaric one. Captured in battle, he had promptly defected. His choice astonished me, but he told me that he now ranked higher and had grown richer, besides learning he preferred the sky to a roof. "In the Empire, it's all birth and patron, is it not? In Hunuguri, it's ability and loyalty. I'd rather be free on the plains than a slave in a palace."

"But you weren't a slave."

"To expectation? Everyone is, in Rome and Constantinople. Besides, I had no rich relatives to ransom me but only my own wits and ability. In the Roman army, I was ignored. In Hunuguri, I'm listened to."

Most irritating was the youngest Hun, a warrior named Skilla just a few years older than I. He had arguably the least rank of any of us and yet exemplified Hun pride. I sought him out the day I arrived and found him squatting by their fire, working on the fletching of an arrow and disdaining to even glance at me. I tried a formal but simple greeting. "Good day to you, companion. I am Jonas, secretary to the senator."

Skilla kept working on his arrow. "I know who you are. You're young to go with the graybeard."

"As are you to go with your uncle. In my case it's because I'm skilled with letters and know your language."

"How do you know Hunnish?"

"I enjoy foreign tongues and Rusticius taught me yours."

"Soon the whole world will speak the words of the People of the Dawn."

Well, that seemed presumptuous. "Or we will live as neighbors and share Latin, Greek, and Hunnish together. Isn't that the point of this embassy?"

Skilla sighted down the shaft of his arrow. "Is our language *all* that you know?" There seemed some secret meaning in the question, but I didn't know what it was.

"I am schooled in many things, like classics and philosophy," I said carefully.

The Hun looked up for a moment to study my face and then went back to his arrow, as if I'd revealed more than I intended to. "But not horses and weapons."

This was annoying. "I've been trained with arms and animals but been educated in much more. I know music and poetry."

"No use in war."

"But of great use in love." I'd wager he coupled like I'd seen the Huns eat: with too much speed, too little care, and a great belch afterward. "Have the Huns heard of love?"

"The Huns have heard of women, Roman, and I have one of my own without need for music and poetry."

"You are married?"

"Not yet, but I have Attila's promise." He finished binding his quill of feathers to the shaft and allowed a smile. "I have to teach her not to scratch."

"It sounds like you need the book and lyre, not the bow and arrow."

"The Hun use books to wipe our asses."

"Because you can't read and have no thoughts worth writing down." Not the most diplomatic rejoinder, I know, but the man's stubborn ignorance was dismaying.

"Yet you Romans pay tribute to us, the Hun."

That was true enough, and it was unclear how this embassy would change that. I finally walked away, wondering what would be accomplished.

V

A TEST OF HORSES

We set out on horseback, the slaves and pack mules extending the total caravan to fifteen people and thirty animals. This was considered modest for an imperial embassy, but again, our mission was a quiet one. We would of necessity be camping. The Roman system of *mansionis*, or inns, located twenty miles apart, had been abandoned after the devastation of the recent wars, so we would set our own ambitious pace, averaging twenty-five miles per day. The Huns would have moved faster on their own, but our Roman baggage train, with its gifts and food, could not move faster.

"You travel so slowly that you need even more food and fodder, which makes you slower yet, and which requires yet more supplies. It is insane," Edeco pronounced.

"We could leave the presents behind," Maximinus said mildly.

"No, no," the Hun muttered. "We will ride like Romans, and I will catch up on my sleep."

It was late spring, the afternoons hot and the mornings cool; and the forests and meadows of Thrace were green and in high flower. Here, close to Constantinople, people had returned to their farms after the gallop of armies and there was a semblance of normality to the landscape. Cattle grazed, oxen plowed, grain was already high, and we would periodically thread through flocks of sheep or gaggles of geese. When we rode farther north and west, Maximinus warned me, the effect of the Hun raids would be more apparent. "The country will become increasingly wild. Bears and wolves have returned to valleys they haven't roamed in generations—and stranger things, too, it is claimed. We live in evil times."

"I would like to see a wild bear." I'd seen only chained ones in the arena.

"I'd like to see peace and resettled farmers."

While I had journeyed as far as Athens by sea, this kind of expedition was entirely new to me. I was unaccustomed to sleeping in a tent, being exposed to the weather, and riding my mare for so long at a time. The first days my thighs and butt were on fire; and while I stoically tried to hide my stiffness, I fooled no one. Yet I also felt a rare freedom. For most of my life my days had been carefully scheduled and my future plotted. Now my future was as open as the sky and horizon.

As the comforting walls of Constantinople fell behind, I studied the young Hun warrior who had taunted me. Skilla rode as if one with his horse like a centaur, his mount a bay gelding and his saddle made of wood and leather softened with sheep's fat. His bow, like all those of the Huns, was that secret combination of wood, sinew, and bone, short but curved backward at the ends, that when pulled made them the terror of the world. Called reflex bows for the added power the bend gave them, they were short enough to be fired from a horse and yet uncannily accurate. The arrows could fly three hundred paces and kill easily at one hundred and fifty. The bow rode in a saddle holster to the Hun's right, next to a whip to lash his pony's flanks. A sword hung from a scabbard on his left, so it could be drawn horizontally by the right arm. A quiver of twenty arrows rode on the man's back. On his saddle was a lariat, used by the barbarians to catch errant livestock and immobilize enemies so they could be enslaved. Unlike Edeco's mail, purchased or stolen from some enemy, Skilla wore a light Asian cuirass of bony scales, cut from the hooves of dead horses and layered like the skin of a dragon or fish. While seeming dangerously light, it was also cool compared to Roman mail or breastplate. He had soft leather boots over his trousers and a conical wool cap he wore in the chill of the evening when we camped, but by day his head was often bare, his long black hair tied back like the tail of a horse. He was clean shaven and not yet ritually scarred like Edeco, and in fact boasted a somewhat noble and handsome look, his cheekbones high and his eyes black and shiny, like stones in a river. His costume was by no means typical because there was no typical barbarian dress. Onegesh wore a strange mix of Roman clothes and Hunnish fur, and Edeco seemed a vain mix of all nations.

My own weaponry was mostly packed away. I had brought the full shirt of mail, helmet, shield, and heavy spear that I had used for the basic military training all men of my class received, as well as my new sword. But only the latter was kept at my side. The rest seemed too heavy for a peace party, so it was bundled on one of the animals. My mare, Diana, bore a padded Roman saddle that borrowed from Hun design, crowned front and back by wood ridges to hold me in place, my legs dangling free. I wore a fine woolen tunic of yellow with blue borders that I had purchased in the forum of Philadelphion, sturdy cavalry trousers, and a fine leather baldric studded with gold coins that held an ivory-handled dagger. A felt skullcap gave me some protection from the sun, and my cape was tied behind my saddle.

I was of approximately the same height and proportion as Skilla, my Greek complexion dark but not as dark as his. I rocked more than he did as Diana clopped down the road, not as at ease on a horse. But then he was useless in a library.

The early part of the journey was uneventful as our group established a pace and learned one another's habits. We camped in early evening, the Romans pitching tents and the Huns sleeping under the stars. I found the nights unaccustomedly dark—I was used to the city, of course—and the ground damp and hard under my sheepskin. I wakened frequently to the sounds of the night and stumbled clumsily when I got up to urinate. When I went out of our tent the first night I saw that the Huns had simply rolled themselves in their cloaks and slept with their heads against their wooden saddles, using for a pillow the same saddle blanket that reeked of horse. From each cloak the hilt of a sword pro-

truded, and near the shoulder their bow and arrows were nestled as carefully as their heads. When I passed near Edeco, he jerked up and then,
recognizing me, sank again in dismissal.

"What do they do when it rains?" I whispered to Rusticius once as
we lay side by side, comparing impressions.

"Get wet, like their horses."

Each dawn we set out again, my own body still tired from a restless
night. And so began a daily rhythm of hourly pauses, a noon meal, and
camp again before sunset, mile succeeding endless mile.

Periodically Skilla became bored with this routine and galloped
ahead for amusement, sometimes looping around and coming down at
us from a nearby hill, yipping as if charging. Another time, he dropped
back to study me. Eventually his stare became a challenge as he searched
for diversion.

"You ride a mare," the Hun said.

Quite the observation. "Yes."

"No Hun would ride a mare."

"Why not? You ride a gelding. Their manners are similar." Castrating stallions was a basic skill in successfully running horse herds, I
knew.

"They are not the same. Mares are for milking."

I had heard the Huns fermented the milk to purify it and drank it
like wine, and I had smelled them doing so. *Kumiss*, they called it. By
reputation it was awful stuff, as rancid as their trousers. "We have cows
and goats for that. Mares have just as good endurance, and better character, than geldings."

Skilla looked at Diana critically. "Your horse is big but fat, like a
woman. All Roman horses seem fat."

Because all Hun horses looked half starved, I thought, ridden hard
and forced to forage. "She's simply muscular. She's a barb, with some
Arabian. If I could afford a pure Arabian all you'd see is her tail this
whole trip." It was time to return some disdain. "Your steppe horse
looks sized for a boy and skinny enough to go to the knacker."

"His name is Drilca, which means spear, and our ponies have made
us master." He grinned. "Do you want to race, Roman?"

I considered. This at least would break the monotony of travel, and I had great confidence in Diana. Nor was I as weighted with weapons. "To the next milepost?"

"To our next camping place. Edeco! How far is that?"

The older Hun, riding nearby, grunted. "Still half a dozen miles."

"How about it, Roman? You are carrying less than me. Let's see if this mare of yours can keep up with my pony."

I judged the barbarian's small, shaggy horse. "For a gold solidus?"

The Hun whooped. "Done!" And without warning he kicked his horse and was off.

Game now, I shouted "Yah!" and set off in pursuit. It was time to put this young Hun in his place. With Diana's longer stride we should catch and pass Skilla's mount easily.

Yet long after we left the main party far behind, the Hun remained elusively ahead. After a brief gallop the barbarian's horse settled into a sustainable canter, Skilla leaning forward in his saddle, legs cocked easily, his hair like a banner in the wind. I put Diana into her own lope to conserve her energy, and yet the Hun's smaller horse seemed to eat ground with an enviable efficiency that my own mare lacked. Despite Diana's longer stride, Drilca kept steadily in front. A mile passed, then two, then three. We pounded past farm carts, couriers, peddlers, and pilgrims. They stared as we passed, Hun and Roman linked.

We entered a copse along a river bottom where the lane twisted through the trees, obscuring the view ahead. I could hear Skilla's mount break into a gallop to lengthen his lead. Determined and increasingly anxious, I did the same, riding hard past the poplar and beech. Yet at wood's end I seemed entirely alone. Skilla had already passed over the rise ahead.

Angry now, I kicked Diana into a dead run. I didn't want Rome to be beaten! We pounded in a blur, gravel flying, and after another mile I had the Hun in sight again. Skilla's horse had once more settled into a rhythmic pace and so now I was gaining, the drum of hoofbeats forcing Skilla to look behind. Yet the Hun's horse didn't mimic Diana's gallop, staying instead in his easy canter. Diana pulled abreast . . . and then the Hun grinned and kicked. We raced together now, neck and neck, our mounts galloping along the ancient road, but my horse began to fade. Diana was losing her wind. I could feel her straining. Not wanting to harm her, I reluctantly let her fall back again, Skilla's dust swirling over us. Drilca's tail became a taunt, its hooves a receding blur. Beaten!

I slowed and glumly patted my horse's neck. "Not your fault, girl. Your rider's."

At a small stream where we planned to camp, Skilla was lounging in the grass.

"I told you she's for milking."

Drilca was tired, too, I saw, its head down. In war, I knew, Skilla would switch to a new mount. Each warrior took four or five horses with him on campaign. Here the lack of endurance was more apparent.

"My mare has more stamina."

"Does she? I think she's longing for her stable. Drilca is more at home out here under the sky, eating anything, bearing me anywhere."

I flipped him the solidus. "Then race me for two of these tomorrow."

Skilla caught it. "Done! If your purse gets light enough, maybe the pair of you can go faster. By then I'll have enough coin to wed."

"To a woman who scratches you."

He shrugged. "She'll think twice about scratching when I return from Constantinople. I am bringing presents! Her name is Ilana, she is the most beautiful woman in Attila's camp, and I saved her life."

That night I brushed my mount down, checked her hooves, and went back to the baggage train to fetch oats I had packed in Constantinople. "A Hun can't feed what he can't grow," I murmured as she ate. "His horse can't draw on strength it doesn't have."

Skilla boasted of the day's victory to the others around our fire that night. "Tomorrow, he promises me two gold coins! By the time we reach Attila, I'll be rich!"

"Today we ran your race," I said. "Tomorrow we run mine. Not a sprint but endurance: whoever goes farthest between sunrise and sunset."

"That's a fool's race, Roman. A Hun can cover a hundred miles in a day."

"In your country. Let's see it in mine."

So Skilla and I set out at dawn, the others in the party making their own bets and cheering us as we departed, joking about the frisky foolishness of young men. The Rhodope Mountains were to the left and Philippopolis ahead. There I first encountered Attila's destruction. We skirted the devastated city at mid-morning; and while Skilla scarcely glanced at it, I was stunned at the extent of the ruin. The roofless metropolis looked like a torn honeycomb, open to the rains. Grass grew in the streets, and only a few priests and shepherds resided around a church the barbarians had somehow spared. The surrounding fields had gone to weeds, and the few villagers peered from huts like kittens from a den.

I had to beat the Huns who had done this.

The road crossed the Hebrus River on an arched stone bridge, crudely repaired by the locals, and became rougher, side hilling along the river's valley. With the rising terrain, my confidence grew. Still we kept within sight of each other: sometimes the Hun riding ahead, and sometimes my determined mount passing him. Neither of us stopped for lunch, eating in the saddle. In the early afternoon we crossed the river again and then the land began to steepen as the road climbed toward the Pass of Succi.

Skilla cursed at the grade.

His lighter pony could keep an easy pace on level ground. On a slope its gait was less even and the horse's lighter muscles and lungs began to strain. My mare was bigger in relation to her rider, her lungs giving her a reserve of air and her oats giving her a store of energy. As we climbed, the Hun's gelding began to slip behind. When it lost sight of Diana, it slowed even more.

The sun was setting over a sea of blue mountains when I reined in at the crest of the pass. The rest of the party wouldn't make it this far today and it would be cold to wait for them at the summit, but I didn't care. I had ridden a smarter race.

Skilla finally came up at dusk, his horse looking ragged, as morose in defeat as he was jubilant in victory. "If not for the mountains, I would have beaten you."

"If not for the sea, I could walk to Crete." I held out my hand. "Two solidi, Hun. Now you must pay tribute to me."

It was such a bold insult that for a moment Skilla seemed ready to balk. Yet the Huns had their own sense of fairness, part of which was acknowledgment of debt. Grudgingly, the Hun handed over the coins. "Tomorrow again?"

"No. We'll get too far ahead of the others and kill our horses." I tossed a coin back. "We each won one day. Now we're even." It seemed the diplomatic thing to do.

The Hun contemplated the coin for a moment, embarrassed at the charity, and then cocked his arm and hurled it away into the dark.

"A good race, Roman." He tried to smile but it was a grimace. "Someday, perhaps, we will race for real, and then—no matter how long your lead—I will catch you and kill you."

VI

THE NEW KING OF CARTHAGE

How far the fight for justice has taken me, thought the Greek doctor Eudoxius.

It was dazzling noon at conquered Carthage on the shore of North Africa, and the rebel physician found himself in a world of bizarre color. Marble and stucco shimmered like snow. Arcades and antechambers were hollows of dark shadow. The Mediterranean was as blue as the cloak of the Virgin, and the sands shone as blond as a Saxon's hair. So different from the hues of Gaul and Hunuguri! How odd to come to this capital that had been destroyed by the Roman Republic so many centuries ago, rebuilt by the Roman Empire, and now captured and occupied by Vandals—a people who had originated in gray lands of snow and fog. Down from the cold the tribe had come, carving like a knife through the Western Empire for decade after decade. Finally they marched through Hispana to the Pillars of Hercules and learned to be sailors, and then they seized the warm and fecund granary of Africa, the capital of which was Carthage. The Vandals, once disdained as hapless barbarians, now rested their boots on the throat of Rome.

As if to fit their sunny new kingdom, King Gaiseric's rude and chaotic court was a rainbow of recruited human color, of blond Vandal and red-headed Goth, black Ethiopian and brown Berber, swarthy Hun and bronzed Roman. All these opportunists had been collected in the migratory conquest and now roosted in a half-deserted and decaying city that no one bothered to keep up anymore. Carthage's palaces had become barracks, its kitchens sties; its aqueducts were falling into disrepair, and its roads were buckling from the assault of sun and rain. There were no engineers left, no scholars, no priests, no astronomers, and no philosophers. All had been slain or fled, and the schools had closed. The barbarians paid no money to maintain them. There was just Gaiseric's powerful army and navy, foraging on the carcasses of the countries they conquered like a tide of ants and wondering how soon they must resume their ravaging march.

Eudoxius believed he knew the answer. Ignorant, arrogant, and illiterate these Vandals might be, but they had seized Sicily and could almost throw stones at Italy itself. As a result, Rome was in the lion's jaw. The top of the mouth was represented by the empire of Attila, occupying the roof of Europe. The bottom was Gaiseric, the conqueror of northwestern Africa. Now the two rulers merely had to be convinced to snap their jaws shut in unison and the oppressive fragment of empire left between them would at last disappear. With it would go the greedy landlords, the heartless slave traders, the pompous aristocrats, the cruel tax collectors, and the corrupt priests who lived like lice on the body of the poor. Had not the Christ himself condemned such leeches? Ever since Eudoxius had realized how the world truly worked—that the strong stole from the weak—he had been determined to change it. Rome was a cancer, and from its excision would rise a better world. These ignorant barbarians would be his unwitting tool to forge a new paradise.

The Greek plied the physician's trade only when hunger and the lack of a patron made it necessary. Medicine was a messy business replete with failure and blame, and Eudoxius didn't really like to work. His real passion was politics, and he imagined himself the liberator of the vast peasantry that Rome had oppressed for centuries. In the early days the Romans had exemplified a golden age of yeoman farmers and free men, the Greek believed, banding together to triumph through virtue as well as courage. But this Republican brotherhood had gradually been replaced by tyranny and sloth and the worst kinds of taxes, slavery, tenant farming, and compulsory military service. In his youth, Eudoxius had preached reform, just as the Lord Jesus had preached his own kingdom in the hills of Judea, but his Greek neighbors jeered at him, too ignorant to understand their own democratic history. So after migrating to northeastern Gaul, where the inhabitants were simpler and less skeptical, he had helped organize an uprising of the Bagaudae tribe against the Romans. His dream was to create a kingdom of free men, with him at its head! Then the great and ruthless General Flavius Aetius had led his mongrel mix of Roman soldiers and barbarian mercenaries against the rebellion, slaughtering the Bagaudae and forcing Eudoxius to flee to Attila. How humiliating! The doctor had been forced to pledge fealty to the worst tyrant of all, the king of the Huns.

At first Eudoxius was in despair. Then he realized that this must all be God's plan and that he had been given an opportunity to create alliance. How shrewd were the mysterious ways of the Almighty! The doctor began to whisper in Attila's ear.

Aetius! The very name was a curse. Romans hailed a man whom Eudoxius considered to be a toad for Emperor Valentinian and his mother, Placidia, a scheming and slippery general who had been sent as a hostage to the Huns in his youth, learned their language, and then hired the Huns to annihilate his ever-changing enemies. Aetius represented the whirlpool of alliance, betrayal, and assault that passed for imperial policy. For decades the wily general had played one tribe against another to hold the rotten toga of Rome together. As long as Aetius existed, Rome existed. And as long as Rome existed there could be no true democracy: nothing, at least, like the great civilization of ancestral Athens. But now Attila had united the Huns, and Gaiseric had seized Carthage and Sicily. It was time for the lion's final bite.

A hairy red giant of a Vandal lieutenant summoned Eudoxius inside for his audience, so he left the blinding courtyard for the cool darkness of its throne room. At first he could barely see, smelling instead the animal rankness of a crude barbarian court. There was the sweat of rarely washed bodies; the stink of the discarded food that the slovenly Vandals could not bring themselves to clean away; the thick incense Gaiseric burned to mask the smells; the tang of sword oil; and the musk of public, shameless sex. Gaiseric's captains were sprawled on heaps of stolen carpets and lion skins. Their women lolled with them, some as pale as snow and others as black as ebony, curled like satiated cats, many with breasts and hips bare and one, snoring, with her legs splayed so obscenely that Eudoxius could scarcely believe these savages had converted even to the heretical Arian creed. Of course, Arians were false Christians, believing the Son inferior to the Father, but worse than this they prayed indifferently while slaying with ferocious intent, mixing Christian creed with pagan superstition. They were, in sum, savages, as apt to quail at thunder as they were to charge a Roman battle line. But these crude warriors were the necessary means to his noble end. His scheme was to let legionary and barbarian destroy each other in a single great battle until none were left, and then build after the slaughter.

Taking breath through his mouth to avoid the smell, Eudoxius made his way to the dim end of the hall.

"You come from Attila." It was Gaiseric, sixty years old now but still tall and powerful, seated on a gilded throne. His hair and beard were like a lion's mane, and his arms had the thickness of a bear's. The Vandal king sat upright and watchful. There were no women at *his* side. Two guards flanked him instead, one a Nubian and the other a pale and tattooed Pict. Gaiseric himself peered with bright, piercing blue eyes as out of place in this climate as ice. How far his people had marched! The Vandal king wore silver chain mail over captured Roman linens, as if expecting an attack at any moment, and a circlet of gold rested on his brow. A dagger was on his belt and a long sword and spear leaned on the wall behind him. He'd been lame since being thrown from a horse as a youth, and his lack of mobility and a life of enemies had made him cautious of attack.

Eudoxius bowed, his robes a curtain around his feet and his gray beard brushing his chest, gesturing with his hand at waist level in the manner of the East. "I come from your Hun brothers, great Gaiseric."

"The Huns are not my brothers."

"Aren't they?" Eudoxius boldly came closer. "Don't both of your kingdoms fight Rome? Are not both of your treasuries hungry for its gold? And is the accession of Attila and your own capture of Carthage not a sign from God, or all the gods, that the time has come for the world to be ruled anew? I have come with Attila's blessing, Gaiseric, to inquire about an alliance. The West has yet to feel Attila's wrath, but he is tempted by the opportunities there. Aetius is a formidable enemy, but only if he has one battle to fight at a time. Were Attila to attack Gaul at the same time the Vandals attacked Italy from the south, no Roman combination could stand before us."

Gaiseric brooded quietly for a while, considering the vast geographies that would be involved. "That is an ambitious plan."

"It is a logical plan. Rome prevails only by fighting the tribes and nations of the barbarians separately or by shrewdly pitting one against the other. The ministers in Ravenna laugh at how they manipulate their enemies, Gaiseric. I am of their world, and I have seen it. But were Hun and Vandal to march together, with Gepid and Scuri, Pict and Berber, then perhaps the man I see before me would be the next emperor."

This discussion was made in the earshot of Gaiseric's followers, in the open manner of barbarians who insisted on hearing a plan before following it. These final words made his lieutenants shout and hoot in agreement, banging goblets and daggers against the marble floors and roaring at the idea of ultimate triumph. Their king as emperor of Rome! But Gaiseric himself was quiet, his eyes probing, careful not to promise too much.

"I as emperor, or Attila?"

"Co-emperors, perhaps, on the model of the Romans."

"Humph." Gaiseric's fingers tapped on the arm of his throne. "Why is it *you* who have come with this proposition, physician? Why aren't you out lancing boils or brewing potions?"

"I've fought Aetius and his minions in eastern Gaul and seen poor men, whose only hope was to be free, slain by Roman tyranny. I barely escaped with my life and sought refuge with Attila, but I've never forgotten my people. Am I a mere doctor? Yes, but I minister to men's health by being their political champion as well as their physician. My role is to see that you and Attila understand how your interests coincide with all good men."

"You have a smooth tongue. Yet this Aetius is *your* enemy, not mine."

Here Eudoxius nodded, having anticipated this very objection. "As Theodoric and the Visigoths are *your* enemies, not mine."

Now the Vandals fell silent, as if a cloud had passed before the sun. Romans were targets, sheep to be harvested. But the rival Visigoths who had settled in southwestern Gaul were a deeper and more menacing opponent, a barbarian power as dangerous as their own. Here was rivalry that went back generations, two Germanic tribes with a long history of feuds. It was to a Visigoth that the Roman empress Placidia had once been wed, and it was the Visigoths who haughtily claimed to be more civilized as a result: as if they were better than the Vandals!

At one point King Gaiseric tried to heal the breach by having his son marry King Theodoric's daughter, to join the tribes with blood. But when the Roman emperor Valentinian later offered the boy his own daughter instead—clearly a more important and prestigious marriage— Gaiseric had tried to send the Vandal bride, a princess named Berta, back to her father in Gaul.

It was then that trouble truly started. The haughty Visigoths had refused to countenance the divorce of their already married Berta to make room for a new Roman wife. But the Roman princess, a Christian, wouldn't agree to polygamy. Visigothic refusal had been followed by recriminations, and recriminations by insult, and finally in a burst of drunken fury Gaiseric himself had slit the nose and ears of Berta and sent her in humiliation back to her father. Ever since, his dreams had been tormented by the possible vengeance of Theodoric: War with the Visigoths was what he feared above all else. "Do not mention those pig droppings in my court," he now growled uneasily.

"It is the land of the Visigoths that Attila covets," Eudoxius said. "It is Theodoric who is the only hope of Aetius. Pledge yourself to this war, Gaiseric, and your most hated enemy becomes Attila's enemy. Pledge yourself against Rome, and the Huns march against Theodoric. Even if he does not destroy the Visigoths Attila will surely wound them. Meanwhile, you can have Italy. But before Attila can march he must know you will distract the Romans in the south. That is the alliance that will benefit us all."

"When will Attila march?"

Eudoxius shrugged. "He is waiting for portents and signs, including a sign from you. Your word alone may help him to finally make up his mind. Can I carry word back of agreement?"

Gaiseric pondered a moment more, considering how he could pit Hun and Roman and Visigoth against one another and then march in to pick up the pieces. The doctor and his miserable peasants would be trampled by them all, he knew, but wasn't that how things were? The weak always gave way to the strong, and the foolish—like this doctor—were there to be used by the wise. How could he use him best? Finally he stood, swaying on his lame foot. "I am going to offer your king the jeweled dagger that I took from the mangled body of the Roman general Ausonius as proof of my word," he pronounced. "All men know that this is my favorite knife. Give it to your new king, and tell the great Attila that if the Romans and Visigoths are his enemies, then I am his friend!"

His captains and their women roared in acclamation of this pledge, banging and screaming; and to Eudoxius it was the sweet sound of wolves, howling at the moon. He retreated with a grateful bow, unable to suppress his jubilant smile, and hurried to take ship with his news.

Later that evening, King Gaiseric drank with his men out in the warm courtyard, the desert they had come so far to conquer glittering under a shroud of stars. "We have accomplished two things this day, my chiefs," he confided when drunk enough. "First, we have encouraged Attila to destroy Theodoric before Theodoric can destroy us. And second, I have gotten rid of that cursed knife I took from the Roman and cut that bitch of a Visigoth princess with. Every time I have worn it since then, I've had bad luck. Let this idiot of a doctor take it to Attila and see if they do any better."

VII

A RUINED CITY

I first truly realized what kind of a world I was journeying into when our Roman embassy camped on the banks of the Nisava River, across from the sacked city of Naissus. The day was late, the sun already gone behind the mountains, and in the dimness it was possible to imagine that the roofless walls still represented a thriving Roman provincial city of fifty thousand people, waiting until the last possible minute to light their lamps. But as dusk deepened, no lamps shone. Instead, birds funneled down in somber spirals to roost in new nests that had been built in empty markets, theaters, baths, and brothels. Bats swirled out from abandoned cellars. The city's stones were shaggy with vines and brambles, and the desolation seemed somber and ominous.

Our camping place became even grimmer when we began to pitch our tents. It was dusk as I have said, difficult to see the ground, and when one of our slaves bent to tie a rope to what appeared to be a brown and weathered root, the peg burst upward from the soil as if rotten. The annoyed slave bent to retrieve the stick and throw it away in disgust, but as he straightened and cocked his arm, he suddenly looked in startled recognition and dropped it as if it were hot.

"Lord Jesus!" He began to back away.

"What's wrong?"

The man crossed himself.

Sensing what it must be, I bent. The stem was a bone, I confirmed, the size and shape clearly human. A gray and brown femur, now jagged at one edge and spotted with lichen. I glanced about, my skin prickling. The displacement of earth had revealed the knobs of other bones and that what had appeared to be a half-buried rock in the twilight was in fact the dome of a skull. How rarely we look down! Now my eyes began sweeping the ground of the riverbank where we were making camp. There were bones everywhere, and what had seemed a shoal of weathered sticks left by a flooding current was in fact a litter of exposed human remains. Sightless sockets, stuffed with dirt, looked blankly at the sky. Ribs held together by persistent sinews of dried flesh curled from the soil like reaching fingers.

I hurried to the senator. "We're in some kind of graveyard."

"Graveyard?" asked Maximinus.

"Or battlefield. Look. There are bones everywhere."

We Romans began scuffling at the soil in wonder, crying out at each discovery and jumping when a crunch told us we had stepped on another fragment of the dead. The slaves joined in the dismayed clamor, and soon the camp was in an uproar. Tents that were being raised abruptly deflated, fires went unlit, and picketed horses whinnied nervously at the human disarray. Each skeleton brought a fresh shout of horror.

Edeco strode over in annoyance, kicking aside the denuded limbs with his boots as if they were autumn litter. "Why aren't you camping, Romans?"

"We're in a boneyard," Maximinus said. "Some massacre from Naissus."

The Hun looked down at the remains, then looked around in sudden recognition. "I remember this place. The Romans fled like sheep, many swimming the river. We crossed ahead and waited for them here. If the city had submitted, they might have had a chance, but they had killed some of our warriors and so no mercy could be shown." He turned, squinting downriver, and pointed to some feature in the gloom. "I think we killed them from here to there."

His voice carried no shame, no remorse, not even the pride of victory. He recounted the slaughter as if recalling a business transaction.

Maximinus's voice was thick. "For the Savior's sake, then why did we camp here? Have you no decency? We must move at once."

"Why? They are dead, and we will be, too, someday. All of us will be bones sooner or later. A bone is a bone, no different here than in a kitchen or waste yard. It turns to dust. The whole world is bone, I suspect."

The diplomat strained for patience. "These are our people, Edeco. We must move the camp out of respect for their remains. We should come back tomorrow to bury and sanctify these poor victims."

"Attila gives no time for that."

"There are too many, senator," added Bigilas, who was translating the exchange.

Maximinus looked gloomily into the dark. "Then we must at least change our camping place. There are ghosts here."

"Ghosts?"

"Can't you feel the spirits?"

The Hun scowled, but his superstition showed. We walked half a mile to get out of the killing field, stopping in the lee of a ruined and abandoned Roman villa. The Huns seemed surprised and subdued by our reaction, as if upset that their companions had taken the battlefield so badly. Death was simply the result of war, and war itself was life.

Since the Hun kit was simple—a cloak to wrap themselves in on the ground—their own move was uncomplicated. We Romans once more laboriously erected our canvas against the starry sky while the unoccupied barbarians built a large fire in the ruins of the house to roast some meat. The flames seemed to push back the haunting. "Come, eat with us, Romans," the Roman turncoat Onegesh called, "and drink, too. Don't dwell on what can't be undone. Think of our mission to Attila and peace in the future!"

We sat in the roofless triclinium, its owners likely lying somewhere nearby. While the walls reflected some of the fire's light and heat, the habitation was sad. Its bright plaster murals were mildewed and peeling, cherubic gods and bright peacocks glazed with the dirt of neglect. The mosaic floor displaying a feast of Bacchus was obscured by litter. Weeds had erupted through the pavers of the courtyard, and its pool was thick with scum. More vegetation crowded the outer walls, and I had the curious feeling that the house was slowly sinking back into the earth, like bones into soil. The Huns had started the flames with broken furniture and were using the detritus of the dwelling to keep it fueled, turning to ash the last evidence that these dead had ever truly lived here. To my dismay, I saw that Edeco was even feeding half-ruined books and scrolls into the fire. The chieftain glanced at some before throwing them in, but often held them sideways or upside down. It was obvious he couldn't read.

"Don't burn those!" I exclaimed.

"Relax. There's no one left to read them."

"That's a thousand years of knowledge and history!"

"What good did it do them in the end?" He threw another into the flames.

We sat uneasily. "By God, even I need a drink," muttered the normally abstentious Maximinus. "I've never seen a boneyard like that." He took his wine unwatered, gulping the first cup. Bigilas, of course, was already ahead of him. The Huns were drinking *kumiss* and the heady German beer, *kamon*.

"Only two times do you see so many together," Edeco said, "when they fight like cornered bears and when they flee like sheep. These were sheep, dead in their own hearts before we slew them. It was their fault. They should have surrendered."

"If you'd stayed in your own country they all would have lived," the senator grumbled.

"The People of the Dawn have no country. We follow the sun, go where we please, settle where we wish, and take what we need. These dead tarried to cut and rob the earth, and the gods don't like that. It's not that we came but that the Romans stayed too long. It isn't right for men to nest and dig. Now they will stay here forever."

"I hope you are as philosophical about your own death."

Bigilas stumbled on the word *philosophical* as he translated and looked to Maximinus for a substitute. "Thoughtful," the senator supplied.

Edeco laughed. "Who cares what I will think! I will be dead!"

"But you destroy what you could seize," Maximinus tried to reason. "You burn what you could live in and kill those you could enslave. You take once, yes, but if you showed mercy and governed the people you conquer, you could live in leisure."

"Like you Romans."

"Yes, like us Romans."

"If we lived like you do we would rule until we became fat, like the people who lived here, and then someone else would do to us what we did to them. No, better to stay on our horses, ride, and keep strong. Who cares that this city is gone? There are many, many cities."

"But what happens when you've raided everything, burned it all, and nothing is left?"

The Hun shook his head. "There are many cities. I will be dead long before then, and like those bones."

At length the drink began to numb us and lighten the Huns. The conversation slowly turned to other things. Both nations had sacked cities, of course. Rome had prevailed by its own ruthlessness, we knew. In the end, it was only the threat of Roman arms that gave our own embassy any meaning. So it did no good to brood on the fate of Naissus, just as Edeco had said. As they became drunker, the Huns began boasting of their mighty home camp and the deeds of their king, who they said had no fear, no greed, and no guile. Attila lived simply so his followers could become rich, fought bravely so his women could know peace, judged harshly so his warriors could live in harmony, talked to high and low alike, welcomed freed slaves into his armies, and led his men from the front rank.

"So let us drink to both our kings," Edeco proposed, slurring his words, "ours on horseback and yours behind his walls." The company hoisted their cups.

"To our rulers!" Maximinus cried.

Only Bigilas, who had been drinking steadily and who had remained uncharacteristically dour and quiet, neglected to join the toast.

"You won't drink to our kings, translator?" the Hun chieftain challenged. The shadows of his facial scars were lit so that his visage seemed streaked with paint.

"I will drink to Attila alone," Bigilas said with sudden belligerence, "even though his Huns killed family I once had here. Or to Theodosius alone. But it seems to me blasphemy for my comrades to raise their cups to both together when all know that the emperor of Rome is a god and Attila is only a man."

The group immediately fell silent. Edeco looked at Bigilas in disbelief.

"Let's not pretend a tent and a palace are the same," Bigilas went on doggedly. "Or Rome and Hunuguri."

"You insult our king? The most powerful man in the world?"

"I insult no one. I speak only the truth when I say no mere man is the equal of the emperor of Rome. One is mortal, one is divine. This is common sense."

"I will show you equality!" cried an angry Skilla, hurling his wine cup into a corner where it clanged, and standing to unsheathe his sword. "The equality of the grave!"

The other Huns sprang up and drew their weapons as well. We Romans stood awkwardly, armed with nothing but the daggers we had been using to eat with. The barbarians looked murderous and could slay us in an instant, as casually as they had slain the people of Naissus. Bigilas stumbled backward. His drink-benumbed brain had finally caught up with his mouth and he realized he had risked us all.

"You fool," Maximinus hissed.

"I only said the truth," he mumbled truculently.

"A truth that could get us stabbed or crucified."

"When Attila speaks, the earth trembles," Edeco growled ominously. "Perhaps it is time you trembled yourselves, Romans, and joined your brethren on the riverbank there." Any pretense of genial debate was gone. I realized that our complaints about the slaughter on the riverbank had gnawed at the Huns. Was there guilt there after all? Now the tension had become manifest.

Bigilas looked uncertain whether to beg or flee. His mouth opened and shut uselessly.

Rusticius decided to come to the defense of his fellow translator, even though I knew he could hardly stand the man's pretensions. "No true Roman trembles, any more than any true Hun," Rusticius tried. "You are brave, Edeco, with your head full of drink and your sword at hand, while Bigilas and the rest of us are defenseless."

The Hun grinned evilly. "Then fill your hands."

"I'll fill them when we have a chance, not to give you another excuse for slaughter like your massacre on the riverbank." Rusticius looked stubborn, and I was taken aback by his courage. I hadn't seen this side of him before.

"Don't test me, boy."

"I'm no boy, and no true man threatens murder and pretends it is combat."

"For God's sake," Maximinus groaned, fearful his mission was about to end before it had properly started. Edeco's knuckles were white on the hilt of his sword. Something had to be done.

"You misunderstood our companions." I spoke up, my voice sounding even to my own ears as barely more than a pathetic squeak. As the youngest and least-threatening traveler, perhaps I could smooth things over. Gulping, I found my normal voice. "Our translator Bigilas doesn't assemble his words well when he's had too much to drink, as all know. He meant to honor Attila, because your king has achieved as much as a mortal as our emperor has with divine powers. He meant a compliment, not an insult, Edeco."

"Nonsense. The young Roman is trying to save himself," sneered Skilla.

"I am trying to save this embassy."

There was a long silence as the Huns weighed whether to accept this dubious excuse. If they slew us, both Attila and Chrysaphius would want to know why. "Is this so?" Edeco asked Bigilas.

He looked confused and nervous, glancing from me to the chieftain.

"Answer him, you idiot," Maximinus muttered.

"Yes," he finally said. "Yes, please, I meant no harm. All know how powerful Attila is."

"And no Roman could detract from that," Maximinus added. "Your lord is the most powerful monarch in Europe, Edeco. Come, come, Onegesh, Skilla. Sheathe your weapons and sit. I apologize for the confusion. We have more presents for you, pearls from India and silks from China. I was going to wait until we reached Hunuguri, but perhaps I will fetch them now. As a sign of our good faith."

"You will drink to Attila first." Edeco pointed. "Him."

Bigilas nodded and hastily hoisted his cup, gulping. Then he lowered it and wiped his mouth. "To Attila," he croaked.

"And you," he said, pointing to Rusticius. He sheathed his sword and stood with his hands open, ready at his side. "You think I am afraid to deal with you like this?"

Rusticius's voice came from a mouth that was a line. "I think all of us should treat each other like men, not animals."

It was not the abject apology the Hun was looking for, and from that moment he would react to Rusticius with a coldness he never showed the foolish Bigilas: Rusticius's courage had made him an enemy. But the Hun provided an exit.

"Then drink to my king."

Rusticius shrugged. "Indeed."

So the rest of us drank as well. "To Attila!"

With that we all finally sat again, and slaves fetched the gifts Maximinus directed. The senator tried to pretend that nothing had happened, but the tension of this night lingered. As soon as was seemly, our gathering broke up.

"Your quickness may have saved our lives, Alabanda," Maximinus murmured to me as we groped in the dark for our tents. "Just as that fool Bigilas might have ended them. You may have the wit to be an ambassador yourself someday."

I was still shaken, believing I had seen the true nature of our barbarian companions for the first time. When crossed, they turned into vipers. "I think I'll be happy just to keep my head attached. I hope Rusticius can keep his. I've not seen him with his back up."

"Yes, he has a stubborn bravery, but it's risky to insult a Hun. You are wise enough to listen before you speak, I sense. Never assume barbarians are the same, young man. The Franks and Burgundians, once arrogant, are now our allies in the Western Empire. The fearsome Celts have become the peaceful citizens of Gaul. Huns have proved coura-

geous mercenaries as well as implacable enemies. The secret is not to an-
tagonize potential enemies but to court potential friends. The Empire
can win only by using barbarian against barbarian. Do you understand
what I'm saying, my scribe?"

Yes, I understood. We were trying to placate jackals.

VIII

THE HOSPITALITY OF
THE HUNS

The next morning, as we proceeded down the Margus valley, Skilla rode his pony next to mine. There was no challenge this time. Everyone's head was fogged from the evening's drinking and quarreling, and conversation had been quiet. Now the Hun warrior simply had a question.

"Tell me, Roman, what god do *you* believe in?"

I shook my head to clear it, thinking it entirely too early for theological discussion. "The Christ, of course. You've heard of Jesus? He's the God of the Roman world."

"But before him the Romans had other gods."

"True. And some Romans are still pagans, passionately so. There is always great debate about religion. If you ask three Constantinople shopkeepers you will get eight opinions. Put a priest in the mix and the arguments are endless."

"So Bigilas is a pagan?"

"I don't think so. He wears a crucifix."

"Yes, I have seen his tree that your god was killed on. Attila learned to use the cross from Romans. But this Christ allows no other gods—is this not true?"

I saw where this was headed. "Yes."

"Yet Bigilas calls his emperor a god—is this not true?"

"Yes. It's . . . complicated."

"It's not complicated at all. He claims to believe first one thing, then another."

"No . . ." How to explain? "Many Christians consider our emperor divine. It is a tradition of many centuries: believing gods are manifest on earth. But not in the way that Jesus is divine. The emperor is . . . well, simply more than a mere man. He represents the divine nature of life. That's all Bigilas meant. He didn't mean to insult Attila."

"Attila has no need to claim to be a god. Men fear and respect him without it."

"He's lucky, then."

"Rome's emperors must be little gods, if they fear a mere man like Attila."

"Rome's emperors aren't just soldiers, Skilla. They symbolize civilization itself. Law and order, prosperity, morality, marriage, service, sanctity, continuity . . . all are bound up in them. That's why they represent the divine."

"Attila is no different."

"But your empire doesn't build, it destroys. It doesn't give order, it takes it away. It *is* different."

"In my empire, the word of Attila is law for a thousand miles. He has given order to a hundred different tribes. It *is* the same, whatever you say."

I sighed. How to reason with a man who hadn't even entered Constantinople, instead sleeping outside like an animal? "What gods do Huns worship, then?"

"We have nature gods, and shamans and soothsayers, and know good signs from bad ones. But we're not obsessed with gods like Romans. We've overrun hundreds of gods and none helped their believers prevail against us. So what good are gods?"

"Three generations ago, the armies of the Christian Romans and the pagan Romans fought a battle on the Frigidus River that the whole world saw as a contest of faith. The Christians won."

"They have not won against us." Skilla galloped ahead.

It was later that day that we encountered a task even more disagreeable than camping near a boneyard. Maximinus had sent word of our progress ahead to what shaky Roman authority survived here, and we were duly met by Agintheus, commander of the Illyrian soldiers who had tentatively reoccupied the ravaged valley. While not pretending to be able to stand before another Hun invasion, this rough militia kept the region from anarchy. Now we carried embarrassing orders from the emperor that Agintheus was to give up five of the men who had joined him after deserting Attila. We were to take them back to the Hun king for judgment.

The five had been prepared for this. They rode without weapons, their hands tied to their saddles, and had the look of the doomed. Agintheus looked ashamed. By their appearance the five seemed to be Germans, tall and fair-haired. The smaller, darker Huns mocked them, galloping around like circling dogs. "Now you must explain yourselves to Attila!" Edeco cried in triumph.

"At your command, I return these men," Agintheus announced. "The other twelve you wrote about are nowhere to be found."

"Their good luck, I suppose," muttered Maximinus.

"Or wisdom." Agintheus sighed. "These soldiers deserve better, senator."

"It is necessary to conform to the treaty."

"It is an evil treaty."

"Imposed by the Huns. Someday . . ."

"See that it doesn't go badly for them, ambassador."

"Attila needs men, not corpses. They'll survive."

As our expanded party rode away toward Hunuguri the five prisoners called back to their general. "Good-bye, Agintheus. God be with you! You have treated us well! Look after our families!" Their new wives ran after them, wailing, but the Hun rode among the deserters and lashed them into silence. At length, their homes were left behind.

"Why are we giving the Huns those men?" I asked Maximinus. "This is wrong."

"It's at the insistence of Attila."

"And they have to leave their families behind?"

"Attila would say they should never have started families."

"But why give back recruits to a despot we've been fighting?"

Maximinus frowned. "Because he is more desperate for men than for gold. Many German allies flee his armies. The Huns are great warriors, but they aren't numerous."

"What will happen when we turn them over?"

"I don't know. Perhaps they will be whipped. It's possible they will be crucified. But most likely they will just be pressed back into his armies. The lesson here, Alabanda, is that sometimes you have to do bad things to do good: in this case, peace."

I rode in silence for a while. "There is another lesson as well, senator."

"What, my youthful friend?"

"That Attila has a weakness, and that is manpower. If the provinces of Rome and their barbarian allies could ever unite and field a truly great army, and make him pay a heavy price on the battlefield, then his power to frighten us would be at an end."

Maximinus laughed. "The dreams of youth!"

I resented the condescension. It was not a dream. If Attila took the time to care about five fugitives, it was reality.

Although the province of Moesia that we traveled through had been Roman territory for hundreds of years, civilization had been abandoned. Hun and Goth had crisscrossed this land for nearly three-quarters of a century; and each invasion had further crippled the economy, stolen tax collections, and beggared repairs. As a result, mills had long since stopped turning, their waterwheels rotted away. Bridges had collapsed, forcing our embassy to detour upstream to fords. Fields were being reclaimed by oak and scrub pine. Granaries had been looted, and broken wagons lay rotting in high grass. Mountains that had not seen a bear for generations now were the home of sow and cubs. At Horreum we passed a cracked aqueduct spilling water uselessly into a new erosive channel.

Most haunting of all were the cities, empty save a few priests, wild refugees, and the dogs that went with them. Frost and rain had cracked the walls, stucco had peeled like tired paper, and roof tiles had cascaded off abandoned houses to heap in piles of red dust.

There were inhabitants still, but they were a peculiarly hard and skittish lot. Shepherds stayed cautiously on slopes high above the road, allowing plenty of time to flee. Surviving farms were tucked into side valleys where they were less visible to roving armies. Groups of armed Roman bandits scavenged like animals. Accordingly, several old Roman villas had been turned into small castles with new walls and towers, their determined owners clinging to ancestral lands. Where peacocks once strutted, now chickens ran.

The road began to drop in elevation, the pines giving way to forests of oak, beech, elm, and alder; and the mountains were left behind for terrain that was flatter, wetter, and more confusing. Roads in the Danube valley wound around marshes like snarled thread: One morning we woke to see our path leading briefly east, not west! Finally we came to the banks of the broad Danube itself, its powerful current opaque and green. This river, once patrolled by the Roman navy, now was bare of ships. The paths on which slaves or oxen had towed the craft upstream were overgrown.

Here was the historic boundary of the Empire: Rome to the south, barbarians to the north. The river retained its majestic serenity. Birds followed its course in flocks so great that at times they shaded the sun, and eddies and sloughs were dotted with ducks and geese. The Huns amused themselves by plucking some of the fowl out of the sky with their arrows. I would have feared losing my shafts, but they never missed.

"How will we get across?" Maximinus asked Edeco.

"River men will take us. There should be some near."

Indeed, we spotted a plume of smoke a short distance upriver and found a crude settlement that was a polyglot of races: old Huns, surviving Romans, refugee Germans, even a black Ethiopian cast up at this outpost, all living together in a warren of log cabins, round houses, ragged tents, and riverbank caves. Naked children played amid wandering geese and pigs. Fly-specked game and fish dried in the sun. On the shore were a dozen log canoes. The crudeness was startling compared to the proud merchant ships and triremes of the Golden Horn. How could such simple people, incapable of building a decent boat, force Nova Roma to come to them in supplication? Yet here we humbled Romans were, bartering for passage with the canoe builders.

We crossed in turns, the villagers paddling while we passengers gripped the canoe sides as if that might somehow help prevent a capsize. Once again, I saw the nervousness of the Huns about water. There was no mishap, however, and our goods stayed dry, the horses and mules swimming at the end of their reins. At length we all gained the wild northern shore and made camp, building driftwood fires.

Rusticius joined me while we sat by the river eating our supper: duck and roots purchased from the village, a pinch of aniseed giving it a little of the flavor of home. "Do you regret your decision to come?" I knew he felt responsible for inviting me, and I had adopted him as my elder brother.

"Of course not." I swallowed the lie. "What an opportunity you've given me, my friend."

"Or risk." He looked gloomy. "These Huns are sour and humorless, aren't they? Edeco is a bully. I hope we don't have trouble in their camp."

"It they wanted trouble they would have made it a hundred miles ago," I reassured him with more confidence than I truly felt. "We have Rome's protection, don't we?"

"Which seems an ocean away, now that we've crossed that river." He shook his head. "Don't let my foreboding affect you, Jonas. You're young and more likable than any of us. You've great things ahead of you. I have less confidence in my own luck."

"You were brave to stand up to Edeco at the ruined villa."

"Or foolish. He expects submission. I don't think he's done with me yet."

Messengers found us with word that Attila was at his camp many days away, so on we went. We found the Tisza River, a broad and gray-green river that is a tributary of the Danube, and followed it northward into Hunuguri. Its banks were lined with timber, like its sister river, and again no ships were available to provide easy passage. Instead, we paralleled it on a great open plain the likes of which I had never seen. While before the sky was hemmed with mountains, now it was a vast bowl that bent to distant horizons. Grass had become an ocean, and animals moved across it in browsing herds. Hawks wheeled high above, while butterflies danced ahead of the legs of our horses.

Sometimes we saw distant curtains of smoke, and Onegesh told us the barbarians kept the flat landscape open by setting fires. Their animals also kept it mowed. Vast collections of horses and cattle roamed seemingly at will, yet the warriors were able to tell at a glance which tribe a herd belonged to: here Gepid, there Goth, now Scuri. Stucco and tile Roman architecture had given way to villages of wattle-and-daub huts or timber cabins. Their smoke holes carried new and foreign smells.

Maximinus, who had studied the maps and reports of travelers, said we were in a vast basin between two mountain ranges, Alps to the west and the Carpathians to the east. "Hunuguri has become their promised land," he told us. "You'd think that having conquered a place better than their homeland they would be content, but instead they have multiplied and become fractious. There's not enough grass to hold them all, so they raid."

For the most part our diplomatic party kept to itself, making better progress by skirting the villages. But on the fifth day after we had left the Danube some freakish weather gave us a taste of Hun hospitality and made me reassess this barbarian people yet again.

The day had been muggy, the sky to the west heavy and yellow. When we stopped for the night at the shore of a large lake, the sun set in murk so thick that the orb turned brown. Vast clouds began to ominously form, their tops as broad and flat as anvils. Lightning flickered in their black bases.

For the first time, I saw the Huns uneasy. If men couldn't scare them, thunder might. "Witch weather," Edeco muttered. Onegesh surprised me by quickly crossing himself. Was the traitorous Roman still a

Christian? The grumble of the storm began to walk across the lake and the water turned gray and troubled, waves breaking and leaving a scud of foam.

"Come in our tents," Maximinus offered.

Edeco shook his head, eyes darting. "We will stay with our horses."

"Your animals will be fine."

"I don't like canvas holes."

Dark tentacles of rain were sweeping across the lake, so we left the Huns to themselves. "They don't have the sense of dogs sometimes," Rusticius said. And, indeed, we'd no sooner huddled inside than the fabric suddenly began a furious rattle and the wind rose to a shriek. A downpour began, the tent twitching under its pounding.

"Thank the Lord we came with shelter," Maximinus said, eyeing the hammered canvas uneasily. The wind rose, the fabric rattling. Our poles leaned from the strain.

"There's nothing on this shoreline to block the wind," Bigilas pointed out unnecessarily, and then the air cracked with thunder, the boom echoing in our ears. The air smelled like metal.

"It will soon be over," Rusticius hoped.

No sooner had he said it than a higher gust struck like a wall and our shelter collapsed, pegs and ropes flying wildly and poles snapping in two. We were trapped, just as Edeco had feared, and the enclosing folds beat on us like flails. We crawled for escape, "Here's the flap!" Maximinus called. We struggled out into a night that was now completely black and howling.

"Where are the Huns?" The senator gasped against the suck of wind.

"They have abandoned us!" Bigilas cried. Indeed, there was no sign of them, the horses, or the mules.

"What do we do now?" I shouted above the sting of rain. Waves crashed on the lakeshore like ocean surf, and spray whipped off their tops.

"There was a village two miles back," Rusticius remembered.

"Tell the slaves to secure our tents and baggage," Maximinus shouted. "We'll seek shelter in the town."

We struggled back along the lakeshore, clinging to each other, and at length stumbled upon the cluster of cabins. We called for help in Hunnish until the portal of the largest house opened.

Stumbling inside, blinking in dim firelight, we saw our rescuer was a middle-aged Hun woman, slight, wizened, and with sad but luminous eyes.

"Ah, the Romans," she said in Hunnish. "I saw you passing and thought I might see you again when I noticed the storm. Edeco tries to avoid me, but now he can't."

"We've lost him," Bigilas said.

"Or they lost you. They will come here looking."

"A woman alone?" Maximinus whispered to me in Latin.

"He seeks to know your husband," I interpreted to her rather loosely.

"My husband is dead. I, Anika, head the village now. Come, let's light more lamps and build up the fire. Sit, have some meat, *kumiss*, and *kamon*."

Chilled, hungry, and thirsty, I gulped the latter. It was a dark and foamy liquid that is made, she explained, from barley. While sour compared to sweet wine, it was rich and warming, and heady enough that I soon saw the hut through a pleasant haze. The wood joinery was quite fine, I decided blearily, and the proportions pleasing: There was more craftsmanship in barbarian dwellings than I expected. The fire pit glowed with hot coals and the storm was reassuringly muffled, hissing against the thatch. Rushes covered the dirt floor, woven blankets hung on the walls, and crude stools gave us places to sit. What a refuge this was, after so many days in camp! Anika ordered her slaves to fetch help, and soon men and women were entering to bring stew, bread, berries, and fish. I drifted in a happy haze. After a time the wind began to die. Eventually Edeco, Onegesh, and Skilla appeared from the storm, dripping wet but apparently well satisfied that they had either safeguarded the horses or outmaneuvered their demons and witches.

"You were not going to say hello, Edeco?" Anika challenged.

"You know the animals needed pasture, Anika." Clearly they had some awkward history. He turned to us. "I told you those tents were no good. Learn to make a yurt."

"Which I have not seen *you* erect," Anika chided him.

He ignored her. "If the horses had stampeded, we would have a long walk to catch them," he explained unnecessarily, perhaps embarrassed that we had been separated by the storm. He sat, looking away.

Maximinus, curious, leaned to him and I translated. "She has authority like a man."

"She has the respect accorded her dead husband," Edeco muttered.

"And who was her husband?"

"Bleda."

Maximinus started at this news.

I had not heard this name.

"Bleda was Attila's brother," Bigilas explained self-importantly. "For a time they ruled together, until Attila killed him. This must be one of his widows."

I was intrigued. "He murdered his own brother?"

"It was necessary," Edeco muttered.

"She's allowed to live?"

"She's kin and no threat. Attila honors her with this village. If he did not, the blood feud would continue. This village is *konoss*."

Again, a word I was unfamiliar with. "What is *konoss*?"

"It is payment for a blood debt. A man caught stealing cattle can be killed, or he or his relatives can give *konoss* by paying the man stolen from. Goods can be paid for a life. A life can be traded for another's. Attila or Bleda had to die—everyone knew that—because they could no longer rule together. So Attila murdered Bleda and paid *konoss* to his wives."

I looked around. This hut seemed meager payment for the life of a husband, a king.

"When you are as powerful as Attila," Bigilas said slyly, "you can decide how generous your *konoss* is going to be."

"When you are a helpless woman," Anika said, who had clearly overheard our whispering, "you must decide how little you will accept to keep the peace." There was an edge of bitterness, but then she shrugged. "Yet I offer the hospitality of the steppes to any travelers. Our women will still warm you to sleep."

What did this mean? As if in answer, soft laughter and the light shuffling of feet caused us to turn. A dozen pretty females slipped into the room, heads cloaked against the now-drizzling rain, eyes bright, their forms draped in intricately embroidered dresses and their feet shod in boots of soft deer leather, soaked from the wet grass. They giggled as they reviewed us shyly, golden girdles cinching their slim waists and lace curving across the hillocks of their breasts. I found myself embarrassingly aroused. It had been weeks since I'd seen young women, and the long abstinence added to my enchantment.

"What in Hades is this?" Maximinus asked, looking more frightened than intrigued.

"Not Hades, senator, but Heaven," Bigilas replied with relish. "It's the custom of the Huns and the other nomads to offer women in hospitality."

"Offer? You mean for sex?"

"It is the pagan way."

Edeco, not embarrassed enough by Anika's history to turn down this opportunity, had already grabbed a plump and giggling girl and was dragging her away. Skilla had chosen a yellow-haired beauty, no doubt the product of capture and slavery. Onegesh was pointing to a redhead. I myself was captivated by a maiden with hair as black as raven's wings and fingers that sparkled with rings. I was both excited and nervous. My father had initiated me in the ways of love with courtesans in Constantinople, of course, but as a bachelor in an outwardly pious Christian city, my opportunities for lovemaking had been limited. What would it be like to lie with a girl of another culture?

"Certainly not," Maximinus announced. He turned to Anika. "Tell her thank you very much, but we are Christians, not pagans, and this is not our custom."

"But, senator," Bigilas pleaded. "It is their custom."

"We will make a better impression on Attila by displaying the stoic dignity of our Roman ancestors, not copying barbarians. Don't you think so, Jonas?"

I swallowed. "We don't want to hurt their feelings."

"Tell her that in our world we have one wife, not many, and that we revere our women, not share them," Maximinus insisted. "They are lovely girls, just lovely, but I for one will be more comfortable sleeping alone."

"For those of us who are not the diplomat . . ." Rusticius groaned.

"Will benefit from my example," the senator said.

Our Hun escort emerged in the glistening morning looking much more satisfied than we were, and their women tittered as they served us break-fast. Then we resumed our journey. Attila was said to be only two days away.

Again, Skilla was curious, riding next to me. "You did not take a woman?"

I sighed. "Maximinus told us not to."

"He does not like women?"

"I don't know."

"Why did he tell you not to?"

"In our world a man marries a single wife and is faithful to her."

"You are married?"

"No. The woman I was interested in . . . rejected me."

"She scratches?"

"Something like that."

"The ones not chosen were very hurt, you know."

My head ached from too much *kamon*. "Skilla, they were lovely. I was simply following orders."

He shook his head. "Your leader is a fool. It is not good to store up your seed. It will make you sick and cause more trouble later."

IX

THE LEGIONARY
FORTRESS

W hat a hollow thing our empire has become, Flavius Aetius thought
as he continued his inspection of the fort of Sumelocenna, on
the banks of Germania's Neckar River. What a hollow thing I have become. A general without a proper army.

"It's difficult to find masons these days, and so we've reinforced the
walls with a timber stockade," the tribune who was his guide was explaining with embarrassment. "There's some rot we're hoping to get to
when replacements arrive from Mediolanum. The local patrician is proving reluctant to contribute the trees. . . ."

"You can't teach your soldiers to lay one stone atop another, Stenis?"

"We've no lime and no money to buy any, commander. We're two
years behind in disbursements, and merchants have ceased delivering because we can never pay. The soldiers today won't do hard work; they say
that's a task for slaves and peasants. These tribesmen we recruit are a
different breed. They love to fight, but to drill . . ."

Aetius made no answer. What was the point? He'd heard these
complaints, repeated with little variation, from the mouth of the Rhine
to this outpost on the eastern side of the Black Forest—had heard them,

in fact, his entire life. Never enough men. Never enough money. Never enough weapons, stones, bread, horses, catapults, boots, cloaks, wine, whores, official recognition, or anything else to sustain the endless borders of Rome. The garrisons scarcely even looked like an army anymore, each man drawing an allowance to clothe and armor himself. They preened in military fashions that were sometimes as impractical as they were individualistic.

Aetius had lived half a century now, and for much of that time he had replaced his absence of military power with bluff, the tattered tradition of "inevitable" Roman victory, and shrewd alliances with whatever tribe he could persuade, pay, or coerce to oppose the menace of the moment. His was a lifetime of hard battles, shifting alliances, truculent barbarians, and selfish emperors. He had beaten the Franks, beaten the Bagaudae, beaten the Burgundians, beaten usurpers, and beaten the politicians in Italy who constantly whispered and conspired behind his back. He'd been consul three times, and, because he ran the army, ran the Western Empire in ways the Emperor Valentinian scarcely understood.

Yet instead of getting easier, each victory seemed more difficult. The moneyed sons of the rich bought their way out of the army, the poor deserted, and the barbarian recruits boasted more than they practiced. The relentless discipline that had marked Roman armies had eroded. Now he feared that the most dangerous enemy of all was casting a baleful eye in his direction. Aetius knew Attila, and knew how the angry, truculent youth he had once played and scuffled with had become a crafty, aggressive king. Aetius had been sent to the Huns as a boy hostage in 406 to help guarantee Stilicho's treaty with the tribe; and later, when his own fortunes were low in the political circus that was the Empire, he had fled to the Huns for safety. In turn, when Attila needed employment for his restless horde, Aetius had used them against Rome's enemies, paying generously. It had been a strange but useful partnership.

That was why the fool Valentinian had written him the latest dispatch.

Your requests for more military appropriations, which increasingly sound like demands, are entirely unreasonable. You, general, of all

people, know that the Huns have been our allies more than our ene-
mies here in the West. It is your skill that has made them a tool in-
stead of a threat. To pretend now that the Huns represent danger goes
against not only all experience but also your own personal history of
success. The needs of finance for the court in Italy are pressing, and no
more money can be spared for the frontiers of the Empire. You must
make do with what you have. . .

What Valentinian didn't understand is that all had begun to change
when King Ruga died and Attila and Bleda succeeded him. The Huns
had become more arrogant and demanding. It changed even more when
Attila murdered Bleda and turned the Huns from marauders to imperi-
alists. Attila understood Rome in ways that Ruga never had, and he
knew when to press incessantly and when to make a temporary peace.
Each campaign and treaty seemed to leave the Huns stronger and Rome
weaker. The East had already been stripped as if by locusts. How long
before Attila turned his eye west?

The weather today matched the general's mood, a gray pall with
steady rain. The drizzle showed all too well how the fortress leaked, and
rather than properly repair stone buildings that were two and three centuries old, the garrison had patched them with wood and wattle. The
trim precision of the old fort's layout had been lost to clusters of new
huts and wandering pathways.

"The men of the Twelfth are nonetheless ready for anything," the
tribune went on.

That was prattle. "This isn't a fortress—it's a nest."

"General?"

"A nest made of twigs and paper. Your stockade is so wormy that it's
ready to fall over. Attila could punch through it with his fist."

"Attila! But the king of the Huns is far away. Surely we don't have to
worry about Attila here."

"I worry about Attila in my dreams, Stenis. I worry about Attila in
Athens or Lutetia or Tolosa or Rome. It's my job and my fate to worry."

The tribune looked confused. "But you're his friend. Aren't you?"

Aetius looked somberly out at the rain. "Just as I am friend of the emperor, friend of his mother, friend of Theodoric at his court at Tolosa, and friend of King Sangibanus at Aurelia. I am friend of them all, the one man who binds them together. But I trust none of them, soldier. Nor should you."

The officer blanched at this irreverence but decided not to challenge it. "It's just that Attila has never come this way."

"Not yet." Aetius felt every moment of his fifty years. The endless rides on horseback, the hurry to every point of danger, the lack of a proper home. For decades he'd loved it. Now? "Soldiers prepare for the worst, do they not?"

"As you say, general."

"True Roman soldiers don't wait for money or permission to repair their walls, they do it today. If they've no lime, they buy it. If they can't buy it, they take it. And if those they take it from complain, they tell them that the army comes first, because in the end the army *is* Rome. Do the complaining merchants want a world of barbarian warlords and petty princes?"

"It's just as I have tried to tell them—"

Aetius stiffened as if coming to attention and thumped himself on the chest with his fist. "What is *in* your nest, tribune?"

"In it?" Again, Stenis looked confused. "The garrison, of course. Some are sick, many on leave, but if we have time enough—"

"What is *within* is what makes reputation. None dare disturb a wasp's nest, because behind its paper wall is a deadly sting. The smallest child could pierce a wasp fort, but even the bravest warrior will hesitate to do so. Why? Because of the fierce sentries inside. Those insects are your lesson! Sharpen your weapons against the Hun!"

"Attila? What have you heard?"

What indeed? Rumors, warnings, and observations that his strange dwarf spy had scribbled on scraps of paper and sent to him from Attila's camp. Did they mean anything? Was Attila increasingly studying the West? Had the disgruntled Frank named Cloda really fled to Attila to demand support for his claim to the throne of his people?

"Make your men into wasps, soldier, before it is too late."

X

KING OF THE HUNS

R omans are coming!"
The words were like flame in a darkened room. "An army?"
Ilana asked.

"Just an embassy," the cook reported.

The captive's heart sank as quickly as it had soared, and yet still it hammered in her breast like an anxious bird. At last, the slimmest connection to home! Since the sack of Axiopolis and the death of her father, Ilana had felt fogged in a vast and noisy Underworld, a migrating Hun capital of unruly children, barking dogs, submissive women, smoke, dirt, and grass. She was only beginning to understand their harsh language, brutal customs, and sour food. The shock of her city's massacre was with her at every moment like the pain of a broken heart, and the uncertainty of her future kept her anxious and sleepless. The dull work she was assigned failed to distract her.

Her situation was better than that of many captives, she knew. Her assignment as handmaiden to Suecca, one of the wives of the chieftain Edeco who had conquered her city, had protected her from the enslavement, rape, and beating that some prisoners had to endure. The Hun Skilla, who had carried her here, had treated her with respect on the journey and made plain his interest in a wife. Ilana knew he had saved her life in the massacre at Axiopolis, and he brought her small presents of clothing and food, a generosity that gave her subtle status but also filled her with uncertainty. She didn't want to marry a Hun! Yet without his favor she was little more than chattel, a prize to be traded. She'd pushed away his early clumsy advances and then felt guilty about it afterward, as if she'd swatted a pesky dog. He'd responded with hurt, amusement, and persistence. He'd warned other men away from her, which was a relief, but it was also a relief when he disappeared with Edeco on a mission to Constantinople.

Now Romans, *real* Romans, had come, back with Skilla and Edeco. Not traitorous Romans like Constantius who served as Attila's secretary, or the strategist Oenegius, who had tried to pretend to civilization by having a slave engineer build him a stone bathhouse, or the lieutenant Onegesh who had been sent south with Edeco. No, these were Romans from the Eastern emperor himself, representing civilization, faith, and order.

"Please, Suecca, can we go watch?" pleaded Guernna, a German captive with long blond braids and impish restlessness. Any task, no matter how light, was daunting to her lazy nature. "I want to see their clothes and horses!"

"What have the lot of you done to deserve to gape and jabber?" groused Suecca, who, despite her grumbling, was not an unkind mistress. "You've enough undone embroidery to last a year, not to mention having drawn neither wood nor water."

"Which is exactly why the sewing can wait!" reasoned Guernna. "Look at sad Ilana there, so quiet as she stitches. Some excitement might wake her up! Come, Suecca, come look with us! Maybe Edeco is bringing presents!"

"Romans are no more special than sheep," Suecca said. Nonetheless, she relented. "Go see them if you must and I'll look for my lout of a husband, if I can even remember what he looks like. Just remember that you are of the house of Edeco, so don't chirp like a nest of senseless chicks. The hearth of the warlord has dignity!"

The handmaidens ran, Ilana among them. Just the physical release from Edeco's wooden compound was enough to pierce her fog. A tide of inhabitants was rushing with them, all curious to see this latest in the steady parade of kings, princes, generals, and soothsayers who came to pay court to the great Attila. Someday, Ilana prayed, Romans would come in real numbers and put an end to her captivity.

Edeco she recognized almost immediately, leading the procession with his horsehair spirit banner held high, allowing just the slightest grin to crack the reserve of his ritually scarred face as he spotted his wife Suecca. Close behind came Onegesh with his paler face, who nonetheless rode with an ease and satisfaction that sometimes made him seem more Hun than the Huns. Finally came Skilla, straight and proud, as if merely visiting the Empire had granted him new status. When his eye triumphantly caught hers, it lit with recognition and possession. She flushed with confusion. He was not ugly like many of the Huns and was quite earnest in his attentions, but he didn't understand that to her eyes he was a barbarian responsible for the destruction of her city; the death of her betrothed love, Tasio; and the end of her dreams. "That is gone," he had told her. "Now you will be happiest if you pair with me."

Behind the Huns came the Romans. At the sight of them, her heart lifted a little. The man in front had draped his riding clothes with the complex ceremonial folds of the ancient toga; and she guessed that he was the lead ambassador, perhaps a minister or senator. Those following did not appear to have his importance, but she eagerly studied them as a reminder of home. Two were in the court dress of aides or interpreters. The shorter man looked uneasily at the throng of Huns as if he feared being found out. The other, who sat straighter and had a pleasanter, more friendly face, kept his eyes carefully ahead as if not to offend anyone. There was also a handsome young man of her age in slightly finer clothes, who peered about with a look of alert and innocent curiosity. He seemed young to have earned a place in an imperial embassy.

The Romans' slaves and pack train were diverted to open grass near the Tisza River that had been reserved for their camping space, deliberately positioned downhill from Attila's own compound. Edeco led the diplomatic contingent itself farther into the vast sea of yurts, huts, cabins, and wooden palaces that rambled on the eastern bank of the Tisza for two miles, representing a central guard of at least ten thousand warriors. Small villages of allied tribes clustered around this crude city like moons circling a planet. The curious crowd moved with the diplomats, flowing around houses like water and chanting greetings to the Hun warlords and good-natured taunts to the Romans. Children ran, dogs barked, and tethered horses whinnied and snorted at the embassy's ponies as they passed, the ponies in turn jerking their necks up and down as if in greeting.

As the Romans and their escort approached the stockade of Attila's compound, Ilana saw that the king's own wives and maids had come out in proud procession under the cloud of cloth, a ceremony she had now seen several times. The tallest and fairest formed two rows, and between their upstretched arms they carried a long runner of white linen, wide and long enough that seven girls walked beneath. All bore flowers that they cast at the ambassadorial party, filling the air with Scythian song. Maids lifted bowls of food to Edeco and his companions, and the barbarian lieutenants gravely ate while sitting on their horses—the consumption acknowledgment of Attila's sovereignty, just as Communion was acknowledgment in Ilana's world of the sovereignty of Christ.

The Romans were given nothing.

They waited patiently.

She noticed that the handsome young man was looking curiously at the horsehair banners before each yurt or house. Each of these spirit banners was made from the hairs of favorite stallions. The richer the owner in horses, the thicker his banner. On the other side of each doorway were horse skulls of favorite past steeds mounted on poles as protection against evil spirits, their large teeth set in permanent grins and their eye sockets empty. Also staked near each house were hides and meat drying on racks, a cloud of flies around each. Mounted on either side of the gate of Attila's own house were two stuffed and snarling badgers, the king's totem. Watching the newcomer take it all in, Ilana was reminded of the powerful stink that had seemed overwhelming to her when first brought to this place: an odor of musty bodies, horses, manure, cut grass, strange spices, and a sallow fog of cooking fires. The Huns believed their odor was an emanation of their souls, and instead of a kiss or a handshake they often greeted each other with a sniff, like friendly dogs. It had taken Ilana a month to get used to their smell.

The Roman's gaze eventually came to rest on her and she saw him pause with interest for a moment, a reaction from men she'd enjoyed before. He registered her beauty as if startled, and she liked to think she still looked Roman, not barbarian. Then his inspection moved on to other people but once or twice returned in her direction, trying to pretend his gaze was casual but nonetheless determined to seek her out.

For the first time since her capture, Ilana felt a glimmer of hope.

And so I, Jonas, came to Attila's palace. It was modest by Roman standards but still more magnificent than I'd expected. I wasn't sure if I'd find the king of the Huns in a tent, hut, or golden palace, but his principal and least temporary headquarters was somewhat between: made of wood but of superior craftsmanship. The Huns, I realized, were caught halfway between their migratory origins and a settled existence, and their city displayed this awkward transition. Yurts, wagons, log cabins, and wattle-and-daub houses all served as homes, scattered haphazardly.

I had already noticed the fondness of Hun warriors for gold jewelry, elaborately styled bridles and harness, fine saddles, and weapons inlaid with silver and jewels. Their boot buckles were apt to be of silver and their waistbands of silk. Now I saw that the women were even more elaborately decorated. Their necklaces and intricate belts were draped over embroidered dresses that came in a hundred colors, meaning I watched goat girls chase their flocks in gowns threaded with silver. Their hair was braided and fenced with circlets of gold on their brows. Gold clasps designed like cicadas held the garments of the queens and princesses at each shoulder, and belt ends looped and dangled to their ankles, the entire length sparkling with metal and jewels. Some of their necklaces fanned from neck to breast as intricately and thickly as a sheath of mail.

Wooden structures showed similar craftsmanship, the timber hauled from long distances and the logs and boards carefully dressed and carved. Attila's palace was finer yet: the planks of its stockade as straight and close fitting as a floor; its guard towers boasting complex balustrades; and the grand home itself as intricate as a jewel box, every board polished to a warm red sheen. Porticos gave shelter on its sides;

outbuildings lined the stockade walls; stepping-stones provided path-ways across the mud; and ovens, storerooms, cellars, and wells made the complex self-sufficient against attack. Window grilles, rafter ends, and eaves bore carvings of horses, birds, and dragons.

"German craftsmanship, done by captives," Rusticius said quietly. "The Huns themselves disdain construction labor. They can't even make bread."

This palace was one of a half dozen such compounds Attila had scattered along the rivers of the Hunuguri plain, Bigilas told us, but this house was reputedly the most impressive. Circling the great hall was a small forest of staffs bearing horsehair banners representing the Hun clans. Again, each staff was topped by the skulls of royalty's noblest and best-loved horses.

More disquieting were poles that bore human skulls.

"What are those?" I whispered.

"Vanquished enemies," said Bigilas.

Each was mounted on a spear tip with the flesh allowed to rot away naturally. By now, most of the heads had been eaten by the crows down to bone, topped only by a few shreds of flesh and strands of hair that fluttered in the wind.

Just as odd were the curiously misshapen heads of some of the Huns. I noticed it first among the bareheaded children and thought that perhaps they were simply imbeciles, malformed at birth. Their foreheads seemed twice normal height, sweeping backward from their faces, so that their heads came to a kind of rounded peak. Politeness forbade me to comment, but then I saw the same feature on some of the male war-riors and even on their women. Add this deformity to their swarthy complexion; dark hair; ritual scars; and small, squinting eyes, and the re-sult was a terrifying visage.

"What has happened to these poor people?" I asked Rusticius.

"Poor? They wear more gold than I will ever see."

"I mean their heads. They look like the kinds of babies best left on a slope."

He laughed. "It's a sign of beauty among these monsters! Some of them flatten their heads deliberately when the bone is soft at birth. They lash a board and tighten the thongs while the baby howls. They think such deformity attractive."

We finally dismounted just steps from the palace porch and Edeco, Onegesh, and Skilla led our little party of Romans into the rectangular great hall of Attila's palace. This reception area was modest by imperial standards, just large enough to hold perhaps a hundred people, and had a wooden floor strewn with carpets and a timbered ceiling that peaked about thirty feet high. This, apparently, was Attila's throne room. Tapestries and captured legionary standards decorated the walls, and small grilled windows let in a modest amount of light. Armed guards stood in the corners and Hun nobles sat cross-legged on the carpets of both sides, the men short, swarthy, and apelike. My childhood idea of barbarians—tall and graceful black Nubians or strapping blond Germans—had been corrupted. These men seemed more like gnomes, squeezed down into compact balls of hard muscle. If anything, this density made them more menacing. They watched us with narrow eyes, their noses broad and flat and their mouths tight and expressionless. Each had a sword by his side and bow and arrows laid against the wall behind him. They seemed as cocked as the trigger of a crossbow.

In the shadows at the far end of the room, on an elevated platform, was a single man, sitting in a plain wooden chair, without weapon, crown, or decoration. A curtain of tapestries hung behind him. This was the king of the Huns? The most powerful man in the world seemed a disappointment.

Attila was more plainly dressed than anyone, his torso erect and his feet firmly planted. Like all Huns he was short legged and long waisted, his head unusually large for the length of his body, and so motionless that he might have been carved from wood. He was, as reputation suggested, a somewhat ugly man: flat nose, eyes so deep set that they seemed to peer from caves, and the ritual cheek scarring that marked so many Huns. Had Attila cut himself after murdering his brother?

The king's wispy mustache drooped in what I had come to think of as the Hunnish frown, and his beard was scraggly and flecked with gray. Yet his gaze was focused and penetrating; his brow large; and his cheekbones and chin hard and pronounced, resulting in a visage that was undeniably commanding. His physique added to his presence. His shoulders were broad and his waist narrow, making him—at forty-four years—as fit as a soldier of twenty. His hands were large and looked as brown and gnarled as exposed roots, the fingers gripping the arms of his chair as if to prevent himself from levitating. There was nothing on his person to give any mark of authority, and yet without saying a word or moving a muscle he commanded the room as naturally as a matriarch dominates a chamber of children. Attila has slain a hundred men and ordered the slaying of a hundred thousand more, and all that blood had given him presence and power.

There was a gigantic iron sword behind him, resting horizontally on two golden pegs. It was rusty and dark, as if of great antiquity, its edge jagged. It was so enormous—it would reach from my feet to my cheek—that it seemed made more for a giant than a man.

Maximinus noticed it, too. "Is that the sword of Mars?" he murmured to Bigilas. "It would be like trying to swing a roof beam."

"The story is that it was found near the banks of the Tisza when a cow cut her hoof on something sharp in the grass," Bigilas answered quietly. "The herdsman alerted Attila, who had it dug out and shrewdly pronounced it a sign of favor from the gods. His men are superstitious enough to believe it."

We were waiting for a sign of what to do, and suddenly Attila spoke without preamble—not to us but to his lieutenant. "I sent you to get a treaty and treasure, Edeco, and you have brought me only men." His voice was low but not unpleasant, a quiet strength to his tone, but his displeasure was obvious. He wanted gold, not an embassy.

"The Romans insisted on addressing you directly, my kagan," the warlord answered. "Apparently they found my conversation lacking, or felt they had to explain their recalcitrance in person. At any rate, they've brought you presents."

"As well as our emperor's wish for peace and understanding," Maximinus added hastily as this was translated. "For too long we've been at odds with the king of the Huns."

Attila studied us like a lion stalking a herd. "We are not at odds," he finally said. "We have an understanding, ratified by treaty, that I have beaten you as I have beaten every army I've encountered, and that you are to pay tribute to me. Yet always the tribute is late or too small or in base coins when what I demanded was gold. Is this not true, ambassador? Do I have to come myself to Constantinople to get what is rightfully mine? If so, it will be with more warriors than there are blades of grass on the steppe." His tone was a growl of warning, and the warlords who were watching buzzed like the warning hum of the hive.

"All respect the power of Attila," the senator placated him, obviously flustered by this rude and quick beginning. "We bring not only a share of the annual tribute but also additional presents. Our Empire wishes peace."

"Then abide by your agreements."

"But your thirst for the yellow metal is destroying our commerce, and if you don't relent we will soon be too poor to pay anything. You rule a great empire, kagan. I come from a great one as well. Why aren't we better friends? Can we not join together as partners? Our rivalry will exhaust both our nations and spill the blood of our children."

"Rome *is* my partner—when she pays her tribute. And returns my soldiers."

"We have brought five fugitives back to you—"

"And shielded five thousand." The Hun turned to Edeco. "Tell me, general, is Constantinople too poor to give me what was promised?"

"It is rich and noisy and crammed with people like caged birds." Edeco pointed to Bigilas. "He showed me."

"Ah, yes. The man who thinks his emperor a god, and me a mere man."

I was startled. How had Attila learned this already? We'd just arrived and already the negotiations seemed to be slewing out of control.

Attila stood, his legs bowed, his torso like a wedge. "I *am* a man, translator. But the gods work through me, as you'll learn. Look." He pointed to the great sword displayed behind him, pitted and dull. "In a dream Zolbon, the one you Romans call Mars, came to me and revealed his sword. He showed me where to find it on the trackless plain. With this weapon, he told me, the Huns will become invincible. With the sword of Mars, the People of the Dawn will conquer the world!"

He lifted his arms and his warlords sprang to their feet, roaring in agreement. Our little embassy shrank, and we clustered together, fearing slaughter. And yet as abruptly as he had stood, Attila dropped his arms, the noise ceased, and he and his chiefs promptly sat again. It had all been an act.

He pointed. "Listen to me, Romans. It is the People of the Dawn who are your god now. It is *our* choice who lives and who dies, which city rises and which is burned, who marches and who retreats. It is *we* who have the sword of Mars." He nodded, as if confirming this arrogance to himself. "But I am a good host, as you were a host to Edeco. Tonight we feast and begin to know each other. Your visit is just beginning. It is over time that we will decide what kind of partners to become."

Rattled by this reception, our embassy retreated to our tents by the river to rest and confer. Bigilas and Rusticius, with the most knowledge of the Huns, were the least disconcerted. They said Attila's aggressive opening was simply a tactic.

"He uses his moods to intimidate and rule," Bigilas said. "I've seen him so infuriated that he writhed on the ground until blood spurted from his nose. I've seen him tear an enemy apart with his bare hands, clawing the man's eyes out and breaking his arms, while the victim waited so frozen in fear that he was incapable of defending himself. But I've also seen him hold a baby and kiss a child, or weep like a woman when a favorite warrior was borne back dead."

"I was expecting patient diplomacy," Maximinus confessed.

"Attila will be more hospitable and less demanding at the banquet," Bigilas said. "He's made his point, just as we've made ours by showing Edeco the strength of Constantinople. It's obvious that word of all that transpired on our journey was sent ahead. The Huns are not stupid. Now, having blustered, Attila will try to forge a relationship."

"You seem very certain."

"I mean no presumption, ambassador. I simply believe that, in the end, things are going to go our way." He smiled, but it was a secret smile that seemed to conceal more than it revealed.

We bathed with water from the river warm in its summer flow, dressed in finer clothes, and returned that night to the same great hall for Attila's welcoming banquet. This time the room had been expanded. The tapestries and partitions that had backed Attila's chair had disappeared, revealing a platform that bore the king's bed, canopied with linens. It seemed odd to me to display one's bedroom, given that Roman chambers were small and secretive, but Rusticius said this intimacy was taken by the Huns as a sign of hospitality. Our host was welcoming us to the center of his life.

At the foot of this platform Attila waited on a couch far more comfortable than the simple chair on which he had received us. Running the length of the hall from the couch to the door was a banquet table. As the guests entered, each was presented with a golden cup that was filled with imported wine. Then we all milled awkwardly, the finely dressed Romans clustering together amid Huns, Germans, and Gepids, all waiting for assignment to sit. I noticed that Edeco was murmuring something to Bigilas as they waited, again as if the two were almost equal in rank. The translator nodded expectantly. Maximinus noticed it, too, and frowned.

Finally Attila commanded us to sit, his Roman-born minister Oenegius on his right and two of his sons, Ellac and Danziq, on his left. The boys looked subdued and frightened, with none of the boisterous energy you would expect of their early teen years. We Romans were told to sit on the left as well, Maximinus closest to the table's head and I at his side to take any notes that were necessary. Then the other Huns took their places, each introducing himself in Hunnish. There was Edeco, Onegesh, and Skilla, of course. But there were many other chiefs too numerous to remember, bearing such names as Octar, Balan, Eskam, Totila, Brik, Agus, and Sturak. Each boasted briefly of his deeds in battle before taking his place, most of their stories referring to defeats of Roman soldiers and sackings of Roman cities. Behind them were more horsehair standards of the Hun tribes with a bewildering thicket of names such as the Akatiri, Sorosgi, Angisciri, Barselti, Cadiseni, Sabirsi, Bayunduri, Sadagarii, Zalae, and Albani. Those spellings are my own, for the Huns of course had no written language and their tongue twists Latin and Greek.

Strapping male slaves who wore iron collars like hounds and had arms as thick as roof beams bore the night's food to us. The vast platters of gold and silver were heaped with fowl, venison, boar, mutton, steak, fruit, roots, puddings, and stews. Women served wine and *kumiss*, and they were without exception the most beautiful women I had ever seen—more beautiful, even, than the maidens chosen to grace Constantinople festivals. How my haughty Olivia would be put in the shade by these blossoms! All were captives; and they bore the looks of their homelands, from Persia to Frisia—their skin as dark as mahogany or as translucent as white alabaster, their hair the color of linen, wheat, amber, mink, and obsidian, and their eyes the shades of sapphire, emerald, chestnut, opal, and ebony. The Huns paid their feminine grace no special heed, but we Romans, except Maximinus, were as transfixed by these captive ornaments as we'd been by the women in Anika's house. I confess to wondering, and hoping, if the same hospitality would be offered here. If so, I was determined to sneak away from the old senator long enough to take advantage of it! How desperately I longed for a respite from constant male companionship, and my body seemed fit to explode. I remembered Skilla's friendly warning.

One of the women I recognized as the dark-haired girl by the gate, whose rare beauty was magnified by her look of intelligence, fire, and longing. This evening she was so light-footed that she seemed to float as much as walk, and I could have sworn that she peeked at me occasionally as my gaze followed her around the room.

"For a man who said he didn't want to lose his head around the Huns, Jonas, I fear it will twist off completely if you keep craning to watch that serving wench." Senator Maximinus was looking agreeably and blankly at a Hun across the table as he gave this quiet scold in Latin.

I looked down at my plate. "I didn't think I was that obvious."

"You can be sure that Attila notices everything we do."

The kagan was again dressed more simply than any man or woman in the room. He wore no mark of rank or decoration. He had no crown. While his warlords feasted from captured gold plate, he ate from a wooden bowl and drank from a wooden cup, rarely saying a word. Instead of alcohol, he drank water. He disdained what little bread there was and touched nothing sweet. He simply looked out at the company with dark, deep-set, all-consuming eyes, as if a spectator at a strange drama. A woman stood like a pillar in the shadows by the bed.

"Who's that?" I asked Maximinus.

"Queen Hereka, foremost of his wives and mother of his princes. She has her own house and compound but attends her husband at state functions like this one."

Attila's sons ate woodenly, not daring to look at their father or speak to the men around them. Then a third boy came in, nodded to his mother, and went up to the king. He was younger than the other two, handsome; and for the first time Attila betrayed a slight smile and pinched him on the cheek.

"And that?"

"It must be Ernak. I'm told he's the favored son."

"Favorite why?"

Rusticius leaned in. "Attila's seers have foretold his empire will falter but that Ernak will restore it."

"Attila will falter?" Now I was curious. First Rome is prophesied doom and now Attila. Competing prophecies! "Looking at him tonight, it seems unlikely."

"He's to falter only after vanquishing us."

Music started—a mix of drum, flute, and string—and the Huns began a round of rousing song. They sang from deep within their torsos, a strange, beelike humming, but it was hypnotic in its own way. While the instruments, noise, and growing drunkenness made translation difficult, I realized that most of the music again celebrated the slaughter of their enemies. There were ballads of triumphs over Ostrogoth, Gepid, Roman, and Greek, sung with no acknowledgment that all those peoples had representatives at the feast. The Huns conquered, and our injured pride was of no consequence.

Then came lighter entertainment: dancing women and acrobatic men, jugglers and magicians, mimes and comic actors. Attila watched it all with an expression as dour and flat as if he were watching the day's shadows move on a wall.

The entertainment climaxed when, with a somersault, a dwarf rolled from the shadows and sprang up wearing a mock crown, bringing howls of delight from all the Huns except Attila. He was a grotesque little creature with dark skin, stumpy legs, a long torso, and a flat, moonlike face, as if an exaggerated caricature of how we Romans saw the Huns. He began prancing and declaiming in a high, piping voice.

"Zerco!" they cried. "King of the tribes!" Attila's mouth had changed to a grimace, as if the jester's was a performance to be endured.

"Our host doesn't like the little one," I murmured. "Why?"

"The dwarf was the pet of his brother Bleda, who Attila doesn't like to be reminded of," Bigilas explained. "The freak was never a favorite of Attila, who is too serious to appreciate mockery. After Bleda died, the king made a present of Zerco to Aetius the Roman, a general who once lived among the Huns as a hostage. But Bleda had rewarded Zerco by allowing him to marry a slave woman and the dwarf pined for his wife, who remained here. Aetius finally persuaded Attila to take the jester back, and the king has regretted it ever since. He insults and torments the jester, but the halfling endures it so he can stay with his wife."

"Is the wife deformed as well?"

"She's tall, fair, and has learned to love him, I've been told. The marriage was supposed to be a joke, but the couple has not conspired with the mockery."

The dwarf raised his arms in mock greeting. "The king of toads welcomes Rome!" he proclaimed. "If you cannot outfight us, at least outdrink us!" The Huns laughed. He scampered over and, without warning, leaped into my lap. It was like the bound of a large dog, and I was so surprised I tipped over my wine. "I said drink, not pour!"

"Get off me," I whispered desperately.

"No! Every king needs a throne!" Then he leaned, impishly sniffed Maximinus, and kissed his beard. "And a consort!"

The Huns howled.

The senator flushed red, and I felt stricken with embarrassment. What was I supposed to do? The dwarf clung to me like a monkey. I glanced wildly about. The woman who had caught my eye earlier was watching me curiously, to see my response. "Why do you mock us?" I hissed.

"To warn you of danger," the dwarf replied quietly. "Nothing is as it seems." Then he sprang away and, laughing maniacally, ran from the hall.

What did that mean? I was bewildered.

Attila stood. "Enough of this foolishness." They were his first words all evening. Everyone fell silent and the gaiety was replaced by tension. The king pointed. "You Romans have presents, do you not?"

Maximinus stood, somewhat shaky from his embarrassment. "We do, kagan." He clapped his hands once. "Let them be brought in!"

Bolts of pink and yellow silk unrolled against the carpets like the flash of dawn. Small chests opened to a shoal of coins. There was a galaxy of jewels scattered by Attila's wooden plate, engraved swords and lances leaned against his bed platform, sacred goblets arranged on a bench, and combs and mirrors set on the skin of a lion. The Huns murmured greedily.

"These are tokens of the emperor's good faith," Maximinus said.

"And you will take back to him tokens of mine," Attila said. "There will be bales of sable and fox, blessing bundles from my shamans, and my pledge to honor whatever agreement we come to. This is the word of Attila."

His men rumbled their approval.

"But Rome is rich, and Constantinople the richest of its cities," he went on. "All men know this, and know that what you have brought us are mere tokens. Is this not true?"

"We are not as rich as you belie—"

"Among the People of the Dawn, treaties are marked by blood and marriage. I am contemplating the latter and want proof of the former. Emperor after emperor has sent the Hunuguri their sons and daughters. The general Aetius lived with us when I was a boy, and I used to wrestle with him in the dirt." He grinned. "He was older, but I beat him, too."

The assembly laughed.

Now Attila pointed abruptly at Bigilas. "You, alone among the Romans who have come to us, have a son. Is this not true?"

Bigilas stood in seeming confusion. "Yes, my lord."

"This boy will be a hostage of your good faith in these negotiations while we talk, no? He will be evidence that you trust Attila as he trusts you."

"Kagan, my son is still in Constan—"

"You will go back to fetch him while your companions learn the ways of the Hun. It is only when your boy gets here that our negotiations can conclude, because only then will I know you are men of your word: so faithful that you trust your son to me. Understand?"

Bigilas looked at Maximinus. Reluctantly, the senator nodded.

"As you order, kagan." Bigilas bowed. "If your riders could send word ahead . . ."

"Some will accompany you." Attila nodded. "Now, I will sleep."

It was his announcement that the evening was over. The guests abruptly stood as if on a string and began moving out of the hall, the Huns pushing their way first with no pretense at politeness. The banquet had ended abruptly, but our stay was obviously just beginning.

I glanced around. The intriguing woman had disappeared. Nor was Hun sexual hospitality about to be offered, it seemed. As for Bigilas, he did not look as downcast at this sudden demand as I'd expected. Did he want to return to Constantinople so badly? I saw him trade a glance with Edeco.

I also spied Skilla, watching me from the shadows at the far end of the hall. The young man smiled mockingly, as if knowing a great secret, and slipped through the door.

XI

A WOMAN NAMED ILANA

"Let me get the water, Guernna."

The German girl looked at Ilana with surprise. "You, Ilana? You haven't wanted to soil your pretty little hands with wood and water since you got here."

The maid of Axiopolis took the jar from the German and balanced it on her head. "So much more reason for me to do it now." She smiled with false sweetness. "Maybe it will help quiet your whines."

As she left Suecca's house to walk to the Tisza, Guernna called after, "I know what you're doing! You want to go past where the Romans are camped!"

It was late morning after the banquet, and the encampment was finally stirring. Ilana hoped the young Roman was awake. The bright reds and blues of the embassy tents were a vivid contrast to the browns and tans of barbarian habitation, making them easy to find, and the hues made her long for the colorful paints and bustling bazaars of civilization. It was astonishing what quiet passion the arrival of the Roman embassy had stirred in her. She'd been half dead, going through the motions of the days and half resigned to union with Skilla. Now she was seized with fresh hope, seeing an alternative. Somehow she had to convince these

Romans to ransom her. The key was the embassy scribe and historian who'd followed her around the banquet room with his eyes.

A year before, the thought of such calculation would have horrified Ilana. Love was sacred, romance was pure, and she'd had a queue of suitors before settling on Tasio. But that was before her betrothed and her father had died, and before Skilla seemed determined to marry her and stick her forever in a yurt. If she acquiesced she'd spend the rest of her days wandering with his tribe from pasture to pasture, bearing Hun babies and watching these butchers bring on the end of the world. She was convinced that ordinary Romans had no idea of the peril they were facing. She believed this because until her own former life had ended, she'd had no idea as well.

Ilana had donned the Roman dress she'd been captured in for this occasion, and carefully washed and combed her hair. A Hun belt of gold links helped emphasize her slender waist, a medallion the swell of her breasts, and Roman bracelets on the raised arm that balanced the jar caught the light of the sun and called attention to her errand. It was the first time since her capture that she'd really tried to look pretty. The jar was seated on a round felt cap on the crown of her head, the posture needed to bear it giving a seductive sway to her walk.

She spied the Roman to one side of their cluster of tents, brushing a gray mare. He seemed handsome enough, curious, and, she hoped, necessarily innocent of female motive. She walked by his field of vision while staring straight ahead and for a moment feared he might ignore her, so intent he seemed on combing his damned horse. She'd have to try again when returning from the river! But, no, suddenly he straightened abruptly and just as he did so she deliberately stumbled and caught the jar as it toppled from her head. "Oh!"

"Let me help you!" he called in Latin.

"It's nothing," she replied in the same tongue, trying to feign surprise. "I didn't see you standing there." She clutched the clay jar to her breasts like a lover.

He walked over. "I thought you might be Roman from your look and manner."

He seemed almost too kind, not yet hardened by life's cruelties, and for a moment she doubted her plan. She needed someone strong. But at least he would take pity!

"I saw you serving at the banquet," he went on. "What's your name?"

"Ilana."

"That's pretty. I am Jonas Alabanda, of Constantinople. Where are you from?"

She cast her eyes down, purposely demure. "Axiopolis, near the Black Sea. The city the Greeks called Heracleia."

"I've heard of it. You were captured?"

"Edeco conquered it."

"Edeco! He's the one we rode here with from Constantinople."

"The warrior Skilla caught me and brought me here on his horse."

"I know Skilla as well!"

"Then we have even more in common than our empire." She smiled sadly.

He held out his arms. "Here, let me help carry that."

"It's woman's work. Besides, it's not heavy until full."

"Then let me escort you to the river." He grinned. "You look like more enjoyable company than Edeco or Skilla."

This was going better than she'd hoped. They walked together, the quick companionship giving a sheen to the pleasant day, the grass suddenly greener and the sky bluer. "You're young to be on such an important mission," she said. "You must be wise beyond your years."

"I merely speak Hunnish and enjoy letters. I hope to write a history."

"You must come from a good family." She hoped he was rich enough to buy her.

"We've had some misfortune. I'm hoping this journey turns it around."

That was disappointing. They reached the grassy riverbank, the Tisza lolling lazily, dried mud showing how much it had fallen since spring. She stooped to dip water, making her movements deliberately slow. "The journey has let us meet each other, at least," she said.

"What house do you belong to here?"

"Suecca, wife of Edeco."

He watched her stand and balance. "I will ask him about you, I think."

Her heart soared. "If you could ransom me, I would serve the embassy on your way home," she said, her words coming more quickly than she'd planned. "I can cook, and sew. . . ." She saw the amused concern on his face and stopped. "I just mean I wouldn't be any trouble." The jar balanced on her head, she carefully began walking back, knowing that Suecca would miss her soon and probably be suspicious of why she'd uncharacteristically fetched the water. "I could tell you much about the Huns, and I have relatives in Constantinople who could contribute . . ."

She was desperate to bind him to her side. Yet even as she babbled, pathetically promising everything she could think of—how she hated to be a supplicant, and helpless!—there was a sudden rattle of hooves and a Hun pony burst between them, butting Jonas aside and spilling some of the water.

"Woman! What are you doing with the Romans!"

It was Skilla, astride his horse Drilca.

"I am only fetching water—"

Jonas grabbed the rein. "It was I who talked to her."

Skilla pointed with his whip. "Let go of my horse. This woman is my uncle's slave, taken in battle. She has no business talking to any free man without permission, and certainly not to you. If she doesn't know that, then Suecca will make it clear!"

"You'll not punish a Roman for talking to a Roman." There was low warning in Jonas's voice, and Ilana realized there was some history between these two. She was both thrilled and apprehensive. How could she use it? How could she be so calculating?

"She's no longer a Roman! And a slave has no business mingling with diplomats! She knows that! If she wants to be free, then let her agree to marriage!"

The Roman pulled on the reins, turning the horse's head and making it sidestep. "Leave her alone, Skilla."

The Hun lashed the hand that held his rein, put his boot on the Roman's chest, and shoved. Jonas, taken by surprise, vaulted backward, landing in humiliation on his rear. Skilla wheeled and scooped Ilana off the ground, her jar falling and shattering. "This one is mine! I told you that!" She struggled, trying to scratch, but he held her like a child, his arm iron. "Keep to your own, Roman!" Jonas charged, but before he could reach Skilla the Hun yipped and galloped his horse away across the encampment, people whooping and laughing as Ilana hung help-lessly, her feet a foot or two off the ground, bouncing like a rag doll until he dropped her rudely in Suecca's doorway. She staggered, breathless, while his exited horse turned in a circle.

"Stay away from the Roman," he warned her, twisting his body to keep her in view as he struggled with his horse. "I am your future now."

Her eyes were afire. "I'm Roman, too! Can't you see that I don't want you?"

"And I am in love with you, princess, and worth a dozen men like him." He grinned. "You'll see it, in the end."

Ilana looked away in frustration. There was nothing more unen-durable than to be loved by someone you didn't want. "Please leave me alone."

"Tell Suecca I will bring her a new jar!"

Then he galloped away.

Never had I felt so humiliated or angry. The Hun had caught me by sur-prise and then disappeared, like a coward, into the sea of his people. I was certain Skilla had no real relationship to the young woman, what-ever he might dream, and I was tempted to dig my weapons from the baggage and call the warrior out. But as a diplomat I knew I couldn't start a duel. Nor, I admitted to myself, was I very certain I could beat him. In any event I'd risked Maximinus's anger simply by talking to a girl. But she was Roman, pretty, and—if this was the one Skilla had boasted would marry him after she'd scratched him—in peril. For a per-son of my age and situation, it was a recipe for infatuation.

I brushed myself off, annoyed at the nearby Huns grinning at my embarrassment, and tried to think what to do.

"You can never win solely by fighting," an oddly pitched voice said in Latin, as if reading my mind. "It requires thought as well."

I turned. It was the dwarf who had performed the evening before. Zerco, they called him. What a little monster he was, waddling up from the trees where he must have been lurking.

"Did I ask your advice?"

"What need to ask, when you so clearly need it?" Daylight made his visage even more pitiable: his skin too dark, his nose flat and lips wide, his ears too big for his head, his head too big for his torso, and his torso too big for his legs. His back was partly humped, his hair a shaggy mat, and his cheeks beardless but pocked. All that saved him from repulsion were his eyes, which were as large and brown as an animal's but blinked with sharp intelligence. Perhaps Zerco was not the fool he seemed when performing.

"You were spying."

"A clown has to observe the betters he wishes to mock."

Despite myself, I smiled wryly. "You plan to mock me, fool?"

"I already did, last night. And between that maid leading you by the sword and that barbarian seating you on your rump, you're doing a good enough job yourself. But I'll pick on your Hun friend next, perhaps."

"That Hun is not my friend."

"Never be too sure who your friends and enemies are. Fortune has a way of changing which is which."

The dwarf's quickness made me curious. "You speak the tongue of the Empire."

"I come from Africa. Discarded by my mother as the devil's joke, kidnapped and sold as a jester, and passed from court to court until I found favor with Bleda, whose idea of humor was simpler than his dour and more ambitious brother's. Other men must work their way to Hades, but I've found it in this life." He put his arm to his brow in a pantomime of self-pity.

"Someone said Attila gave you to Aetius, the general of the West, but you came back for your wife."

"Ah Julia, my angel! Now you have found me out. I complain of hell but with her I've found heaven. Do you know that she missed me even more than I missed her? What do you think of that?"

I was baffled. Bigilas had said the woman was not ugly like Zerco, but I could not imagine what their relationship was like. "That she has peculiar taste."

The dwarf laughed.

"Or that she looks inside the skin as well as outside."

Zerco bowed. "You have a diplomat's flair for flattery, Jonas Alabanda. That is your name, is it not?"

"So you *are* a spy."

"I am a listener, which few men are. I hear many things and see even more. If you tell me something of Constantinople, I will tell you something about these Huns."

"What could I tell you of Constantinople?"

"Its palaces, games, and food. I dream of it like a thirsty man dreams of water."

"Well, it's certainly grander than what we have here: the greatest city in the world now. As for the Huns, I've already learned that they're arrogant, rude, ignorant, and that you can smell one before you see one. Beyond that, I'm not sure there's much to learn."

"Oh, but there is! If you fancy Ilana and despise Skilla, you should come with me." He began walking north along the riverbank, in a rocking gait that was comic and pitiable at the same time, and I hesitated. The crippled and diseased made me uncomfortable. Zerco would have none of it. "Come, come. My stature is not contagious."

I slowed my own habitual pace to match his. Children ran after us, calling insults, but didn't dare draw too close to the odd little monster and the tall, mysterious Roman.

"How did you come to be a jester?" I asked when he didn't say anything more.

"What else could I be? I'm too small to be a soldier or laborer and too ill-formed to be a poet or a singer. Making fun of the great is the only way I've saved myself."

"Including the noble Flavius Aetius?"

"It's the most competent who are usually most willing to laugh at themselves."

"Is that what you think of the famous general?"

"He actually had little use for entertainment, to tell the truth. He was not unkind or conceited, only distracted. He believes in an idea called Rome but lacks the army to restore it. So he fights one day, negotiates the next, buys the third. He's a remarkable man who almost alone is holding the West together, and of course his superiors despise him for it. There is nothing incompetence hates more than virtue. Valentinian will one day punish him for his heroism, mark my word."

"He never marched to help the East."

"March with what? The people tormenting your half of the Empire were the same he was hiring to keep order in his half—the Huns. They'd work for him and take from you. It sounds callous, but it was the only way he could keep the other tribes in harness."

"What can you tell me of the Huns?"

"I don't tell, I show. I help you to see. Learn to think for yourself, Jonas Alabanda, and you will be a hated, feared, and successful man. Now, first of all, look at this settlement along the river. It goes on and on, doesn't it?"

"The Huns are numerous."

"And yet are there more people here than in Constantinople?"

"Of course not."

"More than Rome? More than Alexandria?"

"No . . ."

"Yet the man with the wooden bowl and cup, leading a people who don't know how to sow, forge, or build—a people who prey on others to supply everything they have—believes it's his destiny to rule the world. Because of numbers? Or because of will?"

"They are great and terrible warriors."

"Indeed. Look there." We reached a point on the river opposite a meadow used for grazing and riding. Twenty Hun soldiers were practicing archery. They galloped one by one down the length of their meadow at full speed, plucked arrows from their quivers with deadly rhythm, and fired with frightening rapidity. Their target were melons, erected on poles fifty paces away, and so often did the arrows hit that the warriors roared and jeered only when one missed. Such an error was usually no more than a handsbreadth in either direction. "Imagine a thousand of them, thundering by a clumsy legion," Zerco said.

"I don't have to imagine. By all accounts it's happened far too many times, and again and again we are beaten."

"Keep watching."

After each pass the galloping warrior rejoined the jostling, joking group and then take his turn again, hurtling across the meadow. After three or four sprints each, they sat, spent and happy.

"Watch what?"

"How many arrows do they have left?"

"None, of course."

"How fast are their ponies now?"

"They're tired."

"See? I've showed you more than most Roman generals ever learn. That's what I mean by thought: observation and deduction."

"Shown what? That they can hit an enemy's eye at full charge? That they can lope a hundred miles in a day when our armies march twenty on our best roads?"

"That in far less than an hour they are out of arrows on exhausted horses. That a cloud of arrows came from a handful of men. That their entire strategy depends on breaking the will of others quickly and with-out mercy because their numbers are limited and their endurance is nil. But if they have to fight not for a moment but for a day, against a unity that outnumbers them . . ."

"This was archery. They were *trying* to expend all their arrows."

"As they might uselessly against determined infantry that stands its ground behind its shields. Horses are like dogs. They will catch a fleeing man, but shy from one who stands his ground. An army that is a porcu-pine of spears . . ."

"What you're talking about is the greatest of all battles. Of fighting, after all, not just thinking."

"Of course, fighting! But what I'm talking about is the will to fight *your* battle, not theirs. On your ground: low, armored, patient. Of waiting until your moment. And there is one other thing you should be thinking about as you watch their skill."

"What's that?"

"To match it, if you want to survive. Did you bring any weapons at all?"

"They're in my baggage."

"You'd better get them out and practice as the Huns do. That, too, you should have deduced by watching them. You never know when you will need to fight, as well as think."

The jostling, joking warriors across the river reminded me of the dwarf's leap into my lap the night before. "You claimed that you were warning me of danger at the banquet. That nothing is as it seems."

"Attila invites you to talk of peace, but what Attila *says* may not be what he *means*. And don't be surprised if he knows more about your companions than you do yourself, Jonas of Constantinople. That's the danger I'm warning you of."

Skilla let the wild galloping of his horse release his turbulent emotions. Riding without direction across the flat plain of Hunuguri was like shedding a particularly constricting and burdensome piece of armor. It was a draft of wind that left the complications of camp and tribe and women behind, and restored to him the freedom of the steppes. Attila himself spoke of the tonic of the grasslands. When in doubt, ride.

So why did they leave the steppes ever farther behind?

Until the Romans came, Skilla had been certain that Ilana would eventually be his. He alone had protected her, and when Attila won the final battle there would be no alternative. But now she had flirted with Jonas and dressed like a Roman whore. It enraged him, because he feared the scribe could win simply by being Roman. Skilla didn't want a bed slave. He wanted the highborn woman to love him for what he was, not just make love *to* him, and it frustrated him that she remained stubbornly blind to the Huns and their qualities. The People of the Dawn were better than the hordes that squatted in their stone cities, braver, stronger, and more powerful . . . except that Skilla secretly felt uncomfortable and inferior around the foolish but clever Romans, and hated just that feeling.

That's why seeing Ilana with Jonas had so infuriated him.

It was not just that the Romans could read the thoughts of other men by peering at their books and papers or that they wore fine clothes or built with stone that lasted forever. As near as he could tell, all their wizardry did not make them particularly strong or happy. They could be beaten in battle, worried constantly about money while having more of it than a Hun would ever need, were hapless at surviving away from their cities, and fussed about rank and rules in ways that would never occur to a truly free man. A Roman had a thousand worries when a Hun had none. A Hun did not grub in the dirt, dig for metal, labor in the sun, or go blind squinting in a dark shop. He took what he needed from others, and all men quailed before him. This is how it had been since his people began following the white stag west, conquering all they encountered. And their women shared their haughty pride!

Yet the Romans disdained him. They never said so, of course, lest he chop them down, but he could tell it in their looks and whispers and manners as they had journeyed from the eastern capital. His was the empire that was growing and theirs was the one that was shrinking, and yet they regarded the Huns as their inferiors! Dangerous, yes, in the way a rabid dog is dangerous, but not the Roman equal in anything that mattered, let alone their master. This stubborn confidence tormented him as it tormented his fellow warriors, because no amount of military defeat seemed to convince the Romans that the Huns were their betters. Only killing seemed to settle the issue.

Ilana was the most baffling of all. Yes, she had lost her father and the man she'd planned to marry, and been taken from her city. But Skilla had not raped or beaten her as she might have expected. He in fact had lent her a fine pony for the ride back to the heart of the Hun empire. What other captive had enjoyed such favor? He had fed her well, protected her from the attentions of other warriors, and brought her presents. If she married him she would be the first wife of a rising warlord, and he would plunder whatever luxuries she desired. They would have fine horses, strong children, and live in a society that would let them follow their whims to sleep, eat, ride, hunt, camp, and make love when they wanted. He was already beginning to gather his own *lochus*, or regiment, and his men would protect her from any harm. He was offering her the world, for soon the Huns would be masters of it. Yet she treated him like a pest! Meanwhile, he had seen, at the banquet, how she cast covetous eyes at the young Roman who had nothing and who had done nothing. It was maddening.

Skilla was annoyed that he was so attracted to Ilana. What was wrong with the women of the Huns? Nothing, really. They were nimble, hard workers, and were bred to produce robust children in rugged conditions. They would both couple and bear children in a blizzard or a desert's heat, it mattered not to them, and they were proud of their ability not to cry out in either instance. They could make a meal out of a stag or field mouse, whichever was available; find hearty roots in the mud by a riverbed; load a house into a wagon in a quarter of a morning; and carry twin skins of water from a yoke on their back. But they were also plainer, squatter, and rounder. They did not have Ilana's grace, they did not have her worldliness, and they did not have the fierce intelligence that animated the Roman woman's gaze when she became curious or angry. There was no need for a woman to be smart, and yet he found himself desiring exactly that quality in Ilana for reasons he couldn't fathom. There was no use for it! She represented that Roman arrogance he hated, and yet he wanted to possess that arrogance to assuage his own confidence.

His was a desire that was bewitching every clan and brotherhood, Attila had said. The Hun invasion of Europe had made his people powerful, but it was also changing them. The race was being diluted by marriage and adoption. In the forests to the north and west, the horse was less useful. Men who once fought for the simple pleasures of fighting now talked incessantly of mercenary pay, booty, tribute, and the goods they could bring back to satisfy their increasingly greedy wives. Tribes that had wandered with the seasons were settled in crowded Hunuguri. Attila warned his warriors to be careful, to not let Europe conquer them as they conquered Europe. It was why he ate off plain wooden dishes and refused to adorn his clothing, reminding them of the harsh origins that made them hardier and fiercer than their enemies.

Every Hun knew what he meant. But they were also seduced, almost against their wills, by the world they were overrunning. While Attila ate from wood, his chieftains ate from gold plate, and dreamed not of the steppes but of the courtesans of Constantinople.

This, Skilla secretly feared, would destroy them. And him.

He must destroy Alabanda, take Ilana, and escape eastward. And the best way to do so was to wait for Bigilas to return with his son and fifty pounds of gold.

XII

A PLOT REVEALED

Diplomacy, Maximinus explained to me, was the art of patience. As long as talk went on, weapons were sheathed. While weeks crawled by, political situations could change. Agreement that was impossible between strangers became second nature among friends. So it did no harm to wait in the Hun camp while Bigilas backtracked to fetch his son, the senator assured me. "While we wait there is no war, Jonas," he observed with self-satisfaction. "Just by coming here, we have helped the Empire. Simply by passing time, we are serving Constantinople and Rome."

We tried to learn what we could of the Huns, but it was difficult. I was instructed to do a census of their numbers, but warriors and their families came and went so frequently that it was like trying to count a flock of birds. A hunt, a raid, a mission to exact tribute or punishment, a rumor of better pastures, a chase of wild horses, a story of a drinking den or brothel newly established on the shores of the Danube—any of these things could draw the easily bored warriors away. The numbers I counted were useless anyway because most of the Hun nation was scattered far from where we stayed, a web of empire linked by hard-riding messengers. How many clans? None of our informants seemed able to make that clear. How many warriors? More than blades of grass. How many subject tribes? More than the nations of Rome. What were their intentions? That was in the hands of Attila.

Their religion was a tangle of nature spirits and superstition, the details jealously hidden by shaman prophets who claimed to foretell the future with the blood of animals and slaves. This primitive animism was combined with the pantheons of peoples overrun, so that Attila could proclaim confidently that his great iron relic was the sword of Mars and his people knew what he was talking about. Gods were like kingdoms to the Huns: to be conquered and used. Destiny was unavoidable, these primitive people believed, and yet fate was also capricious and could be wooed or warded with charms and spells. Demons could catch the unwary, and storms were the thunder of the gods, but luck was promised by a favorable sign. We Christians were considered fools to look for salvation in the afterlife instead of booty in this: Why worry about the next existence when it was only this one in which you had control? This, of course, was a misunderstanding of the entire point of my religion; but to the Huns the logical goal was to either make life with a woman or end it with war, and one had only to look at the savagery of nature to understand that. Everything killed everything. The Huns were no different.

Their marriages were polygamous, given the surplus of women due to the ravages of war, with harems the reward for battlefield success. There were also concubines who lived in a social twilight between legitimacy and slavery and who sometimes wielded more influence over their vain masters than a legal wife. Battle death, divorce, remarriages, and adultery were so common that the packs of children who ran screaming through the camp seemed to belong to everyone and no one, and seemed as happy in this state as wolf cubs. The Huns indulged their children and taught them horsemanship with the same earnestness that we Romans taught rhetoric or history; but they would also cuff them with the gruffness of she-bears or hurl them into the river to make a point. Privation was expected as a part of life, and practiced for with fasts, withheld water, long swims, the scorch of fire, or the prick of thorns. Wrestling was encouraged, and archery required. For boys there was no higher honor than to endure more pain than your companions, no greater delight than surprising an enemy, and no goal more important than blooding yourself in battle. Girls were taught that they could bear even more agony than men and that every fiber of their being must be dedicated to making more babies who would someday make still more war.

My guide to this martial society was Zerco, the dwarf seeming to enjoy watching the teasing and torture the children inflicted on one another, perhaps because it reminded him of the torment given people his size. "Anagai there has learned to hold his breath longer than anyone because he's smallest and the others hold him under the Tisza," the dwarf explained. "Bochas tried to drown him, but Anagai learned to wring the bigger boy's balls, so now Bochas is more careful. Sandil lost an eye in a rock fight, and Tatos can't shoot after breaking his arm, so he's catching arrows with his shield. They boast about their bruises. The meanest they make their leaders."

I was toughening myself. The journey alone had developed my muscles to an unprecedented degree, and here in Hunuguri there were no books. Composition of my notes took only a fraction of the day. Accordingly, I set about hardening myself like a Hun. I galloped over the treeless plain on my mare, Diana, improving my horsemanship. And, as Zerco had advised, I dug out my heavy Roman weapons and began to practice earnestly. It made a strange sight for the Huns. My spatha, or cavalry sword, was heavier than the curved Hun blades, and my chain armor was heavier and hotter than their leather and bone lamellar armor. Above all, my oval shield was like a house wall compared to the small round wicker shields of the horsemen. Sometimes Huns came to cross blades for practice and, if I could not match their quickness, neither could they break easily past my shield. They banged on me like on a turtle. I fought several to a standstill, and their initial jeers turned to grudging respect. "Getting at you is like getting at a fox in its den!"

The senator didn't like this. "We're an embassy, Alabanda," Maximinus complained. "We're here to befriend the Hun, not fence with him."

"This is what Hun friends do," I told him as I caught my breath.

"It's undignified for a diplomat to fight like a common soldier."

"Fighting is all the dignity they believe in."

Meanwhile, Skilla's intervention had only increased my interest in

Ilana. I learned that he had been orphaned in the wars, taken in by his uncle Edeco, and had been promised Ilana by Attila himself once he had sufficiently proved his mettle in battle. In the meantime, she served Suecca. Had she agreed to this fate? He claimed that he'd saved her life, and she admitted that her acceptance of presents and protection signaled acquiescence. Yet his generosity also embarrassed her, and it was clear she felt trapped.

I wished I had something to match him, but I'd brought no gifts of my own. Certainly she was a striking woman, with an obvious interest in me as a possible rescuer. Yet she was wary of being seen with me, and I wasn't sure if her interest went beyond my potential utility as a path to freedom. I tabulated her movements, learning to cross paths with her when she emerged from Edeco's household on errands, and she learned to expect me. She walked in a way that made me think of her body even when she was in the plainest and most shapeless clothes, and she smiled encouragingly at me even while seeming reluctant to linger. She knew we most want what we can't have.

"Don't submit to that Hun," I told her in hurried moments. I liked the way her eyes shone as she looked to me as a savior, even while I wondered if I could ever actually help her—I had no money—or if she was using me.

"I've asked Suecca to keep Skilla away," she said. "She's disgusted at my ingratitude and Edeco is amused. These Huns view resistance as a challenge. I'm worried, Jonas. Skilla is getting impatient. I need to get away from this camp."

"I don't know if Edeco would agree to let you go."

"Maybe when your embassy negotiates and favors are being exchanged. Talk to your senator."

"Not yet." I knew her rescue would not make sense to anybody but me. I grasped her hand, even this slight contact thrilling me. "Soon Bigilas will return and opportunity will arise," I promised recklessly. "I'm determined to take you with us."

"Please, my life will be at an end if you don't."

And then Bigilas came back.

•   •   •

The son of Bigilas was a boy of eleven, dark haired and wide-eyed, who rode into camp with mouth open and spine tingling. How could he not gape at this horde of Huns whom Roman boys had exaggerated to mythic proportions? Young Crixus was proud that his father was playing so pivotal a role. He, Crixus, was the guarantee of honesty between the two sides! That his father had seemed troubled and distant on their journey north did not particularly surprise the boy: Bigilas had always been too self-absorbed to be either a proper father or good companion, but he moved with the greats and promised they would someday be rich. How many sons could say that?

When word of Bigilas's return reached Attila, the king invited us Romans to attend him that evening. Despite his proclaimed patience, Maximinus was relieved. We'd been confined to Attila's camp for weeks.

Once again the king of the Huns was on his dais, but this time there were far fewer retainers in his hall. Instead, there were a dozen heavily armed guards and Edeco, Skilla, and Onegesh: the Huns who had accompanied us. Trying to ignore the Hun soldiers, I told myself that perhaps this smaller group was an encouraging sign. Here was private and serious negotiation, not diplomatic ritual and show. Yet I couldn't help but feel greater unease than when I'd first come to the Hun camp, for I'd learned too much about Attila. His charisma was matched by his tyranny, and the humbleness of his attire masked the arrogance of ambition.

"I hope he's in good humor," I whispered to Rusticius.

"Surely he wishes to conclude things as we do."

"You've had enough Hun hospitality?"

"Edeco has never forgiven me for standing up for us and speaking back during our journey, and I've felt his ire in the mood of his followers. They call me the Westerner, as if fundamentally different because I come from Italy. They watch me as if I'm on exhibit."

"I think they're just curious about peoples they've yet to enslave."

Torches threw a wavering light over the scarred faces of Attila's retainers. The king's deep-set eyes seemed to have burrowed even farther into his head than I remembered, rotating to look at this figure or that like creatures peering from protective burrows. His odd, ugly, and impassive face made him difficult to read and, as usual, there was not a hint of a smile. This seemed unsurprising. I'd attended Hun justice councils where quarreling tribesmen took rival complaints; and Attila always adjudicated without emotion, his judgments harsh, strange, quick, and yet curiously fitting his grim people and his own stoic visage. Each judgment day he sat bareheaded in the bright sunlight of his compound courtyard, the quarreling or petitioning parties let in by turn. They would be peppered with hard questions, cut off if they protested too long, and then sent away with a decision from which there was no appeal.

There was no true law, only Attila. Often a wrong could be righted by *konoss*, that Hun practice of a transgressor paying the victim or his family with anything from a cow to a daughter. The Huns usually abhorred imprisonment, for which they had few facilities, and disliked mutilation, because it weakened potential warriors or mothers. But sometimes harsher penalties were applied.

For example, I witnessed Attila's permission for a cuckolded husband in a particularly humiliating case to take revenge by castrating the seducer of his wife with a rusty knife and then stuffing the severed privates into the organ of the woman who had lain with him, locked to her with a chain for the full cycle of a moon.

To steal a man's horse on the empty steppes was tantamount to murder, and so a horse thief was ordered torn apart by having his limbs tied to the ponies he had stolen, their owner and his sons urging the horses slowly forward until his joints popped. Then he screamed in agony for an hour as the animals jostled in place: screamed, at Attila's insistence, until all of our ears ached from it, as evidence of his power. Finally the horses were whipped forward at Attila's command, and it was with great difficulty that I didn't retch. I was astonished at how far the blood spurted and how meaty and meaningless the scattered parts seemed once the victim was dismembered.

A coward in battle was ordered suspended over a pit of planted spears and each member of the unit he'd deserted was told to cut one strand away from the suspending rope. "Fate will decide if you betrayed enough to weaken the rope to the point where you fall into the pit," Attila decreed. Because some of his former companions were hunting or on military missions, it took six days before all returned to camp and took their careful slice. In the end there were just enough strands that the rope barely held, and the victim was finally lowered, gibbering and fever-ish. His two wives sliced their own cheeks and breasts in humiliation be-fore bearing him away.

Each of these incidents was reported and even exaggerated as Huns traveled through Attila's empire. The kagan was just and yet merciless, fatherly and yet cruel, wise and yet given to well-timed rages. What would it do to a tyrant's mind, I wondered, to order such punishments day after day, year after year? How would it shape a leader that only by doing so could he prevent his savage nation from sliding into anarchy? When did such acts take one out of the realm of normal conduct and into a universe that existed only in one's own feverish, self-centered mind? He seemed not so much an emperor as a circus master with whip and torch, and not so much a king as a primitive god.

"This is your son?" Attila now asked, interrupting my thoughts.

"Crixus has come all the way from Constantinople, kagan," Bigilas said, "as proof that my word is my bond." His manner seemed more unctuous and false than ever, and I wondered if the Huns noticed the shallowness of his sincerity or just passed it off as Roman habit. "He's hostage for Rome's honesty. Please, now hear our ambassador." Bigilas glanced once at Edeco, but the Hun chieftain was as expressionless as stone. "I myself am your servant, of course."

Attila nodded solemnly and looked at Senator Maximinus. "This demonstrates the trust I can put in the word of Rome and Constantino-ple?"

The senator bowed. "Bigilas has offered his own son as proof of our good will, kagan, reminiscent of how the God of our faith offered his. Peace begins with trust, and surely this reinforces your faith in our in-tentions, does it not?"

Attila was silent for so long that all of us became uneasy. Silence hung in the room like motes of dust.

"Indeed it does," he finally said. "It tells me exactly what your inten-tions are." Attila looked down at Crixus. "You are a brave and dutiful

boy to come all this way at the command of your father. You demon-
strate how sons should behave. Do you trust the sire of your flesh,
young Roman?"

The boy blinked, stunned at having been addressed. "I—I do, king."
He searched for words. "I am proud of him." He beamed.

Attila nodded, then stood. "Your heart is good, little one. Your soul
is innocent, I think." He blinked once. "Unlike your elders." Then he
let his dark eyes pass over each of us in turn, as if seeing inside our
hearts and selecting different fates for each of us. Instantly we knew that
something was desperately awry. "It is too bad, then," the despot rumbled, "that your father has utterly betrayed you and that you must be
tortured for his sins."

It was as if the air had gone out of the room. Maximinus gaped like a
fool. Bigilas went white. I felt confused. What treachery was this? Poor
Crixus looked like he had not understood.

"We will uncoil your entrails like yarn and let my pigs feed on
them," Attila described without emotion. "We will boil your toes and
your fingers, immersing them one by one so that you will know the pain
of the last before we start on the next. We will cut away your nose, flay
your cheeks, and break out your teeth in turn—one per hour—and
cinch a thorny bramble around your privates and pull until they turn
purple."

Crixus was beginning to shake.

"What madness is this?" the senator croaked. "Why do you
threaten a child?"

"We will do these things—and my wives will giggle at your
screams, young Crixus—unless your father shows the honor that you
have shown." Now Attila's dark gaze swung to settle on Bigilas.

"S-show honor?" stammered Bigilas. The guards, I saw, had quietly
formed around us. "Kagan, what can you—"

"We will do it"—here Attila's voice was rising to low thunder—
"unless the translator here tells me why he has brought fifty pounds of
gold from Constantinople."

We other Romans turned to Bigilas in consternation. What was Attila talking about? The translator looked stricken, as if told by a physi-

cian he was doomed. His legs began quivering, and I feared he might collapse.

Attila turned to his chiefs. "He did bring fifty pounds, did he not, Edeco?"

The warlord nodded. "As we agreed in the house of Chrysaphius, kagan. We searched the translator's saddlebags just moments ago and brought it here for you to see as proof." He clapped his hands once, a sharp report. Two warriors came in bearing sacks, leaning slightly from the weight. They strode to Attila's dais and slashed open the sacks with iron daggers, releasing a shower of yellow metal. Coins rolled at Attila's feet.

The boy's eyes were darting in confused terror. I could smell his urine.

"Edeco, you know what this gold is for, do you not?"

"I do, my kagan."

"This is some monstrous misunderstanding," Maximinus tried wildly, looking to Bigilas for explanation. "Another present sent by our emperor, as proof of—"

"Silence!" The command was as final as the fall of an ax. It echoed in the chamber, ending all other sound. It was an order that made courage desert. What insanity had I enlisted for?

"Only one man here needs to be heard from," Attila went on, "the one who can save his son by practicing the honesty he claims."

Bigilas was staring at Edeco in horror and hatred. The betrayer had been betrayed. Edeco had never intended to carry out his promise of assassinating Attila, the translator realized. The gold was a trap. Now he fell to his knees. "Please, my son knew nothing."

"And what *nothing*, translator, did the boy not know?"

Bigilas bowed his head miserably. "It was a mission entrusted to me by Chrysaphius. The money was to bribe Edeco to assassinate you."

Maximinus looked like he'd been struck by a German long sword. He reeled backward, his face pained. His mission, he understood instantly, was in ruins. What treachery for the chief minister to not tell him of this plot! The proud senator had been made a complete fool. Worse, it probably meant the end of us all.

"To *murder* me, you mean," Attila clarified, "when I was most trusting and most defenseless—while I slept or ate or pissed. A murder by my most trusted warlord."

"I was only obeying the will of my master!" Bigilas wailed. "It was all Chrysaphius! He's an evil eunuch—every man in Constantinople knows it! These other fools were ignorant of the plot, I swear! I was to fetch my son and with him the gold . . ." Suddenly he swiveled toward Edeco, furious. "You gave your word that you were with us! You promised you would assassinate him!"

"I promised nothing. You heard what you wanted to hear."

The translator was beginning to weep. "I was no more than a tool, and my son ignorant. Please, kill me if you must, but spare the boy. He is innocent, as you said."

Attila's look was contemptuous. A quiet that really only lasted moments seemed to us Romans to last hours. Finally he spoke again. "Kill *you*? As if your master would care? As if he wouldn't send a hundred idiots to try again if he thought one of my generals was foolish enough to believe him? No, I won't waste the moment's work required to kill *you*, translator. Instead, you will walk barefoot back to Constantinople with your bag around your scrawny neck, its gold replaced by lead. You will feel each pound with every step of your bleeding feet. My escorts will ask Chrysaphius if they recognize the bag, and he will do so, or you will die. Then you will tell Chrysaphius that you met ten thousand Huns and could not find even *one* who would raise his hand against the great Attila, not for all the gold in the world. *This* is what your Empire must understand!"

Bigilas was weeping. "And my son?"

"If he is foolish enough to go back with you, he may do so. Maybe he will become smart enough to despise you and find a proper mentor. Maybe he will eventually flee the corruption of his father and come live the clean life of the Hun."

Crixus collapsed, holding on to his father as they both bawled.

"God and the Senate thank you for your mercy, kagan," Maximinus said shakily. "Please, do not let this blind foolishness destroy our partnership. The emperor knew nothing of this monstrosity, I'm sure!

Chrysaphius is a vindictive plotter, all men in Constantinople know this. Please, let us make amends and start our talks—"

"There will be no talk. There will be no negotiation. There will only be obeisance or war. You, too, will return to Constantinople, senator, but it will be backward on an ass, and my warriors will make sure your head is always pointed toward the land of Hunuguri as you ponder your foolishness."

Maximinus jerked as if struck. The end of his dignity would be the end of his career. Attila, I was certain, knew this.

"Do not humiliate Rome too much," the senator said in despair.

"She humiliates herself." Attila considered. "You and the one who betrayed you can contemplate my mercy. Yet none dare raise a hand against Attila without someone being struck down in consequence. So he"—Attila pointed at Rusticius—"will die in place of his friend. This man will be crucified to rot and dry in the sun, and his dying words will be to damn to Christian Hell the greedy and corrupt companion who put him in such danger."

Rusticius had gone ashen. Bigilas turned his face away.

"That is not fair!" I cried.

"It is *your* Empire that is not fair or trustworthy," Attila said. "It is *your* country that treats some men like gods and others like cattle."

Now Rusticius fell to his knees, gasping for breath like a landed fish. "But I have done nothing!"

"You joined with evil men you didn't care to know well enough to discover their betrayal. You failed to warn me. By these omissions you doomed yourself, and your blood will be on your friends' hands, not mine."

I was dizzy with horror. "This makes no sense," I tried, heedless of violating protocol. The simplest man of our party was the one who was being sacrificed! "Why him and not me?"

"Because he is of the West, and we are curious how such men die." Attila shrugged. "I may decide to have you switch places. But for now," he said, "you will remain as my hostage against the promise of the return of Senator Maximinus." He turned to my superior. "For every pound of gold Chrysaphius was willing to spend to have me struck down, I want one hundred pounds in penance."

"But, kagan," gasped the senator, "that means—"

"It means I want five thousand pounds by autumn, senator, and only then will we talk peace. If you don't bring it, there will be war and your scribe will have done to him exactly what I promised the young boy there, but done infinitely more slowly and painfully."

The room was a blur, the earth seeming to have dropped from under me. I was to be left alone with the Huns, to watch Rusticius die? And then be tortured if Maximinus did not return with an impossible ransom? The treasury could not afford five thousand pounds of gold! We had all been betrayed by the fools Bigilas and Chrysaphius!

Attila nodded at me with grim satisfaction. "Until then, you are our hostage but a hostage who must begin earning his keep. And if you dare try escape, Jonas of Constantinople, this too means war."

XIII

THE HOSTAGE

Something had gone horribly wrong.

Ilana had been so confident of rescue that she had actually packed and hidden a bag of clothes, biscuit, and dried venison to take with her when she left with the Romans. Surely it had been a sign when the embassy rode into camp and she'd caught the eye of Jonas. God meant for her to be free and to return to civilization. Yet Guernna had run to her, smirking. "Come see your fine friends now, Roman!" Ilana had emerged into a sea of hooting and jostling Huns, some of them flinging vegetables and clods of earth at the three departing Romans. The old man was mounted backward on a donkey, his feet dangling and his fine gray hair and beard dirty and matted. His eyes looked hollow with defeat. Following on foot was the translator who had come back from Constantinople, staggering with a heavy sack around his neck that bent him like a reed. Roped behind was a boy who must be the translator's son, looking frightened and ashamed. A dozen Hun warriors surrounded them as escort, including, she saw to her relief, Skilla. He must be leaving, too. But the Roman tents and baggage and slaves were all remaining behind, the latter conscripted into Attila's army.

Where was Jonas?

"I heard they put one of them on the cross," Guernna said gleefully, enjoying Ilana's dismay. Guernna thought the Roman girl vain, aloof, and useless. "I heard he screamed more than a Hun or a German ever would and begged like a slave."

Crucifixions took place on a low hill a half mile from the river, far enough so that the stench was not overpowering but near enough so that the cost of defiance was always apparent. One or two happened per week, as well as periodic impalings. Ilana ran there, praying. Indeed, there was a new victim, whipped, bound, spiked, and so masked with blood and dirt that at first she had no idea who it was. Only after studying him anxiously did she discern that it was Rusticius, his eyes half hooded, his lips cracked like dried mud.

She was ashamed at her relief.

"Kill me . . ." He was rasping for breath, his own weight compressing his lungs. Rivulets of blood had dried brown on skin blistered from exposure.

"Where is Jonas?"

There was no answer. She doubted he could still hear.

She dared not grant Rusticius's wish, or she would find herself hung beside him. Sickened by her own helplessness, she ran back to the camp, the crowd dissipated now that the humiliated Romans had left. Their tents had already been shared out as if the Romans had never existed. She came to Attila's compound, breathless and tear-stained. "The young Roman," she gasped to a guard. "Please . . ."

"Back like a pup, tied to his father." The man sneered.

"Not the boy, the scribe! His name is Jonas Alabanda."

"Oh, the lucky one. Hostage for more gold. Attila has given him to Hereka until we kill him. Your lover has become a slave, woman."

She struggled to remain expressionless, her emotions a tumult of relief and despair. "He's not my lover—"

"And when Skilla returns, you will be his." He grinned. It was the rare tryst, feud, love affair, or rivalry that did not become gossip in the camp.

Hereka, Attila's first and primary wife, lived in her own compound adjacent to Attila's. Several dozen slaves and servants lived with her; and now Jonas had become one, forced to earn his keep by hewing wood, hauling water, tending Hereka's herds, and entertaining the Hun's primary wife with stories of Constantinople and the Bible.

Ilana tried to get in to see him, but Hereka's gigantic Ostrogoth guards shooed her away. Her rescuer had become a prisoner and hope had evaporated, its memory like a kiss that could never be repeated.

It was two long weeks later that she spied him from a distance driving a Hun cart from the poplar and willow copses where the camp collected its firewood. The sun was low in the west, the sky pinking, when she took a water jar to once more give herself an excuse to walk to the track by the river to intercept him. The day had the warm sultriness of late summer, clouds of gnats orbiting each other. The Tisza River was low and brown.

Jonas reined the oxen when he recognized her, but he looked reluctant. She was surprised by how he'd changed. His hair was matted with sweat from a day of chopping and gathering wood, and his skin had become deeply tanned. Beyond that, he had visibly aged. His face was harder, his jaw stronger, and his eyes deeper and more worried. He had learned in an instant the cruelty of life, and it showed. He'd become a man. She found herself strangely heartened by his grim maturity.

His first words were not encouraging. "Go home, Ilana. I can do nothing for you now."

"If Maximinus returns—"

"You know he won't." He shaded his eyes against the setting sun, looking away from the slight, pretty, helpless woman.

"Won't your own father try to ransom you?"

"What little he could afford would mean nothing compared to the pleasure and object lesson Attila derives from making an example of me. And Rusticius died in innocence, while the creature that created this disaster goes home to Constantinople, a bag around his neck." His tone was bitter.

"Bigilas's master will punish him for failure."

"While I eventually hang on a cross and you become bed slave to Skilla."

Not slave, but wife, she wanted to correct. Was that her fate? Should she accede to it? She took a deep breath. "We can't live expecting the worst, Jonas. The Empire won't forget you. It was a crime to execute

Rusticius, and Attila will sooner or later want to make amends. If we're patient—"

"I can chop a lot of wood and you can haul a lot of water."

There was a long dispirited pause, neither seeing an alternative, and then she laughed, the absurdity making her feel she was going insane. "How gloomy you've become!"

Her laughter startled him. He looked confused, then sheepish. "You're right." He sighed. "I've had another long day feeling sorry for myself."

"It gets tiresome after a while." Her grin was wry.

He straightened. Meek submission to barbarian will was not what Romans were taught. She watched him watching her, each trying to draw strength from the other. "We have to get away from here," he said, obviously trying to force his depressed mind to think.

A glimmer! "Maybe we can steal some horses."

"They would catch us." He thought of his race with Skilla, and the Hun's promise. "They'd send a hundred men. It would be too humiliating for Attila to let us succeed."

"I wish there'd been a real plot," she said fiercely. "I wish Edeco had killed Attila."

"I wish a thousand things, and find it as useful as spit. Our only hope would be a head start, to go when they're distracted. If Attila left on campaign—"

"It's too late in the year for that. There'll be no grass for the cavalry."

He nodded. This girl was smart and observant. "So what should we do, Ilana?"

She thought furiously, knowing word of this conversation would reach Suecca. Yet this lonely and forlorn man was her only chance, unless she wanted Skilla. Despite Jonas's despair there was something good at his core in an age when goodness was in short supply. "We should be ready for that distraction," she said firmly. "My father was as lucky in business as he was unlucky in war, but he said luck was preparation that waited for opportunity. We need to know who we can trust and which horses we can steal. Who can help us, even a little?"

Now *he* pondered, and then suddenly brightened with an idea. He reached for the switch and lashed the ox forward, the cart jolting as he started. "A little friend," he said.

It was dangerous to take Zerco into my confidence and yet who but the dwarf could help us? I was furious at the crucifixion of Rusticius and felt guilty at my own survival. I knew Zerco had no more love for Attila than I did. Indeed, the dwarf was both intrigued about the idea of our escape and thoughtful about its practicalities. "You can't outrun them, even with a diversion," he said. "They'll catch you at the Danube, if nowhere else. But you might outthink them. Go north instead of south, for example, and circle to the west. You need horses—"

"Roman, for endurance."

"You saw the Arabians they've captured for breeding. The Germans have big horses, too. The woman is going to slow you, you know."

"She's Roman."

"This camp has a hundred captive Romans. What she *is*, is pretty and desperate, which is a dangerous combination. Hoist your brain above your belt a moment and tell me what she is to you."

I scowled. "Something Skilla wants."

"Ah! Now that makes better sense. All right, then. You'll need to take food so you can avoid farms and villages as long as possible, and you'll need light weapons. Can you shoot a bow?"

"I was practicing until made hostage. I admit I'm no Hun."

"It will be useful for hunting, at least. Hmmm. You'll need warm clothing because winter is coming. Coin for when food runs out. A waterskin, hooded cloaks to hide your identity—"

"You sound like the commissary of a legion."

"You need to be prepared."

"You're so helpful that I'm suspicious."

The dwarf smiled. "At last you're learning! Everything has a price. My help, too."

"Which is?"

"That you take me with you."

"You! And you talk of Ilana slowing me down?"

"I'm light, a good companion, and I've been where we need to go."

This sounded like madness. "Can you even ride a horse?"

"Julia can. I ride with her."

"Another woman!"

"You started it. Do you want my help or not?"

Ilana and I waited in an agony of impatience. The days were growing shorter, the land yellow and sleepy. Already there was a chill to the night and the first leaves petaled the Tisza. When the weather turned, the barbarian tracks became soup, and travel became difficult. Yet one week and then another slipped by, and no opportunity to leave presented itself. Hereka and Suecca kept sharp watch on us.

Twice we managed to meet for quick reassurance. The first time was at the river, dipping water and murmuring quickly before breaking apart, each of us trusting a person we scarcely knew. The second time was in a ravine through which a seasonal creek fed the river, its bottom dense with brush. Some Huns coupled there, I knew, away from the eyes of their parents or spouses. Now I drew her near to whisper.

These meetings had made her more precious, not less. I found myself remembering moments I didn't realize I'd recorded: the way the light had fallen on her cheek by the river, the wetness of her eyes when she stared up at me on the wood cart, or the swell of breast and hip when she filled her jars at the river. Her neck was a Euclidian curve, her clavicle a fold of snow, her fingers quick and nervous with the grace and beat of a butterfly wing. Now I looked at her ear that gleamed like shell amid the fall of her dark hair, the parted lips as she gasped for breath, the rise and fall of her bosom, and wanted her without entirely knowing why. The idea of rescue and escape magnified her charms. To her, I was a comrade in a dangerous enterprise. To me, she was . . .

"Has the dwarf assembled our things?" she asked anxiously.

"Almost."

"What payment does he want?"

"To go with us."

"Do you trust him?"

"He could have betrayed us already."

She nodded, her eyes glistening like dark pearls. "I think I have good news."

"What?"

"There's a Greek doctor named Eudoxius who Attila sent as an envoy. He's returning and is only a day's ride away, according to gossip. Some think the Greek is bringing important news, and it has been a while since the community feasted. Men have been sent to hunt, and Suecca has started us cooking. I think there's going to be a celebration."

"A Greek doctor?"

"Another traitor, fled to the Huns. It's the end of the summer, and there's an abundance of *kamon* and *kumiss*. The camp is full because the warriors have been returning for winter. They will hold a *strava* to celebrate the return of this Greek and drink, Jonas, drink themselves insensible. I have seen it." She grasped my arm, straining toward me, her excitement making her quiver. "I think this is our chance."

I kissed her.

It surprised her more than I thought it would, and she pulled away, not certain whether she welcomed my advance, her emotions playing across her face like the rippling of a curtain.

I tried to kiss her again.

"No." She held me away. "Not until things are settled."

"I'm falling in love with you, Ilana."

This complication frightened her. "You don't know me." She shook her head, keeping her purpose in mind. "Not until we've escaped—together."

The news that Eudoxius brought back was secret, but his return excuse enough for a *strava*, a grand national party, or a celebration for as much of the fragmentary nation as happened to be camped around Attila at the time. It would welcome back the Greek doctor, mark the harvest that Hun vassals were humbly bringing to their masters, celebrate the humiliation of the treacherous Roman ambassadors, and commemorate a year in which the Huns had exacted a good deal of taxes, booty, and tribute with very little fighting. The relative peace, everyone knew, would not last forever.

The *strava* would take place when the leaves turned golden and the morning plain was white with frost and would last three days. It would be a bacchanalia without Bacchus—a festival of dance, song, games, jesters, lovemaking, feasting, and above all drinking that at its end would leave the participants sprawling. It was this excess that Ilana was counting on to aid our escape. By the end of the first night no one would notice we were missing. By the end of the third, no one would care.

Zerco promised to assemble the saddles, clothing, and food once the *strava* was well under way. There were Roman horses picketed in a meadow across the Tisza. I hoped to find Diana, but if not I would steal the strongest horse I could find. We would swim the river, saddle the animals, and ride north. Once well away we would cut west, following the northern bank of the Danube, and then cross into Pannonia and gallop for the Alps, eventually reaching Italy. From there we could take ship for Constantinople.

I could smell the streets of home.

Because tens of thousands of Huns, Goths, and Gepids were celebrating, the *strava* was held outside. A thousand flags and horsehair banners were erected, fluttering in the wind like a rising flock of birds. A hundred bonfires were built in huge pyramidal pyres. Lit at dusk, they were so bright that they turned the cloudy sky orange, and plumes of sparks funneled upward as if Attila was giving birth to new colonies of stars. Each tribe and clan had its own music. The camp's celebrants migrated from one center of entertainment to the next, each host determined to outdo his neighbor in the volume of song and the quantity of drink pressed into wandering hands. Voices rose and dancing started. Then flirtations. Then fights. A few Huns were stabbed or garroted like fighting wolves, their bodies casually cast behind yurts to be attended to when the *strava* was over. Couples broke away for lovemaking, legs splayed, buttocks pumping, in anxious release before they became too drunk. The warlords and shamans drank mushroom and forest herb drafts and were so exhilarated by their visions that they pirouetted around the fires, roaring nonsense prophecies and staggering after screaming damsels who stayed maddeningly out of reach. Children wres-

132   WILLIAM DIETRICH

tled, ran, stole. Babies cried, half ignored, until their own noise finally put them to sleep.

Both Ilana and I were required to serve. We dragged forth casks and amphorae of wine, bore heavy platters of roasted meat, hauled the insensible to one side so that they would not be trampled, and threw dirt on the worst of the vomit and piss. Despite the cool night air we were sweating from the heat of the fires and the press of bodies. Attached as we were to the houses of Hereka and Edeco, we were at the center of the *strava*'s galaxy, all other fires and merriment wheeling around those of the great kagan and his chief lieutenants.

"Attila has promised to speak," I whispered. "When that happens, all eyes will be on him. Leave, alone, so there is no suspicion. I'll follow."

With no stump or stone on the flat plain, Attila chose a novel means to get attention. A trio of horses was walked into the gathering as the merriment and mayhem built to its first-night climax. Two of the horses had riders, but the third was bare. It was onto this horse that Attila sprang, boosting himself up until he balanced on its back, the flanking riders encircling his calves with their arms to brace him. "Warriors!" he cried.

They whooped in response. A thousand men and women crowded to hear his words, bellowing and singing at the sight of their king. And what a sight he was! Again, Attila wore no decoration, yet what he did wear atop his ordinary Hun clothes was ghastly. The bones of a man had been tied joint to joint and arranged on his front. The bones matched Attila's own frame, jiggling and rattling as the king drunkenly swayed to keep himself standing upright on the back of the nervous horse. The skull was missing, but Attila's own head was far more terrifying. His visage was dark, his hair wild, and two curved horns had been attached to jut from his temples like a demon god's. Lightning bolts of white paint zigzagged down his scarred cheeks, and black paint circled his eyes to turn them into pits. "People of Hunuguri! People of the Dawn!"

They roared their fealty. Attila was giving them the world. Ilana pushed out through the crowd to slip away.

Finally it quieted. "As you know, I am the meekest of men," he began.

There was appreciative laughter. Indeed, who was less ostentatious than Attila? Who wore less gold, demanded less praise, and ate more modestly than the king of the Huns?

"I let deeds replace speeches. I let loyalty speak my praise. I let mercy show my heart. And I let dead enemies testify to my power. Like this one here!" He shook the skeleton hanging on his body, and the Huns howled. "This is the Roman I crucified after his friends tried to have me assassinated. Listen to this Roman of the West, because I have no words to match what his rattle says about my contempt for his people!"

I was sickened. Rusticius's head, I knew, must now be mounted on one of the poles around Attila's house, its fine brown hair blowing in the wind, his once-friendly grin now a skull's grimace.

"You have been patient this year, my wolves," Attila went on. "You have slaked your thirst for blood with water and let tribute substitute for plunder. You have slept, because I commanded it."

The crowd waited, expectant.

"But now the world is changing. New tidings have come to Attila. New insults, new promises, and new opportunities. The Romans must think we are a nation of women, to send a few pounds of gold to kill me! The Romans think we have forgotten how to fight! But Attila forgets nothing. He misses nothing. He forgives nothing. Drink well and deeply, my warriors, because for some of you it will be your last. Sleep deeply and rut deeply, to sow new Huns, and then sharpen your weapons this long cold winter, because the world must never stop fearing its Hun master. All this year we have rested, but in the coming spring, we ride. Are the Cadiseni of the Huns ready to ride with Attila?"

"Ten thousand bows will the Cadiseni bring to the king of the Huns!" shouted Agus, the chieftain of that clan. "Ten thousand bows and ten thousand horses, and we will ride from Rome itself to the bowels of Hades!" The crowd cheered, half crazed with drink and bloodlust. All they really knew was conquest and restless journey.

"Are the Sciri ready to ride with Attila?" the king cried.

"Twelve thousand swords will the Sciri bring when the snows melt in the spring!" promised Massaget, king of that nation. "Twelve thousand who will be first to break the shield wall and let the Huns follow us!" Cheers, hoots, and challenges followed this boast, and there was a friendly and rough jostling as the warlords pushed and jockeyed for position before their king.

"Are the Barselti ready to ride with Attila?"

Another roar. Now I began to push my way out of the crowd, saying I was under orders to fetch more food. Attila would give us the time we needed.

Ilana had initially stumbled in the dark after leaving the area of the great fires, but soon her eyes adjusted. The glow from the clouds cast a lurid red light. As she neared the Tisza the camp seemed empty at its margins, only an occasional Hun hurrying to fetch another skin of mead or chase the rump of a lover. No one paid her any heed. So now she was about to trust her life and future to this young Roman and his strange dwarf friend! It was necessary. Although Jonas and his party had failed to ransom her as she originally hoped, he at least represented the male strength she needed to help escape to the Empire. He'd even said he was falling in love with her. Did men fall in love so easily? Did she at all love him? Not in the way she'd loved her betrothed, the dear Tasio, who'd been shot by that arrow during the siege of Axiopolis. She'd dreamed girlish dreams of marrying him, having a vague but happy future of home and children and sweet surrender to his lovemaking. Now that seemed a thousand years removed, and she could scarcely remember what Tasio looked like, much to her secret embarrassment. She was more practical now, more desperate, more cynical. This man from Constantinople was really just a convenient ally. And yet when *he* kissed her, and looked at her with longing eyes, her heart had stumbled in a tumult she dared not confess. What foolishness to be thinking of such a thing before they were even away! And yet if Jonas and she escaped together, would he try to press himself upon her? And what should be her reaction if he did . . .?

It was while lost in such girlish thought that a wall loomed in the darkness and she stopped abruptly, afraid she was about to crash into a house. But, no, it sidestepped, snorting. She'd been so witless that she'd almost walked into a horse and rider! The Hun who loomed above her leaned drunkenly down, swaying slightly and grinning. "And who is this sweet woman, come to meet me before I'm fully home!" he said in slurred recognition. "Have you been waiting for me, Ilana?"

Her heart sank. What monstrous fortune was this? Skilla!

"What are you doing here?" she breathed. She'd thought him still away at Constantinople, escorting the humiliated Roman embassy.

Leaning precariously, a skin of *kumiss* dangling from one shoulder, Skilla slid off his horse in a half topple. "Finding you, it seems," he said. "What a homecoming! First I find the whole plain alight with celebratory bonfires. Then a sentry patrol passes me some tart *kumiss* so that they don't drink so much that they pass out themselves, earning a crucifixion. And then, following the river path because it's the only one simple enough for my tired horse to negotiate, I find you running out to meet me!"

"It's a *strava* for the Greek envoy Eudoxius, not you," she said. She was thinking furiously. "I've been sent to fetch more *kamon* for the party."

"I think you've come to look for me." He swayed, leering. "I've been thinking of you for a thousand miles, you know. It's all I think about."

"Skilla, it's not our fate to be together."

"Then why did the gods send you to me just now?" He grinned.

Please, please, she prayed, not this, not now. "I have to go." She tried to dart around him but he was quicker than his drunken state made her expect, snaring her arm.

"What beer is out here in the dark?" he objected. "I think it *is* fate that sent you to meet me. And why do you recoil? All I've ever wanted to do is honor you, to make you my wife, and bring you rich presents. Why are you so haughty?"

She groaned. "Please, I don't mean to be."

"I saved you."

"Skilla, you were with the Huns who killed my father. You carried me into captivity—"

"That's war." He frowned. "I'm your future now. Not that Roman slave."

She craned her neck, looking for help. She knew she should try to charm her way out of his grip but she was flustered. She had to get away! Jonas might come at any moment and a confrontation between the two men could ruin everything. She shoved and they rocked backward in a crude dance. "Skilla, you need to sober. We have to part."

It amused him, this smug little flirt, this woman who preened. He yanked and pulled her in close, his breath on hers, the rank smell of travel sweat and dust pungent and disagreeable. He sniffed her sweetness greedily. "In a *strava*? This is when men and women come together."

"I have duties. I serve the wife of Edeco."

This challenged him. "I am the nephew of Lord Edeco and a future lord myself," he growled, twisting her arm so that she remembered who was master. "I am one of those who is going to rule the world and everything in it."

"Only if you prove yourself! Not like this—"

"You could be a queen. Can't you see that?"

She slapped him with her free arm, as hard as she could, and the sound was as loud as the crack of a whip. Her hand stung like fire, the blow jolting her shoulder, and yet he seemed oblivious to the pain of it. He grinned more fiercely.

"I don't *want* to be your queen. Find another. There are thousands who would want to be your queen!"

"But I want *you*. I've wanted you since I saw you by the burning church in Axiopolis. I wanted you all the way to Constantinople these last weeks, prodding that foolish senator seated backward on his ass and hating him for taking me away from you. I wanted you all the way back. You hang on me like that bag of lead hung on the neck of Bigilas, bowing his shoulders, humping his back, until at the end he could barely stagger, weeping, his son leading him by the hand. I'm tired of this foolish waiting."

What to do? His grip was like a manacle. She had to find an excuse. "I'm sorry I slapped you. I'm just surprised. Yes, yes, I know we must marry."

He looked triumphant and greedily kissed her.

She broke with a gasp and twisted her head away. "But Edeco said you must wait for Attila to give me! We must wait, Skilla. You know we must!"

"To hell with Attila." He sought her lips.

She gave him only her cheek. "I'll tell you said that! I'll tell you've interrupted my duties, I'll tell you drank on the way into camp, I'll tell—"

Maddened by impatience he snarled and pushed, as violently as if in battle. She fell, the wind knocked out of her, and bounced her head off the hard-packed turf of the track. She was dazed, her eyes blinded by tiny lights as she looked up at him. He fell to his knees, straddling her, and grasped her dress at its neck.

"No, Skilla! Think!"

He pulled and the garment tore, its strings parting like scythed wheat, and her breasts came free to the cold kiss of the night air. She spat in frustration and defiance, and he cuffed her, dazing her even more, and began hauling her dress up her thighs. He'd gone crazy. The more she squirmed and struggled, the more it seemed to excite him. She clawed at him, and he laughed.

"I told them you'd scratch me."

She screamed, hopelessly, because she knew the scream would be lost in the shouts of this wild night. Skilla was insane, drunkenly wrestling with her clothing and his own. Yet if he raped her, what would it matter? She was a captive and a slave, and he was of the Hun aristocracy.

Then something hurtled in a rush of wind and crashed into both of them, knocking Skilla aside and rolling with him across the grass and dirt. There were grunts and soft curses, and then the newcomer got atop Skilla and struck him.

"Ilana, run for the river!"

It was Jonas.

The Hun snarled, bucked, and finally somersaulted backward. Jonas went over with him, taken by surprise, and lay stunned. The Hun twisted like a wolverine and reached for the Roman's throat. "Haven't they killed you yet?" Now he was on top, pressing down; but suddenly a fist shot upward and Skilla's head snapped back, his grip coming free. Jonas heaved, and the two were separated once again.

"Go to the river!" he gasped to her again.

If she ran for the river she still had a chance to escape. The dwarf could help them find the way, and Jonas could keep Skilla pinned. And yet as the two men struggled, she couldn't run as desperation dictated. Did she feel more for the Roman than she'd admitted? "I won't leave you!" She looked around for a rock or stick.

The Hun, spitting blood from a cut lip, put out his arms to encircle like a bear and charged. Jonas crouched, his arms cocked, and now he struck again—a left, a right, and then a hard jab left—as Skilla was brought up short, standing there stupidly as Jonas hammered at him. Finally the Hun staggered back out of range, confused. Then he stubbornly stumbled forward again. Jonas swung, there was a heavy thud, and Skilla went down.

The Roman stepped back, wary. Ilana had to remember to breathe. She realized that the Hun had no knowledge of boxing, the art that all Roman boys were taught.

Skilla rolled, got to his knees with his back to them, and staggered up, the fermented mare's milk and the drumbeat of punches making him unsteady. From his battered mouth he managed a feeble whistle. "Drilca!" The Hun pony loomed into sight again, nervously dancing.

Skilla fell against the saddle, seemingly spent, and then he whirled, drawing the sword sheathed there. He looked murderous. "I'm sick of your tricks, Roman."

Ilana found a pole from a meat-drying rack and wrenched it free, running back. Jonas had bent and was circling, fists cocked, eyeing the blade to elude it. "Ilana, don't make me waste this. Run, and get away."

"No," she whispered, crouching with the stave, afraid of the sword and yet determined. "If he kills you, he kills me, too."

But then came a new voice, as deep as thunder, and it boomed above all other sounds. "Stop, all of you!"

It was Edeco. Skilla jumped like a small boy caught stealing figs and straightened, his sword lowered. Light flared as torches came near, revealing the blood on the warrior's battered face. His uncle came up with

a crowd of the curious, and Ilana was suddenly aware of her half naked-
ness. She dropped the stave and pulled up her dress to cover her breasts.

"Damnation, Skilla. What are you doing back without reporting to
me?"

The Hun pointed. "He attacked me," he said truculently.

"He was attacking Ilana," Jonas responded.

"Is this true?" Edeco asked.

Emboldened, she let her bodice fall open. "He ripped my clothes."
Some of the Huns gaped, others laughed. Everyone jostled closer—men,
women, children, and dogs drawn by the tableau. She could smell their
acrid breath.

"You'd kill the Roman when he's unarmed?" Edeco asked with contempt.

Skilla spat blood. "He broke the law by attacking me, and he fights
unfairly, like a monkey. Any other slave would be dead by now. And
what is he doing out here in the dark? Why isn't he at his duties?"

"What were *you* doing, trying to rape a woman of your uncle's
household?" Jonas challenged.

"It wasn't rape! It was . . ."

Edeco strode forward and with a contemptuous kick knocked the
lowered sword aside. It rang as it skipped away into the grass. "We will
let Attila say what it was." The warlord sniffed in disgust. "I can smell
the *kumiss* on you, nephew. Couldn't you wait until you got to the
strava?"

"I *did* wait, I'd just gotten to camp, and *she* was waiting—"

"That's a lie," she hissed.

"Silence! We go to Attila!"

But the Hun was already there like a nightmare, pushing gruffly
through the crowd, the bones of Rusticius discarded but his demon
horns still mounted on his head. Like a judging god, he pushed to take
in the scene in an instant. There was a long silence while he looked from
one to the other.

Then Attila spoke. "Two men, one woman. *This* has never happened
before in the history of the world."

The crowd roared, and Skilla's face burned with humiliation. He looked at Jonas with hatred. "This woman is by rights *mine*, from capture at Axiopolis," he protested. "All know that. But she torments me with her haughtiness, and looks to this Roman for protection—"

"It looks to me as if she needed it, and that he protected her well."

The crowd roared with laughter again.

Now Skilla was silent, knowing anything he said would make him look even more foolish. His face was swelling.

"This is a quarrel sent by the gods to make our *strava* more interesting!" the king called to the crowd. "The solution is simple. She needs one man, not two. Tomorrow these two will meet in mortal combat, and the survivor can have the girl." Attila glanced at Edeco, and his warlord nodded once. Both knew what the outcome would be.

So did Ilana. Jonas was a dead man, and she was doomed.

XIV

THE DUEL

Diana shuddered slightly under my unaccustomed weight, and I felt encased and clumsy. *You'll never be the soldier your brother is,* my father had told me, and what had it mattered in Constantinople? I had prided myself on being a man of the mind, not arms, suited to higher callings. But now I wished I had taken cavalry training. Skilla could ride circles around me while I awkwardly charged in my heavy equipment, my big oval shield banging Diana's flank and my heavy spear already tiring my arm. The nose guard and cheek plates of my peaked helmet blocked my peripheral vision. The heavy chain mail was hot, even though the day was cool, and the sword and dagger on my belt felt clumsy against thigh and hip. The only blessing was that the equipment cut my view of the thousands of half-drunken and hungover Huns who'd assembled in a field near the camp to watch what they expected would be quick butchery. The betting was on how quickly I would die.

Skilla's horse Drilca was prancing, excited by the crowd; and the Hun looked as unencumbered as I was swaddled. His light cuirass of hoof bone scales rippled and clacked like the grotesque skeleton Attila had worn the night before, and his legs and head wore no armor at all. He was armed only with his bow, twenty arrows, and his sword. His face was bruised from my blows, which gave me some small satisfaction, but he was grinning past the evidence of his battering, already anticipating the death of his enemy and his marriage to the proud Roman girl. Killing me would erase all humiliation. Ilana stood in a cluster of other slaves by Suecca, wrapped in a cloak that made her shapeless. Her eyes were red and she avoided my gaze, looking guilty.

So much for confidence, I thought. Too bad I can't bet against myself.

I also caught sight of Zerco, sitting comically astride a tall woman's shoulders. His bearer was not unattractive, and looked both strong and kind, the steady companion many men need but seldom wish for or get. That must be his wife, Julia.

"You should not have interfered, Roman!" Skilla called. "Now you will be dead!"

I ignored the taunt.

"Look at him, armored like a snail," someone from the crowd observed.

"And as slow."

"And as hard to get at," a third cautioned.

There were other shouts: about my ancestry, my manhood, my clumsiness, and my stupidity. Strangely, I began to draw strength from them. I hadn't slept since fighting for Ilana, knowing the coming dawn could be my last. My mind had become a whirlwind of regrets and misgivings, and I spent these last hours cursing myself for bad luck. Every time I'd tried to think of the actual combat my brain seemed to shy away from any intelligent planning or useful tactics, skittering away into memories of my race with Skilla, my kiss with Ilana, or that embarrassing but intoxicating glimpse of her bare breasts. I hadn't rested, hadn't concentrated, and hadn't prepared. But now I realized that if I were not simply to be a target as simple as those melons I'd watched the Huns practice on, I must use my head or lose it. I watched dourly as Skilla loped along the line of cheering barbarians, waving his fist in the air and crying in a high yip-yip-yip like an irritating dog. The Hun would shoot me and my horse from a hundred paces, shaft after shaft plunking in until I resembled a field of spiky flowers. It was not so much a fight as an execution.

"Are you ready?" Edeco demanded.

Was I going to sit as target for slaughter? What advantage could I find? *Fight your battle, not theirs,* Zerco had said. Yet what was my battle? "Wait," I said, trying to think. At least, I decided, I could make myself a smaller target. I let the butt of my spear strike the earth and used it as a pole to lever myself off Diana's saddle, landing heavily.

"Look, he's backing out!" the Huns called. "The Roman is a coward! Skilla gets the woman!"

Hefting my shield and squaring my shoulders, I addressed Edeco. "I will fight on foot."

He looked surprised. "A man without a horse is a man without legs."

"Not in my country."

"But you're in ours."

I ignored that. Striding fast to hide my tremors, I made for the center of the makeshift arena, a circle two hundred paces across formed by the wall of thousands of barbarian bodies. There could be no escape.

"Yes, he's a coward!" the Huns called to one another. "Look at him stand still for execution!"

Skilla had pulled up short and was looking at me in bewilderment. Did I hope simply to spare my fat mare from arrows? Diana was in no danger. Skilla's intent, he had promised, was to slay me as quickly as possible and claim the mare for his own.

I stopped at what appeared to be the exact center of the field. *Skilla, you will have to come to me.* I looked back. Attila was seated on a hastily constructed platform, Ilana and the other women pressed against its base. The great iron sword of Mars, pitted and black, was across the tyrant's knees. A man in Greek dress was at his shoulder, whispering commentary. This, I assumed, was the Eudoxius whose return had initiated the *strava.* Why was he so important? The kagan pointed his arm straight up at the sky and then brought it down. Begin! A roar went up from the assembled crowd, where skins of drink were being passed freely.

I watched as Skilla on Drilca made another long loping circuit of the ring, cheers rising as he passed. He seemed to hesitate to attack, as if wondering what I intended to do. I simply followed him by turning in a slow circle, my mail shirt hanging to my knees, my oval shield covering all but my feet and head, my eyes hidden by the shadow of my helmet. My sword was sheathed and my spear remained planted on the ground. I stood like a sentry, not crouched like a warrior, but still well covered. Finally the Hun decided it was time to finish things. He reached and, in a practiced motion almost too quick and smooth to be followed, plucked an arrow from his quiver, drew, and shot. He could not miss.

Unlike a battle, however, where a sky full of bolts and arrows make evasion impossible, I had the advantage of being able to follow a single shaft. I jerked to my left and the arrow passed harmlessly over my right shoulder, flying on toward the crowd. The spectators there surged backward with a yell, some toppling each other, and the missile landed harmlessly at their fringe, plowing into the dirt. The rest of the audience laughed at them.

"One," I breathed.

Skilla, annoyed at my evasion, shot again from the ring's periphery, and again I had time to dodge and duck, the arrow making a sucking sound in the wind as it buzzed by my ear. I cursed myself for the imagination that allowed me to picture it striking home.

"Two." My own voice was firmer now to my ears. I spat and swallowed.

Now a new chorus of yells and catcalls came up from the crowd, which was beginning to back up in order to make a larger arena in respect for the wayward arrows. "The target is the Roman, not us!" Others wondered aloud if my punches had blinded him.

Angry at this mockery, Skilla kicked Drilca into a gallop, still making a broad orbit around me. This time his action was almost a blur. With a speed that seemed almost superhuman but which was practiced until it was second nature to the Huns, Skilla launched a succession of arrows too quickly for me to evade them singly, while riding the circuit at full tilt. They came at me in a fan. Now I crouched beneath my shield and then at the last moment fell into a ball. Three arrows flew over me entirely and three struck my shield at an oblique angle, plowing into it but not penetrating. No sooner had the volley stopped than I bounced up, reached around, and snapped in half the shafts that had stuck in my shield.

"Eight."

Skilla had settled his horse into a lope again, seemingly as baffled by this evasion as he had been by my boxing. He made for where one of his arrows was jutting from the ground and leaned to scoop it up, but a Hun ran forward, yanked it out, and broke it in two. "You only get one quiver!" he shouted.

Sensing the sport, the crowd pulled up and shattered the other spent arrows as well. "A quiver only! Strike home or be damned, Skilla!" Some of the sentiment was beginning to swing to me, I realized. "You couldn't hit your mother's ass!"

Zerco the dwarf had bounded down from his wife and was capering in front of the crowd, crowing excitedly. "The Roman is invisible!" he cackled. "The Hun is blind!"

Scowling, Skilla galloped by and almost ran the dwarf down. At the last moment Zerco scampered back into the safety of the crowd, hooting and turning a somersault as he tumbled to safety.

So the Hun fired again, singly this time, and then again in almost absentminded fashion, giving me time to dodge the arrows.

"Ten."

Yet even as I evaded the tenth shaft, Skilla abruptly changed tactics and kicked his pony straight at me. This time he drew and held, leaning toward me as Drilca neared, the hoofbeats kicking up a blur of clods, clearly intending to shoot from a distance of a pace or two and pinion me once and for all. There would be no time to dodge. Yet as he drew near I stopped pivoting around my planted spear and hefted it, and just before I judged he'd shoot I threw as hard as I could. The spear sailed. Now Skilla was forced to jerk the reins, his horse cutting away; and while the spear missed, so did his arrow, which this time went so high that it soared over the heads of the Huns. A great shout went up, both of excitement and derision, at this near miss by both opponents. Skilla wheeled his horse around, and I ran to retrieve my weapon.

The exchange was repeated, with no different result. Neither of us had yet drawn blood.

"Twelve," I counted, panting now. Sweat stung my eyes.

Edeco stepped out from the mass and grabbed Drilca's bridle as it trotted by. "Are you trying to cool him with the wind from your arrows?" he
demanded. "This is not a game, it's your reputation. Use your head, boy."

Skilla yanked away. "I will give you *his*, uncle."

Now he sped by again, but this time at a distance that was too far for
me to heave my spear. Again he loosed three arrows in quick succession
so that no matter which way I dodged, I could not escape. This time two
arrows thudded home on my shield with enough force to pierce it. One
broke through but was spent enough that it merely punched against my
mail shirt, not penetrating it. The armor saved my heart. The other
arrow struck, however, where my left arm held the shield straps, and
pierced my forearm. I was pegged to my protection. The shock was
enough to make me stop for what was almost a fatal moment, and another arrow flew singing toward my eye. I ducked just in time so that its
head clanged and skipped across my helmet, jarring me with a blow to
the head. I staggered.

"Sixteen." I winced, my ears ringing. A rivulet of blood dripped from
my shield.

The crowd noise fell briefly to a disconcerted murmur. Skilla had
clearly struck his target, but my Roman shield and armor was stronger
than they had expected. What witchery was this? As derisive as they
were of defeated opponents, any prowess or good equipment earned
their respect.

Still the pony cantered around, the crowd screaming encouragement
and abuse at both of us now. Skilla reached around and then hesitated.

He had only four arrows left. How to end this frustration?

With a howl he directed Drilca straight at me again in a thunderous
charge, and as I raised my spear he suddenly veered sharply to the left.
My throw sailed wide, and Skilla cut back to come at my undefended
side before I could turn, his bow drawn. This time I simply fell in panic,
and the arrow sizzled by my ear just before the Hun pony ran over me.
Hooves slammed down on my shield, cracking it, and one hoof struck
my side and kicked me along the ground in a spinning skid. It was as if
the world had been robbed of air. I felt disoriented and in agonizing pain,

a rib cracked. The horse danced, and then it was beyond me, neighing in confusion while Skilla hauled to turn its head around. The sound of the crowd was like a roaring ocean, buffeting both of us with rising emotion.

I had to fight back, but how?

Skilla rode toward me even as I crawled to get my spear. I grabbed it and then twisted around, using my shield like a rock to hide beneath in a desperate attempt to defend myself, as Skilla shot downward again from murderous range. The powerful bow sent the arrow through the shield like paper. Yet the pony was skittering away from my wavering spearhead, and so this shaft missed my chest and plowed through my shoulder instead, driving down with such force that it went completely through and stuck me to the ground. I was more helpless than ever. Skilla drew again, Drilca sidestepping closer. He couldn't miss. This would finish it. I glanced sideways along the ground. Ilana had emerged from the crowd at Attila's dais and had run a few steps into the field, her hand at her mouth.

I would not let him have her.

With an awkward heave I desperately lurched my spear upward and it stuck in the pony's belly. The horse screamed and bucked and Skilla's next to last arrow went at an awkward angle that merely stuck in my shield. Drilca trotted fearfully away, the lance dragging from his underside, blood and piss draining as it weaved. The pony's head shook.

The Huns were going wild, but who they were cheering for and who they were despising could no longer be discerned in the tumult. This had been a far better fight than they had hoped.

I felt as if a horse had fallen on me, so heavy did my shield suddenly feel, and my vision was blurring. It was the shock of wounds. I had to get up! Skilla was getting his horse back under control, and my spear had dropped away from Drilca's belly, kicked and broken in half by the anxious pony. I could hear the spatter of its blood.

I still was pinioned to the ground by that arrow, afraid to move because of the pain. But I had to! Summoning all my courage, I heaved and sat up with a shout that pulled the feathered shaft clear through my shoulder, leaving me dizzy with agony. Then I used my good right arm to lever the shield from my left, wincing as the other shaft through my forearm broke in two as the straps fell away. I kicked, and the shield skidded free, an empty, bloody platter. My mail had a sheen of bright blood now, my shoulder bubbling like a spring, and my head ached from where the one arrow had struck my helmet. Yet somehow I got to my knees and then my feet, staggering, and I marveled at what I could make my body do. "Nineteen." It was a wheezing gasp.

I watched as Skilla drew his final arrow.

Skilla kicked, but Drilca came on at barely a trot, wary now of this man who had wounded him so grievously. The pony's eyes were clouding. The Hun looked triumphant. Noise enclosed both of us like a box, a delirious buffeting; and yet I could see nothing but my opponent, weaving closer. I drew my sword. Skilla's grin grew contemptuous. He would never come close enough to give me a chance to use my weapon.

"Finish him!" Edeco's roar came floating through the cacophony.

I could see Drilca's breast, his high, lathered neck, and Skilla peering just beyond it down the shaft of his arrow. He was only ten paces away.

So I threw, hurling my sword with my right arm and grunting through the pain.

It whirled end over end, a steel pinwheel, and struck Drilca full in the chest, the horse buckling to its knees and tumbling forward. Skilla lurched and lost control of his arrow, which went low. Then Drilca was sprawling, his rider flying out of the saddle and over the horse's head, my sword embedded and lost under the kicking, screaming horse.

Skilla skidded on the grass and dirt, cursing.

I ran past him, a stumbling run, and picked up the half of my broken spear that bore the head.

Skilla still had his sword, but his instinct was for archery. His quiver was empty, but his last arrow jutted tantalizingly from the ground. He crawled for it, even as I staggered in pursuit, my spear poised to strike if I could reach him before he could retrieve the broken arrow and shoot. I was bleeding freely now, and my opponent was largely unhurt. All he had to do was wait for my collapse! Yet that wouldn't fit his pride. Skilla's hand closed over the arrow shaft and plucked it like a flower. He would have one last, clear shot at my chest. Lying on his back, he fitted arrow to bowstring. I braced myself to die.

But when he tried to pull the string, it flapped uselessly. Skilla gaped. The fall had broken his bow.

I charged. Before he could reach for his sword my Roman boot was on his chest and my spear point was at his throat. The Hun started to twist and the tip began to cut. He stopped, frozen, finally knowing fear. He looked up.

I suppose I looked like a great, metal monster, chest heaving, blood droplets from my two arrow wounds spraying us both, my face still mostly lost behind my helmet but my eyes bright and lusting for revenge. Impossibly, I had bested him. The Hun closed his eyes against the end. So be it. Better to die than bear humiliation.

Now the crowd had surged forward, dramatically shrinking the battlefield to a tiny ring, its sound and excitement clamoring, the smell of the pressed bodies rankling. "Kill him, kill him!" they screamed. "Now, Roman, he deserves to die!"

I looked at Edeco. Skilla's uncle had turned away in disgust. I looked at Attila. The Hun king grimly put his thumb down, in mocking copy of the Roman gesture he had heard of.

It would not be a combat kill anymore; it would be an execution. I didn't care. These Huns had crucified Rusticius, enslaved Ilana, slain her father, and trapped me. Skilla had taunted me from the day we'd met. I knew this was not what the priests of Constantinople expected. The final thrust would be a relic from the old world, not this new, saved, Christian one, supposedly so close to Apocalypse. But none of this mattered in my hatred. I squeezed the shaft of my broken spear in preparation.

And then something slight and frantic hit me, butting me aside before I could thrust. I staggered, outraged, and howled with pain. Who was this interloper?

She loomed in my vision. Ilana!

"No." She was weeping. "Don't kill him! Not for me!"

I saw Skilla's eyes blink open, amazed at this reprieve. His hand closed on the hilt of his sword, still undrawn. He rolled to one side to clear it.

And then all went black. I had fainted.

PART TWO

RALLYING THE WEST

XV

THE WINE JAR

I was in a dark, hot place, and some kind of gnome or incubus was leaning over me, perhaps to feast on my aching flesh or carry me to some place even deeper. The roar of the Hun crowd had subsided to a hushed ringing, and Ilana had betrayed me and then disappeared in a fog. I knew I had made some great, irretrievable mistake but couldn't remember what it was. Then the demon leaned closer . . .

"For the sake of your Savior, are you going to sleep forever? There are more important things afoot than you."

The voice was high, caustic, and familiar. Zerco.

I blinked, white light flooding in. So did pain, fresher and more acute than I had felt in my fever dream. The hum of the crowd was merely the noise my ear made while pressed in a cup of wool blanket, and the mistake I regretted was leaving Constantinople and becoming entangled with a woman. I struggled to sit up.

"Not yet." The dwarf pushed me down. "Wake, but lie still." Someone placed something hot on my shoulder.

"Ahhhggg!" It stung like a viper. And I had longed for adventure!

"It will help you heal," a female voice murmured. It was a voice I painfully recognized. "Why did you save Skilla!"

"To save us. And no man is going to die for me. That's silly."

"It wasn't for you—"

"Hush! Rest."

"What kind of a future do you think you'd have if you'd slain Edeco's nephew?" Zerco added. "Let the girl heal you so you can save Rome."

I waited for a wave of nausea and dizziness to pass and then tried to focus. The unbearable light faded as my eyes adjusted to fire and candle. It was actually quite dim in the room, I realized. I was in a cabin with the jester, the leather webbing of the bed creaking as I shifted on my straw mattress. From the smoke hole at the cabin's peak, I glimpsed a circle of gray sky. A cloudy day, perhaps dusk. Or dawn.

"What time is it?"

"The first hour, three days after you humiliated that young rooster," the dwarf said.

"Three days! I feel drained."

"As you are, of blood, piss, and spit. Julia, is it ready?" There was a third person in the room, the woman I had seen holding the dwarf on her shoulders. "Here, drink this."

The cup was bitter.

"Don't turn your head away—drink it! My God, what an unruly patient you are! Finish that, and then you can have some wine and water. That will taste sweeter, but this will make you well."

Obediently, but grimacing, I drank. Three days! I remembered nothing except my own collapse. "So I am alive."

"As is Skilla, thanks to Ilana here. He hates you more than ever, of course, especially since this beauty has been given leave to nurse you. He's hoping she can heal you only so he can try killing you again. No man has ever prayed harder for the recovery of another! I warned him that you'll simply outthink him again. Now he is puzzling how you did it the first time."

Even smiling hurt. I turned to Ilana. "But you feel something for him." It was an accusation. I'd fought for her, and she hadn't let me finish it.

She was embarrassed. "I led him on about marriage, Jonas. I led both of you on, because women are so helpless here. I'm not proud of it.

The duel made me sick. Now I'm out of Suecca's house and soon will be out of this one, and leave you all alone."

"What do you mean?"

"That's the other reason Skilla hates you," Zerco said cheerfully. "When it was apparent neither of you two bucks was going to die, Attila considered like Solomon—and awarded the girl to himself."

"Himself!"

"As slave, not concubine. He actually said you'd both fought bravely. He declared that Skilla was the true Hun but pointed out that he was now in the debt of a Roman. So both of you will now be given a chance to fight for Attila, and whoever distinguishes himself the most will eventually get the woman." The dwarf grinned. "You have to admire his ability to motivate."

"Fight? I want to fight *against* Attila. He crucified my friend Rusticius for no reason. He humiliated my mentor, Maximinus. He—"

"Ah, I see Skilla has shot some sense into you. That's why you need to recover. While you fuss about this pretty morsel, great things are astir in the world, Jonas of Constantinople. Attila has not been asleep, and the world is in peril. Are you planning to nap through all of history or help your Empire?"

"What are you talking about?" My vision was getting blurry again. Whatever Julia had given me was obviously a sleeping potion. Why had they awoken me only to put me back under?

"We're saying that you must sleep to recover, not listen to this little fool called my husband," Julia soothed. "That drink had the medicine of the meadow. Sleep, while your body struggles to heal. You have years ahead to save the world."

"No, he doesn't," Zerco said.

But by that time I was asleep again.

I do not recommend being holed by two arrows. Great heroes bear wounds bravely and without complaint, childhood stories tell. But my arm and shoulder complained loudly and long of having been punched through by two shafts of wood, and every twinge reminded me of my own mortality. My courage would never be so naïve again. Yet I was of that age when confinement in bed seems a torment and recovery comes quickly. By nightfall I was sitting up, even if the hours dragged from pain, and by the following morning I was walking unsteadily around the hut. Within a week I was restless and well on my way to healing, aching but not incapacitated. "By the first snow you'll be chopping my firewood," the dwarf promised.

Ilana and I had spoken at length only once. It was dark, the other two asleep, and fever had brought me awake. She mopped my brow and shoulder, sighing. "I wish the arrows had gone into me."

"Don't blame yourself for a duel ordered by Attila."

"I felt like a murderess and utterly helpless. I thought the death of my betrothed and my father had hardened me, but I couldn't stand to see you two pitted against each other with me as the prize. I don't want to marry Skilla, but do you think I feel nothing toward him after the attention he's given me? I wanted to use you to rescue me, but do you think I don't notice how you looked at me, touched me? I hate fighting. And now . . ."

"It's still a contest."

She shook her head. "I'll not have either of you killing Attila's enemies for him in return for my bed. I won't marry Skilla, but I won't burden you. Pretend you'll fight, and then slip away. Don't worry about me or the Empire. We've damaged you enough."

"Do you really think me such a fool that I was just led around by you? I wouldn't have tried escape if you hadn't encouraged me, Ilana. It's you who was trying to save me."

She smiled sadly. "How naïve your goodness is! You need to heal your mind as well as your body. And that's best done alone." She kissed my forehead.

"But I need . . ." I drifted off again. When I awoke, she was gone.

"Where's Ilana?" I asked Zerco.

He shrugged. "Maybe she's tired of you. Maybe she loves you. Maybe she told Attila you'll live and he decided she'd done enough. And maybe, just maybe, I had more important things for her to do." He winked conspiratorially.

"Tell me what's going on, Zerco."

"The end of the world, the seers believe. The Apocalypse, Christians fear. Messengers are riding out. Spears are being sharpened. Do you know of the Greek Eudoxius?"

"I saw him at my match with Skilla."

"He came with tidings for Attila. Then another party, quieter and even stranger, arrived in camp. I've asked Ilana to keep her ears open. When I entertain in Attila's great hall, she feeds me what information she can, with a whisper here or a written scrap of message there. Thank God we are literate and most Huns are not!"

"What has she learned?"

"Ah, curiosity. Isn't that a sign he is healing, Julia?"

"Curiosity about politics or about the woman?" his wife replied slyly.

"Curiosity about everything!" I shouted. "My God, I've been prisoner long enough of your pots and potions! I need to know what's going on!"

They laughed, and Zerco peeked out the hut's wicker door to make sure no one was listening. "It appears a eunuch has again entered our lives."

"Chrysaphius?" I dreaded hearing that minister's name again.

"No, this one from the West, and considerably gentler by all description. His name is Hyacinth, like the flower."

"From the West?"

"Have you heard of the princess Honoria?"

"From gossip, on the journey. The sister of Valentinian, shamed when she was caught in bed with her steward. Her brother was expected to marry her off."

"What you may not have heard is that she's chosen confinement over marriage, which indicates she's perhaps more sensible than her reputation." He grinned, and Julia poked him. "Actually, this Hyacinth is her slave and messenger, and it seems she may be ever more foolish than reported. Nothing is secret in a royal household, and Ilana has heard he came in the dead of night with a secret message to Attila from the princess. Hyacinth bore her signet ring, and what the eunuch had to say has changed the Hun's entire thinking. Up to now Attila has focused on the riches of the East. Now he is considering marching on the West."

This did not strike me as entirely bad news. Attila had been preying on my half of the Empire for a decade. It would be a relief to have his attention turned elsewhere. "That, at least, is not my concern. My position is from the Eastern court."

"Really? Do you think either half of the Empire will stand if its brother collapses?"

"Collapses? The Huns are raiders—"

"*This* Hun is a conqueror. As long as the West stands fast, Attila dares not risk all his strength against Constantinople. As long as the East gives craven tribute, he satisfies his people by making threats and distributing gold. But now everything is changing, young ambassador. What little standing you might have retained as a member of a failed imperial embassy disappeared two weeks ago when news came that the Eastern emperor, Theodosius, died in a riding accident. General Marcian has succeeded to the throne."

"Marcian! He's a fierce one."

"And you are even more forgotten than you were. Chrysaphius, the minister who sent you and secretly plotted to kill Attila, has finally been ejected from his post at the urging of Theodosius's sister Pulcheria. Rumor says he'll shortly face execution and that Bigilas may find himself rowing a galley. You're simply a diplomatic embarrassment, best forgotten by all sides. Moreover, Marcian has sent word that the days of paying tribute to the Huns are over, that not a single solidus will ever be sent north again. A treaty had been completed with Persia and troops are being shifted from the eastern marches to Constantinople. Attila's demands have gone too far."

"So there's to be war?" I brightened at this chance for rescue, then paled as I realized that Attila had threatened to execute me for far less imperial determination.

"Yes, but with who?" Zerco asked rhetorically, ignoring my expression. "Word of Marcian's defiance had reportedly sent Attila into a rage. His little pig eyes began to bug out as if he were being strangled. His hands balled into fists. He cursed Marcian in seven languages and howled like a crazy man; and he became so frenzied that he flopped on the ground like a landed fish until blood spurted from his nose. It came out in a froth, wetting his beard and flecked his lips and teeth with red. Ilana saw it! None of his henchmen dared go near him during this fit of rage. He vowed to teach the East a lesson, of course, but how? By subduing and uniting the nations of the West, he shouted, and bringing them all, Hun and slave armies, against the walls of Constantinople! Attila said his people had endless enemies and would know no peace until they had conquered the entire world."

"He would do so because of the accession of Marcian?"

"No, because this twit of a Roman princess has asked him to. If this eunuch and her signet ring can be believed, the woman Honoria, sister to the Western emperor Valentinian, has asked Attila to be her protector. He has chosen to interpret this as a proposal of marriage, which he believes would entitle him to half of the West as dowry. Failure to accede to this demand, he is claiming, means war."

"Surely he doesn't expect Valentinian to agree to such an absurdity. People say Honoria is a silly trollop."

"Silly or scheming? Sometimes the two are the same thing. And, yes, Valentinian will *not* agree, unless another threat is so pressing that perhaps he would be forced to come to accommodation with Attila. And now this Eudoxius has brought just that threat, it seems. This wily traitor has become pivotal."

"A fugitive Greek doctor?"

"A self-important troublemaker. He has visited the Vandal king Gaiseric in North Africa and extracted his promise to attack the Western Empire from the south if Attila will attack it from the north. If the Huns and Vandals act in concert, it is the end of Rome."

"Surely Attila is not foolish enough to march west with Marcian showing new defiance in the east . . ."

"Wait, there's more. Have you seen the Frankish prince Cloda?"

"From afar, as one more barbarian envoy. I've been a slave to Hereka, remember?"

"Not just an envoy. The Franks had a disputed succession, and Cloda's brother Anthus seized the throne. Cloda is asking Attila to help him get it back."

I sat, my mind whirling from all these simultaneous happenings. Maximinus had counseled that simply waiting sometimes solved problems between nations, but this time waiting seemed to have compounded them. "The prophecy," I murmured.

"The what?"

"Maximinus told me that twelve vultures Romulus saw in his dream meant Rome would fall after twelve centuries. That would put the end at less than three years away. Not to mention that the priests think that the Huns are a manifestation of biblical prophecy. Gog and Magog and the armies of Satan, or some such thing."

"You understand more than I give you credit for, young man!" the dwarf exclaimed with delight. "Indeed, all signs point to such an end! But now it is the West that must fear, not the East. Edeco himself told me once he was impressed by the triple walls of Constantinople and wondered if the Huns could ever get inside them. Attila might wonder if the Western kingdoms are not easier targets of his wrath. Will the German tribes that have settled there ever unite under the Romans to resist him? It hasn't happened yet. And now Attila has the sword of Mars, which he's claiming is proof that he means to conquer."

"He's never been beaten. There seems little hope."

"Unless Aetius can be warned and Attila's momentum can be slowed, my young Roman friend—until the West can rally together against him."

"But who can do that?"

Zerco gave me the smile of a Syrian rug merchant. "You can. Ilana has a plan."

I could now count two truly foolish things I had done in my short life. The first was naïvely agreeing to serve as scribe and translator to the court of Attila. The second was agreeing to Ilana and Zerco's desperate plan to not just escape by creating a diversion but to take history into our own hands.

Only the prospect of reunion with Ilana convinced me to try. Our dilemma was plain. I had no intention of trying to out-soldier Skilla in Attila's army to win her back or give Skilla a chance to duel with me

again. But the diversion of the *strava* had passed, and no similar opportunity for escape seemed likely . . . unless we made our own. Yet whatever Ilana's guilt or confusion, I was determined not to leave her in
Attila's compound. So Ilana had come up with a magnificently reckless
scheme so lunatic that of course Zerco immediately hailed it a work of
genius. All it needed to succeed, he said, was me. I had little confidence
it would work, but my virtual enslavement and wounds had made me
anxious to strike back before Attila remembered his promise to torture
me to death. I ached to escape from the limbo of my captivity and longed
for Ilana with a desire that was almost overwhelming. Not her body,
though that passed through my mind, too, but her Romanness, her connection to normality and home. What is love? Insanity, I suppose, the
willingness to risk everything for what threatens to be a colossal mental
illusion. Why had she affected me so? I don't know. Our moments were
stolen, our confidences brief, our knowledge of each other meager. Yet
she haunted me in a way that made my feelings for distant Olivia seem
childish and made me prefer to risk all. It made me, finally, ready to kill.

It was Ilana who suggested I be smuggled into Attila's kitchen, but
Julia who came up with how. I was to be carried in the kind of clay amphora that held looted wine. "It's no different from Cleopatra's being carried to Caesar while rolled in a carpet," she reasoned.

"Except that the Egyptian monarch stayed drier and was no doubt
lighter to carry," her dwarf husband joked.

I admitted the idea had a certain simple charm; and while I didn't
know Julia well, I'd become impressed by her calm practicality. She was
that blessed person who made the best of what was, rather than dream-
ing about what should be, and thus was happier with her odd companion than a hundred kings with a thousand wives.

Marriage to the dwarf had been a way out of slavery, though being a
fool's bride wasn't exactly the path to respectability. From the pair's mu-
tual desperation had come an odd and touching form of love, similar to
my own situation with Ilana. Zerco would have adored the allegiance of
even the plainest woman, but Julia was not just attractive, she was en-
gagingly good-humored, smart, able, and loyal, demonstrating faith in
her diminutive husband that most men would envy. She had turned

Bleda's mocking joke of a marriage into partnership. Julia appreciated not just the dwarf's intelligence and determination to survive but that he had voluntarily returned to humiliating bondage with the Huns in order to be with her. Clearly the halfling loved her, and that had been the first step toward her love for him. What kind of sexual arrangement they had, I couldn't guess, but I'd seen them kiss, and Zerco curled in her arms in the evening like a contented pet.

It's odd who we envy.

So Julia had gone to the rubbish pit that smoldered at the foot of the crucifixion hill and found a clay amphora that had been discarded after breaking in two. This wine jar, which swelled from its narrow base like the hips of a woman and then narrowed at the top to a graceful neck, had two handles at its lip and was two thirds the height of a man. Zerco's wife carried it in two trips, past barking dogs on a moonless night, and brought it into our cabin. The clay stank of grape. Now I curled myself to be sealed inside like a chick in an egg. "Your wounds will hurt," she said, "but the pain will keep you awake."

"How am I supposed to get back out?"

"We will give you a Roman short sword and you can chop your way."

"But what if they open the jar before I've had a chance to escape?"

"I'm going to seal the throat of the jar with layers of wax and straw with a little wine between," she said. "We'll drill a small hole in the bottom so you can breathe, and wedge you in with straw."

Zerco was scampering around the cabin in delight. "Isn't she clever?"

I looked at the two pieces. "But the jar is broken, Julia."

"And it will be mended with pitch and the join concealed with clay dust. They carry in provisions at night so as not to disturb the daytime crowd that assembles to hear Attila's judgments. It will be dark. We'll roll you to the wine house, you'll be lifted onto a wagon, and before you know it you'll be stacked in the kagan's kitchens."

Zerco was cackling. "Julia, my muse, who knows every ruse!"

So I let myself be swaddled in the amphora's foul embrace, the jar glued with pitch and coated with yard dust. At Julia's instruction, I reinforced the joint on the inside with a rope sticky with pitch. It was like being buried or sent back to the womb. I was drawn up like a fetus, my gladius clutched like an umbilical cord, and the sensation of being rolled was so disorienting that it was all I could do to keep from vomiting. Soon I was too hot and struggling for breath. Then we came to rest for some time, and from the shortage of air I actually faded, not jolted awake again until the amphora was lifted into a Hun wagon. There was the dull report of a whip and the vehicle shifted into motion.

In little more than half an hour, I was unloaded inside Attila's compound. There were guttural voices for a while, and then silence. It must be the very darkest time of the night, when most are asleep. Following Julia's suggestion, I used the tip of the sword to pry at the stoppers. A shower of wine came down on my head, making me stink even more, but it was followed by blessed air that gave me strength. I saw no light coming through and heard no voices. The kitchen must be empty. So now I sawed at the sticky rope, cutting it to weaken the jar. Finally, summoning my courage, I struck the join and pushed pieces of the amphora aside like shards of egg, letting myself hatch. Then I crawled over the other containers like a sodden chick. How my wounds and muscles ached!

I dropped to the dirt floor of the storeroom and listened. Nothing. Attila's guards manned his stockade, not his pantry.

It was time to find Ilana and try her insane plan to save Rome and let us escape.

Slave barracks lined two sides of the courtyard of Attila's compound. The female barracks, Zerco had reminded me, were on the eastern side so that its windows and porch faced west, giving as many late-day hours as possible for the captives to weave, make baskets, card wool, embroider, sew, and polish at which the Hun females seemed to excel. Those picked for the kagan tended to be young and beautiful, of course, on display and in turn observing, and gossiping about, visitors to Attila's court. Their king kept them for work and decoration, not sex; he slept only with those he married to avoid the political complications of bastard heirs. His multiple marriages—of which that to Hereka ranked first—were usually about alliance, not love. The captives were also an investment. A year or two in Attila's service inflated their value and he would sell them to Hun nobles while their beauty was still at its peak. He used the money to help pay for his armies.

Ilana had told Zerco of a passageway between kitchen and barracks, entered through a hidden pantry door. It enabled the slave women of his household to be served and reach the privy without traversing the more public areas: a scrap of privacy that prevented them from encountering men who could provoke trouble. This would be my own entry. I slipped past the pantry's ranks of hanging game and clay jars of preserves and found the low door in back. It seemed Zerco sized, but once through it the windowless passage became high enough that I could shuffle ahead in the dark without bumping my head. At a second door I cut the bolt's leather thong, lifted the latch, and slid into the room.

The slave chamber was dappled with moonlight, faintly illuminating the forms of two dozen females asleep on floor mats. Their bodies reminded me of the undulating green hills of Galatia, sinuous and rounded; and the place smelled of the sweet musk of assembled women, their let-down hair fanning across woolen pillows and glinting like alluvial plains under a glimmer of starlight. Here a breast peeked from a cocked arm, there a hip made a perfect Byzantine arch.

"Heaven on Earth," I breathed.

I began moving down the double row of sleeping forms, marveling. It was like the assembly of damsels in the village by the lake: here a Hibernian blond, there a Caucasian redhead, and across from them a Nubian black. All exquisite, all captive. It seemed easiest to slip past them all for a quick inspection—the time it took couldn't hurt—and then, my curiosity more fully satisfied, I'd turn back to look more carefully for Ilana.

A toe kicked my ankle.

I bent. Her head came up, hair tousled and her eyes still sleepy: She had nodded off while waiting. The moon painted innocence on her that I hadn't observed before and I realized how much the Ilana I knew was a woman anxious and driven, desperate for alliance. Here for a moment was a younger, softer woman who'd emerged from a dream. I found myself kneeling and caressing her cheek and shoulder before I fully knew what I was doing, aroused by all this female beauty.

"Not here," she whispered, trembling as my fingers slipped down. Light fingers gripped mine. "Jonas, stop."

She was right. I pulled, and we both stood. None of the other girls had moved. My eye wandered over their forms, wondering their eventual fate. Would they suffer for what was about to happen? No, I told myself, the Huns had their own sense of harsh fairness and would know the slave girls were blameless. But, then. Rusticius had been blameless as well . . . Ilana nudged me. Her look had become impatient.

We padded quickly toward the door and then froze as a tawny-headed Scythian groaned and turned, her limbs twitching for a moment like a sleeping dog's. She stilled.

I could hear the release of Ilana's breath.

Then we were through the door and I took a last, wistful glimpse. As we hurried for the kitchen I wondered: Had a head come up?

XVI

ESCAPE

"What took you so long?" Ilana demanded when we paused at the door of the kitchen. "I feared they had found you. I worried all night!"

"Until you fell asleep."

"It's almost dawn!"

"I was delivered on their schedule, not mine, and waited for the kitchen to quiet." I studied her. "We don't have to risk this."

She shook her head. "Yes, we do. Not just for us but for Rome."

Her determination made me braver. "Then find some jars of cooking oil and let's do what you and the dwarf have planned. By first light, we'll either be gone or dead."

The battle with Skilla had hardened me, she could see, just as the sack of Axiopolis had hardened her. Pain had cut some lines onto our young lives, and the hopelessness of rescue had provided desperation. I saw the gleam in my own eyes reflected in hers, and realized we had become wolves. We had, in a way, become Huns. "Yes," she said. "It ends tonight, one way or another."

"Hold still. I'm going to cut your dress."

She caught my wrist. "I don't need help for the distraction you've planned."

"But I would enjoy helping."

She snorted, turned from me, used my short sword herself, then gave it back.

It had to be as simple as it was brutal. I crept along the stockade wall until I neared the rear of Attila's great hall, keeping a wary eye out for sentries on the walls. The silhouettes on the stockade towers, all facing outward, looked somnolent. At the rear door to the hall there was only a single guard, slumped and bored. I signaled my companion by briefly revealing the gleam of the short sword.

Ilana ran wordlessly across the dark courtyard, jars of oil cradled. The guard straightened, puzzled by this approaching female form. She stumbled when she reached the sentry, a sealed jar rolling like an errant ball and drawing his eye. She grasped his knees. "Please!"

He looked down in confusion. "Who are you? Get up."

She leaned back to reveal the provocative tear she had made. "He's trying to have his way with me but I'm pledged to Attila. . . ."

The man stared just a moment too long. I came up behind and thrust. The point of my sword emerged from his stomach as my other hand drew a dagger across his throat. Blood geysered, wetting us all. The man, his cry cut off by the knife, collapsed in the dirt.

"It went through so easily," I said, a little shaken.

"It will go just as easily into Attila. Take his helmet and cloak."

The hall was high, dark, and empty. The table and benches had been pushed to one side and the dais where Attila's curtained bed rested was shadowy, lit only by a single oil lamp. There the chieftain slept with whichever wife he'd picked for the evening, and we could hear the faint drone of his drunken snoring. On the wall, mounted as it had been when I'd first seen it, was the great black iron sword of Mars. It looked huge and ungainly, its haft long rotted away so that only a spike of iron remained. The wavering lamplight played over it. Would stealing it really deter the superstitious Huns?

"Spread the oil and I'll take the sword," I whispered.

She shook her head. "I step lighter."

Dancing across the boards, she hopped up on the dais and made for the weapon. I began pouring oil on the planks of the great hall, the sheen catching the feeble light. Oil splashed on my hands, making the clay slippery; and despite the coolness, I was sweating. How long before another sentry found the dead guard? I finished with one jar, took up the other. If we failed, I did not want to imagine the long death we would endure. . . .

Suddenly there was a thud and I jerked. The unexpected heaviness of the iron sword had twisted it out of Ilana's grasp and its tip had struck the floor. My own grip slipped and the second jar fell and broke, sending oil streaming across the planks.

We froze, waiting. The snoring had stopped a moment, becoming a grumble instead. Yet the curtain of Attila's bed didn't part.

All I could hear was the roar of blood in my ears. Then the snoring resumed.

I remembered to breathe.

Ilana caught the dull blade in her other palm, lifted it, and, bearing the sword, began to carefully make her way to me. Then she would fetch the lamp to ignite the fire. . . .

"The Romans are killing Attila!"

The shout made us jump. It was a woman's voice, coming from the courtyard outside. "Help! The Romans have murdered a Hun!"

Now the bed curtains swung open.

"It's Guernna," Ilana spat.

I leaped our moat of oil to take the sword. "Get the lamp!" I hefted the weapon. No wonder she had dropped it! The relic seemed two or three times the weight of an ordinary blade, as if a god had indeed wielded it. Where had the Huns found it? Who had made it? Then my feet strayed into the pool of oil and I slipped, sprawling, and cursing myself as I did so. At the same moment, the dark form of Attila burst from his bed and he seized Ilana by her hair just as she was lifting the oil lamp.

How could it all go so wrong?

She looked at me desperately as I scrambled to get up, hoping to use the old sword to skewer the barbarian king before I, in turn, was skewered. Then, as Attila bent Ilana's head painfully back and reached for her lamp, she threw.

It struck the oil and a wall of flame roared up, separating me from her.

"Ilana!"

"For the sake of the Empire, run!"

The struggling pair were obscured. I tried to find a way through or around the fire, but my oily leggings ignited. I dropped to press my leg against the floor to smother the flames, wincing at the burn. The fire was growing bigger, and I was coughing from the smoke. "Ilana!"

There was no answer, just fire. The rear door was cut off, but I could see the figure of Guernna, staring at me in the rippling heat. Damn her! Snarling, I charged and leaped, flying through the flames, my clothes smoking.

The German girl yelped and disappeared.

I turned to the dais and Attila's bed, ready to cleave him in two. It was empty. I whirled. I couldn't see the kagan and Ilana anywhere. I began to cough.

Now the wood of the walls was igniting. The heat was a roiling wave, pulsing at me.

"Ilana!"

No answer. Attila's bed ignited, and from its light I saw a hole in the floor leading down into a passageway. Even as I spied it, its entrance burst into flame.

With a whoosh, the rafters overhead ignited. I had to retreat.

I plunged through the flames again to get to the main entrance, ignited, dropped, and rolled. Flames sputtered out even as more pain seared me. Then I staggered toward the front door of the hall, dizzy and coughing. There were shouts and the sound of horns outside the barred main entry. I was still dragging the heavy sword and still wore the Hun helmet. What should I do? The whole point of my escape had vanished in the smoke. I'd lost what I'd really come for: not a sword but a woman. Yet Ilana had sacrificed herself to give me time. *Save the Empire*, she had told me. So had Zerco.

Heartsick at what I must do, I unbarred the door. "The Romans are attacking Attila!" I shouted in Hunnish. Soldiers pushed past me. "Get water to save the kagan!" In the smoke and confusion, no one looked past my helmet and cloak. "He told me to protect the sword!"

With smoke pouring into the darkness and a hundred voices shouting at once, they let me stagger past. Out in the courtyard, all was chaos. Huns were galloping in through the gate to lend help even as the slave women were streaming from the barracks to seek refuge outside the stockade walls. I joined their current, clutching the weapon to my chest. It bumped as I ran. Then I grabbed the reins of a horse that a rider had momentarily abandoned and swung on, looping his lariat around the guard of the sword to hang it from my back. I looked around. Attila's palace was in flames. Ilana was nowhere to be seen. Neither was the kagan.

There was no going back.

So I galloped hard for the Tisza, my heart a stone, my throat burning from smoke, my mind in shock. How I had failed! First I'd lost Rusticius and now Ilana. The fire was mercy if it killed her quickly, I told myself. What Attila would do to her if they had survived by disappearing down that hole, I didn't want to guess.

The entire Hun camp was in chaos. Many, seeing the fire, assumed they were under attack. Half-naked warriors burst from their dwellings with drawn swords or half-strung bows, looking for enemies. Mothers shooed children like tides of mice. Horsemen galloped wildly, passing each other in the confusion. I, looking simply like one more crazed and furious Hun, was able to sprint for the river without being challenged. My mount and I crashed into the Tisza, the spray like milk under the moonlight, and we let the current carry us downstream away from the lurid light of the fire. My horse gained its footing, we splashed onto land, and then galloped across dew-wet grass to the rim of dark trees where the dwarf was supposed to be waiting.

I was nearly in the cover when my stolen pony reared away from some figure lunging with a spear. Before I could react the weapon rammed home in the horse's breast and my mount went over, crashing to earth and pinning one of my legs. Caught! The great iron sword dragged me down. My attacker loomed over the dying horse and another, a scuttling child, was coming with a long knife. Perhaps, given our failure, it was just as well. I tensed for a thrust and then realized who was attacking.

"Zerco! It's me!" I cried in Latin. "Julia!"

The dwarf stopped and his wife paused. She had yanked the bloody spear out of my dying horse and had lifted it to plunge it into my torso, but now she looked down in surprise. "Dressed like a Hun? And where's Ilana? This was not the plan."

I let my head slump back, my voice thick. "I couldn't save her. Attila grabbed her after we started the fire." Tears came, welling on my face.

"Is he dead?"

"I don't know. I don't think so."

Zerco was fumbling at me. "But you've got the sword."

I shoved the dwarf away. "To hell with the damned sword!"

The dwarf came back, cutting the lariat from around my neck and dragging the weapon free. "This is what is important, Jonas Alabanda. This, and what I've stolen as well. I am sorry about your woman, but this will save many women. Many, many women."

"What have you stolen?"

"You aren't the only man who has been busy tonight. I paid a visit to the Greek doctor who would betray the Empire." He grinned fiercely. "He decided to accompany us, trussed like a pig."

"We're taking Eudoxius when we failed to kill Attila?" This was madness atop madness. "Our diversion failed!"

"If Gaiseric is allying with Attila, my master Aetius needs to know about it. He'll be best convinced by the traitor himself. Besides, the doctor's absence might confuse the Huns even more. Perhaps they'll think him a double traitor, secretly in league with Rome. It might slow their plans, if your fire hasn't already done that."

I shook my head in frustration. Nothing was happening as I expected. Stripped of the encumbering weapon, I managed to kick myself free of the horse and dragged myself away. I felt raw: shot, burned, bruised by the fall, exhausted from being awake most of the night in that stifling jar, and devastated by the loss of Ilana. Half a mile away, I could see people running, backlit by the flames of the kagan's palace. "And is what we've stolen worth Ilana's life?"

"A million women's lives, I hope." The dwarf rested the sword on his shoulder like a pole. It was nearly twice as long as Zerco was high. "This sword will be seen as a sign from God. It will help rally the West. I understand your sorrow, but we still have a chance. The Huns are in disarray, and Ilana didn't know which way we'd flee. And if she some-how still lives, this sword may be her only hope."

Suddenly I saw it. "We can trade *it* for *her!*"

Zerco shook his head. "That's not what I meant. Don't torture yourself with temptation. This sword goes to Aetius."

"To hell with Aetius! This piece of iron is all Attila cares about! The Huns will give anything to get it back!"

"How long do you think any of us, including Ilana, will live once you stop to parley with the barbarians? Have you learned nothing in all your months here?"

He was right, but I was stubborn. "They have their own honor."

"Which must now be avenged for the murder, or attempted mur-der, of Attila. And you want to walk back into their camp with his stolen sword?"

I opened my mouth to argue and then closed it. The dwarf was right. Escape was insult enough, but we'd risked everything by violating the chamber of Attila. This would not be forgiven. Ilana had coura-geously gambled and lost. Just as I'd lost her.

"If she lives your only hope is to defeat Attila," the dwarf went on, "and the best way to do that is to take this sword to Aetius. Come, the horses are waiting." He began dragging the sword toward the trees.

I felt I couldn't move. "I failed her, Zerco," I said miserably.

My tone made the dwarf stop. Finally he came back and pressed the old weapon into my hands. "Then make up your failure, Jonas. The last thing Ilana would want is for you to be found at dawn standing foolishly in a meadow, her sacrifice in vain."

The sky was beginning to blush. So we mounted the horses and rode hard, desperate to be well out of sight by full daylight.

Eudoxius, bound to a saddle, was gagged, his eyes glaring furiously. I'd expected that Zerco might have stolen my own mare, Diana, but the dwarf said that would have aroused too much suspicion: both when he took the horse and when she was found missing. Diana's presence, in contrast, might confuse the Huns enough to think that I died in the fire. So the dwarf had instead stolen Arabians. Julia and Zerco shared the same mount, Eudoxius was on the next, and I on a third. The fourth we let go again, for Ilana was not there to ride it.

XVII

PURSUIT

It was startling how the witch Ansila has been right, Skilla thought. Fortune had given him a second chance after all.

After his combat with Jonas, the Hun had been so humiliated that he wanted to drown himself in the Tisza. It was terrible enough that the Roman had bested him. But he'd been saved by a woman! The reprieve had meant other warriors treated him like a ghost already dead but somehow still annoyingly among the living, a reminder of rare defeat. Skilla burned for revenge and the recapture of his honor, but Attila wouldn't allow a combat rematch. And mere murder would not erase his shame. A stab in the back was the mark of a coward. So until war came, there was no opportunity to prove himself, and war was an agonizing six months or more away. Every waking moment became a torment, and every dream a nightmare, as Jonas recovered with Ilana as his nurse. So finally Skilla went to the Hun witch Ansila and begged her to tell him what he should do. How could he regain his old life and eliminate the cursed Roman?

Ansila was an ageless crone who lived like a burrowing animal in a clay cave, paved with straw and beamed with tree roots in the riverbank. She remembered much of the past and saw far into the future, and every warrior both feared her and bribed her, for visions. A gold-studded bridle and bit, looted by Skilla during the raid on Axiopolis, was the fee he paid for her prophecy. He went to her at midnight, squatted morosely as she built up her fire to heat sacred water, and then watched impatiently as she scattered herbs on its surface and looked into the steam.

For a long time nothing seemed to happen, the prophetess standing motionless over her iron pot, her lined face and gray hair wreathed in the vapors. Then her pupils dilated and her hands began to tremble. She recited her message in a singsong rhyme, not looking at him but at things impossibly far away:

> You will not have to wait long,
> For your frustration to be gone,
> Young warrior.

> The one you hate is tempting fate.
> He will light a fire that will bring desire,
> And steal what will ultimately heal.

> On a darkling field you will have met,
> When the greatest fire is not yet set.

She staggered back from the steam, breathing deeply, her eyes shut. Skilla waited for explanation, but there was none. The closeness of the cave made him giddy.

"Steal what, Grandmother? What fire? I don't understand."

Finally she peered at him, as if remembering he was there, and gave a crone's grin of missing teeth. "If you understood life, little fool, you could not bear to live it. No man could. Be thankful you're as ignorant as a goat in its field, for you're happier because of it. Go now, be patient, and prepare for everything to change." She turned from him in dismissal, grasped the bridle, and tottered across the cave to secrete it in a chest. Later, she would trade it for food and clothing.

For a week Skilla had stewed in frustration, confused by the prophecy and waiting for some obvious sign. Had Ansila been wrong? Had he wasted the bridle? Then Jonas set fire to the kagan's house, trying to kill Attila, and Ilana had been caught. In a single night of flame and confusion, everything *had* changed.

No bodies had been found in the ruins of the great house. Attila himself had escaped with Ilana and his third wife, Berel, who had been sharing his bed that night. The king had pushed the two women beneath his bed through a hole that led to a tunnel specifically constructed to keep him from being cornered. It had been too dark and smoky for the king to be certain just who had attacked, but Guernna said it had been the young Roman.

Ilana, battered from Attila's beating of her in his early rage, claimed Jonas was kidnapping her. "I was trying to save the sacred sword when you awoke," she said in the gray ash of morning, her high chin failing to control the quaver in her voice. "He was trying to steal it and me."

None believed this, and yet it provided a plausible excuse for what was to come next. Attila's chiefs had assembled by the smoking ruins, several murmuring that the Roman girl should be crucified or worse. Their king had a different idea. The loss of the sword deeply disturbed his superstitious spirit. This was a message, but what? To reveal misgiving would be to invite a usurper, but to fail to keep alive every opportunity for the sword's recovery would be to tempt fate. Better to use the loss to spur on his warriors, and use the woman until he got the sword back.

"It seems the god of war is testing us," he told his followers. "First he allows us to discover the sword in a common field, meaning for us to find it. Then he steals it away just as easily. Do we deserve his favor? Or have we become soft as the Romans?" His warlords looked down in embarrassment and resentment. All had heard Attila's warnings of decay many times. Was this finally a sign of divine disfavor?

"Now we will become hard again," Edeco vowed, "hard like Mars."

"What do we know?" Attila asked. "Is the Roman here?"

"His horse is here."

"Which means nothing." He thought. "The war god is revealing our proper direction. He wants us to march to wherever the sword is and wrest it back."

"But the Romans will have it!" Onegesh exclaimed. "They will use it against us!"

"How can they use what they do not understand? This is my talis-man, not theirs."

Edeco looked glum. "I would rather they not have it."

"So let's get the woman to tell us where he went," Onegesh said.

They eyed her. Ilana said nothing.

"No," Attila finally said. "I am not going to damage this woman for what she probably doesn't know. She's better used as bait. All know how much the Roman who must have the sword desires her. Guernna said he leaped the flames to try to follow." He pointed to Skilla. "I also know the longing of our own young hothead. So nothing has changed except this test. This fire is a sign that the Hun must return to the open sky. My survival is a sign that Mars still finds me worthy. Any sword that has been through the fire is stronger for it. So now we plan in earnest. This girl goes in a cage. This hothead finds where the sword has been taken and gets it back—or, when we find the Roman, we trade the woman for the sword." He looked pointedly at Skilla.

"There will be no trade because the Roman will be dead and I will bring the sword back to you!" Skilla cried. And, elated that Ansila's promises seemed to be coming true, Skilla took thirty men and rode out in pursuit.

He followed the Tisza southward to the Danube, reaching it in two and a half days of hard riding, but there was no trace of Jonas. The ferry-men in their canoes swore they hadn't seen any fugitive. Villagers didn't report any strange travelers. The best hunters in the group could find no trail or sign.

Skilla was anxious. Was he about to be humiliated again?

"Maybe he is so slow we've gotten ahead of him," a warrior named Tatos, one of Skilla's closest friends, suggested.

"Maybe." Skilla pondered. "Or maybe so fast that he slipped across on a log or a stolen boat, or even swam the river with his horse. It's not impossible. Nor is it impossible he drowned." *That would be a bitter theft,* he thought. "All right, two will search downriver, one on either bank. Two more upriver. Five of you will cross here and ride toward the Pass of Succi, questioning every person you meet and offering a reward for the

Roman. But I don't think he came this way. He has another purpose in mind."

"What?"

"My guess is he's gone another direction."

"East?" asked Tatos.

"That takes him farther from everywhere he knows."

"West?"

"Eventually, perhaps. But not at first, because he'd risk running into our patrols. I say north first, but not forever. The Germans would never hide him from us—they know better than that. My guess is north and then west . . . west to Aetius." He tried to remember the maps of that area he'd seen. The Huns didn't have the knowledge to draw maps, but they had learned to read them. How strange that an enemy would tell you the way to his homeland! "If we follow the Danube to the old Roman provinces of Noricum and Raetia, far up the Danube valley, we may intercept him. Tatos, return to Attila with word of what we're doing and see if anything more has been learned in the camp. The rest of us will ride northwestward, toward the great bend of the Danube. I've ridden with Romans before and know well how slow they are. We still have time."

So they set out, and when Tatos rejoined them five days later he had intriguing news. "The dwarf and his wife are gone, too."

"The dwarf?"

"The fool, Zerco. He's disappeared."

Of course! The jester had not just help nurse the Roman in his hut, the pair had become conspirators. Not until they lived together had Jonas shown the boldness to set fire to Attila's palace. How much of what happened had been the fool's idea?

"And something even stranger, Skilla. The Greek Eudoxius has disappeared, too."

"Eudoxius! He's no friend of Zerco."

"Or of the Roman. Unless he's been playing a double game."

Skilla thought. "Or they have taken him prisoner."

"Perhaps as a hostage," Tatos said, "or for the Romans to torture."

"It's clear, then. They're riding for Zerco's old master, the Roman general Aetius. So we ride toward news of Aetius, too. Anyone who sees them will remember a dwarf, a woman, a Roman, and a Greek doctor. They might as well be a traveling circus."

Our quartet of fugitives rode ever deeper into the barbarian world. Zerco's plan was to travel a great arc into Germania, going first north-west and then southwest, striking the Danube again somewhere be-tween Vindobona in the east and Boioduram to the west. He said we would cross the river into the relative safety of Noricum, that province north of the Alps still partly under Roman control. From there we could learn the whereabouts of Aetius or go on to Italy.

The chance of discovery by roving patrols of Huns or Germans forced us from the main tracks and required us to move slowly. We rested during the middle of the increasingly short days as autumn ad-vanced, but rode into the night and rose again before dawn, as stealthy as hunted deer. Fortunately, we were away from major rivers or trading routes and settlement was sparse. Log huts crouched in clearings amid forest as old as time, the smoke of cooking fires curling away into thick ground mists. Trunks were as fat as towers, their limbs the outstretched hands of giants. Leaves rained down, and the days were growing cloudy and cold. The world was growing darker.

This was country different than I had ever seen before, different even than the mountains we'd crossed to get to Attila. It was dim in the forest and hard to tell direction. Shapes moved in the night, and occa-sionally we saw the moonlit gleam of animal eyes, of which kind I can-not say. The air was always chill and damp, and our reluctance to light a fire, because of its revealing smoke, made our meals cold and cheerless. My only consolation was that I believed the Huns would like this path-way even less, given their love of open sky and rolling grassland.

I could have ridden faster by myself, I suppose, but it would have been with a sorrowful recklessness likely to get me caught. The elation I'd expected from fleeing Attila's camp had instead become sadness at the loss of Ilana. In this somber mood, the company of the dwarf and his wife was a comfort, relieving me of having to make the decisions of where to go. They were gentle at my remote and troubled manner—

only much later would I think to thank them—and Julia, who had come from such country, instructed us in the ways of camping. Zerco tried to explain the intricacies of imperial politics to me. So many kings, so many alliances, so many treacheries! Animosities reaching back two and three hundred years! The sword, perhaps, would help temporarily unite them.

The kidnapped Eudoxius, in contrast, was a misery as company. The Greek, once his gag was removed, was tireless in complaining not just about his capture but also about the weather, the food, the route, the hard ground at night, and the companionship. "I consort with kings, not jesters," he ranted. "I am on a mission to free a captive world. I am Pericles! I am Spartacus! I am Gideon! I can hear the pursuing hoofbeats now! Listen, you've sealed your own doom by capturing me!"

"Listen?" Zerco replied. "How can we not? You're louder than a mule and twice the trouble, and your braying makes just as much sense."

"Let me go and I'll trouble you no more."

"Slit your throat and you'll trouble us no more! You are gabbling your way toward a bright red necklace, believe me!"

"Let's do it now," I suggested irritably.

"He's met Gaiseric," the dwarf replied wearily. "That's what Aetius will be interested in. Trust me, he's worth all his noise."

Zerco knew more than I suspected. His fool's antics had allowed him to be ignored like a dog during some of the Hun councils, and he'd learned much about the location of barbarian tribes, favored routes to the west, and where provisions might be bought or stolen. Riding like a stocky child in front of his wife, his head cushioned pleasingly against her breasts, he led us by the map he'd formed in his mind. At an unmarked crossroads or at the hovel of a sutler where we might buy food, he'd clamber down and leave us waiting while he played the mysterious and misshapen pilgrim. Eventually he'd waddle back with information and bread. "This way," he'd announce confidently. Then we'd be on our way again. Never seen was the great sword that was swaddled in rags and slung across my back.

The traveling was more rugged than my journey to Attila. The autumn rains were chill and this part of Germania seemed a maze of low hills, cloaked by dark forest that extended as far as the eye could see. Our sleep was restless, and there were no slaves to pitch a tent or prepare a meal. We huddled like animals.

It was on the fourth night that Eudoxius tried to escape. I'd tied the captive's hands behind his back, hobbled his feet, and strung another rope from the Greek's ankle to my own to alert me of any mischief, but in the deepness of the night I shifted slightly, my leg stretching, and realized the tether had gone slack. I came sharply awake. Someone was moving because I could hear his anxious breath.

The quarter moon came out from behind a shred of crowd, and I saw a dark form crouched over my saddle where I had placed the great iron sword.

I reacted without thinking, hurling a faggot of wood that took Eudoxius by surprise. It bounced off him, drawing a grunt, and then the Greek was running hard for the darkness of the trees, abandoning the sword he'd tried to steal.

I snatched up the Hun bow I'd been practicing with and had taken, but Zerco, also awake, stayed my hand. "Aetius needs him." So I ran, too, and here my youth stood me in good stead. I steadily gained on the lumbering doctor, hearing his panicked wheezing.

It was when I was about to tackle him that he whirled and almost killed me, lashing out with a bright knife I didn't know he had. So that is how he'd cut himself free! It barely grazed my side before I was inside his reach and plowing into him like a bull. We both flew; the knife was knocked free and crashed. Then the same boxing skills I had used on Skilla were employed again. I wasn't sure what I was more furious about—my own laxness at searching him, his greed for the sword, or his attempt to kill me—but I pummeled him thoroughly for all three. In moments he gave up resisting and curled into a ball.

"Please, mercy! I only wanted to go back to Attila!"

I stopped, panting. "Where did the knife come from?"

He peeked and smirked. "From the small of my back to my inner thigh to the stitching on my saddle—wherever I could hide it."

Zerco came and spied the knife in the moonlight. He picked it up. "This could have ended all three of us, if he'd been brave enough to go for our throats while we slept." He turned its jeweled hilt. "A pretty blade. Look at the workmanship!" The dwarf squatted. "Where did you get it, doctor?"

"What care is that of yours?"

Zerco pricked the doctor's throat. "So I'll know who to send it for cleaning!"

"It was a gift from Gaiseric," Eudoxious squeaked. "He took it from a Roman general. He sent it as a token of his word to Attila, and Attila gave it to me as a reward."

The dwarf handed it to me. "And now you've bestowed it on Jonas, while you'll be trussed each night like a pig." He gave a kick to the prostrate doctor. "That's for disturbing my sleep." He kicked again. "And that's for having to listen to you for the last four days."

"I'll speak my truth!"

"And I'll kick you again."

We traveled on. With no Roman mileposts and few promontories to judge our progress, this new world seemed as endless as the sea. Crude forest tracks wound underneath patriarch trees that had sprouted before Romulus and Remus were born. This was a world Rome had never conquered and never wanted to, a place of shadowy stillness; gray marshes; and dark, tunneled brooks. The sun of the Bosporus seemed impossibly distant, and when we encountered settlement, the primitive state to which people were falling after the rampages of the Huns was depressing. At the ruins of Carnuntum we passed by a small party of Gepids living like animals in its corners. How I longed for a Roman bath! And yet the baths were a ruin, the pools empty and the boilers unlit. The only water left running was through the abandoned community's sewage drains, and it was here that the hapless barbarians washed themselves and their clothes.

We bought food, and passed on as quickly as we could.

I learned more about the peculiar marriage of Zerco and Julia.

"The union was meant to mock me," Julia explained. "I was captured from the Scuri tribe when a child and sold by the Huns to a Gepid master as brutal as he was stupid. He thought he could force affection by the whip, and meant to take me to wife when I reached thirteen. I was comely enough to excite his lust, and he was ugly enough to extinguish mine. He proclaimed one night I was ripe enough to give up my virginity, but I put foul meat in his stew and gave him a night at the privy instead. His neighbors laughed at him. He threatened to kill me, but the Huns warned him not to, so he went to Bleda demanding his money back. Bleda, who didn't want to offend the Gepids at that moment, paid for me himself from money he owed his own jester. Then he awarded me to Zerco instead, as an insult to me and in punishment for my mischief."

"Not that I minded losing coin I might never see anyway," the dwarf chimed in. "I'd no hopes of marrying, and then suddenly I was presented with this angel. The Huns thought it hilarious. They offered to lend us a stool."

"What others treated as a joke we saw as salvation," Julia said. "Zerco was the first truly kind and gentle man I'd ever met. We had a bond: our fear of a future dominated by Huns. Attila is a parasite on better people."

"And he is driven by two great fears," Zerco added. "The first is that his people are being corrupted by the booty they acquire and will become soft."

"Not likely by spring," I said. "And the second?"

"He fears his own failure. Do you realize what it must be like to be a tyrant who rules by terror and cannot trust one? How does he know a follower's loyalty is given or extorted? How does he know that sex is love or coerced? The very might that makes a kagan all powerful can also make him all doubting. He gains support only by winning. If he falters, all might come undone."

"You think he'll falter without the sword?"

"That's my hope."

"And Attila sent you to Aetius, and Aetius back to spy."

"Our marriage was an excuse to send Zerco back to where I was trapped with Attila," Julia went on. "And there my dwarf saw a way to solve all our problems."

"How?"

"By getting you to steal the sword, of course. It will demoralize Attila and encourage Aetius. If we can get to the Roman army, the captured sword may help the army to rally, and if the Romans win, Zerco and I can live in peace." She nodded happily, as if the fate of the world were an easy enough thing for me to arrange.

XVIII

THE AVALANCHE

Skilla's Huns were tired and far from home, riding in a frontier region not firmly held by any nation. The once-inviolable northern boundary of the Roman Empire had long been breeched. Far south of the Danube the Romans still held sway, in order to guard the passes into Italy. Far north of it the Germans dominated in the deep forests that deterred all conquerors. But along the Danube itself, order had devolved to a rabble of semi-independent governors, warlords, and chiefs who had carved out fiefdoms in the dying Empire's disorder. A party as large and deadly as the Huns could move through this landscape with relative impunity, but Skilla's group dare not linger long in case a local duke or renegade centurion decided to treat them as a threat. The Hun's task was to recover the sword and kill Jonas, not provoke a skirmish with provincial bumpkins. So he and his men skirted the walled villas and new hilltop forts as carefully as the fugitives did, muttering at the gloom of the trees, cursing the frequent grades, and grumbling at the weather. Their bowstrings were continually damp, detracting greatly from their killing power, and even their swords showed spots of rust. To add to their unease, the Alps loomed to the southwest. Snow was creeping down the autumn flanks.

Zerco was key. At any one time there were hundreds of couriers, peddlers, pilgrims, mystics, mercenaries, and witches wandering the crumbling roads, making it hard to track a single fugitive such as Jonas. But a dark dwarf riding with a full-stature woman and two other men, one of them bound, was a curiosity that even these strange parts did not see every day. As Huns followed the river upstream toward Lauriacum, they began to hear stories of an odd quartet who had emerged from the forests of the north. The newcomers were filthy and exhausted, and yet the halfling had paid in gold for a hired courier to take a message upriver. The rumor was that the document was a missive for the great Aetius himself. Then they crossed to the river's southern bank and aimed in the direction of the alpine salt mines where Roman garrisons still soldiered. One of the fugitives carried a strange bundle on his back: long, narrow, and as high as a man was tall.

If the fugitives could find a powerful Roman escort, their escape would be completed.

The Huns had to find them first.

They galloped hard for Lentia and the last standing bridge on this part of the Danube, its stone piers cracked and mossy and its wooden span a crude replacement for long-destroyed Roman carpentry. Yet the bridge remained passable. It was manned by ruffians who demanded tolls; but no sooner had these toughs heard the sound of hooves, and swung shut their gate of thorns, than they smelled the rank odor of Huns, like smoke on the wind. The bridge keepers reconsidered. By the time the barbarian party broke free of the trees and galloped onto the bridge like wolves from the steppe, several with bows in hand and their brown faces mottled with scars, the gate was open and its toll takers in hiding. All they saw was a blur of clods, accompanied by the excited yips of barbarians aimed eagerly southward.

On the warriors went like a dark and urgent cloud, collecting scraps of rumor at this place and that. Somewhere on the highway to Iuvavum fled four tired fugitives. One of them gabbled in Greek.

Skilla found himself thinking of Ilana more than he wanted to, despite the humiliation of her both rejecting him and then saving him from Jonas. He knew she lived, and the thought of winning her back still haunted him. Why had she pushed aside Jonas's spear from that final thrust? If she hated killing, why had she later tried to burn Attila, instead of simply fleeing with Jonas? She baffled him, and it was her mystery that kept her in his mind. He had visited her in captivity before setting out, bringing her food as an excuse and hoping she might give some clue about the fugitives, torn between pity, obligation, and exasperation.

"None of this would have happened if you had come to me," he had tried.

"None of this would have happened if you and your kind had stayed where you belong, out on the oceans of grass," she'd replied. "None of this would have happened if I'd let Jonas win the duel."

"Yes. So why didn't you, Ilana?"

"I wasn't thinking. The noise, the blood . . ."

"No. It's because you're in love with me, too. You're in love with both of us."

She had closed her eyes. "I'm Roman, Skilla."

"That's the past. Think of our future."

"Why do you torment me!"

"I love you. Accept this, because I'm going to free you from this cage."

She had spoken with the weariness of the terminally ill. "Just leave me, Skilla. My life is over. It ended in Axiopolis, and it's some kind of monstrous mistake of misguided destiny that I've been left to witness this other. I'm a dead woman, and have been for some time, and you need to find a wife of your own kind."

But he didn't want his own kind—he wanted Ilana. He didn't believe she was dead at all. After he killed Jonas, retrieved the sword, and won her back, everything would become simple. They would scratch and buck like wildcats, but when they coupled, what sons they would make!

The country became steeper, reminding him of his horse race with Jonas on the journey from Constantinople. Skilla sensed the Roman was near as he sometimes sensed a deer or wild horse was near, and yet he felt blinded in these hilly woods. He was growing discouraged—had the Huns somehow galloped past them in their haste?—when one of his men shouted and they reined up at a wondrous discovery: a bright Greek ring, left like a golden beacon beside a track that led off the main road. Eudoxius!

So the Huns rose long before dawn to ride quietly on the sidetrack, finally spying a pillar of gray smoke. Had the fugitives become so foolish or so overconfident? Then the smoke disappeared, as if someone realized the mistake. The Huns quietly ascended ridges that overlooked where the plume must have come from, dismounting to lead their ponies through the trees. It was the grayness before dawn, the mountains ahead a soft pewter and the trees a dark foundation. At the crest, Skilla spied three horses in a hollow below.

Now he would be revenged! But Skilla didn't have much practice yet at leadership, his band was young, and before he could order a proper ambush his warriors whooped and charged. A dwarf and a woman? This would be easy.

It was the noise that saved Jonas. He sprang up, shouting, just as the first arrows, fired at too long a range, arced into his campsite to stick in the ground. He seized one horse, mounted it, and dragged some other man—the Greek doctor?—across its neck with him. The woman and dwarf grabbed another as the third animal simply reared and plunged out of reach. It ran toward the attackers until Hun arrows thudded into the mount's breast to make sure their quarry couldn't use it, bringing that animal with a shudder to its knees. Now the fugitives were kicking their two surviving mounts furiously as arrows rained around, all of them precariously mounted bareback. The Huns had them! But then the Arabian horses seemed to explode with speed, weaving almost instinctually, and in a flash they were obscured by the branches. The warriors cried in excitement and frustration and whipped the flanks of their own ponies in pursuit, embarrassed they had not encircled their prey. But the fugitive horses were fresh from a night's rest and the Hun horses, already exhausted from these mountains, had been climbing for two hours and had sprinted in attack. In moments, what should have been easy capture turned into dogged pursuit.

Skilla was furious. Each of his men had abandoned the tactics they'd been taught since childhood in hope of the individual glory of retrieving Attila's sword. Now they'd all spoiled it for one another. The warriors blamed as they rode, pointing, while their prey's powerful horses slipped around the shoulder of a ridge, ending any chance of shooting them. By the time the barbarians crested the hill, the fugitives were streaking for the valley below, where an arched Roman bridge led over a foaming stream.

"We'll still run them down," he grimly told his men.

"They're carrying too much," agreed Tatos.

The Hun horses were whipped downhill in a ragged line, the warrior's bows still strung, swords bouncing against their thighs. They watched their quarry pause a moment on the bridge, as if to break or block it. Then the fugitives seemingly gave up and rode across, leaving the Roman road to ride through a gap in the trees on the far side of the stream and struggle directly uphill. They were desperate now, Skilla guessed, leaving the track in hopes of losing their pursuers in broken country. It was a foolish and fatal move because his men would not slacken, not when their quarry's scent was like the spoor of a wounded stag.

His men need cross only one more bridge, and they had them.

The attack of the Huns had come as a complete shock to us three escapees but not at all to our prisoner, the wily Eudoxius. After crossing the Danube and riding southward toward the Alps, we had foolishly assumed that our circuitous route had been successful, and we had slackened our pace, giving our tired horses some rest. Yet even when the passes to Italy seemed almost in sight, I still didn't dare light a fire or abandon habitual caution. I'd taken the risk of purchasing some charcoal when we crossed the Danube, and its heat had since kept us alive. I believed it gave no smoke.

Until that morning.

Ever since we'd escaped Attila's camp, Eudoxius had been doing anything he could to attract attention. It raised too many questions to gag him, so he'd spoken Greek at every opportunity. He had offered medical care to the endless parade of the sick and crippled that any traveler encounters. One by one he had plucked silver and gold rings off his fingers and left them on boulders or logs in the remote hope a pursuing Hun might spot them, and it was only in the foothills of the Alps that Julia furiously noticed that his fingers had become bare. The doctor had listened for pursuit every night when his head touched the ground. He had not so much seen or heard Skilla as felt him, I think—felt as if an arm were reaching for him as he sank under water. The closer we drew to the Alps, the more his hopes perversely rose. Finally, it was my last charcoal fire that was our undoing. We warmed our dinner and I kicked it out, but the dirt locked in the heat and quiet coals remained. Late at night when Julia had nodded from exhaustion, Eudoxius stretched his bonds enough to reach a fallen fir bough damp with dew. At dawn, he slipped the branch onto the embers before the rest of us stirred and smoke began to roll upward. Julia finally jerked awake, shouting, but by the time Zerco kicked the limb aside and kicked our prisoner, it was too late. Shortly afterward, we heard the yip of the Huns.

Now we were desperate. Unable to break the old timbers of the bridge, we'd abandoned the Roman track and were climbing through trees. Eudoxius thought we were trying to hide.

"Better to give yourselves up," he counseled as I clutched him like a sack of wheat across the front of my mount, wondering for the hundredth time if his potential value to Aetius was worth his trouble as a captive. "Trying to hide is as ineffectual as a child covering his eyes in hopes of not being seen. The Huns will find you. I've seen them shoot out the eye of a stag at two hundred paces."

"If I die, you will too."

"You won't know the arrow is coming until it is through your breast."

I punched him in frustration and he swore.

"Leave me and the sword and maybe the Huns will break off their pursuit," he tried. "I'll trade you your life for it."

"The sword I might abandon," I said. "You, I'll keep as shield."

Given time and a tool more effective than the old iron sword, we might have sabotaged the bridge. It was obvious no repairs had been made in a generation, and the rotting timber deck had been patched only crudely by the rare traveler charitable enough to care about who came after him. Gaps revealed the white water below. Yet even as I pondered the possibility, the Huns began spilling down the slope behind like a brown avalanche. This forced me to look ahead, and what I saw inspired me.

"Where the devil are you taking us," Zerco gasped as our two horses struggled up the mountainside, gravel skittering.

"We can't outrun twenty or thirty men forever," I replied. "We have to stop them."

"But how?" Julia cried. An arrow, fired from so great a range that it wobbled, rattled into the trees.

"See that slope of rubble and talus above the bridge? If we can jar it loose, we can send down an avalanche."

"And ourselves with it," Zerco predicted. But what choice did we have?

We came out of the trees at the base of a cliff that loomed high above the ravine that the bridge spanned, casting the stream in shadow. Following the cliff base, we climbed along a rubble slope until the loose shale became so thick that all vegetation ended. The horses began slipping as if on ice. Far below, we could see the Huns riding down to the crossing.

"Zerco, truss this damned doctor like a sacrificial goat. Julia, come with me!" I grabbed a stout pine pole lying amid the rubble and we slid partway down the talus slope, zigzagging to a point above the span.

The Huns were like ants, bunched at the bottom, pointing up to where they spied us. One was angrily ordering the others further, and his posture and gestures were all too familiar. Skilla! Would I never be rid of my rival?

I saw what I was looking for. A rock larger than the others had slid down the talus and was perched precariously upright at one end, wedged in place by smaller rocks around it. I planted the pole under, using a stone as a fulcrum. "Help me push!"

Julia pressed desperately.

The Huns, leading their ponies, began filing over the bridge.

"I can't do it!" she shouted.

"Throw your weight against it!"

"I am!"

And then a smaller ball of energy sprang down the slope and hurtled onto the pole. Zerco! The dwarf's impact, his weight multiplied by speed, was just enough. Even as the lever snapped, the rock sprang high enough to topple forward; and as it did other rocks broke loose and began sliding like a ruptured dam.

Zerco started to slide with it, his wife catching his tunic. For a moment she swayed at the edge, about to tip.

I hauled at them, retreating upward. "We have to get out of the way!"

Now the hillside was roaring, beginning to slide in a sheet. We clambered to the cliff pass, grabbed solid rock, and turned. What a sight!

We'd triggered a major avalanche. Falling stone smashed into falling stone, rupturing the delicate equilibrium of the mountain. Dust was hissing upward in a geysered plume. The rumble grew in volume, at first inaudible to the Huns below and then so loud that it overcame the sound of the rushing water. The barbarians looked up, staring in stupefaction at the lip of the cliff. A spray of talus burst over and arced down.

They turned their horses and ran.

Now hundreds of tons of rock were sluicing over the precipice like a stone waterfall, and when they struck the bridge there was an eruption. Planks kicked skyward as if catapulted. Aging beams exploded into a spray of splinters. The avalanche punched through the bridge as if it were paper, taking two Huns and their horses with it, and then the plume of rubble hit the torrent with a titanic splash. Bridge bits rained down.

We climbed to the top of the talus, where Eudoxius was, and looked back. I was jubilant. It was as if a giant had taken a bite out of the mountain. A haze of dust hung in the air. Below, the middle of the bridge had disappeared.

The surviving Huns had reined in on the far side of the stream and stared upward, quiet at the damage.

"It will take them days to find another way around," I said with more hope than knowledge. "Or at least hours." I patted Zerco. "Let's pray Aetius got your message."

XIX

THE ROMAN TOWER

The guard tower of Ampelum overlooked the junction of two old Roman roads, one going west to the salt mines around Iuvavum and Cucullae, the other south to Ad Pontem and the mountain passes beyond. The tower was square, fifty feet high, crenellated at its crest, and topped by a tripod-hung kettle in which oil could be lit to send signals to distant towers like it. The fire had been lit many more times than help had ever arrived, given the depleted nature of imperial resources; and so this garrison, like so many, had learned to depend on itself. Rome was like the Moon: ever present and far away.

Around the tower's base was a wider fortification of stone walls eight feet high, enclosing a courtyard with stables, storerooms, and workshops. The dozen occupying Roman soldiers slept and ate in the tower itself, relying on cows stabled on the ground floor to provide some warmth. This animal heat was supplemented by charcoal braziers that gave the air a stale haze and, over the centuries, had stained the beams black.

To call the garrison "Roman" was to stretch the historic meaning of the term. It had been ages since legions consisted primarily of Latins marching out of Italy. Instead, the army had become one of the Empire's great integrating forces, recruiting men of a hundred conquered nations and training them under the common tongue. Slowly, the uni-

versality of language, custom, and armament had slipped away, and so
what manned the tower now was a collection of mountain farm boys
and recruited vagabonds, all under the command of a gruff decurion
named Silas who originated in the marshes of Frisia. One soldier was
Greek, one Italian, and one African. Three were Germanic Ostrogoths,
one a Gepid, and the other five had never ventured more than twenty
miles from the fortress and thus were simply inhabitants of Noricum.
While these men owed nominal allegiance to Rome, they principally
guarded themselves, plus a few villages in surrounding valleys from
which they extracted provisions and a few coins in taxes. Travelers
passing the crossroads were required to pay a toll. When reminders
from the clerks in Ravenna became insistent enough, a small portion
of this levy was shared with the central government. The soldiers did
not expect, and did not receive, anything in return. They were responsible for providing their own food, clothing, weapons, and any material needed to repair the guard tower. Their reward was permission
to levy taxes on their neighbors.

Still, these men had at least nominal allegiance to the idea of Rome:
the idea of order, the idea of civilization. I hoped they represented refuge.
Our destruction of the bridge several miles back had delayed but not
necessarily stopped the Huns. A Roman garrison might force Skilla to
give up and go home.

"What the devil is *that?*" greeted the commanding decurion Silas,
who had come to the gate and, after observing that four of us were
crowded on two exhausted horses, was peering at Zerco.

"An important aide to General Flavius Aetius," I replied, reasoning
it would not hurt to exaggerate the truth.

"Is this a jest?"

"His wisdom is as tall as his stature is short."

"And that sack of grain across your saddle?" He looked at the
trussed and gagged Eudoxius, who wiggled to communicate outrage.

"A traitor to Rome. Aetius wants to question him."

"An aide, a traitor?" He pointed to the woman. "And who is she, the
queen of Egypt?"

"Listen. We've important information for the general, but need help. We're being pursued by a party of Huns."

"Huns! This *is* a joke. Any Huns are far to the east."

"Then why are four of us on two horses while our other grows Hunnish arrows?" Zerco piped up. He slid down from his mount and waddled over to the Roman captain, peering up. "Do you think a man as big as me would stop in a sty like this if I weren't in dire peril?"

"Zerco, don't insult our new friend," Julia interjected. She too dismounted. "I apologize for his rudeness. We're being chased by Attila's men, decurion, and only the collapse of the bridge below saved us from capture. Now we ask your protection."

"The bridge collapsed?"

"We had to destroy it."

He looked as if not certain whether to believe anything we said, and to dislike us if he did. "You're with him?" The commander nodded from Julia to me.

"It's this rude one who is my husband." She put her hand on Zerco's shoulder. "He's a fool and sometimes makes jokes that others don't find humorous, but please don't mind. He's taller in spirit than men twice his size, and it is true, he serves the great Aetius. Do you know where the general is?"

The soldier barked a laugh. "Look around you!" The tower was mossy and cracked, the courtyard muddy, and the stabled animals thin. "I'm as likely to see Aetius as I am Attila! There was a report he was in Rome or in Ravenna or on the Rhine, and even a report he was coming this way, but then there was also a report of a unicorn in Iuvavum and a dragon at Cucullae. Besides, he never stays anywhere for long. With winter coming on, he may retire to Augusta Treverorum or Mediolanum. If you're to reach him, you need to move quickly before the passes are snowed in."

"Then we need food, fodder, and another horse," I said.

"Which means I need a solidus, a solidus, and another solidus," Silas replied. "Let's see your purse, strangers."

"We have no more money! We've escaped from Attila's camp.

Please, we have information that Aetius needs to hear. Can't you requisition help from the government?"

"I can't get anything myself from Rome." He looked at us and our meager possessions dubiously. "What's that on your back?"

"An old sword," I said.

"Let me see it. Maybe you can trade for that."

I considered a moment, and then climbed down and unwrapped it. Black and rusty, it looked like it had been pulled from the mud. Which it had. Only the size was impressive.

"That's not a sword, it's an anchor," Silas said. "It wouldn't cut cheese, and looks too big to swing. Why are you carrying that piece of scrap?"

"It's a family relic that's important to me." I wrapped it back up. "A token of our ancestors."

"Were your ancestors ten feet tall? It's ridiculous."

"Listen, if you won't provision us, at least let us spend the night. We haven't slept under a roof in weeks."

He looked at Julia. "Can you cook?"

"Better than your mother."

Silas grinned. "I doubt that, but better than wretched Lucius, without a doubt. All right, you will cook supper; you will fetch water; and you, little man, will carry wood. Your prisoner we'll tie to a post in the tower and let him sputter. Agents of Aetius! The garrison at Virunum will laugh when I tell them that one. Go on, I'll let you fill your bellies and sleep in my fort. But you're on your way in the morning. This is a military post, not a *mansio*."

If the decurion seemed a reluctant host, his bored soldiers welcomed our company as entertainment. Julia cooked a hot and hearty soup; Zerco sang them ribald songs; and I told them of Constantinople, which to them seemed no more or less distant and incredible than Rome or Alexandria. Eudoxius, his gag removed, insisted he was a prince of the Huns and promised all of them their weight in gold if they would free and return him. The soldiers thought him as funny as Zerco. They assured us that Huns did not exist in these parts or, if they did, were no doubt on their way home by now. Forts less than a day's ride apart guarded the approaches to Italy, and we could travel from one to the next. "Sleep well tonight," assured Lucius, "because we don't allow bar-barians in upper Noricum."

At the gray smudge of dawn, that time when sentries finally become dark silhouettes against a barely lightened sky, just two Romans were still awake in our small outpost.

Both died within moments of each other.

The first, Simon, was at the gate and looking in sleepy boredom down the lane. He hoped that Ulrika, a local milkmaid who had udders like a cow, might make her delivery before he was called off duty to breakfast. He was thinking of her breasts, round as melons and firm as a wineskin, when a pony trotted out of the gloom and, before he could call challenge, a Hun arrow took him squarely in the throat. He gurgled as he sank numbly down, wondering what the devil had happened to him, and what had happened to Ulrika. It is oft remarked that a common ex-pression on the dead is surprise.

The second man, Cassius, was at the top of the tower and was pac-ing back and forth to keep warm. It was a strange humming that caused him to look up before a dozen arrows hissed down like a sudden squall. Four of the arcing missiles found their mark, and the others rattled on the tower roof like hail. It was this, and the thump of his body, that woke me and the others.

"Huns!" I cried.

"You're having a dream," Silas grumbled, half asleep.

Then an arrow sizzled through the chamber's slit window and banged off the stone wall.

We heard a rumble of hooves as Skilla's men galloped to the com-pound wall in a rush, leaped from their pony's backs to the lip of the wall, and then streamed over like a ripple of shadow. So far, remember-ing the lesson of yesterday, they had not let their voices make a sound.

They dropped lightly down into the courtyard like the softest of warnings, the quiet broken only by a dog that barked before it could be speared and a donkey startled and braying before it was brained by an ax. It took the barbarians a moment to explore the kitchen, storerooms, and stables, running lightly with swords drawn. Then, learning quickly enough that all of us were in the tower, they charged its door and found it barred. Now Roman heads were popping from the tower windows and shouting alarm. It was Silas who was the first to strike back, hurling a spear from a third floor window. It struck so fiercely that it staked the Hun it found like a tent peg.

"Awake!" he roared. "Grab your sword, not your sandals, you oaf! We're under attack!" He stepped aside an instant before another arrow whistled through the window. It struck a beam and quivered.

I'd rolled out of my sleeping mat with loincloth and the Roman short sword I had killed Attila's sentry with. Julia still had the spear with which she'd gutted my horse. Beyond that and the dagger I'd taken from Eudoxius, we fugitives were virtually unarmed: my skills as an archer were still indifferent. Now I ran for the rack of javelins, grabbed one, and peeked outside. It was barely light, and the Huns below were scuttling back and forth across the courtyard like spiders. One paused, looking up, and I threw. The man saw the motion and dodged. There was something familiar to his quickness. Skilla?

Now more Romans were throwing javelins or firing crossbow bolts, even as Hun arrows clicked and ricocheted off the stones of the tower.

"Who in Hades is attacking us?" Silas demanded.

"Those Huns you said would be scurrying home by now," I responded.

"We have no quarrel with the Huns!"

"It appears they have a quarrel with you."

"It's you! And that prisoner, isn't it?"

"Him, and that rust you called an anchor."

"The sword?"

"It's magic. If Attila wins it, he will conquer the world."

Silas looked at me in wonder, once again not certain what to believe.

"Julia, heat the soup!" Zerco cried, gesturing toward the pot of beef and millet broth that remained warm in an iron pot. Then the little man ran up the stairs toward the top of the tower, his boots pounding.

Heat the soup? Then I realized what the dwarf had in mind. Julia was fanning and feeding the coals. Meanwhile I looked and waited for another target from my window. Finally a Hun made a dash for the door at the base of the tower. Reminding myself of my combat with Skilla, I waited for a covering arrow to clang off the stonework and then leaned out and threw. The weapon fell like a thunderbolt, and the Hun fell with it, dying halfway to the door.

I felt nothing but satisfaction. I was not the boy I had been.

The Romans were fully aroused now and the growing light was helping. But with our dead and wounded—two more had been struck by arrows—we were outnumbered more than two to one. More ominously, the Huns were dismantling the shed roof of the stable, loosing the tile covering from its posts and gathering men around it. Their intention was obvious. They would use the roof as a shield to get themselves to the gate. Other Huns were gathering straw and timber to start a fire at the door.

With both sides fully alert now, the arrow volleys were slackening as the battling warriors became wary about exposing themselves. Our supplies of missiles needed to be hoarded. Insults in Latin, German, and Hunnish echoed back and forth across the bloody courtyard in lieu of volleys.

"Give up our slaves!" Skilla called in Hunnish.

None of the Roman garrison could understand his demand.

Zerco came pounding back down the stairs, his eyes bright with excitement. Penned as he was in a fortress, he was something of an equal in this fight or even had an advantage, since he didn't have to crouch so much to stay away from the arrows. "I lit the signal fire. Lucius and I have loosened some of the stones at the top to throw down on them when they charge the door. Is the soup hot?"

"Beginning to bubble," said Julia.

"Get Jonas to help you pour. Stick that bench plank out the window to make a sluice. When their makeshift roof breaks, pour our lunch down on anyone in the wreckage."

"What if I get hungry?" one of the soldiers tried to joke.

"If you can't get to the courtyard kitchens by the time your stomach growls, you're already dead," the dwarf replied. Then he pounded back up the stairs.

Outside there was a shout and a volley of arrows shot upward again, many keying accurately through the windows.

"Keep down until our friends drop the stones!" Silas ordered. "When the Huns run back for cover, rise and use the crossbows!"

I watched from one side of the narrow slit window. The detached stable roof suddenly rose, rocked slightly as the Huns positioned themselves better to carry it, and then began to trundle forward. Crouching toward the rear were warriors with combustibles and torches. The rhythm of Hun arrows from their archers discouraged us from trying to hit the oncoming barbarians. I couldn't help but flinch each time a missile whizzed through the narrow windows. There was a thud as the lip of the roof struck the base of the tower, and then harsh shouts as hay, wood, and torches were passed forward.

"Now!" came Zerco's piping cry from above.

I could hear the rush of wind as the parapet stones plummeted. There was a brutal crash, cries, and oaths as the stones, half the weight of a man, punched through the roof and shattered its tiles.

"The board!" I ordered. A soldier slid the bench out the window and tilted it downward to direct the soup away from the walls. Then I and Julia, our hands wrapped in cloth, hoisted the black pot off the hearth fire, staggered with it to the window, and poured. It was clumsy, a gallon or two of good food splashing inside our chamber, but most of the hot liquid gushed outward as planned and hissed downward in a plume of steam to strike the Huns entangled in the wreckage. Now there were screams as well as curses.

The Huns broke, running, and the aim of their companions faltered as the barbarians came streaming back. Now we Romans filled the windows to shoot or throw, and two enemies were hit in the back and fell, skidding, as they tried to flee. Two more lay insensible or dead in the roof wreckage, and a few more were limping or staggering.

The odds were beginning to even.

We cheered until smoke began ominously rising up the face of the tower. I risked ducking out the window to look, jerking back just in time as an arrow bounced by my ear.

"A fire has started in the wreckage and it's against the door," I reported. "We need water to put it out."

"No water!" Silas countermanded. "We barely have enough for a day, let alone a siege."

"But if the door burns—"

"We pray it doesn't, or kill them on the stairs. We need to be able to wait for help."

"What help?"

"Your little friend's signal fire. Let's pray that your Aetius, or God, is watching."

The Huns were beginning to shout and howl in excitement at the sight of the flames burning outside the tower door. One suddenly darted across the courtyard with an armful of hay and wood and hurled it into the makeshift bonfire, then dashed back before any Roman could successfully hit him. A second pulled the same trick, and then a third.

The fourth who tried it was killed, but by that time the fire was roaring. Smoke made it hard to see from the tower windows. Silas and I ran to the ground level to see the effect. The cows penned inside the tower were lowing in panic, their eyes rolling as they pulled on their stable bridles. Smoke was filtering through every joint in the door and drifting upward, and I could hear the Roman soldiers above us beginning to cough. We could feel the heat.

There was a howl above. Another Roman had been hit with an arrow.

"Let me go!" cried Eudoxius from the post where he was tied. "It's me they want! If you give me to them, I'll tell them to spare your wretched lives!"

"Don't listen to him!" I shouted to no one in particular.

"When they rush us we'll use the cattle," Silas muttered to me. "Julius and Lucius will be waiting with crossbows. We have to kill enough to make them tire of this game."

"Aim for their leader if you can," I told the crossbowmen. "He's the one who won't give up."

The Huns were chanting now, singing a death song for us. A third of each side had been killed or wounded.

Skilla let the fire eat at the door for a full hour while he busied his warriors with dislodging a heavy beam from the kitchen. The Huns used cleavers to sharpen a blunt point. Holes were drilled and handles hammered into each side, giving the nomads an air of industry I'd never seen before. This would be their battering ram. They were as energetic at war as they were indifferent to farming.

Finally the fire began to die. The door was still standing, but it was a sagging, blackened hulk. A new flock of arrows soared skyward, providing cover, and the Huns charged under its shelter, holding the ram. In a rush they were across the courtyard and the beam hit the door with a crash. It burst inward.

"Yes!" Skilla cried. The Huns hurled the beam in with it and drew swords.

Yet suddenly the doorway filled with horn and hoof. We were beating the flanks of our cows, and cattle crashed into the grouping of surging Huns like Carthaginian elephants, knocking them askew. The Huns tried to drive them back the other way, but the momentum was ours. Horns twisted, goring, and hooves trampled any Hun who fell. In the moment of confusion more stones and spears rained down, and two more Huns fell in the maw of wreckage. Finally the attackers had the sense to let the cows burst outward, but all their speed had been lost. When the surviving attackers crowded through the doorway once again, determined to end things once and for all, we were ready.

Two crossbow bolts sang and two more Huns fell, tripping those pushing behind. I cursed that Skilla wasn't at the forefront. All the advantages the horse warriors had in normal battle had been lost in this close-quarter contest, and I knew the casualties were maddening to the enemy. If we lost, there would be no mercy.

Silas's soldiers were furiously cranking to recock their crossbows, backing up the stairs as they did so. But the Huns with bows pulled and shot.

Lucius and Julius came tumbling down the stairs.

Another charge upward and now our iron soup pot was hurled down at the Huns, knocking them backward. Spears stabbed out, one striking home and another grabbed and jerked away. The fighting on the

stairs was desperate; and Skilla could see me among the Romans blocking the way, chopping with a sword in grim determination. I saw it in his
eyes. *Now I have you!*

Suddenly someone *behind* the attackers was calling in Hunnish in a
familiar, irritating voice. "I am a minister of Attila and you answer to me!
Fight harder! Get the sword!"

Eudoxius!

"How did he get loose?" I shouted in outrage.

"A fool soldier cut the man free, thinking he could parley," Julia answered from behind me, passing javelins we could throw. "The Greek
stabbed his benefactor through the throat and leaped out the window."

"Burn the base beams and the tower will fall!" Eudoxius advised.

"Another crossbow!" Silas demanded, clubbing a Hun backward
with a shield. He was bleeding from wounds, and no one answered.

Step by step, grunting as they pushed us upward, the Huns climbed.
There were too few of us left. I hurled down the bench we'd used for the
soup and they knocked it aside with a snarl. We gave them the first floor
and tried to use furniture to block the entry to the second. Arrows thudded into it.

"Burn them, burn them!" Eudoxius was screaming.

And then far above I heard the dwarf's high, piping voice. "Cavalry!
Cavalry!"

There was a distant, distinct call of a Roman lituus; and the Huns
milling below us looked at one another in consternation. Reinforcements? Our survivors, recognizing the sound, began to cheer.

Skilla was using a small trestle table to shield himself from whatever
we hurled at him. Now I saw him hesitate in an agony of indecision. His
enemy and Attila's sword were so close! Yet if the Huns were penned inside this fort by a fresh force of Roman cavalry, all would be lost.

One last attack!

"Tatos! What's happening!" he called anxiously.

"Romans are coming! Many of them, on horses!"

"We still have time to kill them!" Skilla lifted the table.

I took a crossbow and shot. The bolt punched through its surface,
narrowly missing his nose, and his head jerked backward.

With his face turned, he saw that his men were melting. "We have to flee!"

"The sword! The sword!" Eudoxius was pleading.

Skilla still hesitated.

I was cranking desperately.

Finally he leaped downward as I fired again, the bolt missing him by inches. Then he was running out of the shattered doorway, hurtling the bloody mess. The badly wounded Huns were left to Roman justice while the rest ran for their ponies that had been picketed outside the wall. Skilla jumped from the parapet and landed neatly on his horse's back, slashing to cut its tether. Even as we hooted in triumph, the Huns were getting away.

I craned out a window to look. There was a flash of armor in the rising sun, and an unusually well-uniformed and well-armored company of cavalry began to round the brow of a hill to the south, where the high mountains lay. Skilla lashed his pony and rode north the other direction, back the way the Huns had come. His retreat was downhill, and no soldiers anywhere were better at melting away than the light cavalry of the People of the Dawn. By the time the Roman cavalry had thundered up to the beleaguered tower the Huns were a mile distant and galloping fast, scattering until they could regroup later.

The battle was over as suddenly as it had begun.

We gaped. The leader of the reinforcements was on a snow-white stallion, his cape red and his helmet crested in the old style. His breastplate bore an inlaid swirl of silver and gold, and it seemed for a moment as if Apollo were descending from the rising sun. He galloped through the fortress gate and up to the wrecked door of its central tower with a *turma* of cavalry behind him, reining up to stare in wonder at the havoc. We defenders staggered out to meet him, and what must he have thought: a woman whose sweaty hair hung in tendrils on her face; a grimy dwarf; and me, bearing in two arms a great old iron sword almost bigger than I was.

The officer blinked in recognition. "Zerco?"

The newcomer's surprise was no more than the dwarf's. He, too, let his mouth open in shock and then fell to one knee, displaying a humility he had never displayed to Attila. "General Aetius!"

"Aetius?" Silas, bleeding and triumphant, stared as if he were indeed observing that rumored unicorn. "You mean this fool was telling the truth?"

The general smiled. "I doubt it, from what I remember of his slyness. So what in Heaven and Hell are you doing here, Zerco? I got your summons, but to actually find you . . ." Aetius was a handsome and weathered man, still hard muscled in his fifth decade, his face lined with care and authority, his hair an iron gray. "We saw the signal fire. You always did have a knack for trouble."

"I was looking for you, lord," the dwarf said. "I have decided to change employers again, since Attila has tired of my company. This time, I brought my wife with me."

Julia bowed.

"Well, the saints know we need laughter at perilous times like these, but it doesn't look like you've been joking, fool." He looked at our bloody mess with a grim kind of satisfaction. "It appears you've started what I barely have hopes of finishing. I'm inspecting our alpine posts because of your warnings of war, in case Attila advances on Italy. Your message of escape caught up with me two days ago."

"More than warnings, general. I've brought you dire news from Attila's camp. And I've brought you a new companion, a Roman from Constantinople who almost killed the kagan himself." Zerco turned. "You have a gift for him, do you not, Jonas Alabanda?"

I was happy to be rid of it. "Indeed." I walked up to his horse with the sword.

"You tried to kill Attila?"

"I tried to burn him, but he has the devil's luck. My luck was this talisman." I raised the pitted relic. "A gift, General Aetius, from the god of war."

XX

THE DRUMS OF ÁTTILA

A.D. 451

S now came, and the world seemed to slumber. Yet from the capital of
Attila on the frozen plains of Hunuguri, a hundred couriers were
sent to a thousand barbarian forts, villages, and camps. No mention was
made of the loss of the fabled sword. Instead, Attila evoked other magic,
telling his followers that Rome's own prophets had foretold the city's
final end. All the historic currents—the plea of Honoria, the promise of
Gaiseric, the defiance of Marcian, and the petition of Cloda for help winning the throne of the Franks—made a river of destiny. In all the world,
no land was sweeter, greener, richer, or more moderate than the lands
still farther to the west: Gaul, Hispania, and Italy. Every Hun should
ready himself for the final battle. Every ally and vassal should renew his
pledge. Every enemy would be given a last chance to join the barbarians
or, if they balked, utterly destroyed. In spring, Attila would unleash the
most terrifying army the world had ever seen. When he did, the Old
Age would come to an end.

As pledges of fealty, the couriers brought back the horsehair standards, cloth banners, and sacred staffs of the subject tribes. The warlords would be allowed to retrieve them when they joined their forces
with Attila. Boards were drilled and the poles that carried the tribal in-
signia were erected in the newly rebuilt great hall, its wood raw and

green. By winter's end, with the grass blushing green and the sun once more climbing the clear blue sky of Hunuguri, the chamber was entirely full of standards, and Attila and his chiefs were meeting outside.

Ilana had to watch all this. She'd been let out of her wooden cage after two months of confinement and exposure threatened to kill her. She slept in a corner of the kitchen now, fed on scraps, and walked with a chain connecting her ankles. Guernna rejoiced in the haughty Roman girl's subjugation and would have liked to give her periodic abusive kicks. The first time she tried it Ilana had slapped her back, so now Guernna kept her distance. Ilana's burns and bruises had healed, and her heart once more held desperate hope. Skilla had come back, and with him word that Jonas was still alive.

The Hun brought back the Greek named Eudoxius but not the sword. Skilla was uncharacteristically quiet, more mature and more somber, and he did not visit her. The rumor was that he'd fought bravely but that the young Roman had beaten him again. Despite this, Edeco treated him with new respect, promising him a finish to things in the spring. Attila, in contrast, pointedly ignored Skilla, a silent rebuke that kept him in anxious agony.

The grass grew higher, and the first flowers appeared. Animals fattened for slaughter and fodder was plentiful. It was time when marching armies could be fed, and thus time for war. Attila signaled his intentions by ordering an assembly at the old Roman fortress of Aquincum near the great bend of the Danube. There, next to the roofless barracks and weedy arena, the Huns would prepare to strike west. Attila announced he'd been asked to be the rescuer of the princess Honoria, sister of the Roman emperor! He would marry her and become king of Rome.

The Hun host came from all points to the ruined fort and consisted of not just the myriad Hun tribes but their barbarian allies. Riding or marching into the sprawling encampment were the Ostrogoths, the Gepids, the Rugi, the Sciri, and the Thuringi, as well as representative contingents of Vandals from Africa, Bagaudae refugees from Gaul, and seaborne raiders from the frozen lands across the Baltic. Some came in armor and some came in rags, some favored the spear and some the ax, some were bowmen and some were swordsmen, but all sensed that

Rome had never seen an invasion such as this. The growing army, and rumors of its might, created a gravity that drew in runaway slaves, fugitive thieves, exiled politicians, discredited aristocrats, unemployed mercenaries, and old soldiers bored with retirement. Many brought wives and children with them to help carry the booty as long as their husband and father stayed alive, and to claim it should he fall. There were whores, conjurers, seers, wizards, priests, prophets, merchants, horse traders, armorers, tanners, cobblers, wheelwrights, carpenters, siege engineers, sutlers, gold dealers, and Roman deserters. The tent city grew, and grew, and grew still more, the grass trampled into spring mud and a third of the army soon sick and coughing. Attila began sending forward contingents of cavalry up the Danube simply to make supply of the mammoth camp feasible. As each advance division left for the west, the kagan had them march through one of the ruined arched gates of Aquincum, as if through a triumphal arch of Rome.

"The whole world is in motion," Skilla murmured to his uncle as they watched fresh troops march out toward the west, even as newcomers were arriving from the east. "I didn't know so many people even existed."

Edeco smiled grimly. "There will be fewer by season's end."

At the new moon of late spring, Attila called the most important warlords to a final conference before a great pyramidal bonfire. This would be his last opportunity for some time to address them all in person with his charismatic intensity. Once the host fully set out and spread like an engulfing wave, he could communicate only by messenger until they gathered again for battle. Once more he dressed humbly, his armor plain, his head bare, his clothes rugged. The only concession to ornament was a gold brooch to hold his cape, in the shape of a golden stag. The Goths wore the oath rings that pledged loyalty, and the Gepids the colored sashes of their clans. Attila's eyes held them all like a fist.

"The People of the Dawn," he began, "are destined to march as far as the setting sun. This is our fate, and has been since the white deer led us out of our homeland."

There was solemn nodding by the Huns in the assembly.

"We will rule from the endless grass to the endless ocean, which none of us have yet seen. All men will unite under us, and any of you here will have your pick of a hundred women and a thousand slaves."

There was a low growl of anticipation.

"The campaign ahead will not be easy." Attila's look was stern. "Rome's western emperor is a fool; all know this. But his general is not a fool, and Aetius, who I know well, will do all in his power to oppose me. As children we were the best of friends, but as men we have become the deadliest of enemies. It must be so, because we are too much alike and want the same thing: empire."

Another murmur of assent.

"The princess Honoria has begged me for rescue from her insipid brother. As the greatest king in the world, I cannot ignore her plea. She yearns for my bed, and who can blame her?"

The warlords laughed.

"Moreover, I've had communication from our brothers the Vandals. Their king Gaiseric has sent word that if we strike the West, he will as well. Cloda will bring his Franks to our side. Rome's own prophets forecast our victory."

Another solemn nodding of heads. All knew that fortune was on the side of the Huns.

"Here is what will happen. We are not going to raid. We are going to *conquer* and stay, until all men swear fealty to the People of the Dawn. We are going to destroy the West in what has become its heart, Gaul. We will defeat the Romans there, enlist their German allies, and descend on Italy and Hispania and make ourselves masters. Then I shall marry Honoria, and rut with her, and make new Attilas." He grinned.

They roared, stamping their feet in an enthusiastic drumming. "Attila! Attila! Attila!" Only his eldest sons scowled.

"Then, with all the West under my banner, I will destroy Marcian and the East."

"Attila!" they cried. They bayed like dogs and screamed like eagles. They howled and yipped and growled. They drummed the ground with spear butts in a rumble so loud that all the camp could hear their enthusiasm.

Attila held up his hands for quiet. "The Hun will win, and why? Because he is not soft like the Roman. A Hun needs no roof, though he can take one. He needs no slave, though he can conquer one. He can sleep on horseback, wash in a stream, and shelter under a tree. The People of the Dawn will triumph not because they come with much, but because they come with little! Every battle has proven this. Cities turn men into weaklings. Their burning will make our women sing."

There was less certainty this time. These men had learned the comforts of a snug hearth or heated bath. They liked fine jewelry and gilded swords.

"Listen to me, all of you! We are going to make the complicated places simple! I want the purity of fire. I want the cleanliness of the steppe. Leave no stones together. Leave no roof intact. Leave nothing but the ashes of new birth, and I swear to you by any god you hold holy, victory will be ours. This is what the gods truly wish!"

"Attila!" they roared.

He nodded, grimly satisfied but knowing the human nature of his followers. "Do this," he promised them, "and I will make you rich with the wreckage."

Like thunder heralding the approaching storm, rumors and reports of the Hun assembly filtered steadily to Aetius. He had made his winter headquarters at Augusta Treverorum in the valley of the upper Mosel, a city with the same hollow heritage as his army. Once a headquarters for emperors, Augusta Treverorum had been sacked, rebuilt, and rewalled. Constantine's palace had become a church, since no imperial delegations came this far north anymore. The baths had closed and the newcomer Franks and Belgicans had turned them into apartments, wooden floors subdividing what had once been great arching halls. The games were no longer held, so the arena had become a marketplace.

Yet Treveris was the most intact and strategic Roman city left in the region. From there, Aetius took ship on the Rhine and traveled up and down, anxiously preaching the strengthening of defenses and the need to burn the river bridges when the time came. Messages went out to the Alans, the Burgundians, the Franks, the Armoricans, and the Saxons,

warning that the Hun aim was to destroy the West and make them vassal nations. Only by uniting, he warned, could they hope to stand.

The barbarian kingdoms answered him cautiously. Most sent
queries about a great sword they had heard of, the sword of Mars, which
Aetius had somehow captured from Attila. Did it really exist? What
power did it have?

Come to me in the spring and see for yourself, Aetius replied.

At the same time, spies from Attila reached these same courts and
urged surrender and obeisance as the only chance of tribal survival. The
coming invasion could not be withstood, they warned, and to ally with
the tottering Roman Empire was folly.

The key, for both Aetius and the wavering tribes, was Theodoric,
king of the Visigoths and the most powerful of the barbarian chieftains.
If he joined with the Romans he gave Aetius and his allies a slim chance
of victory. If he remained neutral or went over to Attila, then all was lost.

Theodoric was well aware of his own strategic importance, and wary
of the wiles of Aetius. The general had manipulated the Germanic tribes
too many times before. In response to every missive and every blandish-
ment, he kept putting Aetius off. "I have no quarrel with Attila and none
with you," he wrote the Roman general. "It is winter, when men should
rest. In spring, the Visigoths will make a decision in our best interests,
not yours."

The emperor Valentinian seemed equally oblivious to the danger. In
response to Aetius's pleas for more men, weapons, and supplies, he responded with lengthy letters complaining about the incompetence of tax
collectors, the miserly ways of the rich, the dishonesty of bureaucrats,
the treasonous plotting of his sister, and the selfishness of military plan-
ners. Couldn't the army appreciate the problems of the imperial court?
Didn't Aetius understand that the emperor was doing all he could?

*I suspect your spies are quite misinformed about the intentions of At-
tila. You may be unaware that Marcian has suspended the tribute
payments that the East has made to the Huns and has recalled troops
from Persia. Isn't it more likely that the Hun's wrath will fall on Constantinople? Isn't Attila one of your oldest friends? Have not the Huns*

served bravely as mercenaries in your own campaigns? Is not my half
of the Empire poorer than Marcian's? Why would Attila attack here?
Your fears are exaggerated, general. . . .

It was like the prattle of a nagging and self-pitying wife, Aetius thought
bitterly. He knew Valentinian had committed large portions of the budget to circuses, churches, palaces, and banquets. The new emperors refused to acknowledge they could no longer afford to live like the old.
Legions were at half strength. Contractors were corrupt. Equipment was
shoddy. Maybe the prophets are right, the general thought. Maybe it's
Rome's time to die. My time, as well. And yet . . .

He looked out at the green Mosel, swollen with spring rains. This
river had long since lost the thick traffic of imperial trade but still led to a
remnant of Roman agriculture and commerce in the northern reaches of
Gaul. The barbarians might disdain Rome, but they also copied it in inferior, almost childlike, fashion. Their churches were rustic and their
houses crude, their food plain, their animals unkempt, and their contempt for literacy impregnable to reason. Still, they pretended at Romanness, preening in plundered clothing and living in half-ruined villas, like
monkeys in a temple. They tried to cook with aniseed and fish oil. Some
men cut their hair short in Roman style, and some women traded their
clogs for sandals, despite the mud.

It was something. If Attila won, there would not be even mimicry.
The future would be a return of wilderness, the eclipse of all knowledge,
and the extinction of the Christian Church. Couldn't the fools see it?

But of course one fool could: Zerco. It was odd how the dwarf had
become a favored companion. He was not just funny, he was perceptive.
He came back not just with information about Attila's power but about
the Hun himself: His fear that civilization was corrupting. Aetius remembered Attila as the quietest and most sullen of all the Huns he'd
met while a hostage in their camp. Aetius had wondered if the unhappy
man, nursing some secret wounds, was simple.

The opposite was true, of course, and while Hun warlords had
preened and boasted, Attila had made secret alliances with a fierce, quiet
magnetism. He had proved to be as masterly a tactician off the battlefield

as on. While others had strutted, he had risen, wooing, allying, and killing. And what had been a plague of raiders had turned, under Attila, into something far worse: a horde of would-be conquerors who wanted to go back to a salvation of animal-like simplicity.

All this Zerco tried to explain and more: that the core of the Hun army was not huge, that the barbarians often quarreled like dogs over a scrap of meat, and that their spirits were winded quickly if they could not prevail. "They will win only if the West believes they *must* win," the dwarf argued. "Fight them, sire, and they will back off like a jackal looking for an easier meal."

"My allies are afraid to stand up to them. They have cowed the world."

"Yet it is often the bully who is the most fearful and weak."

The young man Zerco had brought with him, this Jonas from Constantinople, also had spirit. He was in love with a captive woman—ah, the age when such longing could consume you!—and yet hadn't allowed it to entirely cloud his reason. He had proved to be an able diplomatic secretary, despite his fantasies of rescue and revenge. While the youth chafed under his scholarly duties—"I want to fight!"—he was too useful to waste as a mere soldier. He was as interesting as Zerco, recounting how he had outlasted the arrows of a rival in a duel and arguing that Rome could do the same. As dusk fell in a March chill, Aetius ordered a fire lit and these two friends brought to him. Leaves were budding, and as soon as the grass was high enough to feed their horses, the Huns would come. On this side of the Rhine, every ally would be watching to see how many would unite under the Roman general. If he could not hold firm, all would come apart.

"I have a mission for each of you," Aetius told them.

He could see the Byzantine brighten. "I've been practicing with your cavalry!"

"Which will serve, eventually. In the meantime, there's a more important and pressing task."

The young man leaned forward, eager.

"First, Zerco." He turned to the dwarf. "I'm going to send you to Bishop Anianus in Aurelia."

"Aurelia?"

"It is the capital of the Alan tribe, whose name the new rulers corrupt in their tongue so that it sounds like 'Orleans.' It is the gateway to
the richest valley of Gaul, the Loire, and the strategic key to the
province."

Zerco stood up in self-mockery, his eyes at belt level. "I am certain
to stop him if he gets that far, general." His eyes twinkled. "And enjoy
myself if he doesn't."

Aetius smiled. "I want you to listen and talk, not fight. I send you to
Anianus as a token of friendship and, indeed, one of your tasks is to befriend him. I'm told he is a particularly pious Roman who has inspired
great respect among the Alans; they think him holy and good luck.
When the Huns come he will be watched closely by the population. You
must convince him to lead in our cause."

"But why me, a halfling?" Zerco protested. "Surely a man of greater
stature—"

"Would be watched too closely by Sangibanus, king of the Alan
tribe. I have received word that Sangibanus is listening to emissaries
from the Huns. He fears Attila, and wants to keep what he has. Once
more I need you to play the fool, caper in his court, and pass me your
judgment on which side he's leaning toward. If he betrays Aurelia to Attila, then all of Gaul is opened to invasion. If he holds, we have time to
win."

"I will learn his mind better than he knows it himself!" Zerco
promised.

"And if there is a plot of betrayal then I will fight to stop it," Jonas
chimed in.

Aetius turned to him. "No, you have an even more important and
difficult task, Bringer of the Sword. I am sending you to Tolosa."

"Tolosa!" Far in the south of Gaul, it was two weeks' journey away.

"Somehow King Theodoric must be persuaded to ride with us. I
have reasoned, argued, and begged in correspondence, and still he re-
fuses to commit. Sometimes a single visit is worth more than a hundred
letters. I am making you my personal envoy. I don't care how you do it,
but you must bring the Visigoths to our cause."

"But how?"

"You know Attila. Speak your heart."

While Zerco and Julia set out for Aurelia, I ascended the Rhine by boat. All seemed quiet in the greening valley, war a distant dream, and yet change was in the air. Cavalry clattered by on the old Roman roads, evidence of preparations, and when the ship put in to deliver goods and messages or take on provisions, there was a solemn and watchful atmosphere in the riverside villages and old Roman forts. In the evenings the men honed weapons. The women smoked meat and loaded the last of the previous year's grain into bags in case flight became inevitable. All had heard rumors of stirrings to the east. Few had ever seen a Hun. At inns I warned of Hun ferocity. At fortresses, I reviewed troops in Aetius's name.

Aetius had asked me to detour to the legionary fortress of Sumelocenna. "I told the tribune named Stenis there to make his men into wasps," the general recalled. "I want you to see if he has succeeded and write me the result."

The fort seemed low and unimpressive as I approached, one tower broken and its paint long peeled away. Yet as I drew nearer I took heart from what I saw. The ditches had been cleared of brush and weeds. A hedge of wooden stakes had been planted within crossbow range to ward off siege towers and battering rams. The old walls were dotted with pale new stones. Peasant recruits were drilling in the courtyard.

"We are a nut Attila might not want to bother cracking," said Stenis with rare and welcome pride in his voice. "A year ago a child could have captured this outpost, and Aetius recognized that in an instant. Now I'd like to see an army try. We've built twenty new catapults, a hundred crossbows, and recruited seventy-five men."

"I will tell this to the general." I decided not to reveal the size of Attila's army.

"Just tell him that I am ready to sting."

I traveled southwest to the Rhone where a barge carried me downriver toward the Mediterranean. As I traveled south, the sun brightened and the land grew lush. It was beautiful country, greener than distant

Byzantium, and I wondered what it would be like to live here. Yet the oncoming rush of spring also heightened my apprehension. Time was hurrying, and so would Attila. How could I persuade Theodoric?

I bought a horse near the river's mouth and took the main Roman road west toward Tolosa and the Visigoths, occasionally spying the glittering sea far below to my left. How far I had come! From home. From Ilana. From dreams to nightmare.

It was late April when I finally came to the Visigothic capital in the old Roman city, its central fortress rearing above the red tile rooftops. I paused a minute before the city's gray stone walls and wondered how I would convince these semicivilized barbarians to ally with the Empire they had half conquered, resented, envied, and feared. Frighten Theodoric with stories of Attila? My mission was absurd.

Yet destiny has its own devices. Unknown to me, watching secretly from a slit window high in a tower, was my answer.

XXI

THE SCOURGE OF GOD

The armies of Attila were too huge to advance on any single road or path, so they ascended the Danube valley in a series of parallel columns, engulfing the ancient border between Rome and Germania like a wave. The Hun cavalry went first as the tip of the arrow, striking ahead of any warning and overpowering weak garrisons before they had time to prepare. The heavier Ostrogoth cavalry came next, their big horses, heavy shields, and long lances crushing any line that resisted. Should the inhabitants instead try to seek refuge in a tower, fort, monastery, or church, they then would be left for the long snake of infantry, its ranks speckled with mercenaries and engineers with the skill to build catapults, siege towers, and battering rams. Roiling columns of smoke marked where each pocket of resistance had been overcome.

Never had the Huns assembled so great an army, and never had its supply been so challenging. They stripped the land like locusts. Those who hid emerged to desolation. The upper Danube valley had become a wasteland. Every house was burned. Every granary was emptied. Every vine and fruit tree was chopped down. It was not so much conquest as depopulation. After slaughtering the men and raping and enslaving the women, the Hun cavalry took particular care to kill infants and pregnant women. No generation would be left to seek revenge. The few surviving orphaned children shivered in the woods like animals. Abandoned dogs went feral and fed on the corpses of their former masters.

One by one the outposts of civilization became ruins. Astura, Augustiana, Faviana, Lauriacum, Lentia, Boiodurum, Castra Batava, Castra Augusta, Castra Regina . . . all were erased from history. It was as if the earth was swallowing civilization. Ash drifted in the air instead of apple blossom, and every smashed home had the forbidding smell of burnt timber, rot, and damp decay. Dried blood spattered intricate mosaics. Wall murals were smeared with the brains and effluent of the owners who died looking at them. The prophets were right: The armies of doom were signaling the end of the world. Never in a thousand years would Europe forget this march. Evil had come on shaggy steppe ponies, and the angels had fled. It was the spring when days grew darker.

Attila was well pleased.

He paused one afternoon to eat the looted rations of a ruptured Roman fort called Sumelocenna, its garrison massacred with particular fury because it fought so uncharacteristically bravely. Attila rested his boots on the body of a tribune they said had been named Stenis, noticing that the dead man's tunic was closed by a golden clasp in the shape of a wasp. The king bent to rip the brooch free. He had never seen its like before and would give it to Hereka. "The man who wore it stung," he would tell her.

No officers had trained Attila in the arts of war. No courtiers had coached him in the grace of nobles. No singer had persuaded his rough fingers to touch harp or lyre. No woman had soothed his constant anger, that simmering rage from a childhood of beatings and harsh training and a manhood of treachery and war. No priest had explained to his satisfaction why he was here, and no prophet had dared suggest he could fail. He was a primeval force, sent to cleanse the world.

Huns were different from other men, he believed—so different that perhaps they weren't men at all but gods. Or perhaps there *were* no fellow men but rather that his people preyed on a world inhabited by odd forms of lower beings, mud men. He didn't know. Certainly the deaths of these Romans had no meaning to him. Their lives were too foreign, their habits inexplicable. He understood that life was struggle, and the joy that some found in simple existence utterly baffled him. One was either a killer or a meal. This belief that life was pitiless colored everything he did. Attila would lead his Huns to glory but he trusted no one. He loved no one. He relied on no one. He knew there would never be any rest, for to rest was to die. Wasn't it when he'd slept that the Roman bitch had almost set fire to him? What a lesson *that* had been. He slept only in snatches now, his features aging, his dreams troubled. Yet this was how it *should* be. Killing was the essence of life. Destruction held the only promise of safety.

Attila was no strategist. He couldn't envision the lands he planned to conquer. Their desirability, or lack of it, was almost immaterial. Attila understood fear, and he was concocting a catastrophe, but a catastrophe that was to fall on Aetius. For every Roman he killed, two or three went running to his target in Gaul. Each had to be fed. Each carried panic like a plague. In every story his horsemen grew uglier, their aim more deadly, their stench more rank, their greed more insatiable. This use of terror was necessary. His horde, vast though it was, was small compared to the millions upon millions in the Roman world. Its strength was its seeming invincibility. Huns were never defeated because no one believed they *could* be defeated.

He didn't know that Aetius began to intercept tens of thousands of fugitives like a net, drafting the men into his forces and sending the women and children to help farm.

Attila had no intention of fighting Aetius if he didn't have to; the man was too good a soldier. But if he did fight him it would be when Aetius was nearly alone, his allies fragmented and quarreling, his cities burning, his food supplies stripped by the homeless, his legionaries sick and demoralized, his emperor wavering, his lieutenants betraying. Attila had never lost a fight because he never fought fairly. Surprise, deception, treachery, superior numbers, terror, and stealth had let him win every contest, from the murder of his brother to the destruction of the eastern provinces. Only the loss of the old sword secretly troubled him. He knew it was only a talisman, shrewdly invented by himself, but his followers believed in its magic. Leadership was all about belief. Its disappearance was never spoken of, but it planted a seed of fear.

Victories would make up for the loss of symbol. The barbarian led his entourage of warlords and messengers up a grassy slope to look back down the Danube valley at the long winding columns making up his attack force, stretching back to a hazy horizon, the hard men resting on tough ponies that cropped the grass. Attila never lost because if he did lose, he knew, these jackals would turn against him. His warlords could be kept in harness only with the booty that was corrupting them. The more they took the more they craved, and the more they craved, the more like Romans they became. Attila saw no way out of this dilemma except to destroy everything. In desolation, he believed, was the salvation of the Hun.

He looked forward to the wasteland.

And to what he would finally do to Ilana when his sword was recovered.

It was the way of the world, a cycle that could never end.

Ilana had become an exhibit in Attila's bizarre zoo.

Like Attila's wives and slave girls, she had been brought for the invasion. But instead of a comfortable rolling wagon with felt canopy and carpets, her home was a trundling cage of wooden poles, its grid roof open to sun and rain. It was one of a dozen wagons in a train that included some captured bears; a lion liberated from a Roman villa; a pacing wolf; three captured Roman generals squeezed into a single iron enclosure; and squalling badgers, Attila's favorite animal. The wagons were normally used for transporting slaves and prisoners, but any Roman slaves were pressed into Attila's great army and any liberated criminals were simply executed. So Attila had decided to load the transports with curiosities— among them the woman who had tried to burn him alive and who, for purposes not yet fully explained, had been allowed to remain living.

His temporary mercy was torment. Ilana's life had been reduced to animal-like squalor as she sat dully in the lurching wagon amid a great, dusty, fly-plagued army: her clothing filthy, her privacy gone, her station abased. At noon she was hot and at night she was cold. She got barely enough water to drink, let alone bathe. Her keeper was Guernna, who enjoyed mocking her from a safe distance.

"I'm sure he'll come to your rescue at any moment," the German girl cooed to the Roman when she brought her scraps of food. "He'll cut his way through a half million men with that sword he stole."

"He's waiting for both of us, Guernna," she replied with more spunk than she really felt. "Your liberation, too. When battle is joined we'll both have a chance to escape to the Romans."

"Do you think there'll be any Romans left, Ilana? Edeco says this is the biggest army the world has ever seen."

Ilana believed it. The wagon had bogged down once in a rut at the crest of a hill. While a dozen Gepid infantry heaved to clear it, she'd had a chance to gaze backward in wonder at the great host stretching to the horizon. Fields of spears rocked like wheat in a breeze; herds of horses churned up dust like thunderheads; and wagons heaped with tents and booty crawled across meadows like elephants, grinding the grass to stubble.

"Aetius and Jonas will have a great army, too."

Guernna smiled. "We are all wondering what Attila will eventually do to you, Ilana. Most of the women suggest fire, since that is what you nearly did to him. Some think crucifixion, and some think a rape by Ostrogoths or perhaps by animals. Some think you will be flayed; and some think Attila will wait until he has enough Roman gold to melt and pour down your throat, burning you from inside out and making a cast of your body."

"How amusing all this speculation must be. And what do you think, Guernna?"

"I think he is devising an execution so clever that none of us has thought of it yet!" Her eyes danced at the thought. Guernna had little imagination and admired it in others.

"And you will help him."

Guernna looked reproachful. "Ilana! I am the only one feeding you. You were wrong to attack our master, yet still I bring you water and throw a bucket to wash out your filth. Don't you expect the best from me?"

"The best, as you know, would be a spear between my ribs. I think I could expect that from you, given your betrayal when we tried to escape that night."

Guernna smiled. "Yes, killing you *would* consummate our relation-ship. But I must think of the other women, too, sweet Ilana. It is always exciting to watch torture. We have all discussed it, and what we really want to do is hear you scream."

Aetius had planned to burn the Rhine bridges, but Hun cavalry arrived three days before defenders thought it possible. They swept across at midnight, arrows plucking away the engineers, and so crossed the Rhine as if the great barrier of the river hardly existed. Attila himself crossed two days later, watching with interest the bodies from upstream floating by on the current, bloated and bearing Hun arrows. His soldiers were doing their work. Aetius had established his own army at Argentorate, a hundred miles to the south, and the Hun plan was to outflank him through the forested highlands of northeastern Gaul and break out east of Luttia. The cavalry could then sweep southward over the fertile flat-lands, take the strategic crossroads of Aurelia, and hold the strategic cen-ter of the West.

Attila rode toward horizons of smoke, with more smoke behind—a ring of smoke that marked the devastation of his armies in all directions. No cohesive resistance had formed. The Franks had retreated, and the other tribes were hesitating. If the Huns struck hard enough and quickly enough, they would annihilate Aetius before he could gather a credible force. Cities were emptied, armories were captured, aqueducts were de-liberately broken, and granaries were looted. Crows were so bloated from feasting on the dead that they staggered on Roman roads like drunken men.

Thousands of opportunists, traitors, and the fearful were joining At-tila's invasion: craven chieftains, escaped slaves, greedy mercenaries. Some were fleeing a bad marriage, broken heart, or debt. There were not as many as the Hun king had hoped, but those who did enlist joined the slaughter with a kind of hysteria. All rules had ended. Hell had tri-umphed over Heaven. Anarchy and pillage provided opportunities to set-tle old scores, act on resentment against the rich, or take by force a maiden who had spurned earnest advances. As each law was broken, the next seemed easier to shatter. The indiscipline carried into the Hun army itself, where quarrels quickly turned murderous. The warlords had to separate feuding soldiers like snarling dogs, and maintained some semblance of order only by whip, chain, and execution. So huge was the army, and so far-flung were its wings and columns, that it was barely controllable.

Attila knew he was riding a whirlwind, but he was the god of storms.

It was at a clearing in a wood in Gaul that he encountered the Roman holy man who would give him a different title. A patrol of Huns had roped a Christian hermit who was apparently so stupid that he'd been making a pilgrimage right into the path of Attila's army. The cavalry laughed as they trotted the pilgrim first one way and then another, jerking on the lines. The hermit was screaming, perhaps trying to egg on his own martyrdom. "Enjoy your triumph because your days are numbered, Satan's spawn!" the old man cried in Hunnish as he staggered. "Prophecy foretells your doom!"

This interested Attila, who believed in destiny and had bones thrown and entrails read. After killing a few prognosticators in blinding rages, his prophets had learned to tell him what he wanted to hear: so much so, that they bored him. Now this hermit had a different view. So he ordered the Hun soldiers to back up their horses until the ropes were taut and the man was trapped in place. "You speak our tongue, old man."

"God gives me the gift to warn the damned." He was ragged, filthy, and barefoot.

"What prophecy?"

"That your own sword will smite you! That the darkest night heralds dawn!"

Some warlords murmured uneasily at this mention of a sword, and Attila scowled. "We are the People of the Dawn, hermit."

The man looked at Attila quizzically, as if scarcely able to believe such nonsense. "No. You come in dust and leave in smoke, and blot out the sun. You are night creatures, sprung from the earth."

"We are restoring the earth. We don't cut it. We don't chop it."

"But you feed off men who *do*, old warrior! What nonsense Huns spout! If Attila was here, he'd laugh at your foolishness!"

The Huns did laugh, enjoying this little joke.

"And where do you think Attila is, old man?" the king asked mildly.

"How should I know? Sleeping with his thousand wives, I suspect, or tormenting a holy pilgrim instead of daring to face the great Flavius Aetius. Aye, easier to pick on the pious than fight an armed foe!"

Attila's face lost its amusement. "I will face Aetius soon enough."

The hermit squinted at the rider more closely. "You're Attila? You?"

"I am."

"You wear no riches."

"I need none."

"You bear no sign of rank."

"All men but *you* know who I am."

The holy man nodded. "I wear none, either. God Almighty knows who *I* am."

"And who are you?"

"His messenger."

Attila laughed. "Trussed and helpless? What kind of God is that?"

"What god do you have, barbarian?"

"Attila the Hun believes in himself."

His captive pointed to the haze of smoke. "You ordered that?"

"I order the world."

"The innocents you have slaughtered! The babes you have made orphans!"

"I make no apology for war. I'm here to rescue the emperor's sister."

The hermit barked a laugh, and his eyes lit with recognition. He waved his finger at Attila. "Yes, *now* I know who you are. I recognize you, monster! A plague! A whip, sent out of the East to punish us for our sins! You are the Scourge of God!"

The king looked puzzled. "The Scourge of God?"

"It is the only explanation. You are a tool of the divine, a wicked punishment as dire as the Great Flood or Plagues of Egypt! You are Baal and Beelzebub, Ashron and Pluto, sent to lash us as divine punish-ment!"

His men waited for Attila to kill the crazy man, but instead he looked thoughtful. "The Scourge of God. This is a new title, is it not, Edeco?"

"To add to a thousand others. Shall we kill him, kagan?"

Attila slowly smiled. "No . . . the Scourge of God. He has explained me, has he not? He has justified me to every Christian we meet. No, I *like* this hermit. Let him go—yes, let him go and give him a donkey and gold piece. I want him sent ahead, sent to the city of Aurelia. Do you know where that is, old man?"

The hermit squirmed against the ropes. "I was born there."

"Good. I like your insult, and will adopt it as my title. Go to your native Aurelia, hermit, and tell them Attila is coming. Tell them I come to cleanse their sins with blood, like the Scourge of God. Ha! It is *I* who am His messenger, not *you!*" And he laughed, again. "I, Attila! A tool of the divine!"

XXII

THEODORIC'S
DAUGHTER

Tolosa had been a Celtic city, then Roman, and now Visigothic; and the new rulers had done little more than occupy the decaying buildings of the old. Their famed prowess in battle was not matched by any expertise in architecture. The strategic city on a ford of the Garumna had long dominated southwestern Gaul, and when the Visigoth king Athaulf agreed to give up Iberia and send the Roman princess Galla Placidia back to Rome in return for new lands in Aquitania, Tolosa became the natural capital. The barbarians did front the old Roman walls with a ditch and dike, but inside the city it was as if a poor family had moved into a fine house and added tawdry touches of their own. The stone and brickwork was old and patched, the streets were potholed and poorly repaired, paint was older than the inhabitants, and dwellings of stucco and marble had additions of timber, daub, and thatch.

Yet under the great barbarian king Theodoric—who had reigned so long, thirty-six years, that most of his subjects had known no other king—Tolosa throbbed with activity. As Roman culture had been layered upon Celtic, so now was German tribal culture layered upon Roman; and the result was a fusion of pagan artisan, imperial bureaucrat, and barbarian warrior that had given the city an energy it hadn't seen for a hundred years. Traders and farmwives bawled in half a dozen tongues from the crowded marketplaces, Arian priests ministered to thick crowds of illiterate tribesmen, and children chased each other through the streets in numbers not seen in living memory.

Their ferocity was still there, however, and it was this ferocity that Aetius hoped I could somehow help harness. The Visigoths were as haughty as Huns and as regal as Greeks. They were as famed for the long lances of their heavy cavalry as Attila's men were for their bows; and the palace guards looked like mailed, bearded giants, their pale eyes glinting from beneath the brow of iron helmets like bright, suspicious jewels. Their legs were like tree trunks, their arms like thighs. When the tips of their long swords rested on the chipped marble floor, the pommels came to their chests. Here were men who should have no fear of Huns. Why weren't they riding with us?

Perhaps they hesitated because their ancestors had been put to flight by the Huns three generations before. Had the Visigoths journeyed across Europe only to be faced with this peril once again? Would they at last make a stand? Or become vassals of Attila? I had to convince Theodoric that survival was with Aetius and the hated Romans.

My arrival had already been promised by correspondence from Aetius. A Visigothic captain helped stable my horse, gave me watered wine to quench my thirst, and finally escorted me to Theodoric. There was a courtyard in the palace, familiar enough except that its fountain was dry because no one could be found with the skill to repair it, and its plants dead because no barbarian could be bothered to keep them alive. Then we entered the reception hall beyond. The old Roman standards and symbols of office were long gone, of course, the pillars hung now with the bright shields and crossed lances of the Goths. Banners and captured tapestries gave color atop faded paint, and the marble floors were obscured by rushes that had been strewn to catch the mud of barbarian boots. High windows let in a crosshatch of light. Nobles clustered and gossiped behind a railing that separated Theodoric's carved wooden throne from petitioners and courtiers. A single aide stood by to make notes—could the fifty-six-year-old king read?—and the monarch's crown was a circlet of simple steel. His hair was long, his beard gray, his nose curved, and his expression set in a permanent frown. This was a man used to saying no.

Theodoric beckoned me forward through the wood railing to stand where we could talk without being overheard. I bowed, trying to remember the formal manners of Maximinus, my diplomatic mentor, and marveling at the odyssey that had brought me here. "I bring you greetings, King Theodoric, from your friend and ally Flavius Aetius. Great happenings shake the world, and great deeds are needed."

"General Aetius has already sent me such greetings a hundred times in missives this winter," the barbarian replied with a deep, skeptical voice. "The greetings always come with tidings, and the tidings with requests. Is this not so, Hagan?" He turned to his scribe.

"The Roman wants us to fight his battle for him," the scribe said.

"Not for him, *with* him," I corrected. "Attila is marching on the West, and if we don't stand together, all of us will perish separately, frightened and alone."

"I have heard this talk from Aetius before," the king replied. "He is a master at playing on the fears of the tribes. Always there is some dire peril that requires us to muster our armies for Rome and shed *our* blood for *his* Empire. Yet even as he begs for our help, he is reluctant to promise how many legions *he* will muster or what *other* tribes will join. Nor can he explain why Attila should be my enemy. I have no quarrel with the Huns."

This would be difficult. "The world has changed, sire." I recited what Theodoric already knew: the plea of Honoria, the accession of Marcian in the East, and the claim of the Frankish prince Cloda in the north. He listened impatiently.

"And then there is the matter of the Greek doctor Eudoxius," I tried.

"Who?" The king turned in curiosity to Hagan.

"I think he is referring to the man who stirred up the Bagaudae in the north," the scribe said, "an intellectual who led a rabble."

"In the revolt that Aetius crushed a few years ago," I added.

"Ah, I remember this Greek now. What about him?" Theodoric asked.

"He fled to Attila."

"So?"

"He persuaded Attila to send him as embassy to Gaiseric in Carthage. It was when Eudoxius came back from the Vandals that the Huns decided to march on the West." At these words something moved in the shadows, jerking as if startled. It was a shrouded figure, I realized, listening from an alcove. Who was that?

"Gaiseric?" Theodoric's gaze narrowed at mention of the Vandal king. "Why is Attila talking to the Vandals?"

"An equally pressing question, sire, is why are the Vandals talking to the Huns?"

I had at last struck a nerve. Attila was distant, and the Roman emperor Valentinian impotent, but Gaiseric and his haughty Vandals were the one group the Visigoths truly feared. They were a powerful tribe of Germanic origin like themselves, lodged in Africa, and no doubt they coveted Aquitania. I could see that this news had a powerful effect. I remembered hearing that the Vandals had humiliated the Visigoths by rejecting and mutilating Theodoric's daughter. "Gaiseric is marching with the Huns?" he asked.

"Perhaps. We don't know. We only know that to wait and do nothing is folly."

Theodoric sat back on his throne, fingers drumming as he thought. Gaiseric, whose warriors were the equivalent of his own. Gaiseric, who alone matched Theodoric in age, longevity of rule, and list of bloody victories. Gaiseric, who had shamed him as no man ever had by scarring Berta, his beloved child. He squinted at me, this young Roman before him. "What proof do you have of what you say?"

"The word of Aetius and the favor of God."

"The favor of God?"

"How else to explain my possession of the sword of Mars? Have you heard of this relic? I stole it from Attila himself and carried it to Aetius. It is reputed to be a sword of the gods that Attila has used to arouse his people. Now Aetius is using it to rally the West."

Theodoric looked skeptical. "That's the sword there, on your belt?"

I smiled at this opportunity to cite more evidence, and lifted out the knife I had taken from Eudoxius. "This is a dagger I took from the Greek. For the sword, imagine something a hundred times larger."

"Humph." He shook his head. The hooded figure in the shadows, I noticed, had disappeared. "The Huns are advancing on Aetius, not the Visigoths," Theodoric insisted. "What proof do you have of Vandals? I want to know about Vandals, not Huns."

I hesitated. "Eudoxius himself told me that Gaiseric had pledged to make war with Attila, meaning the Huns and Vandals are one. Gaiseric hopes Attila will crush you."

"Yet how do you *know* this?"

"We captured the doctor. I was captive in the Hun camp, and when we made off with that sword we took the Greek with us."

"So this Greek could tell me himself."

Here I dropped my head. "No. The Huns pursued us, and there was a fight at a Roman tower. He escaped."

The Visigoth king laughed. "See? What proof for any of what Aetius claims!" His secretary Hagan smiled scornfully.

"The whole Empire and world are in peril!" I exclaimed. "Isn't that proof enough? With you, Aetius can win. Without—"

"What proof?" Theodoric demanded softly.

My jaw was rigid with frustration. "My word."

The king looked at me quietly a long time, and finally softened just a little. "I do not know who you are, young man, but you have spoken as well as you could for a master who is notoriously elusive. My frustration is not with you but with Aetius, whom I know too well. Go, let my stewards show you lodging, while I think about what you have said. I do not trust Aetius. Should I trust you? I tell you only this: When the Visigoths ride, it will be for a Visigothic cause, not Rome's."

I was depressed. Theodoric's faint praise seemed only to presage failure. That happy moment when my father first announced that I had an opportunity to accompany an embassy to Attila seemed an age ago. What I had hoped would make my future seemed only to cloud it. Our diplomacy with the Huns had been a disaster. My attempts to win or rescue Ilana had come to nothing. Now, here I was again, a fledgling diplomat, and the one proof I needed to persuade the Visigoths—the testimony of Eudoxius—I had lost at the tower. So *this* embassy seemed unlikely to be any more fruitful than the earlier one! I'd never really persuaded anyone, now that I thought of it, from the fetching Olivia in Constantinople to this barbarian king. What a joke that I was an envoy at all!

I could wait here in Tolosa for the end, I supposed. My presence would make little difference to the poor army of Aetius, and it would take a while for Attila to ride this far. Or I could return and hurl myself into battle and end things sooner: There was a certain finality in that. There would be no unity against the Huns; Rome was too old and too tired. There would only be hopeless battle, fire, oblivion. . . .

A knock came on the door to my chamber. I was in no mood to answer, but it came again and again with insistence. I finally opened the door to find a servant bearing a tray with dried fruit and meats, a gesture of hospitality I hadn't expected. The figure was wearing a long gown with a hood pulled over her head. "Sustenance after your journey, ambassador," a woman's voice said.

"I'm not hungry."

"Even for company?"

I was wary. "What kind of offer is that?"

"To hear more of what you know."

Hear more? Who had heard any of my quiet discussion with Theodoric? Then I remembered. "You were listening from the shadows, from that pillar behind the throne."

"As one who understands your warning better, even, than you."

"But who are you?"

"Hurry." The tone was nasal. "I'm not supposed to go to a man's chambers."

So I let her in. To my surprise she kept her head covered, her face in a dark hole. She put the platter down on a side table and stood back. "I need to watch you eat."

"What?"

"I'll explain."

I looked at the food doubtfully.

"It's not poisoned."

I took a dried apple and bit tentatively, then sipped from the ewer of water. There was nothing peculiar. So I took out my dagger and cut a piece of meat.

"Yes." Her breath was a hiss. "Where did you get that knife?" The question was as sharp as a slap.

I glanced down, suddenly realizing what her interest was. "From Eudoxius, the Greek doctor. I took it from him when he tried to escape. He almost stabbed me with it."

"And where did *he* get it?"

I looked more closely at the weapon. Once more I noticed the fine carving of the ivory handle, the inlaid ruby, and the pretty glint of the blade. "I don't know."

"I do."

I looked at her in mystification.

"Surely you must know who I am by now. The whole world knows the shame of Berta." Reaching up, she pulled back her hood like a curtain.

Involuntarily, I gasped in horror.

She was a woman, yes, but a horribly disfigured one, puckered with pink and purple scars. One ear was almost entirely missing and another slit so that its two pieces ended in wrinkled points. Her lips had been sawn crosswise, turning any smile into a grimace. Worst was her nose, its tip cut off and the remainder flattened so that her nostrils were like those of a pig.

"Now you know who I am, don't you?"

My heart was hammering. "Princess, I did not imagine . . ."

"No man can imagine my shame or the humiliation of my father or the need to banish mirrors from my quarters. My own king cannot bear to look at me, and keeps me locked away unless I cover my head or mask my face. I scuttle in the shadows of this palace like a ghost, an unwanted reminder of the arrogance of the Vandals."

"You were the wife of Lochnar the Vandal." I said it with pity.

"Daughter-in-law to the great Gaiseric himself, a symbol of unity between my people and his. How proud I was on my wedding day! Great armored regiments of the Goths and Vandals lined the processional path in Carthage, and Gaiseric paid a small fortune in dowry to my father! And yet when Valentinian offered Lochnar a Roman princess instead, I was forgotten by him in an instant."

"But why . . . ?" I was shocked at her ugliness.

"Lochnar demanded a divorce so he could marry a Roman Christian, but no daughter of Theodoric is going to be so easily cast aside. My father wouldn't give him one. So finally my father-in-law, Gaiseric, in a drunken rage at our intransigence about giving his son a divorce so he could ally himself with Rome, turned me into a monster. It would have been kinder if he had murdered me."

"Why do you ask about my dagger?"

"Because I know who owned it." She looked bitterly at the weapon. "I knew of your mission and watched you ride here from a tower window. I know Gaiseric as well as you know Attila, and I've been warning my father that the one is simply the twin of the other. Then you strode into our chambers and I almost fainted to see the hilt of that knife at your side. That"—she pointed—"is the blade that Gaiseric used to cut me."

I dropped it as if it were hot. "I didn't know! Please, I'm sorry! Eudoxius tried to cut *me* with it, so I took it from him!"

"Of course you didn't know." Her tone was calm as she walked forward and picked the weapon up, balancing it in her palm. "Even the bravest or craziest fool wouldn't bring this into my father's house if he knew its history. Only someone innocent, from ignorance, would do that."

"Eudoxius must have gotten it from Gaiseric—"

"To show Attila." Her voice was low but bitter. "To unload his own sin. Do you know what Gaiseric said to me? That because of my stubborn pride no other man would ever have me and that I would have a face to frighten children and revolt lovers. He said he hoped I lived a hundred years, and that every day of those years I think of my folly for having dared defy a prince of the Vandals."

"Lady, it was a truly monstrous thing that he did."

"Can you imagine my hatred? Can you imagine my burning desire for revenge? Yet so embarrassed is my father that he sits frozen in this old palace, too afraid to challenge Gaiseric by himself and too proud to ask for Roman help. But now Rome asks for him! Now my deepest enemy has become allied with yours!" Her eyes flashed fire. "You are a gift from God, Jonas Alabanda, a messenger sent like the archangel to shake my father from his lethargy. He allows himself doubts, but I had none when I saw your dagger. You have a token of challenge from the Vandals, which you didn't even know you bore."

I saw hope. "Then you must convince your father that what I say is true!"

"I will demand the justice that is every Visigothic woman's right. Attila thinks he has guaranteed his victory by allying with Gaiseric. But I say every person who bargains with that wicked Vandal is poisoned by fate, and Attila will be, too." She held up the knife, her knuckles white and fist trembling. "By the blade that ended my happiness, I swear that my people will ride to the aid of Aetius and Rome, because to join with him is to defeat Hun and Vandal . . . once and for all!"

The signal fires were lit and the horns sounded from ridge crests to the deepest valleys. All Aquitania was stirring, from the shores of the great western ocean to the peaks of the central massif. The king was calling the Visigoths to war! The arrows fletched in the long dark days of winter were bundled and strapped, the long swords of the Germans were rasped on oiled stones, and the stout lances with their leaf-shaped tips of silver were carried forth. Great shields were shouldered, armor strapped, and helmets polished. Anxious boys were chosen for the campaign, while, groaning disappointment, their younger brothers were ordered to care for home at least one more season. Somber wives packed satchels of dried meat and grain while daughters stitched campaign clothing and wept at what might come. The Visigoths were going to war! Saddles were oiled, boots soled with new leather, belts cinched, and travel cloaks tied. The gathering men could be seen coming down from a dozen hills into every village and from a dozen villages into every town, rivulets becoming streams and streams becoming rivers.

The word had gone out. At long last, Berta would begin to be avenged.

In Tolosa, a thousand knights were waiting on horseback for their king. Their horses were huge, the hooves heavy, the tails tied with ribbons and the manes decked with coins. The Visigothic helmets were high peaked and plumed, their horse shields oval, and their spears were as high as a roof. It thrilled me to wait with them.

Finally stepping out onto the old Roman portico was Theodoric himself, tall and resplendent in gilded mail and a shield embossed with bright bronze. His sons Thorismund and Theodoric the Younger came with him, just as proudly armored and armed; and at the sight of them the assembled warriors roared greeting with a cry that made me shiver.

Their king spoke deeply but quietly, his words repeated like a ripple through the crowd. "Our fathers wrested this rich land. Now, it is our turn to defend it. Hun and Vandal have joined in league, and if either wins then our world is lost. My daughter asks vengeance. So hear me, my warlords! We ride to seek it!"

A thousand spear shafts banged against a thousand shields in acclamation. Then Theodoric mounted, raised his arm, and they were off. A thick, muscled parade flowed down the streets of Tolosa for its great Roman gates, thundering out to meet the far greater hordes of fellow tribesmen waiting in the fields and woodlots beyond. Thousands would become tens of thousands, and tens of thousands an army. The host of the Visigoths would ride to join Aetius, and the West would rally behind them.

Would it be enough to stop Attila?

I galloped ahead to bring my general this glad news, looking back at the tower that Berta watched from. Now she would have her revenge.

PART THREE

THE BATTLE OF NATIONS

XXIII

THE SECRET STOREROOM

Aurelia was a walled Roman city that stood in the path of any armies marching through the lowlands of Gaul. Situated on the Loire River, it was the heart of Rome's most fertile province. If the Huns could occupy it, they would have a strategic capital from which to dominate western Europe. If the Romans could hold it, their defense would be simplified.

Attila hoped that treachery would deliver the city. Sieges were costly; betrayal cheap.

It was one of the ironies of history that the Alan tribe that had come to control Aurelia, and the Loire, were distant cousins of the Hun. They now were part of that patchwork confederacy of Roman, German, and Celtic peoples that made up the Western Empire. The tribal migrations that had upended the region two generations before had settled into an uneasy coalition of chieftains, generals, and opportunists who had carved out spheres of influence. Each tribe owed nominal allegiance to the Empire, and yet each enjoyed a measure of independence, because that empire was weak. Each tribe had been placed by the emperor to check its neighbor. The barbarians depended on Rome, envied Rome, disdained Rome, feared Rome, and yet thought of themselves as newly Roman.

If the Visigoths were the most powerful tribe, the Bagaudae, Franks, Saxons, Armoricans, Liticians, Burgundians, Belgicans, and Alans each had territories and armies of their own. Two months before the Hun armies marched, emissaries had come to Aurelia to sound out the king of the Alans, the wily Sangibanus. Attila was coming with the greatest army the West had ever seen, the king was warned. Sangibanus could fight for the Romans and be destroyed, or join the Huns and remain a king, albeit a vassal.

It was a grim choice, made worse by the fact that Sangibanus's own belligerent warriors had no intention of submitting to anyone. Worse, if the king's treachery was discovered before the Huns arrived, Aetius might make an example of him. Yet to fight Attila was to risk annihilation.

"You cannot sit out this war—you must choose," insisted the young and rising Hun sent to persuade Sangibanus. "You can rule under Attila, or you can die under the Romans."

"My people won't follow me to the Huns. They already flatter themselves that they're Romans and Christians. No one wants to go back to the ways of our grandfathers."

"*They* need not make the choice. *You* must, for their safety. Listen, I have a plan so that even the gate guards need not choose. Here is all you have to do . . ."

The Hun's name was Skilla.

"A child to see you, bishop."

"A child?"

"He doesn't have the manners of one. Or any manners at all, as far as I can see. He says it's about the safety of the church. It's really quite peculiar."

"This is a bold child." Bishop Anianus looked thoughtful.

"He insists on keeping his head covered. Were he an assassin—"

"Bertrand, I am the easiest of all men to kill. No one need send a child to do it, in a cape. They could assault me in the street, stampede a wood cart across me, drop a brick from a parapet, or poison the daily sacrament."

"Bishop!" But of course this was true. If this visitor was strange, their own bishop was stranger. He had the habit of disappearing for weeks at a time as hermit and pilgrim, talking in his own way to God.

Then he would suddenly reappear as if never absent. He visited the sick and lame without fear of contagion, gave penance to murderers and thieves, and conferred with the powerful. In an increasingly lawless world, he represented divine law. His piety and good works had made him not only popular but also a leader.

"But they don't harm me because it is God's will," Anianus went on. "And it is His will, I think, that I see this mysterious visitor. These are strange times, and strange people are afoot. Demons, perhaps. And angels! Let's see which he is."

Their visitor had overheard. "Too ugly to be an angel and too charming to be a demon," he proclaimed, pushing back his hood. "Of strangeness, I will confess to."

Bertrand blinked. "Not a child but a dwarf."

"An emissary from Aetius, bishop. My name is Zerco."

The bishop's face admitted surprise. "Not the usual representative."

"When I'm not representing my master I amuse him." Zerco bowed. "I admit to being unusual but not useless. Not only am I a fool by profession, but I came through the gates with Burgundian refugees. No one notices a halfling if there are children all around."

"I thought it was the business of a fool to be noticed."

"In less perilous times. But there are agents of Attila in Gaul as well as agents of Aetius, and I'd prefer not to meet them. I bring you greetings from the general and a warning that Aurelia is in the path of the Hun. Aetius wants to know if the city will hold."

"The answer to that is simple. It will hold if Aetius will come."

"His army has temporarily retreated to Limonurr in hopes that, by offering such proximity and support, Theodoric will bring his Visigoths. If Aurelia can buy my general time while he rallies the western tribes—"

"But what are the Visigoths going to do?"

"I don't know. An able friend has been sent to urge them to join us, but I've had no word of his success or failure. My assignment is to know what Aurelia is going to do."

Anianus laughed. "Everyone is waiting for everyone else! Surely there is a parable about such meekness, but I can't remember it now. Yet what choice do all of us have? If the Huns succeed, the Church is finished before it has properly begun, and I will be roasted as a preview of eternal punishment. I know more of Attila than you might expect, halfling—enough to have taken the time to learn Hunnish! There is no question what *I* intend to do: resist, and resist with all my breath. But the king has shut me out of his councils. His soldiers don't want to submit to the yoke of a new empire, but neither do they want to die for nothing. Every man is asking if the next man is constant, and none has the courage to be the first to step forward. The Franks are feeling out the Alans, the Alans the Burgundians, the Burgundians the Saxons, the Saxons the Visigoths and the Goths, I suppose, the Romans! Who, besides Aetius, is going to stand?"

"Let it start with you and me, bishop."

He smiled. "A man of peace and a dwarf? And yet isn't that the message, in essence, of our Church? Of taking a stand against evil? Of belief in the face of fear?"

"Just as you know something of Attila, I know something of you. People sang your praises the closer I came to Aurelia, Bishop Anianus. They will unite behind you if Sangibanus allows it. But Aetius fears that the king of the Alans has no faith in him or anything else and will sell himself to the Huns."

Anianus shrugged. "I am bishop, not king. What can I do?"

"I will listen to Sangibanus, but I need the eyes and ears of your priests, nuns, and prelates to find out what is really going on. If there's a plot to betray the city we need to learn of it and stop it, and convince the Alans to hold until Aetius comes."

Anianus looked sober. "If he doesn't, Attila will kill us all."

"If you give up Aurelia and put Attila in a position to win this war, he will kill the entire Empire, bishop, and with it the Church. The world will go dark, and men will live like beasts for the next thousand years. I, too, know more of Attila than most men, because I've played the fool for him. One thing I always remember: I've yet to make him laugh."

If the Huns had an emissary in Aurelia he was well hidden, but the news from the east was grave. An ever-growing flood of refugees was pouring into the city. Mediomatrica had been entered on the eve of Easter, its inhabitants slaughtered and its buildings burned. Durocortorum was destroyed when its population fled. Nasium, Tullum, Noviomagus, Andematunnum, and Augustobona went up in flames as Attila's vast army split into arms to sustain itself. The bishop Nicacius was beheaded, and his nuns raped and speared. Priests were crucified, merchants flayed until they revealed the hiding place of their valuables, children enslaved, and livestock slaughtered. Some Aurelians were already fleeing toward the sea. Yet the news produced grim determination as well. In the depth of despair, some people were finding courage. Aurelia was bitterly divided—as Axiopolis had been, far to the east—on whether to resist or surrender.

In the end, Zerco's discovery depended on luck. A boy assisting a new unit of hastily organized militia had gone to the city's weapon shops and had curiously slipped through a narrow passageway briefly revealed by a shifting of shelves. Inside, the boy glimpsed a glittery cache of weapons and armor. The youth always prepared earnestly for the sacrament of the Sabbath, but always had difficulty during confession to find some sin with which to practice penance. It was hard to be venial enough to occupy the confessional's time when you were only eight! He finally remembered to confess his trespass, and it was the room's very existence that caught the priest's ear. He thought the hidden cache of weaponry peculiar enough to mention to a prelate, who in turn remembered the bishop's request to report anything unusual. Anianus mentioned it to Zerco.

"It seems strange to lock armor away."

Zerco thought. "Saved for an elite unit, perhaps?"

"For when? After the city has fallen? And that's not the only peculiar thing. The boy said all the helmets and shields and swords looked alike."

Now this was intriguing. The tribesmen who had settled in Gaul retained individual taste in weaponry. Every man had his own armor, every clan its own colors, every nation its own designs. Only the thin and depleted Roman units managed by Italians retained a uniformity of equipment. Yet Roman troops were far away, with Aetius.

"Perhaps it is innocent or a boy's imagination. But I'd like a look at this storeroom, bishop. Can you get me in there?"

"That's the province of the marshal, just as the altar is mine." He considered. "But I might send an altar boy to fetch Helco, the youngster who made his confession. Someone of your stature, in a vestment, might just get close enough. . . ."

"An altar boy I shall be."

Zerco was helped by the confusion the approach of the Huns had caused. Men were assigned to the armory at morning and reassigned to a tower by noon, and then posted to the granary at dusk and a well by midnight. Private arms were being sold, donated, and redistributed. As a result, a small altar boy with a concealing hood, sent by the bishop to find another lad, did not cause much notice at first. Zerco spied a narrow opening behind the regular armory storage, and when eyes were turned tried to slip inside.

But a guard challenged him. "Hold up, boy. That back there is not for you."

"The bishop has sent me to fetch Helco. The captain said to look there."

"The captain of the guard?"

"Ask him if you must. But Anianus is impatient."

The man scowled. "Stay until I come back."

Once the guard left, Zerco didn't pause. There was a tight twist in the rocky corridor and a wooden door with a heavy lock. The dwarf had brought a hammer and chisel, and with a bang, the lock parted. If he was caught, his means of entry was the least of his worries.

The room was dark, so the dwarf lit a candle to reveal the gleam of steel and leather. It was much as Helco had described, except the boy had omitted a crucial detail.

"Roman!" There was enough Roman armor to equip a troop of cavalry, yet no Roman troops would come to Gaul unequipped, and none would report to Sangibanus before reporting to Aetius. This was for barbarians, but why? And why was this equipment kept secret? Because any men wearing it would be assumed to be Roman. . . .

Zerco heard voices and snuffed out the candle, melting into the shadows. He discarded the hood and took out the signet medallion assigned him by Aetius, in hopes it would make the guards hesitate long enough for the dwarf to remind them that Anianus knew where he was.

The corridor filled with approaching light and then the broken door-way filled with men and oaths. There was the guard who had challenged him and a second, older, grizzled soldier, probably his captain, angry at the broken lock. These two put their hands to the hilt of their swords. A third man, shorter and stockier and with a brimmed hat concealing his face, stepped up behind them. They came inside with a torch.

Zerco, his discovery inevitable, stepped out. Even as he displayed the medallion, the dwarf could see the third man's eyes widening.

The stranger spoke in Hunnish. "Little mouse!"

It was Skilla.

"That man is a Hun!" Zerco cried in surprise.

The guard captain shook his head. "We warned you not to come here."

Skilla spoke to the Alans in Latin, his accent thick. "I know this dwarf. He's an assassin, kidnapper, and thief."

"I'm an aide to Aetius and Anianus! Harm me at your peril!"

"If allowed to speak to your bishop," Skilla warned, "he will mislead him."

"He's not going to speak to anyone." Blades were drawn.

"Listen to me! This is a trick to betray your city—"

A sword swung with a whistle, narrowly missing. Zerco hurled his hammer at Skilla's head, but the Hun knocked it away, scoffing at the at-tempt. The dwarf dropped and tried to scuttle, but blades clanged against the stone floor, blocking his way. So he somersaulted backward instead, knocking over a rack of spears and shields to slow his tormen-tors. The men laughed. This was play!

"The Huns are going to enslave you!" the dwarf warned from the darkness.

A spear sailed at the sound of his voice and nearly pinioned him. "Come out, little mouse," Skilla called in Hunnish. "The cat is here to eat you."

He needed a mouse hole. There was no back door and no window. A drain? He hadn't noticed one. He looked for a spot darker than the darkness, the boots of his assailants treading heavily on the stone as they moved to corner him. And there, in the corner where wall and ceiling met . . .

The men charged, and the dwarf leaped. He sprang past a sword thrust and clutched at the mail of the guard who had challenged him, temporarily blinding the man with a poke that elicited a howl. Then he clambered like a squirrel to the man's head and leaped, half landing in a tight cavity. His fingers scrabbled for a hold.

"Get him! Get him! I can't see!"

A hand slithered on his ankle. Zerco kicked, connecting with something hard, and pulled himself upward with all his might, wriggling up a passageway as narrow as a pipe.

"Boost me up!" someone cried.

He could hear an arm thrashing behind him. "He's like a damned rabbit. It's too small! There's no way I can follow."

"What is that hole?" Skilla asked.

"Who knows? Probably a vent, to give air."

"Can he get out the other way?"

"There are grates on the outside to keep out animals. He can't go anywhere, but we can't get him, either."

"Maybe if we boost up a dog . . ."

"Why bother," Skilla said. "Aren't men working to reinforce the walls? Get some stones and a hod of mortar. We'll seal him in and have no corpse to explain."

Even as they worked, Skilla felt cursed by the dwarf. The little man was grotesque and scuttled like a spider, and he seemed tied to every moment of the Hun's torment by Jonas and Ilana. The witches had told him forest legends of squat and scabrous gnomes from the German woods who plagued ordinary men with magic and tricks. The annoying Zerco was one of these, Skilla believed, and sealing him in a stone tomb would be a gift to the world.

The warrior watched impatiently as the guards clumsily bricked. How Skilla hated it down here! No Hun liked crowded, dark, or confined spaces; and these underground passageways that the Romans had built were all three. He was proud of having been assigned the mission of conspiring with Sangibanus—it was a mark of his uncle's growing trust in him, despite his setbacks—and he knew success would eventually bring him overdue recognition, and Ilana. But the past week in Aurelia was almost more than he could bear. It was never quiet in the city. His senses were battered with noise, color, crowds, and ceaseless clanging. How he longed for the countryside! But soon Sangibanus would betray his own capital and Aurelia would fall. Soon the Huns would be masters of everything, and the clever men who made life complicated would be no more.

The king of the Alans dared not simply surrender his city, Skilla knew. His own warlords, who distrusted their cousin Huns as much as they distrusted Romans, might turn on him. Sangibanus could not convince them of the West's weakness without seeming a coward. Nor could he simply organize a party of traitors to overwhelm the sentries at his own gate. If too cowardly to fight Attila, he was also too cowardly to murder his own soldiers, because the chance of betrayal and civil war was too high. So instead Skilla had offered a different way. With Roman armor and a persuasive Aurelian officer, a party of Huns could seize the gate with a minimum of bloodshed, holding it open just long enough for other Huns to gallop through. With that, the battle would be over before it began, and no one—including King Sangibanus—need die.

Now they had to act more quickly than planned. If Zerco had found this hidden armory, who else might know? Aurelia must fall before the dwarf was missed.

XXIV

THE GATE OF AURELIA

There are few things more difficult, Zerco supposed, than listening to men brick up your tomb. He tried to laugh at his predicament, just as he had tried to laugh at his entire bizarre life. How he'd wanted to be an equal in the councils of the big people! His humor was a mask for his bitterness about his own ugliness, of course—just as it covered up his astonished wonder that he could marry a woman as fine as Julia or have a friend as promising as Jonas. Now he would pay for pride and ambition! Sealed in a little catacomb without the mercy of oblivion. Should he back out before they finished and hope for a quick death instead of torture? Or stay out of reach and suffocate instead? For a little man who depended on agility and wit, the latter seemed a particularly pathetic way to die. Yet life had taught the dwarf to keep hoping. He was a freak who advised generals and consulted with bishops. So perhaps it was not time to wiggle backward to certain death but to squirm forward. Even as the final stone was wedged into place, Zerco was climbing the steep incline of his tunnel to find where it led.

What followed, his mind would long shy from remembering. He would not recall if he had been suspended in darkness for hours or days, and if the overwhelming feeling had been of cramped heat or numbing cold. He'd simply remember wedging himself ahead. A ridge of stone could seem as insurmountable as a mountain, and he'd peck at it with his fingers, loosening key bits and letting them rattle down behind him. Then he'd shimmy, expelling all air to shrink and surge forward some impossibly small amount. He'd jam, gasp, his middle squeezed by what felt like the entire weight of the Earth, ears hammering, expel air again, wriggle forward, breathe, gasp against the pain, expel . . . again and again and again until finally his hips would be past the obstacle and he would lie panting in a tube no roomier than a cocoon, his heartbeat the only sound, his sweat the only lubricant. Somewhere, fresh air was keeping him alive. As his clothes disintegrated he left the pieces behind except for strips with which to wrap his hands. His blood made him slippery; and as it leaked, he shrank. *Never before have I wanted to be small,* he thought, drawing himself out like a snake. Occasionally he started to panic, his lungs working wildly, but stifled any scream by thinking of Julia. *"Stop sobbing and get yourself out of the hole you climbed into,"* she lectured him. *"What is so hard about crawling forward? Babies can do it!"*

So he did. He passed an even smaller hole, its rank smell tying it to an old Roman sewer, slimy effluent dripping down like a baptism from Hell. Praise God! It made him slicker! The worst came when he spied a glimmer of light but only beyond a narrowing of the cavity that at first seemed too small even for him. *As tight as the cunt of a virgin,* he cursed, as if he'd had all that many virgins. But what choice did he have but to be reborn? He put his arms forward as if diving, his already-narrow shoulders pressed to his ears, and kicked forward like a fish. Each rib clicked by the stones like a bead on an abacus, the pain as excruciating as if he were being flayed. Then his stomach was through and his hips jammed tight—*I'm as wide as a woman!*—until he found handholds and pulled the last inches by brute strength, jamming his teeth against the agony. Then the air was cooler and fresher, the light brighter. He came with his nose to an iron grate.

Thank the saints for rust and the laziness of barbarian conquerors. The metal had been no better maintained than Aurelia's walls, which is why the Alans were working so frantically now. With his last bit of strength he pounded on it like a madman, on and on, until suddenly it fell away with a screech and clang. He waited for shouts but heard nothing. He was still far under the city's central fortress. Zerco popped out into a wider tunnel, big enough to crawl on all fours, lit by light coming down from grated shafts too narrow and sheer to climb. The new passageway seemed a hopeless labyrinth, making him panic all over again, but finally there was the sweet smell of steam and the chatter of laundry girls in a fortress washroom. A pipe from the room vented the steam, and Zerco was the only inhabitant small enough to slip down. He popped out into a clothing pile, a demon sheathed in bright blood. One laundress screamed and fled; another fainted and would later tell tales of the end time. Zerco merely stole a sheet and crept back to the bishop.

"I think I know what they're planning," he announced.

Then he collapsed.

No wonder Romans fought so clumsily and slowly.

Skilla felt as encased as a sausage in the heavy Roman armor, his vision restricted by the hot helmet and his torso confined by the weight of mail. The oval shield felt as unwieldy as the door of a barn. The lance was a log, the sword as straight as their rigid roads, and the heavy clothing wet with sweat. Once they got inside the gates of Aurelia he would abandon this nonsense and reach for his bow, but in the meantime the disguise would get them unchallenged to the city wall. Once the portal was seized, Edeco's division of five thousand men could follow and the hapless Sangibanus would remain blameless.

It was midnight, the moon dark, the city sleeping, and the Huns supposedly far away. Edeco had led his division two hundred miles in three days, outdistancing any warnings. Now his men waited in the woods while Skilla's disguised company of a hundred men trotted toward Aurelia's wall with a great clank and creak of Roman equipment. As always, Skilla found himself studying the walls with a soldier's eye. The ramparts and towers of fresh stone glowed noticeably lighter than the weather-stained wall below, even in starlight. A few torches flickered to mark the gate, and the Hun could see the heads of Alan guards peering down as he approached.

The Alan captain, paid well to keep the armory a secret, had left the city with Skilla and came back with him now, the new gold jingling in his purse as he rode.

"A company from Aetius to reinforce Sangibanus!" the henchman cried when they came under the central tower. "Open the gate for friends!"

"We've had no word of Romans," a sentry responded cautiously.

"How about word of Huns? They're not far, you know. Do you want help or not?"

"What unit are you?"

"The Fourth Victorix, you blind man! Do we look like Norican salt merchants? Open! We need to eat and sleep!"

The gate began to ponderously swing. It was going to work!

Then it stopped halfway, giving just a glimpse of the city beyond. A voice called. "Send in your officer. Alone."

"Now!" Skilla cried.

They charged, and even as the soldiers began to swing the gate against them the Hun horses bashed into it and knocked the sentries backward, pushing the entryway wide. Through the short arched tunnel that led through the wall was the courtyard beyond. The Huns kicked their horses.

And a wagon lurched from one side of the inner arch and rolled to block their way. A torch made oiled hay explode in a fireball of flame. The ponies reared, screaming, and warriors cursed, reaching awkwardly for the unaccustomed Roman weapons. Before they could act a dozen arrows buzzed through the fire, some igniting as they flew, and struck home. Men and horses spilled in the crowded portal. The Alan captain's gold coins of betrayal spilled with him, rolling on the stones. Meanwhile, men beyond the flames were yelling alarm. "They're not Roman— they're Hun! Treachery!" A bell began to ring.

Priests were running past the burning wagon and charging at the front rank of horsemen with long pikes. The butts of the wicked weapons were planted in the ground and the spearheads set to form an impenetrable hedge of steel. Horns began blowing. In the light of the fire, Skilla could see soldiers were spilling from nearby buildings and dashing to the wall. Buckets of rocks began raining on the Huns bunched behind. Then sluices of oil came raining down and ignited. The trick had become a trap.

Skilla's horse wheeled uselessly at the hedge of pikes. Had Sangibanus double-crossed them? No . . . who was this halfling taking aim?

On a stairway to one side of the gate, a midget was whirling a sling.
Skilla cursed and reached for his bow. Could it be?

A rock whizzed by Skilla's ear even as he drew back his bowstring.
Then Tatos grabbed his arm. "There's no time!" An iron portcullis was
rattling down to cut off the Hun leaders from their followers.

"Blow the horns for Edeco!" Skilla cried.

"It's too late!" Tatos jumped down and hauled Skilla from his horse,
an action that saved his life when another volley of missiles scythed into
the gateway and toppled half a dozen more men and horses. Skilla's own
horse screamed and went down. The gate had become a slaughterhouse
of kicking hooves, broken legs, and discarded Roman weapons. Skilla
and his companion ran to where the portcullis was descending, slid, and
rolled. They made it to the outer side just as the grate bit into the causeway. Behind, the priests who had attacked his men charged with a howl
and began killing the wounded with axes and scythes. Here was none of
the meekness of the monastery.

Skilla stood at the outer end of the portal. Everything was chaos.
Huns were on fire. Others were milling helplessly. One stone struck a
warrior's head and it exploded like fruit, spraying them all with blood.
Hundreds of Alans were running to man the wall. Skilla heard with
dread the thunder of Edeco's charge and ran to turn it back.

The oaken gate itself slammed shut again against them.

It was all the damned dwarf!

"Fall back! Fall back! The Wolverine retreat!" Yet even as his men
tried to flee out of range, Edeco's huge division of screaming Huns swept
Skilla's stunned company forward like a wave against the wall, the formation breaking against the stone like surf. The Alans were electrified
by this sudden appearance of their enemy, bells pealing and horns
sounding all over the city, and any opportunity for Sangibanus to surrender had disappeared in an instant. Instead, the Huns found themselves mounting a cavalry charge against a wall fifty feet high.

There was a brief period of confusion and slaughter before the failure to breach the gate was at last fully communicated to Edeco's surging

Huns and they all pulled back. By that time scores were dead and wounded, and flaming ballista bolts chased them for four hundred paces. The ruse had become a disaster.

"The priests were waiting for us!" Skilla seethed.

"So much for the promises of Sangibanus," Edeco said.

"It was Zerco, alive from the dead, who warned them!"

"Zerco? I thought you buried that damned dwarf."

"He passes through walls like a ghost!"

Edeco spat. "He's just a sly little man. Someday, nephew, you're going to learn to truly finish your enemies, from that ugly dwarf to that thieving young Roman."

I rode to an Aurelia that had a halo of orange, the glow of fires casting a corona against the night clouds, that I could see from ten miles away. Well past midnight I came to the crest of a hill overlooking the Loire River and saw the besieged city on the northern bank in a dramatic play of light. A thousand Hun campfires ringed the town. Buildings within Aurelia sent up plumes of glowing smoke. Catapults on both sides shot flaming projectiles that cut lazy parabolas of fire across the darkness, like a tracery of filigreed decoration. It was quite beautiful and quiet from a distance, like stars on a summer night, but I knew full well how desperate the situation must seem within. The hope I carried was vital to Aurelia's resistance.

If the city could hold, Theodoric and Aetius were coming.

I was in temporary disguise. I'd become a Hun by killing one, a straggler I caught looting the farm of a slain peasant family. The hut's plume of smoke and a chorus of faint screams had drawn me, and I'd cautiously observed the warrior, drunk on Roman wine and weighted with booty, staggering from outbuilding to outbuilding, looking for more. The bodies of the family he had murdered were scattered on farmyard dirt, smoldering from the hut fire that had driven them outside to their slaughter. I'd taken my own bow, with which I'd been earnestly practicing, and slain the Hun from fifty paces, the man grunting in perplexity as he went down. Such a kill no longer seemed momentous to me, given the apocalypse that was enveloping us. Taking his clothes and shaggy pony, I'd set out under a dirty Hun jerkin for Aurelia, knowing dried blood would arouse no suspicion in these dark days.

Now, under cover of darkness, I rode down into the Hun encampment. Unlike a Roman one, the encirclement was a haphazard affair. The Huns erected no fortifications of their own, as if to dare the defenders to come out and fight them. Their lines were thin south of the river, the Loire inhibiting assault or escape. Accordingly, this part of the barbarian encampment had a desultory air. The Huns were huddled around campfires, watching the city wall across the river.

"I'm looking for the Rugi," I said in Hunnish, knowing my features and accent would betray any pretence I was a Hun. "I satisfied myself with a wench too long and lost my *lochus*. Now I've been riding two days to let my sword catch up with my cock."

Such a confession would earn me a flogging in a Roman army, but the barbarians laughed and made a place for me by the fire, offering *kumiss*. It burned my throat as I drank, and they laughed again at my grimace. I grinned foolishly and wiped my mouth. "How long do we have to wait at this stink hole?"

This was not the kind of battle a Hun liked to fight, they said. Their cavalry had outrun their engineers, so there were not enough siege engines. Besides, the Huns preferred to fight in the open like men, not crouched behind machines of war. Yet the cowardly Alans wouldn't come down from their walls. And while the Huns enjoyed shooting at the helmeted heads of defenders, so many thousands of arrows had been used that Edeco had finally ordered a halt to the sport until the attackers were ready for a coordinated assault. That left the warriors bored, some drifting away to loot, like the Hun I had killed.

"I thought you Huns tricked your way in," I said.

The plan to open the city had been betrayed by a dwarf, it was said, which seemed like an ominous joke. Now the Alans were as aroused as ants. Good Huns had been killed trying to take a place these men no longer wanted. "We should go home."

"But it's a rich land, is it not?" I asked.

"Too many trees, too many people, and too much rain."

I left them as if to piss and made my way to the river. A firebrand arced across the water, leaving a path of pink. The Loire was broad but dotted with sandbars that I could rest on as I swam. I slipped into the cold and began swimming on my back, kicking off my rancid Hun garments as I did so. My head was like a little moon against the current, and I waited anxiously for a bolt from either side, but none came. I paused on a bar to catch my breath, studied the walls, and then swam on my belly for the stone quay of Aurelia. In the shallows near it were carcasses of the city's boats that had been burned and sunk to prevent the Huns from using them. I grasped one of the iron docking rings to lift myself. Was there someone I could call to?

As if in answer, there was a flicker, and a projectile banged next to my cheek. I dropped back into the water immediately, still hanging on to the ring. Crossbow! "Don't shoot! I bring a message from Aetius!" I called in Latin.

Another bolt ricocheted, drawn by my sound.

"Stop! From Aetius!" The name, at least, they should recognize.

I waited and finally someone called down in Latin. "Who are you?"

"Jonas Alabanda, an aide to Aetius! I've come through the Hun lines with a message for Sangibanus and Bishop Anianus! Throw me a rope!"

"What, you want in? All of us wish we could get out!" But a line uncoiled; and I heaved myself onto the quay, crawled, and grasped.

"Pull quickly, because the Huns are bored!"

They hauled so fast I almost lost my grip. I was dancing upward on the rough stones, trying not to think of the drop below, when a fresh firebrand soared overhead, illuminating the wall. I heard excited shouts across the river and knew what it meant. "Hurry!" Mailed arms reached out to seize me. There was a sigh, and a nearly spent arrow pinged off the stone by my shoulder. "Pull, damn you!" Another missile whisked overhead and a third clipped my ankle. Then I was through the gap in the stone and could collapse on the parapet, wet, cold, and gasping for breath.

A gnomelike face peered down to check mine. "You missed me so much that you've come to Hell to see me?" Zerco looked raw, half swaddled in bandages, and entirely satisfied with himself.

I sat up and looked back at the ring of fires around the city. "I've come to promise you salvation."

At dawn the garrison of Aurelia gathered in the city's great church, built from the Roman temple of Venus, to hear Bishop Anianus tell them what to do. Their king Sangibanus was present as well, but this dark-featured and dour man stood to one side, surrounded by his lords and also half shunned by them. Sangibanus had protested he had no knowledge of the ruse that nearly captured the gate, but his protests were too quick and too loud, and the rumors from priest and prelate too sober and convincing, to absolve him of blame. Was their monarch a coward? Or a realist, trying to save them all? In any event it was too late: Battle had been joined, and the city's only chance now was resistance. A Roman courier had climbed over the walls the night before, bringing news for bishop and king. Now Anianus had called them to hear it. The assembly knew there was not much time. The Huns had begun a great drumming, signaling preparations for attack, and the rhythmic pounding carried inside the thick walls of the church.

Anianus commanded not just from faith but by example. Had he not, with the dwarf's help, organized a secret defense of the gate that gave soldiers time to rally? Had he not marched around the walls during the attacks since, bearing a sacred fragment of the True Cross and exhorting the soldiers to stand firm? Had not Hun arrows not always missed his mitered head? Already, people were murmuring of sainthood and miracles. As the Huns drummed, at last he spoke.

"You cannot fail."

The words hung there, like the haze of incense in the morning's growing light. The soldiers stirred, a mongrel mix of eastern horseman, gruff German, sturdy Celt, aristocratic Roman—the mix, now, that made up Gaul.

"You cannot fail," the bishop went on, "because more than the lives of your families are at stake. More is at stake than this city of Aurelia, more than my own diocese, and more than the lineage of your own king or your own pride." He nodded, as if to confirm his own words. "You cannot fail because this Church is part of a new truth in the world, and that truth is part of a great and venerable Empire. We are inheritors of a tradition that goes back twelve hundred years, the only hope mankind has ever had for unity. You cannot fail because if you do—if the Huns breach these walls and overthrow your kingdom and win the strategic heart of Gaul—then that Empire, that tradition, and that Church will come to an end."

He held them in silence a moment, his gaze circling the room.

"All life is a fight between light and darkness, between right and wrong, between civilization and barbarism, between the order of law and the enslavement of tyranny. Now that fight has come to Aurelia."

Men unconsciously straightened. Fingers flexed. Jaws tightened.

"You cannot fail because the Holy Church is behind you, and I say to you this morning that God is on the side of our legions and that Heaven awaits any man who falls."

"Amen," the Christians rumbled. They put their hands on the hilt of sword, mace, ax, and hammer.

Anianus smiled at this ferocity, his gaze circuiting the room and seeming to rest for a moment on each man in turn. He spoke softly. "And you cannot fail, brave warriors, because a messenger came to us last night with great tidings. Theodoric and the Visigoths have joined the alliance against Attila, and even as we speak they are riding with Aetius to the relief of Aurelia. They are just days, perhaps hours, away. That is why you hear the drums, because the Huns are panicking and wish to conquer us before reinforcement arrives. They will fight desperately to get inside these walls, but they will not succeed because you cannot *allow* them to succeed. You need only fight and win for a little while, and then deliverance will be at hand."

Now the assembly in the church was stirring and whispering, realizing that in an instant the entire complexion of the war had changed. Without Theodoric any resistance was desperate. With him, there was a chance to defeat Attila's entire horde.

"Can you fail?" Anianus asked in a whisper.

"No!" they roared.

And then the bells and trumpets began sounding the alarm as the barbarian horns rang out from beyond the walls. The great attack was beginning.

The Huns had outridden their best mercenary engineers and couldn't make a proper siege. What they did have were arrows, ladders, and an abundance of courage.

They attacked Aurelia from all sides but the river, a wild rush designed to stretch the defenders thin. As the scale of the attack became apparent, it was necessary for nearly every inhabitant of the city—from unarmored women to children as young as ten—to join the men on the ramparts and hurl down stones, tiles, and cobbles. The air was thick with flying shafts, each side shooting back some of the arrows shot at them; and there was an ominous humming in the air like the sound from a hornet's nest. Scurrying priests and nuns gathered spent Hun shafts in baskets to carry back to their city's own archers; and occasionally a plunging arrow would catch one of the clergy in the crown of the head, plunging with such force that its point would jut through the lower jaw and sew the mouth shut so tightly that the dying couldn't scream. He fell, but another priest picked up his burden.

As the missiles flew, the barbarians surged, boiling, across the ground outside the city, hundreds struck by the defenders' salvos but thousands more bunching at the base of the walls. Pots of oil and boiling water, poured from the ramparts, cut swathes of fire and pain in the ranks. Plunging stones snapped limbs and shattered helmets. Yet all this seemed a dent. There were simply too many Huns. Scaling ladders soared skyward like an uncurling fist of claws. Hun archery began in earnest, each volley of arrows timed to follow the last so that it was impossible for the Alans to poke their heads above the protective stone crenellation without being killed. At the same time, attackers swarmed up the ramparts. So the Alans crouched and pitched rocks over the lip of the wall blindly, waiting for that cease in the hiss of arrows that would signal when the first Huns reached the top. Then a great shout went up, and they rose in their iron and leather to clash with the snarling attackers, wrestling on the lip of wall. Here a ladder was overthrown, there the

Huns gained a toehold; and desperate battle raged back and forth on the parapet.

The ferocity of the fight made the combat in the lonely tower of Noricum seem leisurely in comparison. Here was battle of an entirely new scale—men swinging, chopping, and biting like animals because even a moment's pause meant instant death. Some of those wrestling toppled off the wall together, throttling each other as they fell; and if a defender somehow survived such a plunge the Huns waiting below dismembered him and hoisted his limbs as bloody trophies.

I'd borrowed armor to join the battle, now that my message had given hope. I felt more practiced at this grim craft now, rising after the arrow volleys to slash with sword and club with shield, sinking out of sight when more arrows came, and then rising once again. A misstep in this rhythm and I was dead. There was no courage to it because there was no time to be afraid. To lose meant death, so I did what all of us did, what we had to do. We fought.

Soon the parapet was littered with the fallen, defender and attacker alike, some groaning and some already still, festooned with arrows. Many of the dead were women and children, yet new ones constantly clambered up the steps on the city side to drag them aside and bring fresh stones, arrows, or pots of hot oil and grease. At the base of the wall many of Attila's men were thrashing on the ground and twisting in agony from cruel burns or trying to crawl away on broken legs. The luckiest rocks we dropped struck the ladders themselves, snapping enough in two to seriously limit the routes the attackers could take. Yet to aim a rock was to invite a dozen arrows, and many a broken ladder was purchased at the price of a defender's life.

On the eastern side of the city where I was stationed and where the Hun concentration was greatest, the defenders had erected a Roman *tolleno*, a huge pivoting beam with a hook on its end that could be manipulated by a counterweight to swoop down outside the walls like a bird of prey. The hook whistled down, snared a Hun, and hoisted him, kicking, high into the air before the wetness of his entrails made him slip off. The machine did not kill that many, but the huge whir it made as it dived was cruelly effective in throwing the attackers into disorder.

Yet all this furious fighting was really a mask for the primary Hun assault, which was the advance of a wheeled battering ram to destroy Aurelia's main gate. What the attackers had not gained by stealth they would break open by brute force. The ram rumbled forward, surrounded by a swarm of upended shields like an undulating roof, and our arrows against it were feeble as rows of Hun archers suppressed our own.

The ram, we knew, could spell disaster. Shouts of warning attracted our bishop, and Anianus waved his cross like the standard of a general to draw more troops to this crisis point. Yet what could we do? And then Zerco appeared. Where he'd been I had no idea, but just as he'd shown at the Roman tower in the Alps, he seemed to have a presence of mind in battle the rest of us lacked. Now he stayed below the wall's lip, busily tying a huge grappling hook to a rope stout enough to tether a ship with. "What are you doing here, little friend?" I wheezed when the fighting momentarily slackened. "You're likely to be stepped on."

The dwarf smiled. "But not shot. Envy me, Jonas. I do not have to duck."

"Don't try to be a hero in a sword fight."

"Hero! I scuttle between their legs, and they dance like chickens. Here, let the others hack at the Huns while you help me finish my toy. My brain is as big as anyone's, but I'll need a broad back like yours to make this work."

"What is it?"

"A ram snagger. The *tolleno* gave me the idea."

The battering ram traversed the last few yards, running over broken bodies; and then with an ominous boom it slammed into the oaken gate. The entire wall trembled. Our garrison let loose a small avalanche of rocks and they crashed on those pushing the log, momentarily stunning or scattering some of them; but then the wounded and injured were dragged aside, new hands took the handles of the wheeled device, and it struck again. Inside, yellow cracks appeared in the gate like the ruptures of an earthquake. We were running short of stones; and those defenders who rose to hurl what we had left were picked off by arrows.

"They'll pull it back in a moment to get some momentum for the next attack," Zerco said. "When that happens, be ready. Anianus! Get us some strong backs to help!"

The bishop quickly understood what the dwarf was trying to do. He shouted for men to stand in a line along the rope, his clear, earnest voice quickly assembling a company.

I, too, saw what the dwarf intended. "We'll be skewered by arrows."

"Not if our archers aim for theirs. Get them lined up and ready."

The dwarf scuttled along the parapet, line uncoiling as he dragged the heavy grappling hook. He was counting his paces as he walked. Finally he got to a point as far from the gate as the wall was high, and stopped. At his direction, I drew the line taut. Other men crouched behind me, holding the hemp. The dwarf was looking at an angle through the crenellation, watching what the Huns were doing. Finally we could hear the hoarse shouts as the ram was readied to be hurled against the gate again, perhaps breaking it this time.

"Ready?" Zerco shouted.

I nodded, wondering if this could possibly work.

"God be with us," Anianus intoned.

The Huns roared a command to advance, and we used it as a signal to fire a volley of arrows. They flew toward the Hun archers, momentarily spoiling their aim. Zerco took the brief opportunity to stand on tiptoes and push out the hook while I held the line above the gate. The grappling hook clanged on the outside wall, bounced, skipped past a ladder, and dropped in a predictable arc for a point directly below where I held the rope. Just as the battering ram surged forward, the hook slipped neatly into the side of the pointed log like a hook in a fish.

"Now!" the dwarf cried.

We heaved, straining backward. The rope came up and with it the snout of the ram, jerking it clear of the gate. The rear end swerved, and Huns cursed as they lost their grip on their weapon. Higher and higher the front of the ram rose as we pulled, the attackers milling in consternation and leaping futilely to cut our rope. We'd bested them. Only one brave and clearer-thinking Hun started scrambling up a scaling ladder, since our trick had momentarily robbed a stretch of wall of defenders as we pulled. Clearly, he meant to cleave the rope from above. I left my own place to intercept him.

I got there as he was coming over the wall, and we met on a charge, swung, clashed, and recoiled. I swung again, the man parried, we pushed off each other with a grunt and then crouched to duel, sweating. This one had rare courage, I acknowledged.

Then I recognized him behind his captured helmet, as he did me.

"You!" Skilla breathed.

"Zerco thought maybe he'd killed you," I said.

"As I thought I had killed your little rat friend." He edged sidewise, looking for an opening. "Where's the sword you stole, Roman?"

"Where it belongs—with Aetius."

Skilla attacked, swinging, and I blocked the blow, my hands throbbing from the ring of steel. Again we swung and again, and then we were apart once more, looking for weakness. I'd lost all thought of the main battle.

The Hun grinned. "When I kill you, I will once more have Ilana. Attila has her ready with him, in a cage."

That cost me my concentration. "She's alive?"

It was enough for the Hun to charge before I was ready. My parry now was one of desperation. I stumbled backward over a body and fell as Skilla swung down. But then Zerco came from behind, stabbing with a dagger, and Skilla howled in frustration to turn and swat at the little man who had cut his leg. I scrambled up as Skilla retreated, and risked a glance over the wall.

Now the wheeled ram was completely vertical, its end dragging in the dirt as fifty men strained to take the weight.

I looked back at Skilla. He had frozen, too, watching this contest.

Hun arrows started slicing toward the suspending rope, fraying it. Finally it snapped, spilling the hauling crew backward but letting the ram fall sideways. It hit with a crash that snapped all its axles. Wooden wheels rolled like scattered coins.

Taking advantage I lunged at Skilla. He leaped back, his eyes flicking with doubt. He was alone on the wall, and Hun horns were blowing retreat. Free of the rope, Alan soldiers ran up to support me, forming a half ring around my opponent. I stayed their attack.

"You're on the wrong side, Skilla," I gasped. "Aetius is coming. Don't fight for your monster."

"I want Ilana!"

"Then help us rescue her!"

"I can rescue *her* only by killing *you*." It was near despair. And then, knowing the odds had become impossible, he turned and leaped.

I thought it might have been to the death and ran to see, surprised by my sudden feeling of dread. I didn't want to be robbed of this Hun. But Skilla had caught the fragment of rope where the ram had broken and was swinging now, halfway between the top of the wall and the ground. He let his sword drop at one end of the swing and then dropped at the other, falling thirty feet and rolling, even as arrows and spears tried to pin him. Hun arrows arced up to cover his retreat, catching one defender in the eye and another in the shoulder; and then the fighter was up and limping back to his own lines, pausing to help a comrade carry one of the wheels that had sheered from the battering ram. They would fix it to a new one, I knew. Skilla would never give up.

I could see him looking back at me as he withdrew. The other Huns were drawing off into the trees as well. Had we beaten them?

"We should have killed him," Zerco said.

I looked around. The parapet was a charnel house. Bodies littered it so thickly that rivulets of blood were running down the gutters and spouts like rainwater. Half Aurelia seemed in flames; and everyone was blackened, bloody, and exhausted.

We could not survive such an assault again.

So we slumped, wondering how long it would take the enemy to prepare a new ram. Women and old men clambered up to bring skins of wine and water. We drank, blinking at a sun that seemed to have gone stationary. Then someone shouted about glitter spotted in the trees to the south, and we heard Roman horns. Aetius!

XXV

A GATHERING OF ARMIES

The Huns melted away like snow. One moment it seemed as if Aurelia was being strangled by enemies, and the next as if the death grip was an illusionary nightmare. Siege engines were abandoned, a new ram undone, campfires left to smoke unattended. The barbarians mounted their horses and rode back northeast, away from the tramp of Roman and Visigothic troops approaching from the opposite direction. We looked at our retreating tormentors almost in disbelief. Yes, our bishop had promised deliverance, but who in his deepest heart had really trusted? And yet there from the southwest came Aetius as promised, with tramping legions, Gothic cavalry, old veterans, and raw teens. I had tears in my eyes as I watched them approach. Zerco capered gleefully, singing a nonsense song.

I watched the allied leaders march through the battered gate with a combination of pride and impatience. Yes, my mission to Tolosa to convince the Visigoths to join the alliance had been a success. Yet this vast maneuvering of armies seemed suddenly inconsequential compared to Skilla's momentous news. Ilana was alive! How, and where, the Hun hadn't said, but the news set afire my whole being, making me realize how quietly her loss had been gnawing at me since escaping from Attila.

A burden of guilt was lifted, and a burden of worry replaced it. I knew how selfish such sentiment was in this time of peril, and yet in turning over Skilla's brief statement, uselessly picking at it for meaning, a hundred memories came rushing back. She had saved Skilla at the duel, yet nursed me afterward. It had been her idea to set the fire and steal the sword for Aetius. Her voice, her manner, her eyes . . . I wanted to ride after Skilla right now, trailing the Hun as the Hun had once trailed me. Perhaps I could disguise myself as a barbarian again, skirting Attila's armies while I gathered information . . .

"Jonas Alabanda?" A centurion had found us on the wall.

I stood, stiffly.

"The general is waiting for your report."

The council of war that evening gave only brief thanks for lifting the siege of Aurelia. All knew a far greater task lay ahead. Some of the Alan captains who had been present at the morning assembly were now missing, having died on the walls. Their place was filled by men from neighboring barbarian kingdoms. Most had never joined in alliance before. Aetius was our acknowledged leader, and yet there were few present who hadn't fought or quarreled with him at some point during his decades of maneuverings. Each tribe was proud of its individuality, even while assembling for the unity of Rome. Theodoric and his Visigoths were the most numerous and powerful military contingent. Sangibanus and his Alans were the bloodied hosts of the gathering, the heroes of Aurelia. But there were also the Riparian Franks from the banks of the Rhine; the Salic Franks; the Belgicans; the Burgundians; the Saxons of the north; the Liticians; the Armoricans; and the Roman veterans, the Olibriones. Their weaponry was as varied as their tactics and origins. We Romans fought in traditional fashion, with shield walls and war machines, but the barbarians were as individualistic as their clothing and armor. Some favored the bow, some the ax, some the stout spear, and some the long sword. Hired Sarmatian bowmen would match their expertise with the Huns, and slingers from Syria and Africa would add new missiles to the fray. There were crossbowmen, light infantry with javelins, heavy cataphract cavalry who depended on the shock and weight of their armored horses, sturdy infantry with long pikes, and fire wizards specializing in tipping missiles with burning pitch.

All this expertise depended on our combined will to stand up to Attila. That's what Aetius wanted to cement this night, in the afterglow of our first great victory. "Attila's foremost column is retreating," Aetius told the kings and warlords around him. "He's lost control of his broader army, scattered across northern Gaul. If we strike now, fast and in concert, we can defeat him once and for all."

"Is he retreating or regrouping?" Sangibanus asked warily. "Let's not risk losing the victory we've already won."

"A war half fought is a war almost certainly lost," Aetius replied. "The Huns exploit every hesitation. Is that not right, Zerco, you who have lived among them?"

"We've defeated a finger of Attila's army, not Attila," the dwarf said. "Had there been any disloyalty in Aurelia, we would have failed to do even that."

The comment hung in the air.

Sangibanus glowered. "We Alans have done more than our share already, little man. You can hear the wailing as the dead are carried off our walls. I had no quarrel with Attila to begin with, and cease to care about him if he leaves my kingdom."

"And where does your kingdom stop?" Aetius asked.

"What do you mean? In this river valley, given to us by the emperor of Rome. We have answered his call by defending our holdings and his. Who knows what Attila will do? Maybe he will go back all the way to Hunuguri."

The others laughed at this suggestion, and Sangibanus flushed.

"I *mean*, Sangibanus," Aetius went on, "that as long as Attila threatens Rome, he threatens all of us. Including you."

"I've heard this argument a thousand times. To hell with your Empire! It means my warriors die for the rich of Italy!"

"It means that failing to unite means the end of what your people migrated here to get. Rome has stood for more than a thousand years. Gaul has been Roman for five centuries." He turned to the rest of us. "Listen to me, all of you. Your ancestors came to the Rhine and Danube and found a world of power and riches beyond all imagining. The deeper you marched into it, the more you wanted to be a part of it. The emperors have granted you lands, but only on the condition that you defend the civilization that accepted you. Now you must pay that debt. If Attila succeeds, the world will fall into permanent darkness. If he is defeated, your kingdoms become heir to a thousand years of civilization. Your choice is simple. You can fight to live as free kings in a world of promise. Or wait to be destroyed individually, one by one, your people enslaved, your daughters raped, your wives tortured, your houses burned. Are we cowards, throwing ourselves on the mercy of the Huns? Or are we the last and the greatest of the legionaries?"

There was a low rumble at this speech, most muttering that Aetius was right. There were already too many fallen cities, too many refugees, and too many stories of Hun slaughter. Now there was a chance for revenge.

"The Alans are no cowards," Sangibanus said sulkily, knowing that Aetius had challenged his courage before every man in the room.

"Indeed they are not, as this siege has proved," Aetius replied with seeming generosity. "Which means that I give *your* people the place of honor, Sangibanus: the middle of our line, in the coming battle."

The king started. The center would undoubtedly mark some of the hardest fighting. It was also the place most difficult to flee from, or switch sides. Once placed in the center, Sangibanus could only fight against the Huns for his life.

Aetius waited. Every eye was on the king of the Alans, knowing that the Roman had outmaneuvered him with words, challenging his manhood and the reputation of his people. Sangibanus gloomily regarded the hundreds of warlords watching him. Then, swallowing, he haughtily raised his head. "The Alans will fight nowhere *but* the center, and *I* shall be in their front rank."

A shout of acclamation went up. Now the assembled kings debated over who should have the honor of occupying the dangerous but potentially decisive right wing. That task was finally acceded primarily to Theodoric and the Visigoths.

One by one, the other kingdoms were assigned to a rough order of battle. Princes preened and boasted as their roles became known. Anthus, king of the Franks, wanted to lead the attack on the left in hopes of forestalling the claim to the throne of his brother Cloda. The veterans called the Olibriones asked to stiffen the Alans in the center. The Burgundians wanted a crack at the Ostrogoths.

"What about me?" Zerco piped up, getting a laugh.

"You will be my adviser, little warrior."

"Let me ride on your shoulders, general, and together we will tower over Attila! He is as squat as he is ugly!" The men laughed again.

"I have a better use. You know the Huns and their language better than almost anyone. Some will be captured and others wounded. I want you to interrogate them about the condition of Attila's army. If he is indeed regrouping his forces, it will probably be in the rolling farmland beyond the Seine where his cavalry can maneuver. But he will be assembling in a wilderness he has burned. I want to know how long he can feed his men."

"The rest of us will give him fewer men to feed," I boasted.

Aetius turned. "No, Jonas of Constantinople, I have a special task for you as well. Rumor persists that this war began in part because Gaiseric and his Vandals agreed to aid Attila in an attack upon Rome. So far, no word of such an attack has come, but if it does all our efforts may be in vain. We desperately need help from Marcian. I need you to return to your home by ship, with my signet ring, and try to persuade the Eastern emperor to march on Attila's rear."

"And thus force the Hun to retreat?" I said.

Aetius smiled. "You have a growing grasp of strategy, young man."

I bowed. "But not the heart, general."

He raised his eyebrows.

"You do me a great honor by showing so much confidence," I went on. "What you wish is indeed important. But it will take me many weeks to reach Constantinople by even the fastest horse and ship, and— even if I persuade him—many months for my emperor to muster his armies and march to Hunuguri. Or to fight Gaiseric. It seems doubtful he could do so this season. So there is time, my lord, to make such a plea this winter, when the West and East can plan together. Our own battle with Attila will be decided long before then. Please don't make me miss what I suspect will be a contest sung of for a thousand years."

"Surely you've had enough blood already, Alabanda."

"I've had enough for a lifetime. But more than almost any man here, I've seen what Attila represents. I watched him crucify a friend for no reason. He kept me from my love, humiliated my embassy, and sent men to kill me and Zerco. Let me stand in the ranks."

My words drew approval from the assembly. A personal grudge the tribesmen understood.

"I admire your courage," Aetius said slowly, "and know too much of your cleverness to believe that serving as a common soldier is all that's on your mind."

I shrugged. "Attila still imprisons the woman I love, general. I intend to kill him, cut my way through to her, and beg her forgiveness for having left her."

Now there was laughter and shouts of encouragement.

"You fight for love, not just for hate?" Aetius asked.

"I fight for the idea of a good, simple life."

Theodoric abruptly stood. "As do we all!" he thundered. "Let the boy ride with us for his woman, as I do for my daughter! Let him ride with me!"

"For our women!" his chieftains cried.

Aetius lifted his hands for quiet. "No, Theodoric, I think I'll keep him with the legions," he said with a smile. "He fights for himself, but something tells me that Alabanda was sent to us for other reasons and that his full usefulness is not yet revealed."

One hundred miles to the east, Attila's vast train of wagons had been halted for two days. Ilana didn't know what this meant. The sun was near its summer's peak, and the fields were hot and hazy from the dust of countless thousands of horses and driven livestock, spilling across the rolling Catalaunian Plain of Gaul. Ilana had never dreamed the world was so big until she'd been driven like a penned animal across it, and now she wondered if she was coming to its end. Augustobona, called Troyes by its more recent inhabitants, was to the south, her driver had told her. Durocatalauni, the place the Franks called Châlons, was to the north. Or rather, had been. Columns of smoke marked where each had existed.

The driver's name was Alix, he had lost half a leg to a battle with the Byzantine Romans, and now he earned his keep by being a teamster in the kagan's train of captured plunder, wives, and slaves. The thousand-mile trek had turned his initial contempt for the caged would-be murderess into something closer to pity. Ilana was bruised from the constant jouncing, filthy from the weeks of dust, thin from being fed only table scraps, and stiff from being confined in a cage. She spoke little, simply watching as they trundled across the famed Rhine, wound through wooded mountains, and now came to this open country reminiscent of Hunuguri. Only when they stopped did she begin to grow dimly curious. Had Attila finally found a place he liked enough to stay? Had Jonas and Zerco escaped somewhere ahead? Were the Huns finally near the fabled ocean?

Probably not, Alix told her. There had been a battle ahead, and the Huns were falling back to gather their strength.

This was intriguing news.

Ilana had thought it her fate to rock hopelessly westward forever, but now more and more wagons were arriving to make a vast laager of wagons, surrounded by another that was bigger still. Regiments of Huns were beginning to congregate. Something in the tempo of invasion had changed.

Then Attila himself arrived, with a thundering contingent of warlords.

As always, his arrival caused an eruption of excitement. He traversed the broad front of his forces like the wind, dashing from one wing to another, sending back an endless stream of looted treasures; captured food; jars of wine; stolen standards; pillaged church relics; kidnapped women; shocked slaves; and the ears, noses, fingers, and cocks of his most prominent enemies. He was the Scourge of God, punishing the world for its sins! He played the role like an actor. He could laugh at an efficient massacre, weep for a single dead Hun, and impose his will on his lieutenants by rages so complete that his eyes rolled and blood gushed from his nose. Now, with news that Aetius had marched to the relief of Aurelia, he had come to this cavalry ground of open, rolling hills. So the Romans had marshaled their forces, winning over even the reluctant Visigoths. Then so would he! All would be decided on a single great and bloody day, and when it was over he would either be dead or king of the world.

Never had he felt such excitement.

Never had he felt such foreboding.

That night, with his thousands of campfires an infinite mirror of the heavens overhead, he disdained most food, drank sullenly, and then, unexpectedly, sent for Ilana.

"Clean the girl, dress her, and make her beautiful. Then bring her to me."

She came at midnight. Her hair had curled after its washing, its darkness gleaming like wave-washed stones on a moonlit beach. Her gown was red silk, captured from the Romans, brocaded with silver and girdled with gold chain studded with rubies. A larger ruby the size of a goat's eye was at her throat, and her sandals were silver. Under threat of death if she demurred, rings of slain matrons had been slipped onto each of her fingers, and the heavy earrings she'd been made to wear hung like trophies. Her eyes were lined with lampblack, her lips highlighted with red ochre, her skin had been scrubbed and moisturized with lanolin-rich sheep's wool, and her breath purified by chewing mint leaves. The woman who had crouched in her cage like an animal just hours before now stood stiffly, like a child bewildered by fine new clothes. She'd no more choice in this dressing up than in being imprisoned, and it seemed equally humiliating.

"Kneel before your kagan," he ordered.

Eyes lowered, cheeks blushing with anger, she did so. To refuse would only result in her being pushed down by Attila's guards. From the corner of her eyes she looked for even the feeblest of weapons. Ilana had no illusions that she could kill Attila, but she knew that he or his guards would kill her, if she tried. That would be release, wouldn't it? Did she have the courage? But there was nothing to even threaten him with.

"Do you wonder why I brought you here?"

She looked up. "To your tent or to Gaul?"

"I could have ordered you a hideous death a thousand times, and yet I stayed my hand," Attila said. "It amused me to watch young Skilla long for what I hate. From all reports he's fighting like a lion to win my favor and your company. It reminded me to be wary of desire and greed, because they change like the weather and have no more explanation. This is why I eat from a wooden plate, sleep in animal skins, and spit out soft bread in favor of meat and gristle. To long for too much is to risk losing it."

Somehow, she found voice. "To fear to hope is the mark of a coward."

He scowled. "I fear nothing but the stupidity of those I must deal with. Like you, who longs for what is out of reach: the past. A Hun like Skilla would make you a princess. A Roman like Jonas has reduced you to a cage."

She rocked back on her heels, her carriage more upright now. "It is *your* cage, kagan. And I know you can slit my throat in an instant. So, yes, why did you bring me here?"

He leaned back in his camp chair, lazy in his power. "Alabanda is alive."

Instantly she was tense. "How do you know this?"

"Skilla saw him on the walls of Aurelia. They fought, but again there was no decision." He saw her confusion, not just at this news but at his willingness to tell her. He was quiet for a while, amused by her little dreams, and then spoke. "Have you ever considered that I brought you to Gaul to give you back to him?"

She trembled. "Give me or trade me?"

"Sell you, if you want to call it that, for the sword."

"You don't even know he has the sword."

Attila sat abruptly upright and his fist crashed onto the arm of his chair, making her start. "Of course I do! Why else does Theodoric ride with Aetius? Why else do the tribes of Gaul refuse to join me? Why is there no news of Gaiseric and his promised Vandals? Because Rome has been given courage by the sword of Mars, that's why! But that sword is mine, by discovery and by right. He stole it from me, and I want it back before the battle!"

"You brought me all this way for that?" It was odd how courage ebbed and flowed, and now came unbidden. She even smiled. "Surely you know the Romans would never trade the sword for me. Even Jonas wouldn't do it."

Attila's fingers drummed in that habit he had, his dark, sunken eyes regarded her dourly. "He will if you ask him to. He'll only do it if you ask him to."

Her heart began to hammer.

"Why do you think I've dressed you like a Roman whore, had the pig smell scrubbed off you, and painted your lips the color of your cunt? Why would I do this to a witch who helped the thief steal what was rightfully mine and who set my house on fire and who almost burned me in its flames? To persuade your lover."

"I wish we *had* all burned," she said quietly.

"We will, witch, if I lose the coming battle because I have lost my sacred sword. We will burn together, you and I, on a pyre that I will build of my choicest possessions—and while I might stab my own heart to quicken things, you'll be left to the flames."

"You fear the Romans, don't you?" she said in sudden realization. "You, the king who professes to fear nothing. The Westerners are uniting to fight you. That's why we've stopped. You fear Aetius. You even fear Jonas. You regret that you've come here. It is all going wrong."

He shook his shaggy head. "Attila fears nothing. Attila needs nothing. But it will spare many lives, Roman and Hun, if the final battle is an easy one instead of a hard one. If you meet Jonas, and he brings the sword, I will let you go with him."

"What about Skilla?"

"Skilla is a Hun. He will forget you in a year. I'll have a thousand women for Skilla, all of them more beautiful than you. Just help me get back what you stole."

She looked at him in wonder, this king trying to strike a bargain with the most helpless member of his retinue. "No. If you want the sword back, then take it from Aetius."

Attila sprang out of his chair and towered over her, his face enraged, his voice a howl. "I want it stolen back from Aetius! Do it or I kill you right now! I can rape you, strip you, flay you, and give you to my soldiers to use and my dogs to eat!"

His rage was weakness, and it gave her hope. "You can do anything you wish, but it will not bring back the sword," she said quietly. Here *was* power, she realized, the power to play on his fears. He had the look of a man haunted by nightmares. "I *have* cursed you, but it's a curse you earned when Edeco treacherously killed my father. Rape me, and the curse is redoubled. Kill me, and I'll be at your shoulder in the battle, whispering the breath of the grave. Abuse *me*, and you'll lose your empire."

His look was wild. "If we lose this fight, you will burn on my pyre!"

"And go happier that way than living to watch you win."

XXVI

FIRST BLOOD

The Huns who had assaulted Aurelia were but a tree in a wood. Now we were approaching the immensity of the full forest.

Attila was gathering his forces on the Catalaunian Plain, and that is where Aetius would face him. A hundred kings and warlords rode from the council to direct a hundred armies into one mighty host. Some were from the decimated garrisons of cities and forts that had fallen. Some were proud retinues of the high kings of the Germans. Some were Roman legions whose standards and histories dated back centuries, marching now to this last and greatest battle. And some were the hastily organized regiments of men who had fled in fear and now, with a mixture of desperation and hope, wanted to recover their pride and avenge their burned homes. The Huns had put more than a million people to flight, creating chaos, but also churned up a vast reserve of potential manpower that Aetius was now furiously arming. Some of these men were old veterans. Others were untried youths. Many were merchants and craftsmen with little knowledge of war. Yet all were able to hold a spear and swing a sword. In the havoc to come, skill might not count as much as numbers.

I felt swept up in the current of a river, carried toward Ilana by an irresistible flood. My decision not to go as an envoy to Marcian in Constantinople had reduced my importance from diplomat to soldier and aide, but I found my new anonymity strangely comforting. I need do nothing more complicated than take orders, fight, and wait for an opportunity to find the woman I'd been forced to leave behind. As the columns marched forward, long glittering spears of men on the straight Roman roads, it seemed to me we marched with the ghosts of countless Romans who had gone before us: with Caesar and Trajan, Scipio and Constantine, legion upon legion who had imposed order on a world of chaos. Now we faced the greatest darkness. It seemed ominous and appropriate that in the heat of late June a range of thunderheads formed to the east, lightning crackling in the direction of Attila's army. The air was humid and heavy, and the storm seemed symbolic of the test to come. Yet no rain fell where we were, and huge columns of dust rose as herds of men, horses, and livestock moved toward collision. Ordinary life had stopped, and every soldier in Europe was migrating toward the coming contest.

Zerco rode with me on his own short pony, saying he wanted to see the finish of what we had started. We trailed Aetius like loyal hounds. Accompanying us, strapped to a staff like a standard and carried as a talisman by a veteran decurion, was Attila's iron sword. Its presence was proof, Aetius told his officers, that God was with us, not them.

We gained a slight rise and paused to see the progress of our alliance. It was thrilling to see so many marching under the old Roman standards, rank after rank on road after road, to the left and right as far as I could see. "It looks like veins on a forearm," I remarked.

"I've seen boys of twelve and old men of sixty in the ranks," Zerco said quietly. "Armor that was an heirloom. Weapons that a few days before were being used to turn soil, not kill men. Wives carrying hatchets. Grandmothers with daggers to still the wounded. And a thousand fires that mark where Attila has been. This is a fight of revenge and survival, not a test of kings."

He was proud, this little and ugly man, that we'd had some small role in this. "Don't get lost in the battle, doughty warrior," I advised him.

His seriousness retreated. "You're the one who is going to cut his way through the entire Hun army. I'm going to stay on Aetius's shoulders, like I said."

The landscape we traversed was rich and rolling, fat with lush pastures, ripening fields, and once-tidy villas. In many ways it was the loveliest land I'd ever seen, greener and more watered than my native Byzantium. If my body was to fall in Gaul, it would not be such a bad place to stay. And if I were to survive . . .

That night I stood in the background of the headquarter's tent as Aetius received reports of each contingent and its direction. "There's a crossroads called Maurica," Aetius told his officers, pointing to a map. "Any armies crossing between the Seine and the Marne will pass there, both the Huns and us. That's where we'll find Attila."

"Anthus and his Franks are drawing near that place already," a general said. "He's as anxious to find his traitorous brother as that boy there is to find his woman."

"Which means the Franks may stumble on Attila before we're ready. I want them reined in. Jonas?"

"Yes, general."

"Exercise your own impatience and go find impatient King Anthus. Warn him that he may be about to collide with the Huns. Tell the Franks to wait for our support."

"And if he won't wait, general?" I asked.

Aetius shrugged. "Then tell him to take the enemy straight into Hell."

I rode all night, half lost and nervous about being accidentally shot or stabbed, and it was mid-morning before I found Anthus. I had snatched only a little sleep, and felt I needed hardly that. Never had I been so anxious and excited. Lightning flashed without rain, leaving a metallic scent, and when I dismounted to rest my horse I could feel the ground quivering from so many tramping feet.

The Frankish king, helmet off as the day's heat rose, listened politely to my cautious message and laughed. "Aetius doesn't have to tell me where the enemy is! I've run into some already, and my men bear the wounds to prove it! If we strike while the Huns are still strung out, we can destroy them."

"Aetius wants our forces collected."

"Which gives time for the Huns to do the same. Where *is* Aetius? Are the Romans mounted on donkeys? He's slower than an ore wagon!"

"He's trying to spare the men's horses for the battle."

Anthus put his helmet back on. "The battle is here, now, if he would just come to it! I've got the enemy's butt in my face! Not Huns, but other vermin."

"Gepids, lord," one of his lieutenants said. "Hun vassals."

"Yes, King Ardaric, a worm of a man hoping for a scrap of Hun favor. His troops look like they've crawled from under a rock. I'm going to put them back."

"Aetius would prefer that you wait," I repeated.

"And Aetius is not a Frank! It isn't his homes that are being burned! It isn't his brother who has gone over to Attila! We wait for no man and fear none. This is our land now. Half my men have lost families to these invaders, and they starve for vengeance."

"If Attila turns—"

"Then I and my Franks will kill him, too! What about it, Roman? Do you want to wait another day and yet another, hoping the enemy will go away? Or do you want to fight him this afternoon, with the sun at our backs and the grass as high as the bellies of our horses? I heard you boast you'd cut your way to your woman! Let's see it!"

"Aetius knew you wouldn't listen to me," I confessed.

"Which means he was sending you to battle!" He grinned, his eyes glinting beside his nose guard. "You're lucky, Alabanda, to taste war as a Frank."

Ram's horns were lifted to begin the call. Heavy Frankish cavalry trotted forward, each kite-shaped shield bearing a different design and color, their lances thick as axles and tall as saplings. The knights' hands were gloved in dark leather, and their mail had the leaden color of a winter pond. Their helmets were peaked, and the cheek guards were tied so tightly against chins that those who shaved in the Roman fashion had white lines pressed into their faces. Barbarian long hair and beards, I realized, served as padding.

As I joined them a hundred smells assaulted me—of horseflesh and droppings, dust and sweat, high hay and timothy, honed metal and hardwood shafts. War is a stink of sweat and oil. It was noisy in a cavalry formation, too, a vast clanking and clumping as the big horses moved forward, men shouting to each other or boasting of their prowess in war or with women. Many of the words had the high, clipped sound of men under tension, afraid and yet mastering their fear, waiting for the charge they'd trained their whole lives for. They were as different from the Huns and Gepids as a bull from a wolf: tall, thick-limbed men as pale as cream.

Only a minority of the Franks could afford the expense of horse and heavier armor. Thousands more were paralleling the wedge of horsemen by loping on foot across tall grain. Their mail shirts ended at thigh instead of calf and their scabbards rocked and banged against their hips. These would take the Gepids on the ground.

Our foe was an undifferentiated mass of brown ahead, bunched against a slow but deep pastoral stream at which they'd paused to drink. Half had already waded the chest-high water to join Attila's main force to the east. Half were on the near bank closest to us. I saw that Anthus was not just hotheaded but a tactician, whose scouts had told him of this opportunity. The enemy formation was divided by deep water.

"See?" the king said to himself as much as to anyone. "Their cursed bowmen won't want to risk crossing to our side. Their distance will give us an edge."

Now the enemy seemed to be milling with indecision like a disturbed ants' nest, some urging a quick retreat across the creek, which would turn it into a protective moat, and others a braver fight with the oncoming Franks. Attila's orders to regroup had been obeyed with bitterness by warriors used to driving all before them. And now their foes had come to them: not the rumored vast army of Aetius but just a wing of eager and reckless Franks who'd pushed too far ahead!

We watched King Ardaric, marked by his banners of royalty, ride off looking for Attila, apparently wanting the Hun to tell him what to do.

It was just as Anthus hoped. "Charge!"

I had expected more fear, but what drunken pleasure to join them! The sheer power and momentum of the Frankish cavalry was intoxicating, and never had I felt more alive than when galloping ahead with this stampede of knights. The ground shook as we pounded, and there was a great cry on both sides as the distance closed, the Frankish horse and the more numerous Gepid infantry hurriedly forming a line.

When we neared, they shot and threw, a heave of javelins meant to swerve our charge. There was a curling wave as some of our foremost horsemen collided with this bristle and fell, skidding into the Gepid ranks. Then the rest of us crashed over and past them, shredding the enemy line, the Franks spearing and hacking all the way to the bank of the river before turning to take the survivors from behind. The violence of the attack was a shock to the Gepids, who had become used to having their victims flee. The big Frankish swords cleaved enemy spears and helmets in two, even as Gepid infantry desperately speared the flanks of Anthus's horses, spilling some of his knights on the ground where they could be overwhelmed. For a perilous moment the Gepids vastly out-numbered us, but then Frankish foot began swarming in support, pour-ing into the edges of the fight with great cries amid a cacophonous beating of drums.

For long minutes it was pitched battle that could have gone either way. I used my horse to butt and unbalance the Gepid infantry, striking down with my sword, but I also saw Frankish nobles swallowed by the maelstrom. Then the fury of the Franks began to tell, Gepid courage began to break, and the enemy was pushed to the water. There they re-alized their peril. The bank was steep and if they slid down it they couldn't properly fight, so their choice was either to abandon their com-rades and swim for safety or be speared or shot by Frankish bows where they stood. They began shouting for help to their comrades on the far bank. Some plunged in to come to their aid while others called for with-drawal before it was too late. It was chaos, and the Gepid generals, ac-customed to being under the domineering thrall of Hun warlords, seemed at a loss whether to counterattack or withdraw. As more and more Franks came up to the battle, the beleaguered Gepid troops be-came packed and they panicked.

A regiment of Huns rode up on the far side and began firing arrows in support, but, as Anthus had hoped, distance and the melee of combat made the volleys ineffective. The Hun archers killed as many Gepids as they did Franks. Had the horsemen crossed upstream and circled to the Frankish rear, they would have had better effect, but they were loathe to be cut off from Attila.

Yet the Gepids on the far shore were equally reluctant to abandon their kinsmen by retreating. They fed themselves piecemeal into the fray, plunging into the water and wading or thrashing slowly across, some picked off by arrows, some simply drowning. The survivors clambered up the Frankish side to try to stiffen the barbarian line even as it was dissolving. This prolonged the fight but did not change it. Our cavalry chewed huge gaps in the Gepid formations, swords and axes hewing down at the tangled footmen and grinding them under hoof. Meanwhile, Frankish infantry exploited the gaps to take the Gepids from the side and rear. The fight began turning to a rout, and then the rout into slaughter. Attila's henchmen broke to plunge back into the river, desperately pushing, and Frankish archers tormented them from the bank. As each invader tried to save his own life, most died in a waterway that had turned red.

Our victory won on the western shore, a few of Anthus's cavalry splashed across to continue the pursuit; but now the enemy had the advantage of a high bank and greater numbers, and these impetuous Franks either died or were forced to a quick retreat. Finally the Gepids themselves drew back farther, both sides temporarily disengaging from the embattled river, and this preliminary battle died. Raggedly forming, the shattered rear guard of Attila's army shambled up and over the far hill. The supporting Huns, mustered from Attila's main force, rode back and forth on the crest as if to continue the fight, but finally thought better of it. The day's shadows were long, the western sun was in their eyes to blind bow aim, and they could see the shine of other Roman formations coming up in support of the Franks. Better to wait for the morrow, when Attila could bring his full might to bear.

They turned, and vanished from the crest.

I caught my breath. My arm ached from the shock of striking shield, helmet, and yielding flesh. My sword was red and myself, miraculously, unhurt. I looked back at the carpet of bodies, thousands of them, and was appalled to realize that this was only a beginning. It wasn't the first time I'd seen battle corpses, of course, but the sheer number sobered me. The bodies lay still and strangely deflated. There was no mistaking the dead.

At the same time I felt exhilarated by my survival, as if infused by the glow of the storm's earlier lightning. Was it a sign that no missile or blade had touched me? We'd crushed the rear guard as the Frankish king had predicted, and for a briefly insane moment my greatest fear was that the Huns would keep running before I could get to Ilana.

Anthus hauled off his helmet again, his sweaty hair in strings and his eyes bright with triumph. "Come, let's get a look at the rest of them before we lose all the light!" he roared. "This battlefield is mine, and I want to claim that hill!"

A thousand Frankish cavalry foamed across the stream in a body, now that the enemy was gone, and rumbled to the crest of the ridge that the enemy had just left. We reined in, the ground pockmarked with hoofprints, and looked eastward in awe.

The dying sun emphasized the darkness of the clouds to the east, turning them jet-black, while bathing in gold the panoply before us. The effect was dazzling, and the panorama was one I will never forget. We were seeing, it seemed, every person born east of the Rhine.

A few miles away the lines of the Hun camp began, great swaths of men settling in for the night. There was an enormous double-laager of wagons beyond, canvas hoop tops and yurts blossoming like gray mushrooms. We could see the crossroads of Maurica in the far distance and tens of thousands—nay, hundreds of thousands—of Attila's warriors around it like a vast browsing herd. There were also chains of ponies, flocks of bleating sheep, and pens of oxen. The very ground seemed to move and twitch like an animal's skin. The smoke of ten thousand cooking fires created a purple haze, and the metal of countless stacked spearheads sparkled with menace. It was as if every man from every place was at last coming here, to settle world supremacy once and for all.

"Look and look well, my brothers, for no man has seen such a sight in a thousand years," Anthus solemnly said. "Does it look like a fight worth fighting?"

"It looks like every nation on Earth," a Frankish captain said in awe. "My hands ache from swinging my sword, lord, and yet we've barely begun."

"Aye, but the Romans and the Visigoths and the rest of them are coming up now, so they'll help finish what we started. We've shown them how to do it." We turned and saw tramping columns of our allies converging from all directions, swallowing the last few miles before Attila's camp. Their dust had turned the setting sun bloodred, and their armor looked like an advancing tide of water.

"Look at this sight and hope to remember it for your children," Anthus murmured. "Look and never forget." He nodded, as if to himself. "Not only has no such gathering ever happened but never will it happen again."

"Never?" the captain asked.

The king shook his head. "No. Because by nightfall tomorrow, many of them—and us—will be dead."

XXVII

THE BATTLE OF NATIONS

What I remember of the night before the great battle is not fear and not sleep but song. The Germans were great singers, much louder and more demonstrative than we quiet and methodical Romans; and as regiment upon regiment, division upon division, and army upon army marched up to take the places that Aetius assigned them, settling down to a restless night on the grassy plain, they sang of a misty and legendary past: great monsters and greater heroes, of golden treasure and bewitching maidens, and of the need for each man to convince himself that on this night, of all the nights of his life, it was necessary to conquer or die. If dead they would pass to an afterworld, a jumbled mixture of the pagan great hall and Christian Heaven, and take their places in a pantheon of heroes and saints. If they survived, they'd live free of fear. As the words lifted to summer's great starry night, the air warm and still humid from the thunderstorms that had dissipated, song built on song into vast resolve, giving our soldiers courage.

The Huns sang as well. In the aftermath of their invasions they have been remembered as virtually inhuman, I know: an Eastern plague of such unworldly ferocity that they seemed to belong to Satan or older, darker gods. Or, as Attila called himself, the Scourge of God. Yet while I knew they had to be defeated, I also knew them as people: proud, free, arrogant, and secretly fearful of the civilized world they had hurled them-

selves against. Their words were hard to catch from such a distance—
overladen as the songs were by the Germans' singing nearby—but its
hum was strangely softer and sadder, sung from deep within their squat
frames. The Hun songs were of a home they had long left, of the freedom of the steppes, and of a simplicity they could not regain no matter
how hard and far they rode. They sang for a time already gone, no matter who won this battle.

The Romans were quieter at first, trying to sleep or, giving up on
that, sharpening their weapons and wheeling into place hundreds of ballistae that would hurl bolts capable of cutting down a dozen enemies at a
time. Their habitual discipline was silence. But near dawn of this short-
est of the year's nights, the mood caught some of them as well. They finally sang, too, choosing new Christian hymns. Bishop Anianus had
followed us from Aurelia; and now I watched him walk among these
rude soldiers, dressed like a simple pilgrim, blessing and confessing the
believers and offering encouragement even to those who had not yet
been won by the Church.

The sun rose as it had set, red through smoldering cloud. It glinted
in our eyes, and Aetius ordered his generals and kings to brace our
disorganized ranks in case the Huns used the light at their backs to
charge while we were relatively blinded. But the enemy was no more
ready for combat than we were. Such numbers had never been assembled for a battle; and there was considerable confusion on both sides
as men were moved first here, then there, grumbling about the anxious waiting as the sun climbed higher and hotter. There was a small
stream that tantalizingly ran between the armies, but it was within
bowshot of either side so none dared venture there. Instead, women
passed down the ranks with skins and jars of water drawn from the
captured river in our rear. The men drank thirstily, sweating in their
armor and pissing in place until, by the time it was noon, the battlefield already smelled like a privy.

"When will it start?" we grumbled.

The plans of the two sides were opposites of each other. Attila
placed himself and his Huns at the center of his line, clearly hoping to
use his cavalry, the fiercest of his forces, to split our army in two.

Attila's Ostrogoths with King Valamer were on his right, facing our Roman left, as were his battered Gepids and the rebel Bagaudae. Cloda, the Frankish prince who wanted the crown, would there face his brother, Anthus.

The Rugi, Sciri, and Thuringi tribes allied with the Huns were, in turn, on Attila's left. These were stiffened by a force of several thousand Vandals who had come to kill Visigoths.

Aetius, in contrast to Attila, put his best troops on either wing and, as promised, Sangibanus and the Alans in the center. "He does not have to win. All he has to do is hold," Aetius said. This force was stiffened by fresh troops as yet unblooded, the Liticians and the Olibriones. What the old Roman veterans lacked in youthful vigor they more than made up in experienced determination.

Theodoric and his Visigoths formed the Roman right flank. They were the most powerful cavalry we had, arrayed against the Rugi, Sciri, and Thuringi.

Finally Aetius and his Roman legions—combined with the Franks, Saxons, and Armoricans—made up the Roman left. Except for the Frankish heavy cavalry that had fought so well the afternoon before, these were primarily foot soldiers, shield linked to shield in unbroken walls, who would advance like a lumbering dragon against the German infantry on the enemy side. What Aetius hoped was that as the Huns hurled themselves against his center, he could close on the Hun allies on either side and push the invaders together, trapping and slaughtering them as the Romans had been slaughtered at Cannae by Hannibal or at Hadrianopolis by Fritigern and the Goths.

"All will depend on two things," he told us. "The center must hold, or Attila will run rampant in our rear and cut us down with arrows from behind. Second, our own wing must seize that low ridge before us, because from there our infantry can hurl spears down on any enemy charge and turn it back. The decisive blow will then be delivered by Theodoric and his Visigoths. If the Huns are in confusion, his cavalry can win the day." He put his helmet on his head. "I told Theodoric all the riches of the West and East are waiting in Attila's camp. He told me that in that case, he will either be wealthy beyond measure or dead by the nightfall." His smile was grim, and not entirely reassuring. "That prophecy works well enough for all of us."

History has recorded these battle plans as simple and clear. The reality is that both sides were a babble of languages and a coalition of proud kings; and so neither the patient diplomacy of Aetius, nor the terrifying charisma of Attila, could easily maneuver men into position. We could scarcely understand one another or grasp the scale of the field, which ran for miles. It could take half an hour to relay an order.

How many were assembled that day no man will ever know for sure. Tens of thousands of escaped Roman slaves had swelled the ranks of Attila. Tens of thousands of merchants, shopkeepers, farmers, scholars, and even priests had swelled the Roman ranks, knowing Aetius offered the only chance to sustain civilization. Any attempt at counting was impossible in the milling throngs and swirling dust, but the numbers on each side were in the hundreds of thousands, I believe. It was as if this *was* Armageddon, the final battle in the history of the world, and every man had pledged his soul on its outcome.

Accordingly, hour upon hour passed with the two armies essentially in awe of each other, and still separated by more than a mile. The ridge remained unclaimed, and the tempting brook was a pale line in high grass promising water to the first army that could seize it. Yet neither was ready to advance for some time, because to go forward in disarray was to invite annihilation. I grew tired of sitting on my restless horse, and the infantry grew so weary of standing that many sat in the grass.

I said I remember the night as one of song, but the noon was one of stillness. It was apparent by midday that both sides had achieved some semblance of order and that combat must soon begin, and a curious quiet descended on both sides. For some it was silent determination, I suppose, for others fear and for still others prayers and superstition— but all knew that the test was finally at hand. I had nothing useful to say, either. Never had the Romans faced such a fearsome enemy. Never had the Huns faced such a determined foe: our backs, in a sense, to the great western sea, even though the ocean was far away. There were at least a thousand standards and banners held upright among the endless ranks of soldiers, and they formed a thicket as quiet as a grove before the storm. I saw the golden legionary standards of the Romans; the horse-hair banners of the Huns; and the flags, crosses, and pagan symbols of all the diverse tribes and nations that had gathered here, each man iden-tifying himself in part by the symbol that was before him. The suspense seemed almost unbearable, my mouth dry paper despite the water I sipped, and I wondered where past that vast and innumerable horde At-tila's own laager might lay. That was the goal I must fight toward, be-cause that was where Ilana would be.

I had no idea what she might look like after months of imprison-ment, whether she had been burned and tortured, whether she felt I'd abandoned her to the Huns or done what she wanted by fleeing with the sword. It didn't matter. She was Ilana, a memory as sharp and vivid as a steel blade. The greater this conflict became, the more I cared about my own small happiness. No matter who won this day I myself would know no peace until I found her, won her back, and took her from this night-mare. Kings fought for nations. I fought for my own peace.

As if he read my thoughts, a lone horse and rider detached himself from the Hun center and began a long, easy lope that angled toward our lines, the horse a chestnut color and the Hun erect and proud, his queue bouncing as he rode, his quiver of arrows rattling. The clop of the hooves was startling in the pregnant silence. He splashed across the lit-tle stream, but no one shot at him; and at a hundred paces from our lines he turned slightly and rode parallel to our ranks, coolly surveying the thousands upon thousands upon thousands of men we'd arrayed, his gaze clearly searching for someone. Then, as he drew abreast of the Roman formations on the left I recognized him at last and knew pre-cisely who it was he was looking for: me.

It was Skilla.

His horse slowed as he came abreast of the little forest of standards around Aetius and his officers, hunting for my face, and with a feeling of dread and destiny I dully raised my arm. He saw my gesture, and I took off my helmet to make sure of his recognition. He halted his pony and pointed, as if to say it was time to renew our fight. I saw him grin, a flash of teeth in the tan of his face. Then he wheeled and galloped back to his own army, taking a place on the Hun right now, roughly opposite my own. The men of his new *lochus* cheered.

"Who was that?" Aetius asked curiously.

"A friend," I replied without thinking, and surprised myself by what I said. But who better understood me than the man who wanted Ilana for himself? Who more intimately shared my experiences than the man I'd battled so often?

Aetius frowned at my reply, regarding me a moment as if it were the first time he had really seen me and wanted to lodge this curious sight in his memory. Then he nodded to Zerco, and the dwarf waddled forward, almost staggering under the weight of Attila's great sword of Mars strapped to its pole. The general leaned to take it and then, the muscles of his arm straining, he lifted the weapon as high overhead as he could. Ten thousand faces swung to look at it, and then, as word filtered down the ranks, ten times ten thousand and more. Here was the signal at last! Even the Huns stirred, and I knew they could see it, too—this talisman that had been stolen—and I could well imagine Attila exhorting his followers to look at the long black blade held against the sky of the west and telling them that the man who won it back would win his weight in gold.

Then, to the steplike thud of drums, the long lines of the Roman and allied infantry picked up their resting shields and in easy unison swung them forward like the closing of a shutter. With that, our wing started for the ridge.

I was mounted like the officers, giving me a better view. On my horse, I and the other cluster of aides followed our ranks at a slightly safer distance, marveling at the disciplined cadence of the sea of heads with rocking spears and helmets that marched to a steady beat before us. Beneath the sound of the drums was the background sound of creaking leather and clanging equipment and the tread of a hundred thousand feet. It was as if a great, scaled monster had at last roused itself and was advancing from its cave, hulking and hunched, its gaze fixed with dire intent. As we neared the low hill that Aetius meant to seize, the Ostrogoths opposite us were momentarily lost to view, but as the ground began to rise we heard a great shout from the far side and then an eerie rippling scream like the screech of a thousand eagles. It made the hair bristle on our necks. The invaders were charging to reach the crest before we did. So now our own drums doubled their tempo and our own ranks began to trot, then run. I drew my sword, the blade rasping as it cleared my scabbard, and the surrounding officers did the same. All we could see was the green sward of the gentle ridge now, and yet the pounding of the Gothic infantry charging toward us was so loud and heavy that the vibration of the earth could clearly be felt.

Then the sky went dim as it filled with arrows.

How can I describe that sight? No man had seen it before, or is likely to ever see it again. It was like a wind of chaff, a canopy of clattering wood, a hiss of missiles that tore the very air apart with a sound like the ripping of a sheet. It was a hum like a plague of locusts. Now the legions were running in awkward formation, lifting their oval shields overhead, and the first storm broke on us even as another volley—and another and still another—followed in an endless pulse of wicked shafts.

The arrows struck with a rattle like hail, the unlucky screaming or whoofing as some missiles found gaps in the shield ceiling and they went down. In an instant my own horse was hit and pitching forward, spilling me into what had become a meadow of wooden shafts jutting from earth and men. I landed hard, stunned, and at first wasn't sure what had happened. Then another rattle as the next volley came down, miraculously missing my sprawled form. The screams of my horse made me realize that arrows were steadily punching into its neck and flanks. Finally gaining some breath and wits, I yanked at the shield of a dead man and pulled it over me just in time before the next salvo came sluicing at me. How many arrows were fired in those first moments? A million? And yet it was just the prelude to what would be an endless day.

Now I heard the air being rent anew with an angry sizzle, and dared to peek up. It was the heavy bolts and flaming projectiles of our own Roman artillery, returning the volleys. And I saw our own archers running forward. Now arrows flew in both directions, so many that some collided in midair and spiraled down to earth like fluttering seedpods. As men fought, the shafts broke and crackled underneath like a skin of ice.

There was a vast roar, a sea of voices. Then a clash as the two charging wings, Roman and Ostrogoth, met at the crest of the desired ridge.
The bang of the collision actually echoed across the battlefield like a clap
of thunder, a great violent shock of wall hitting wall; and here the discipline of Aetius's Roman line began to tell. They bent and rippled but did
not break, even as the Ostrogoths recoiled slightly.

I crawled out from under my protective shell and hoisted the shield
to my arm. With the melee joined, the storm of missiles had slackened.
Three arrows were stuck in my oval disk of protection, reminding me of
my earlier lone combat with Skilla. I was still somewhat stunned by the
squall of arrows, and had to remember what my task was. Ilana! Life!
The thought of her jolted into my consciousness again, and it energized
me for the work at hand. For the moment I was an infantryman and as
desperately needed as every other Roman that day. The two sides were
locked together in front of me in a vast scrum, and when enough men
went down to provide a gap I waded atop groaning bodies and added my
own sword and muscle to the clamor. Ahead I could see the Ostrogoth
Valamer and his brothers Theodimer and Valodimer urging their troops
on, and our crazed Anthus trying to hack his way toward his rival
Cloda. Romans and Huns fought for empire. The allies on both sides
fought ancient feuds.

I wish I could tell you of swift parry and clever thrust, but I remember nothing like that, or much of any skill at all. Just a sea of Gothic
heads, some with helmets and some without, pushing up the ridge and
we Romans grunting and pushing and stabbing and slashing down it.
Each side shoved against the other. By the grace of a few paces, we had
gained the tiny advantage in altitude that made all the difference. I held
up my shield while things hammered on it, like intruders trying to break
down a door, and cut blindly with my own blade, usually hitting something hard that reverberated in my hand . . . but sometimes striking
softer things that howled. Men clutched at my ankles, and I swore and
stabbed at them. A man beside me lurched backward, his face cleaved
with an ax: I remember that because the gore sprayed like a fan, spatter-
ing half a dozen of us all around. I don't recall much else. Entire ranks
seemed to go down on both sides, as if swallowed by the earth, only to

have replacements close in right behind. I tripped on something, a body or a spear, and fell with an awkward gasp, exhausted already. I was down on all fours, my back exposed, and I tensed myself for a final thrust. But, no, the line moved past me, fresh Romans taking my place. Goths were toppling, retreating, as Aetius's legions pressed. I was to learn later that this first fight was vital, giving our armies an advantage we never surrendered in the long nightmare to come, but the significance of this early action wasn't apparent to me then. I stood upright in time to see the mounted Skilla being carried backward by the sea of retreating Goths and Gepids, shouting at them in Hunnish to stand firm. They cried oaths in their own language, trying to reorganize after the death of so many of their chiefs. I doubt he saw me; I was too low.

Horns blew and Aetius halted his advance just downslope of the crest of the hard-won hill. Thousands of bodies marked its summit, some utterly still and others twitching and moaning as blood gushed out, their jutting and splintered bones jostled by reinforcements as our men dressed their ranks. The Romans killed those Ostrogoths they found who were still alive, even as the Ostrogoths took the few Romans they'd captured and gutted or dismembered them before our eyes. Here, where height gave the throw of Roman javelins a few yards' advantage, we caught our breath.

And now the battle began in earnest.

If the ground had trembled before, now it shook—and it shook with violence reminiscent of the earthquakes that had toppled the walls of Constantinople a few years before. Survivors told us later that Attila had disdained lending his cavalry to help the Ostrogoths struggle for the ridge, because he thought the hillock insignificant in the context of great cavalry charges. He shouted to his warlords that the unmounted Romans were slugs who could be covered by dust and ignored, while the real battle would be decided by horsemen. So with a shout he led the cream of his army at Sangibanus and his Alans in the center, vowing to ride down the king who had somehow failed to surrender Aurelia. If Attila cleaved through there, the battle would be over. The Huns rode with a high, wavering yip, firing sheets of arrows. I remembered Zerco's early lesson in war by the Tisza River and wondered just when, if ever, these horsemen would run out of shafts—and whether it would be too late when they did. I also wondered if Aetius had been wise to bet his center on Sangibanus, because our general seemed in no hurry to envelop the Huns with his two wings. Until he did, the battle would ride on the Alans, Liticians, and Olibriones. We held our breaths as the Huns charged.

Our armies tried to slow them with missiles, our arrows fewer but our heavier artillery cutting wicked furrows in the oncoming assault with stones, ballista bolts, and flaming kettles of fire that tripped whole swathes of Huns. At the same time, the Alans were charging forward on their horses, many with their own deadly scores to settle with these eastern barbarians who had besieged their city and killed members of their families. The combined ranks were riddled with arrows as the space between the two cavalries closed, men sinking. With a few more volleys, perhaps the Huns could have cleared a gap for themselves and sliced our army in two. But even the steppe warriors could not fire fast enough; and their numbers were so huge that instead of simply being overwhelming, they were getting in the way of one another. None of the nations assembled had experience controlling such an assembly. So at last the centers met, and that collision dwarfed what I had seen on the ridge, a slamming together not just of men but heavy horses. I hadn't seen the western ocean yet, but I sensed this is what it must sound like, the boom of breakers against rock, as tens of thousands of horsemen plowed into one another. Horses neighed and screamed, lances and shields splintered, and some collisions were so violent that spear tips, helmets, armor fragments, or even pieces of bodies erupted into the air. The bits cartwheeled lazily, seeming suspended for hours, before raining down.

All was then swirling confusion, but the Huns were not equipped for the kind of brutal close-quarters hacking that the bigger and more heavily armored Alans had adopted in the West. Hun ponies were eviscerated, running backward with dead riders entangled in their tack, dragging their own entrails. Light lamellar and leather armor were punctured and shredded under the assault of hard Alan steel. Horsetail banners that had not fallen for generations toppled. Whole clans of Huns were trampled under in the desperate center, their long family sagas snuffed out in a few anxious moments of carnage. Even as the Ostrogoths were advancing again on our Roman lines, Aetius was exulting and waving the huge iron sword, one arm already bandaged and bloody. "They're holding! They're holding!" Now the center's infantry was coming up, and the Hun horses were balking even as their masters urged them against the ranks of spearmen. I could imagine Attila's frustration.

Line after line of Hun cavalry went down, and to continue this close-quarter mismatch was madness. The barbarians broke to retreat and re-form, even as still more horns and drums sounded and Attila's left wing began to advance toward Theodoric and his Visigoths on the right. If they could not break us at one point, then maybe at another!

Now the battle was well and truly joined along miles of front, great tides of men surging back and forth under the singing arc of un-countable arrows. There was no hope of any one man controlling the fury that followed. It was the havoc of horse and foot, spear and arrow, sword and biting teeth. Whole companies seemed to be swallowed, and yet as soon as they disappeared in the slaughter, fresh companies pushed ahead.

The Ostrogoths charged us Romans again and then again and then yet again, surging up the ridge to try to take the advantage. Each time they had to clamber up a slope slick with blood and thick with the bod-ies of their comrades, a hedgerow of stiffening limbs and broken weapons. The Gepid king, Ardaric, went down with a spear wound and was carried away, delirious; and the ambitious Cloda the Frank sank somewhere in the carnage, his corpse deliberately trampled by the hooves of his brother's steed. Each time the Ostrogoths charged, the disciplined legions made them come through a wave of javelins. Hun-dreds of Goths grunted and went down with each volley. The Goths clawed and spat and stabbed at us, but the loss of the ridge crest was proving catastrophic to them. Too many warriors were dying, and At-tila's right flank was weakening. What if Aetius could begin to squeeze them upon the Hun center, as he hoped?

But the sun was still high; fresh Ostrogoths kept appearing, their

numbers seemingly as endless as grains of sand. We Romans could not
be dislodged, but neither could we advance. Men were staggering from
exhaustion after each attack, chests heaving, the blood running down
their limbs in bright sheets. During pauses they let their shields slump
to the ground and crouched behind them for a while in an attempt to recover and to keep from being shot.

I found myself back with Aetius and was given the horse of a dead
centurion. Mounted once more, I could better see the battle, but reunion with our general was not entirely reassuring. Clearly he was now
growing as frustrated at this failure to break the Ostrogoths ahead of
him as Attila had been frustrated at failing to crack our center. "We have
to fold them and we can't!" he muttered. "This fight may finally be settled elsewhere." He glanced worriedly down the rest of the line.

Indeed, now Attila displayed his talents as a tactician. On the right
of our forces, far to the south, Theodoric and his Visigoths had accomplished what we'd hoped. In a great, heroic charge their cavalry had
hurled themselves on the Vandals, Rugi, Sciri, and Thuringi. It was like
a snowy avalanche against sapling timber, a great barbarian nation charging against lesser or less-numerous ones, and our right wing seemed destined to crumple their left. Again the price was terrible, a generation of
warriors falling to the remorseless scythe of arrows, but then the lances
of the Visigoths struck home and their foes were hurled backward toward Attila's laager. So swiftly did Theodoric and his men advance, crying for revenge for Berta against the Vandals, that they rode far in
advance of our center. A dangerous gap began to open between them
and the rest of our army.

Attila saw this and charged into it, leading his Huns against the
Visigothic flank.

It was as if Theodoric's men were a charging, snarling dog, suddenly
brought up short by a chain. The Huns struck the side of their advance
like a shock of lightning, pouring in a volley of arrows at brutally short
range and then riding over the fallen to cut at the Visigoths with their
swords. The Visigothic charge faltered, the retreating Hun allies turned,
and suddenly Theodoric, the spear tip of his people, found himself in a
sea of enemies.

I could see this struggle only at long distance, and made little sense of it, but the songs afterward recalled how the high king of the Visigoths, father of the mutilated Berta, his hair iron gray and his anger made of iron, spied Attila. Instead of retreating he kicked his horse toward the Hunnish king, roaring that he had found the devil himself and meant to kill him, and Gaiseric next. Attila was equally maddened by the roar of battle, urging his own horse toward his foe, but before the leaders could close, a pack of snarling Huns surrounded the Visigothic king's entourage and cut it off, puncturing it with arrows and stabbing with swords. One, two, three, and then four arrows thunked into the torso of Theodoric. He reeled, dizzy, crying in his last moments to his old pagan gods as well as to his newer Christian one, and then spilled from his saddle where he was trampled into bloody pulp. The Huns screamed with triumph and the Visigoths broke in disorder, fleeing back to their original starting point. Yet Attila's men were also in such disorder after charge, countercharge, and melee that he couldn't immediately follow. Many had drifted within range of Roman artillery and crossbows, and the Huns—who Attila had so carefully conserved over the years by forcing their allies to do the hardest fighting—were dying in unprecedented numbers.

It was now that all hung in the balance. The Visigoths had retreated in disarray, their king dead. The Alans had lost half their number in the desperate center, and only the support of the Liticians and the sturdiness of the Olibriones kept them from breaking entirely. The wing of Aetius with its Franks and Saxons and Armoricans held the high ground but was still unable to advance; and Attila himself still had a vast force milling in front of us, encouraged now by the fall of Theodoric.

Both sides had scored triumphs. Which would prevail?

The two armies hurled themselves at each other again, more desperately than ever.

And then again.

And again.

Hour followed hour. The rain of arrows slackened because, as Zerco had predicted, not even Huns had an inexhaustible supply. The longer the fight went on the more they were forced to come to grips with the heavier Western cavalry, and the more grievous their own losses became. The dwarf's forecast was proving grimly right. This was no lightning raid or standoff archery contest; this was the brutal and fundamental kind of close-quarters fighting that western Europeans excelled at. None of us on either side could fight endlessly without rest, however, and so ranks surged, battled, and then, exhausted, retired while new men took their places. The ground became pocked with bodies, then marbled, and then carpeted with a meadow of carnage such as chroniclers had never imagined. Nothing approached the cost of what some would call the Battle of Châlons, some Maurica, and some simply as the Battle of Nations. Men sensed that here was a hinge of history, the difference between darkness and light, oppression and hope, glory and despair; and neither side would give up. If their swords broke they fought with broken swords, and if their weapons snapped again at the hilt, then they rolled on the ground, grappling for each other's throats and reaching for each other's eyes, gouging and kicking in a frenzy of unreasoning fury. Each death had to be revenged, each yard lost had to be retaken; and so instead of slackening the battle grew ever more intense as the afternoon wore on. It was hot, a huge pall of dust hazing the battlefield, and wounded men screamed equally for their mothers and for water.

The butchered who still breathed crawled to the thread of the brook between the armies in order to drink, but the human body holds more blood than one can ever imagine. It gushed out in sheets on the ground, soaking it to capacity, and then formed rivulets that became brooks and then turned into streams, a vast tide of blood soaking across the trampled meadows. The blood finally filled the little stream that men crept toward, so that when they reached it they found only gore. They died there by the hundreds, choking on the blood of their comrades.

I threw myself into the fray like everyone else, still mounted, my sword once more sheathed so that I could use a longer spear to stab down at the Ostrogoths and dismounted Huns who'd become mixed in the swirling confusion. My weapons came up red but I have no idea who I killed or when, only that I thrust desperately as the only way to preserve my own life. All reason had left this combat, and all strategy, and it had come down to a brutal test of will. I realized finally that it had slackened on the right flank because the Visigoths were holding back after the death of Theodoric, meaning the Huns had more ability to push against our own wing. I feared that without Theodoric's leadership the Visigoths might abandon us altogether.

I had no understanding yet of the Visigothic heart or their desire to avenge the king. They were not withdrawing but re-forming.

Meanwhile, Attila was concentrating his force on our left and center. The battle was beginning to pivot. Aetius and his heavy infantry were making progress against the Ostrogoths, forcing them down the slope of the ridge and across the bloody brook, bending them toward the Hun center and the laagers of his wagons. But at the same time the Alans, even braced by the stoutness of the Olibriones, were bending as well, the gap growing between them and the Visigoths on our right flank. The whole combat was slowly wheeling. The Huns were the key, and with charge after furious charge they crashed against our lines, each time driving a little deeper, their horses hurdling mounds of the dead. I found myself fighting at the junction of the Romans and the Alans, intercepting Huns who broke through the infantry ranks. I dueled with a deadly, remorseless efficiency, realizing how much the past year had changed me. Killing had no shock anymore. It had become the ceaseless business of this ceaseless day. Shadows grew long, the grievously wounded bled to death before they could crawl to any help, the field became a mire of trampled grass and bloody mud. Still it went on.

And then came Skilla.

Once more he'd spotted me. Then he fought his way to me so that here on this vast field of carnage he and I could come to a final end. The duel I should have finished in Hunuguri would now be finished here.

His quiver was empty, arrows long since spent, and he was as spattered with blood as I was, whether his own or others I cannot say. A year of frustration had lit a dark fire in his eyes; and while neither of us could control the outcome of this huge battle, we could perhaps control each other's fate. He used his horse to butt aside a wounded legionary, the man stumbling long enough that another Hun killed him, and then he came at me, our horses snorting as they wheeled and bit. I threw my spear and missed, narrowly, and once more reached for my scabbard.

Our swords rang and we twisted in the fight, trying to keep each other in sight as our tormented steeds turned, snapping; and I was as eager to kill him as he was to kill me. But for him, I would long since have escaped with Ilana! But of course we would *not* have escaped, the war would have come anyway, except Attila may have come with his magic sword as well. Was that part of Skilla's frustration—that he had unwittingly become a part of strange destiny? How inexplicable the Fates are.

I was weary and past weariness by this time, as exhausted as I've ever been in my life. And yet Skilla came with a fresh ferocity as if none of this long battle had ever happened. I felt my wrist turning under his blows. I was sweating with fatigue and fear, waiting for him to make a mistake and yet finding none. I was making too many. Finally I parried a blow badly, my blade nearly flat to his stroke, and my spatha snapped in two.

For a moment I was stunned, looking at the stunted weapon stupidly. Then he swung again, his throat gushing a victorious "yah!" that sounded half strangled, and I avoided decapitation only by leaning so far backward on my horse that I felt its tail on my head. In desperation, I tumbled off my horse into the scrimmage below, a hell pit of churning limbs and dying men. I looked for a weapon, crawling between horse and human legs, soldiers grunting above, as Skilla cursed and tried to urge his frenzied horse after me.

I found an ax, its dead owner still gripping its haft, and yanked. It took a heave to break it free because the owner's fingers were already beginning to freeze. Then I scooted sideways on the ground. A hoof came near and I swung at its foreleg. Skilla jerked his pony away, eyeing me but also looking around as he backed in case some other Roman came at him from behind. I stood now with the ax, planning to unhorse him as I had in Attila's makeshift arena, kill him once and for all, and finally hack my way to Attila's camp. I was insane with exhaustion and desperation. All I wanted was to seize Ilana and flee this madness forever. But Skilla was wary, remembering the same combat I did, and I saw him finger his quiver with regret that he didn't have an arrow. There were hundreds around us on the ground, of course, some broken but others whole, and I grimly waited for him to reach for one, figuring that was the time to charge at his horse and kill it.

Then I was dimly aware of horns blowing at a volume not yet heard in this battle, and the song was so great and so high that it reminded me of tales of angels ascending and Joshua at Jericho. What was going on? I could see nothing but struggling men and churning dust, the light now low in the west. This long day was drawing toward darkness. Then Skilla sidestepped his horse into a gap in the fighting and bent to pluck an arrow.

I ran at him, raising the ax.

On clear ground, perhaps, I could have done it. But I stumbled on a corpse, his pony skipped out of reach of my swing, and in an instant Skilla had three arrows in his hand and was nocking one on his bow. There was no room for me to run, no shield to lift, and he was too close to hope that I could dodge. I felt defeated, and a vast regret settled on me as if I could have avoided all this if I had only done . . . what?

He pulled to kill me.

And then suddenly a wave of Huns spilled into us like an avalanche, crashing into the flank of his pony, and the shaft went wide. The Hun warriors were in disarray, their eyes wild and their voices hoarse, yelling warning even as they scooped up their fellows and carried them away from us like a retreating wave. They were fleeing, and a cursing Skilla was helplessly caught up in their panic.

Pushing against the Huns, I saw, was a stormy wall of my own cavalry, a scrambled mix now of Roman and Visigoth and Frank and Alan, yelling themselves hoarse as they rode over Huns too slow to escape. I ran myself, sideways, to get out of the path of careening horses. Now all the horns were blowing, Roman and Hun alike, and the whole field seemed in vague motion from west to east, as if we were on a plate that had been tilted. The battle was sliding off toward Attila's camp.

I found a mound of dead and clambered up on it to see what was going on. What I observed stunned me. The Visigoths had not broken from the battle, as I had feared. They had rejoined it. But this time they came in an unstoppable wave under Theodoric's son Thorismund, and their charge was carrying all before it like a flood from a dam. Here was revenge for the death of their king and the mutilation of their princess! Many Huns were still fighting furiously, others were ridden under, but tens of thousands were retreating to the wagon laagers that Attila had arranged as crude forts, taking refuge there.

They were whipped.

The sun was glimmering on the western horizon. "Advance!" Aetius was roaring as he rode among us. "Advance!"

Had the old iron sword worked? Was this to be the final destruction of Attila?

I went forward with the others, but for most of us it was more a stagger than a charge. We had been ferociously fighting for the day's full second half; the battle had become an apocalypse of death; and it was hard to merely lift a weapon, let alone wield it. The Huns were in no better shape. Yet when they reached the wagons they reached water, and it revived them enough to take up their bows and fill the sky with defensive arrows. Our own bowmen and war machines were out of range, and so when this black rain fell out of the dusk none of us had any missiles to return or the stomach to go further. Not even me, who wanted Ilana. I was astonished to be alive, drunk with fatigue, and unable to fight longer. We retreated out of range of the Hun arrows, the battered armies separating by a mile again, and collapsed in the charnel house that was our field of victory. The sun was gone, and darkness seemed a blessing. So I found a skin of water on a slain legionary, drank, and faded into exhausted oblivion.

XXVIII

THE SWORD OF MARS

I came to my senses some hours later. The moon had come up to illuminate the field of the dead. The butchered stretched as far as I could
see, farther than any man had ever seen: None would recall any battle as
huge and horrible as this one. Who could stand to count? No one ever
tried to bury them all. We instead fled from this place when it was all
over, letting nature reclaim the bones.

It was an eerie, haunted night, the moans of the wounded creating a
low keening and their anguished crawling producing scuttling noises like
small animals or insects. Dogs long abandoned by their masters in the
summer's invasion came to eat at the edges of the carnage. So, I was later
told, did wolves, their eyes gleaming in the moonlight. Howls and snarls
lilted at the edges of the armies.

It had taken the entire world, it seemed, to stop Attila, and even
now none of us was certain he had been stopped for more than an
evening. He had retreated, yes, but would he ride out of his laager again
on the morrow? Alternately, could Rome sustain another assault on his
wagons? An entire generation had been half wiped out in a single long
afternoon and evening, and the cost of this battle would be remembered
and whispered for centuries. Never before had so many died so quickly.

It was not just men but horses, thousands of them, too. By the
moon I could see the corpses of soldiers and animals formed curious pat-

terns: lines, crescents, and circles that marked where the fighting had been the fiercest. It was like the design of an intricate, macabre carpet. Some of those who survived were wandering the field looking for friends or loved ones, but most on both sides had simply collapsed in exhaustion so that the dead were swelled by vast numbers of the sleeping and unconscious. There was already the stench of blood and piss and shit. By tomorrow's noon there would be the smell of rot as well, but for now our army nested among the fallen.

I had not the slightest idea what I should do. I'd seen so much horror in the past year that life had become incomprehensible. I felt disconnected, drained, dreamy. Only chance had kept Skilla from killing me this time. Why? What was God's purpose in all I had seen? I could find Aetius, but to what end? I could crawl toward Ilana, but she seemed as elusive and remote as ever. Attila's surviving army still stood between us. I could again fight Skilla but he, too, never seemed to die. Oddly, he'd become the one warrior I felt closest to. We shared a love, battles, and a historic journey; and I wondered if, when this was over, we could stop fighting and simply share wine and kumiss in front of a hot fire, trying to remember the cocky young men we'd once been before the slaughter here.

Was he gone forever, swept away by the Visigoths' charge? Or hunting for me still with taut bow and arrow?

I explored my body and was astounded to find no wounds despite my bloody clothing, and my bruises and sores. I was not equal to three-quarters of the warriors who had died and yet here I was, breathing, when they were not. Again, why? I once thought experience would solve the mysteries of life, but instead it seems only to add to them.

So I sat with these foggy thoughts, as useless as my own broken sword, until finally I noticed a dark form weaving toward me through the dead, as if looking for a fallen companion. The task would not be easy. Inflicted wounds had been so brutal and the slain so trampled that many were past recognition. I admired this figure's loyalty.

It turned out to be loyalty of a different sort, however. His form became disquietingly familiar, and suddenly my exhaustion was replaced with anxiety. I stood, swaying. He stopped, the moon behind him and on my face, and spoke softly to me from thirty paces away. "Alabanda?"

"Don't you ever rest?" My voice quavered with weariness.

"I've not come to fight you. I'm tired of killing. This day wasn't war—it was insanity. It has destroyed my nation." Skilla gazed out at the moonlit bodies. "Ilana needs our help, Jonas Alabanda."

"Ilana?" I croaked the name.

"Attila has gone mad. He fears final defeat tomorrow and has built a pyre of wooden saddles and his richest possessions. If Aetius breaks through the wagon wall, he intends to light it and hurl himself into the flames."

My heart hammered at this unexpected information. Were the Huns really that desperate, or was this some kind of trick? "If Attila dies, perhaps Ilana goes free," I suggested groggily.

"He has chained her to the pyre."

"Why are you telling me this?"

"Do you think I would come to you if I didn't have to, Roman? You've been a plague to me since I met you. I came within moments of killing you yesterday, but the gods intervened. Now I know why. Only you can save her."

"Me?" Was this a trap? Had Skilla decided to win by guile what he'd been robbed of in repeated combat?

"It's impossible to rescue her," he said. "The pyre is surrounded by a thousand men. But Attila will still take the sword for the woman."

So this was it. "The sword of Mars."

"He blames its loss for the evil that has befallen our people this day. Half the Hun nation is gone. We cannot attack anymore, that's obvious, but we can retreat as an army, not a mob. Attila's sword will give my nation back its heart."

"It is you who has gone insane!" I cried. "I don't have the sword, Aetius does. Do you think he wants to give it back now that final victory is within our grasp?"

"Then we must steal it, like you stole it from Attila."

"Never!"

"If we don't, Ilana will burn."

I looked out into the darkness, my head aching. Had I come so far, and fought so hard, only to see the one I loved consumed by flames because of victory? How could destiny be so cruel? And yet what Skilla was asking me to do was to risk sure Roman triumph for a single woman, to put into Attila's hands the symbol he needed to rally his battered army. I had no guarantee the Huns would let Ilana go if I turned over the sword. They might simply burn both of us for amusement. Maybe this was Skilla's way of killing me—by luring me to his camp with the promise of Ilana.

Or maybe he truly loved her, too, loved her so much that this madness somehow made sense to him. So he thought it should make sense to me.

I stalled, trying to think. "If we save her, which of us gets her?"

"That will be Ilana's choice." Of course he would tell me that, because I would assume she'd choose me. She was Roman. Yet what did I really know? The only word of her survival had come from Skilla himself. For all I knew she'd died in Hunuguri or had married Attila or even had married Skilla! He would tell me anything to get the sword. And yet, looking at him—this man I'd come to know too well through too many combats—I knew he was telling the truth. Knew it in my gut more than my mind. War had given us a curious comradeship.

If I did nothing, she would die. If I acceded to Skilla's plan, there was a good chance that both Ilana and I would die. And so no chance existed, or did it? The seed of a desperate alternative began to form in my brain.

"I'm not even sure where the sword is," I said as I thought. What if it now served a different purpose—to demoralize instead of empower?

"Any fool knows where it is. We saw Aetius lift it. Where your general sleeps, there sleeps the sword."

"This is madness."

"The madness is men's preoccupation with that old piece of iron," Skilla said. "You and I both know it has no power beyond what superstition gives it. That relic will not change what happened here, or what must happen tomorrow. My people cannot conquer the West—there are too many to conquer. But the sword saves Ilana and it saves my kagan. It saves my own pride."

I looked at him, wondering how my plan could possibly work.

"We must work together, Jonas. For her."

At the outer fringes of the battlefield, where the Roman armies rested, tens of thousands of surviving soldiers were sleeping as if clubbed, every fiber drained by the fight we had just been through. Thousands more wounded had been carried or had crawled here to die. Fresh troops were still coming up to the field, so universal had been the response of resistance in Gaul. The work of war went on. These newcomers were making lanes of advance through the dead by piling them like cordwood. They were bringing fresh supplies of food and water, wheeling catapults and ballistae forward, and were readying for a resumption of battle on the morrow. Others were being sent into the battlefields to retrieve spent bolts and unbroken arrows. I paused to speak quietly to a carpenter working on a catapult, and took the tool he charged eight times too much for.

Torches lit the way to the complex of tents that marked the headquarters of Aetius. I'd left Skilla behind, telling him to lie still like one of the Hun corpses to avoid discovery. I would get the sword by persuasion or not at all; the two of us could not hack our way through an aroused Roman army. I went by myself knowing that my general would think me a lunatic. Yet didn't I have some claim to the weapon? Could I tamper with the sword? Was a gamble any worse than renewed slaughter?

If Aetius needed any reminding what his profession was, the night's sounds provided it. I could hear the shriek of the wounded from all points of his headquarters compound. Trestle tables had been set up within a stone's throw; and limbs were being hacked, set, sewn, and bound for those unlucky enough to be grievously wounded and yet still alive. It was a demons' chorus, despite the vaunted skill of Roman surgeons. A ditch and wooden stockade had been erected around this nexus of the army, and I worried that I might be stopped from entering, ending my ploy before it began. But, no, Jonas of Constantinople was well known as the general's aide, envoy, spy, and adviser. With my face wiped clean, I was let pass with a salute of respect from the sentries. I walked toward the sword, listening to the cries of the dying.

What is one more dead? I asked myself. *Even if it was me?*

"We thought you had perished," one centurion remarked with more prescience than he knew when I came to the tents. I saw Visigothic and Frankish sentries and a little galaxy of lamps in one of the tents and heard a low murmur. The highest-ranking kings and generals were still awake, apparently, debating what to do when the sun came up. Aetius would be in there, but I needed to speak to him privately.

So where would Aetius have put the old sword? Not on the council table as a symbol of his own luck. He would diplomatically leave it aside and pay attention to the pride of the kings he'd bound to him. This triumph must be theirs as well as his. The weapon would wait in his sleeping chamber.

"The general has asked me to fetch maps and the great sword," I lied. Aetius traveled with charts of the entire West, poring over them in the evenings the way a merchant might a budget. As his aide, I'd fetched them a hundred times.

"Is he ever going to sleep?" the sentry asked, betraying his own wish to do so. He looked heartsick, like all of us.

"When victory is final," I replied. "Let's hope the sword will end things."

I lifted the flap, peering inside for additional sentries. None. So I hesitated deliberately, knowing that an errand which might not arouse suspicion in an exhausted sentry would nonetheless puzzle a loyal fool. Something moved around the corner of the outside of the tent, small and furtive, and I was satisfied. I went inside.

It was dark, so I lit a single clay lamp. There were the trunks and stools of his kit I'd seen many times: here his bed, there his folding desk, and there a heap of sweaty and blooded clothing. But where was the sword? I felt with my hands. Ah! It lay blanketed on his cot like a courtesan, as necessary as love. I caressed the familiar roughness of pitted metal, heavy and ungainly. How odd its size! Had gods really forged it? Was it fate that Attila had found it, giving him courage to try to conquer the world? And more fate that I had delivered it to Aetius? How life plays with us, favoring one moment and fouling the next, raising us up and then dashing our hopes. Again, the sense of it all eluded me.

I took out the file I'd purchased and set to work.

Shortly afterward, someone big filled the entry of the tent. "So you decided to take back what you gave, Jonas Alabanda?" the general asked softly.

"I've decided to give it in a different way."

"I was told by a special sentry that I might want to see what you were up to."

I smiled. "I relied on that sentry to be on duty."

A small shadow emerged from behind. "I'd get far more rest if I didn't have to look after you, Jonas," Zerco said.

"Please, sit." I gestured to the camp stools as if this tent were mine. "I'm as surprised that you two are on your feet as I'm surprised I'm on mine."

"Yes," said Aetius, taking my invitation. "How important all of us must be, to be so tireless. And what are you planning to do with that? Kill Attila? Are you trying to file it sharp?"

I put the file aside. "I've been informed the woman that I love is chained to a funeral pyre. She's to be burned tomorrow with Attila, if we attack and he loses the battle. A Hun told me this, and I believe him."

"Skilla," the dwarf surmised.

"I seem as bound to him as you seem bound to Attila, general, or you seem bound to Aetius, Zerco. Bound by fate. He's a young warrior, the nephew of the warlord Edeco, who I fought in Noricum when you first encountered me and the sword."

"Ah, yes. A bold Hun, to have followed you so far into Roman territory. Is he the one who saluted you this day?"

"Yes."

"Now I have a better idea why. He wants you to trade the sword for this woman?"

"Yes."

"He loves her, too?"

"Yes."

"And you believe Attila will accept this trade?"

"No. He will take the sword, of course, but he wants revenge for our setting fire to his palace. I'll die if we go to his camp, and accomplish nothing."

The general smiled. "Then I fail to see the logic in your plan."

"There's no possibility of escape from Attila's laager. No possibility of rescuing Ilana. And for me, no possibility of life without that rescue. I've watched many men die for what they believe in, and now I'm prepared to die for what I believe in: her."

The general looked bemused.

"I plan to ask Skilla to take her and trade myself for her life. The Huns have a word for it, *konoss*. A payment of debt. It's the way families and clans settle disputes. I will pay *konoss* with my life for hers, and *konoss* to Skilla with the sword, in return for his solemn promise to care for her as best he can."

"Letting Attila rally his troops with this symbol, after all we did to get it here," Zerco accused, "so one woman can be given to one Hun, instead of burned!"

"Yes." I shrugged. "I can't bear the thought of her dying, not after so many others have died. Could you bear the thought of losing Julia, Zerco?"

There was a long, uncomfortable silence. Then Aetius spoke again.

"I acknowledge your willingness to sacrifice, but do you really think I'll let you take the sword for such a pointless exchange?"

"Not take it, exactly."

"What then?"

I explained my plan.

They were quiet a longer time now, turning over the risk in their minds.

"Attila must be distraught and defeated if he is planning to throw himself on a pyre," Aetius finally said.

"Indeed."

"My own army is in no better shape. My men have endured casualties on a scale none of us have ever imagined, and the havoc is threatening to break our alliance. Thorismund leads the Visigoths after the death of his father, but his brothers thirst for the kingship just as much as he

does. The Visigoths who charged with such implacable fury and unbroken unity at sunset will be a divided people by dawn. Similarly, Anthus
has been satisfied with the body of Cloda and fears further sacrifice. The
Franks have already fought two days in a row. Sangibanus hates me for
putting him and his Alans in the center. The Olibriones scarcely have
endurance to go another day; they are not young men. And so on. Our
horses need more water. Our war machines are short of ammunition.
Our quivers are empty. All the problems that plague the Huns plague us
as well. But we have one more. Attila is a tyrant, and as long as he lives
he can keep his coalition of Huns and subject tribes united by fear. My
power, in contrast, is simple persuasion, and only the threat of Attila has
persuaded our nations to unite. Even as Attila threatens to destroy the
Western Empire, he has perversely welded it together. If he's annihilated
in our attack tomorrow, our own unity disappears instantly and with it
the influence of Rome. Our allies won't need us anymore. Attila is as
necessary to Aetius as Satan is necessary to God."

I was puzzled. "You want him to prevail?"

"I want him to survive. Neither of us can afford an attack tomorrow.
But if he withdraws crippled but with face, I have the tool—fear of the
Hun—that I need to keep the West together. Two days ago, his existence was the greatest threat to Rome. Tomorrow, his absence would be
the greatest threat. I've held this Empire together for thirty years by balancing one force against another, and it's how I'm going to hold it now. I
need him to retreat, demoralized, but not lose."

"Then you'll give me a chance to try this?"

The general sighed. "It is risky. But the sword has done what it can
in my hand."

I grinned, dizzy with relief and fear.

Zerco laughed at my expression. "Only an amateur fool, exhausted
by battle and heartsick with love, would come up with an idea as absurd
as yours, Jonas Alabanda!" He nodded, to confirm this judgment to himself. "And only a professional fool, like me, could think of absurdities to
improve it!"

XXIX

THE LAAGER OF ATTILA

Skilla and I struggled across a battlefield as treacherous as a marsh. The moon had set to a deeper darkness but now the sky was blushing in the east, giving barely enough light to illuminate the grotesque path we must take. We stepped carefully to avoid the blades, arrows, spear tips, shards of shattered armor, and bodies. On and on the havoc stretched, thousands upon thousands upon thousands. Worst were those who were still alive, twitching feebly, crawling blind as snails, or begging pitifully for water. We had none, so we passed quickly by. There were too many! By the time we drew near the Hun encampment, I was finally and forever done with war.

Once more I had strapped the great sword of Mars on my back, but this time it felt like I was carrying a cross. Could this gamble possibly work? I was about to find again, and possibly lose forever, the one person I truly cared about. Having once escaped the lion's den, I was walking back into it. Fool, indeed.

Skilla had tethered his pony on the field's edge, a dark silhouette with neck down as it munched dew-wet grass, oblivious to the historic carnage. Nearby was another horse with a form that seemed gladly familiar.

"We will ride, not walk, to see Attila," he said. "I brought your horse."

"Diana!"

"I added her to my string after you fled." He turned to me in the pearl gray light and grinned that familiar flash of teeth. "She's only good for milking, but I kept her anyway."

Suddenly I felt a rush of a feeling of brotherhood with this man, this Hun, this barbarian, that so flooded my body that it felt disorienting. My most hated enemy had become, after Ilana, the one I felt closest to: closer, even, than Zerco. We were partners trying to save a life, instead of taking one. And yet I was planning to betray him.

We mounted and rode. My Roman dress drew attention, of course, but Skilla was well known even in this vast army, and the light had grown strong enough that he was easily recognizable. Huns sentries rose warily from the meadow grass but stepped aside to let us pass. We reached the great circle of Hun wagons, a laager half a mile in diameter with similar, smaller laagers scattered about it like moons. Weary Hun ponies grazed between in vast herds. Ranks of Hun archers still slept in the shadow of the wagons, ready to be roused if the Romans advanced.

Our horses jumped one of the wagon yokes and we went on, encountering a second line of wagons inside it, like the second wall of Constantinople. I wondered if Edeco had recommended this from his memories of my home city. We jumped that as well and came to the tents and the awful, carefully prepared funeral pyre of Attila. The pyre towered twenty feet high, a riotous jumble of saddles both fine and plain, silks, tapestries, carved furniture, furs, robes, jewelry, perfumes, staffs, and standards. Much had been looted in just the past few months. Clearly the kagan intended to not only take his own life if the Romans broke through but also prevent them from capturing his possessions.

I recognized Ilana, huddled against the heap of saddles, and my heart was wrenched. She was asleep, or at least slumped, with her eyes closed. I had expected a beaten and emaciated slave, but instead she was dressed in a spectacular silken gown and dotted with jewelry. What did this mean? Had Attila taken her as a wife or concubine? Was this last journey for nothing?

I touched Skilla's arm, stopping him and his horse. "Listen. I want you to promise to care for Ilana and take her far away from this place, far from all these armies."

"What?" He looked at me in confusion.

"Attila is not going to let us go. You know that. But he may let *you* go, with Ilana, if I offer myself as *konoss*. My life and the sword in recompense for the fire at his palace, in return for yours and Ilana's."

He looked at me in disbelief. "I did not bring you here to die, Roman. If I wanted that, I'd kill you myself."

"It's not what you want but what Attila wants. Think! This is Ilana's only chance—to be given to you. Attila will expect you to marry her and serve him. But give me your word you'll slip away from this madness so she can live a normal life. You've seen the Empire, Skilla. Live with her within it."

He shook his head stubbornly. "You never understand a thing, Roman! I've seen your Empire and I don't like it! Too many people, too many possessions, too many laws!"

"But it's *her* world. She'll never be happy in yours. You know this, and you must accept it. This is what you must promise, if I give myself as *konoss*."

"And if I don't?"

I reached behind my back to loosen the big sword, lifting it clear and laying it across the front of my saddle. "Then I will die trying to kill Attila, Ilana will probably perish, and you yourself will be crucified for bringing me to his tent."

He shook his head in disgust, troubled by my proposal, and it occurred to me that perhaps he felt fellowship for me as I felt for him: that perhaps he had sought me out on the battlefield not just from calculation but from loneliness. It's also unlikely he fully trusted me. But finally he shrugged. "Very well, sacrifice yourself. I will go wherever Ilana asks me to take her."

"Thank you." I gave a slight bow, strangely content. All my diplomacy had led to catastrophic slaughter, and all my efforts to free Ilana had led to her being imprisoned more hopelessly than ever. Bargaining my own life, after the sacrifice of so many others, felt oddly liberating.

I'd expected, however, some degree of surprise and gratitude. Instead, he seemed to regard me with irritated impatience. "Just don't kill yourself until we get Ilana."

We rode the last few yards and dismounted. How bizarre this reunion with Attila seemed! Here I was, a lone Roman amid thousands of Huns after the worst battle on Earth. Men clustered around us like sniffing dogs. One, with a bloody bandage, looked particularly familiar and I peered closer. It was Eudoxius, the Greek doctor! Here he was, in the army he'd dreamed of, and his old nemesis Aetius might crush him at any moment. He recognized me, too, and his look was one of loathing.

Not just Ilana but a dozen beautifully dressed women were linked with light chains to the pyre, awake now and looking frightened. Attila's lust for conquest had led his people to disaster, and if he must die he wanted to bring those closest to him down with him.

Ilana herself was looking at Skilla and me with wonder. She'd come groggily awake at the noise of our approach, and then her eyes had widened with recognition in the growing morning light. She seemed bewildered by our apparent partnership: We stood together as allies, both of us spattered with dried blood and grimed with the filth of combat. Then she saw the sword and her eyes clouded. I knew she wanted Roman victory, and revenge on Attila, more than her own life.

The kagan erupted from his tent.

If the Scourge of God had slept at all, it was in the battle mail and animal skins of yesterday, spotted with the gore of his enemies. His hair was wild and stringy, his thin beard grizzled, and his piercing eyes rimmed and red from worry, or lack of sleep. I was shocked and I think Skilla was, too: Attila seemed to have aged a decade since I'd seen him, and perhaps a decade in a day.

"You!" he cried, and I confess I jumped. I'd seen him wield power too often. But now he looked as if the shock of this battle had thrown him from the mount of reason. Never had so many Huns died so quickly. Never had Attila retired from a battlefield, victory not in his grasp. Now he was hunched behind his wagons, waiting for Aetius to finish destroying him. I hadn't realized until this moment how decisively the Romans had won. The kagan's spirit had been broken.

I lifted the sword for him to see. "I come from Aetius, kagan."

He looked at me suspiciously, but instantly native craftiness replaced surprise. "He wants to parley?"

"No, I do." I pointed at Ilana. "That woman is blameless for what happened in Hunuguri; I stole her from your compound, took your sword, and set the fire. Her only sin was to be kidnapped by me. I've come to offer *konoss*. I've brought you back the sword and for her life I offer myself. Kill me, but let the woman go."

Attila's eyes narrowed. He turned to Skilla. "What is your role in this?"

"I pledged I would bring back the sword. I have."

The king grunted. "And do you still want what I promised in return?"

He nodded. "Ilana is to go with me."

She cried out. "Jonas! This makes no—"

I interrupted. "I've come unarmed to save the woman I love. My life is a small price to pay for hers. Give her to Skilla, and let their blessing be on the sword of Mars."

He looked from one of us to the other, a trio about to become two. "You care this much for a *druugh?*" It was a Hunnish nickname for her genitals.

I swallowed. "Put me in the flames instead."

Still Attila hesitated.

"It's *konoss*, kagan," a chieftain spoke up. "You must accept it." I started in recognition at the voice and realized Edeco had come up. He wasn't looking at me but at his nephew Skilla with curiosity.

The king scowled. Was this a trick? "I have to accept nothing." His look became narrow and greedy. "Give me the sword." His warlords were nodding, eager to have this talisman back to rally their men.

"Let her go to Skilla first."

"Give me the sword first. Or should I just kill you now?"

I hesitated, but what choice did I have? I walked to him, and he grasped the iron haft, resting its heavy tip in the grass. We were inches apart.

His look was a half smile. "Now it will not be so easy."

I put my own hand back on the sword. "I made a bargain."

"Which I am going to change." He turned his head and ordered. "Unchain the girl."

I was sweating, despite the cool of the morning. They unlocked Ilana and she rose stiffly, perplexed and wary.

Attila raised his voice so others could hear. "She can leave, *konoss* will be paid, but no Roman assassin will dictate the payment." He grinned at her. "*She* will choose who goes with her . . . Skilla or the Roman."

"What?" she exclaimed.

"The other will take her place on the pyre."

"No!"

"What madness is this, kagan?" Edeco demanded. Skilla had blanched, looking at his king in bewilderment.

"She refused a better bargain when I offered it two nights ago. So let her make one now. Which of her suitors does she choose to kill?"

"I cannot make that choice. It's monstrous!"

"Then I will lock you back to that pyre with the other women and set fire to it now! Which one!"

I felt sick, things spiraling out of control. Where were my allies? Would Attila really kill Skilla instead of me? What kind of unjust game was this, to play with people's lives, to threaten the three of us with the arbitrary fate he had given poor Rusticius? How many innocents must this tyrant condemn? As I watched Ilana stand there, stricken, horrified, confused, my rage boiled over. Maybe it was Chrysaphius who was right, not Aetius. Eliminate Attila and our greatest problem was solved!

I shoved, butting him; and because of the surprise, I, Attila, and the sword went sprawling on the ground. Before the surprised older man could gather himself I'd wrestled myself behind him with the blunt but still-lethal sword at his neck, dragging both of us toward the pyre so I could use it as a shield for my back. The sword was so long it was like holding a pike pole against his throat.

"This sword has become his curse!" I cried. "Harm us and I take off his head!"

"Roman trick!" Edeco roared. His hand was at his sword. Other Huns raised weapons. But all hesitated because Attila was my shield. Eudoxius, I noticed from the corner of my eye, was slipping sideways out of sight. Now what?

"No trick, warlord!" another voice cried out. "Beware its curse, Attila!"

At last! Two figures on horseback were pushing through the small mob of Huns that was gathering around us, ignoring their angry muttering like men ignoring the growl of dogs. They were on a single horse, the smaller one looking at my desperate stance with wonder.

"So you have a found a lover, Alabanda," Zerco called.

Hun attention swung momentarily from me to the newcomers.

"Think what has happened to your people since you found that sword!" the tall one was shouting. "Think where it has been, with the Romans!"

"What is this?" Attila gasped in frustration against my hold. "Can any man in the world walk into my camp?"

A chieftain in escort fell to his knees and looked in stupefaction at the tableau we presented: Attila and I locked like wrestlers, Ilana and Skilla white-faced in shock, Edeco looking murderous. "He said he had an urgent message from Aetius," the Hun pleaded. "He said if I didn't let them through it would doom us all. I remember the dwarf. He's a demon, lord. But most of all I remember this holy man."

"Holy man?" Attila squinted harder. "By the gods! The hermit!"

Edeco started, too. He seemed to recognize a man I knew as Bishop Anianus.

"The halfling I loathe," Attila said. "And you, I remember you. . . ."

"As I remember you, Scourge of God," said Bishop Anianus. I was baffled. Had these two met? "You have scourged the West of its sins as intended. Now it is time to go back to where you crawled from. Leave the sword. The thing you lusted for has been corrupted for your kind."

"Corrupted?"

"Bathed in holy water, blessed by high bishops, and anointed by a vial of blood from the savior. Do you think Aetius is fool enough to let this youth give back a tool of Hun power in exchange for a single woman! This is no longer the sword of Mars, Attila. It is the sword of Christ. For you, it has been cursed, and if you take it with you, your people will be utterly destroyed."

Attila twisted angrily, so I pressed the blade anew. "Let us go and I let you go," I whispered.

"You dare come here to offer bad prophecy?" the king challenged the bishop.

"I come here to offer fair warning. Think! Could this young fool steal the sword from the tent of Aetius? Or did the general let him have it? Ask him."

Attila twisted his head. "What is true?"

"Aetius said he wanted you to survive—"

"Think!" interrupted Anianus. "That sword has brought you no luck, Attila."

I could almost feel the king calculating. "Then it curses the Romans as well," he tried. "Look at the battlefield, warlords. They lost more than we did."

Zerco laughed. "Which is why you cower in your laager!"

Now Edeco's sword was half out of its sheath, but I shouted warning. "Don't!" I bent to the king's ear. "My life for yours. Ilana for the sword. I can't hold you much longer. I must slice and kill us both, or leave."

There was silence. Sweat spotted us both. Ilana seemed to have turned to marble. Skilla seemed dazed by all that was happening.

Finally Attila grunted. "All right." None of us moved, not certain we had heard him right. "Go. You and the witch. Go, and be a plague on Aetius instead! You've both cursed my camp since you came to it. Leave the sword and I give you safe passage."

I sensed movement at the edge of the pyre, coming behind me. We didn't have much time. "I have your word?"

"You have my word. But if I see you in battle again, I will kill you."

I released him and stepped away, holding the old sword at the ready and careful of treachery. Attila's eyes were like the point of a spear, but he made no move toward me and issued no command. Eudoxius, I saw, had been trying to sneak behind the pyre to get a shot at my back with a bow and arrow, but now he stopped, too, the arrow half drawn.

Attila rubbed the red welt at his neck. "The sword, Roman."

Stooping carefully, I laid it in the grass, then began backing for Diana. "I need a horse for Ilana," I said.

"Give her one," the kagan growled.

I swung up onto Diana and Ilana mounted her horse. Skilla looked at us with quiet sadness, finally accepting that he'd never have her.

"Skilla, come with us," I tried.

He straightened then, proud, contemptuous, confident. "I am a Hun," he said simply.

"Skilla . . ." Ilana spoke, her voice breaking. "I know what you've—"

"Get out of here," Attila interrupted, "before I change my mind."

Skilla nodded. I wanted to offer my strange enemy-friend something, but what? Not Ilana. She was quietly weeping, tears running down her cheeks.

"Go," Skilla said in a choked voice. "Go, go, Romans, and stop corrupting us."

"*Now!*" Zerco whispered urgently.

I was dazed that I was alive, that Ilana was behind me, that Anianus had appeared, that the sword I had carried so long lay untouched in the grass. Our horses began to move, Huns reluctantly stepped aside, our own lines glinting on the horizon. It might work!

I heard a familiar voice. "Here's a better ending, kagan."

Our heads swiveled and I saw Eudoxius, his face contorted with hatred, draw his bow. The iron of the arrowhead trembled slightly as he aimed at Ilana.

"*No!*"

He shot as Skilla leaped without thinking, trying to spoil the aim. Instead the arrow struck him and the Hun was pitched forward by the impact, falling onto his back. He looked in disbelief at the shaft jutting from his breast.

Eudoxius gaped in horror.

"A Hun keeps his word," Skilla gasped, a red froth at his lips.

There was a roar of outrage, and the Greek turned and flinched. Edeco's sword came whistling down and cleaved the doctor nearly in two.

"Now, now!" Zerco cried. "Ride! Ride for our lives!"

Attila howled and picked the great iron sword out of the grass with two hands and came running at us like a madman. I kicked my horse between him and Ilana, and he swung, hard, and narrowly missed. I felt the wind of the passage. The massive blade cracked the rim of my saddle, nearly buckling Diana.

And broke. The old iron shattered into fragments that flew like a broken glass, spinning at the circle of startled Huns and making them duck in superstitious horror. The Hun king looked at the iron hilt in disbelief.

"You have cursed yourself!" Anianus shouted.

Then we kicked and bent low over our horses. A Hun had stepped out to grab my reins, and I rode over him. Then another caught at Ilana, dragging. I looked. The German girl Guernna! My love clubbed with her fist and the slave dropped away, braids flapping as she rolled.

The wall of the inner laager loomed, and we made for the low wagon tongues. Now a couple arrows buzzed past but they were high, the archers fearful of hitting fellow Huns. Shouts rang out, but they were ones of confusion. Who had shot Skilla? Who had Edeco killed? What had seemed to be an orderly parley had turned into chaos.

I glanced back. Attila and Edeco were frozen, staring at the shards of the sword. My file had done its work.

I let Ilana get ahead of me and saw her horse bunch and jump. In an instant, I followed her over the wagon trace. Now we had the inner laager obscuring and shielding us from the Huns at Attila's tent and we sprinted for the outer one, some Huns just now waking up, groggily staggering to their feet as we galloped past.

We blasted through a campfire, scattering pots and people, and came to the second laager. A few Huns moved to stop us but they were bowled over. Again we leaped, hooves clicking as they nicked the edges of the wagons, and then we were onto the battlefield beyond, racing over the forms of the dead. Something winked up high, and I glanced up to see missiles falling. "Arrows!" I shouted.

They hissed as they fell around us, but none struck.

Now Romans were shooting in return. Ilana rode grimly on, arrows plunking the ground, her gaze horrified as she saw closely for the first time the full butchery that had occurred, the endless carpet of bodies. We rode fast amid and over them. Then we were past even that horror, men cheering Anianus, and finally reined up at the compound of Aetius. Winded, I looked back in wonder. Attila's laager was two miles safely behind, and Ilana was flushed and bright beside me.

We were free.

The Roman general was already mounted and in armor, ready for battle if it came to that. "What happened?"

"Skilla saved us," Zerco said.

"And the sword broke," Anianus added. "A sign from God."

The general nodded. "Indeed." He smiled knowingly at me.

"When I held it to Attila's throat I feared it might break instead of cut."

"Attila's throat!"

"It's called diplomacy, general. He's alive, demoralized, and beaten, as you wished."

Aetius shook his head, as dazzled as I by the turn of events. "And this is the woman you were ready to risk whole nations for?"

"You helped save her from burning."

"I can see why. So, what will Attila do next, young diplomat?"

I took breath and considered. "He seemed in shock at the battle and at the shattering of the sword. If you give him the chance, I think he'll withdraw."

"Bishop, do you agree?"

"I think his followers will take its breakage as evidence of Christian power, commander. I'd hold my attack. If you advance, you may win or lose, but if you wait . . ."

"I don't think men will follow my advance. They're too sickened."

"Then guard your lines, gather your dead, and pray. What you began yesterday with your victory, Alabanda has finished today with that sword."

I was reeling with exhaustion, sorrow, and exultation. Skilla dead, the sword broken, Ilana back, Attila beaten . . .

She put her hand on my arm. "Let's go home," she whispered.

But where, after all we'd seen and done, was home?

Once more the horizon was filled with smoke, but this time of retreat, not advance. Attila did not ignite his pyre, but he burned surplus wagons and the plundered goods that were too numerous for his depleted army to carry. Then he started back the way he'd come, his invasion of Gaul over. Aetius followed slowly and at careful distance, not anxious to provoke another fight. The Visigoths peeled away to take their fallen king back to Tolosa. Anthus rode out with his Franks to solidify his claim. The huge assembly was breaking up.

The thunderclouds rumbled on and on and then finally let loose a torrent of rain that began to wash away the bloody pollution of the tiny brook. Armor began to rust, bones to powder, seeds to sprout. The greatest struggle of the age began to sink slowly into the earth.

Zerco and Julia elected to remain in the entourage of Aetius. "I'm too malformed to live an ordinary life," he told me, "and too easily bored to lead a serious one. My future is with the general."

"It's still a dangerous road."

"But not boring. See if you don't join me on it, after you farm a year or two."

Aetius had given ample money for my services, and offered far more if I'd stay and serve as aide and diplomat. I was not tempted. Ilana and I went west.

I will say little of our reunion, as it was a private thing, except there were a thousand things to say and a thousand things that could go unsaid. Anianus married us in a grove of poplar. We clung to each other afterward like limpets holding fast to a rock against a raging sea, until our lovemaking left us sated and exhausted. Then we rode with the bishop back toward Aurelia, away from Attila.

What were we looking for? We didn't know, and scarcely spoke of it. There were a thousand depopulated farms we could have stopped at, but each seemed to hold too many memories of the families who had lived there. So we came to Aurelia and passed by its battlements, finally taking a boat down the Loire River. How lazy the summer current was, and how soothing! When we met people who wanted to share rumors of the movement of armies, we ignored them. We didn't want to know.

At last we stopped at a high-banked island in the river, a mile-long refuge from the tumult of the world, its grass tall and yellow and the air golden with late summer. Flowers spilled down its banks, birds flitted through the lacy trees, and insects gave a soft buzz. We walked its length, burrs of seeds clinging to our clothes.

My purse was enough to hire labor to build a house and farm, I judged. Here was the land I'd fought for, against all expectation, and here new nations were rising from the ashes of the old. The West had been saved but changed, irrevocably. The Empire was passing. It had fought its last great battle. Something different—something we and our children would forge—was taking its place.

We walked the meadows of the island to choose a house site, eating wild apples in the sun. My initial preference was for its eastern end. "So we can look back to where we came from," I told Ilana.

She shook her head, walking me back through the trees to the island's western point, facing the warm afternoon sun. "I want to look to the future," she whispered.

So we did.

EPILOGUE

Attila was defeated at the battle of Châlons, in A.D. 451, but at Aetius's urging was not destroyed. The balance of power that "the Last of the Romans" tried to achieve among the barbarians required that the Huns be contained but not extinguished. Had Aetius not used Hun warriors many times to chastise other tribes? Did Attila's threat not justify the continuation of the Roman Empire? It was the grimmest kind of realpolitik, but wise in its realism. Attila would never truly recover from Châlons, and in all the centuries hence, no eastern barbarian would ever penetrate that far again. The alliance had saved Europe.

History did not stop, of course. The emperor Valentinian, who had hidden in Rome during the bitter contest, was as jealous of the great victory as he was thankful for it. He grasped at this news of peace and mercy. He also blamed Aetius for letting Attila get away.

Certainly the Hun's ambitions were not yet sated. After licking his wounds, Attila invaded northern Italy the following year with his depleted army, hoping to rebuild his reputation by sacking Rome itself. But his weary forces entered a region suffering from famine and plague. Disease killed more Huns than swords did. When Pope Leo met Attila to plead that he spare Rome, the kagan was looking for an excuse to retreat. It was his last great campaign.

The next year Attila took another bride, a young beauty named

Idilco, as if to assuage his failure. But after bringing her to his bed on his wedding night, he had a nosebleed while in a drunken stupor. In A.D. 453, he drowned in his own blood.

His bizarre death marked the end of the Hun empire. None of his heirs had the charisma to unite the Huns as Attila had, nor to hold other tribes in thrall. The Huns tore themselves to bits, a storm that had passed.

The success of Aetius doomed him in the jealous eyes of the Western emperor, of course, who took the general by surprise by leaping from his throne and running him through with a sword just one year after Attila's death. A year later, in 455, the general's followers assassinated Valentinian. Just as Attila was the last great Hun to make his people a menace, Aetius was the last great Roman to hold the Empire together. With his death, disintegration of the West into new barbarian kingdoms accelerated. Within a generation, the Western Empire was no more. The vision of Romulus seemed indeed to have come to pass.

And Honoria, the vain and foolish princess who had helped start such great events? She too disappeared from history, a Pandora who haunts the fields of Châlons.

HISTORICAL NOTE

Few subjects are more deserving of the label "historical fiction" than a novel about Attila the Hun. The most unbelievable things about this story—the plea to Attila for rescue by a Roman princess, the assassination plot of Chrysaphius, the mutilation of Theodoric's daughter by the Vandals, the sword that Attila claimed came from the god of war, and the existence of such characters as the rebel Eudoxius and the dwarf Zerco—are true. It is the prosaic details of how the people of the fifth century dressed, ate, traveled, and lived that must be surmised and guessed at by the novelist, from the meager findings of archaeological and historical research. The few Roman commentaries we have of the period pay little attention to the everyday details we would find so fascinating now, and this author was pressed into using more educated invention than I would have preferred. What I have described is as accurate as I could make it, based not just on book research but on exhibits in France, Austria, Germany, and Hungary, and Roman archaeological sites across Europe. This novel is not an anthropology text, however. Even the most tireless scholars of the Huns admit to how little we truly know.

Since the Huns and the barbarian nations they encountered had no written language, our primary information about them comes from the Romans and Greeks, who understandably had their own prejudices on the subject. The archaeological record is meager because steppe nomads could carry only a small amount of material with them, almost all of it perishable. The Huns minted no coins, carved no stones, forged no tools, sowed no crops, and made no permanent likenesses of their kings. There is gold jewelry that can be attributed to their era, and some pottery and bronze cauldrons that almost certainly belonged to them, even if made by someone else. We know the stories of head flattening are true because we have Hun skulls that show the deliberate deformity. But their songs, legends, and language have vanished. We have far more information on much older societies, such as the Babylonians, or more exotic ones, such as the Mayans, or more geographically remote ones, such as the Eskimo, than we do the Huns.

It is all the more fascinating, then, that with the possible exception of Genghis Khan, Attila the Hun is the most famous barbarian in world history. In fact, he's the one barbarian king whose name ordinary folk, uninterested in history, recognize in casual conversation—even if they aren't precisely sure who he was or what he did. That Attila remains so well known after nearly sixteen centuries is testament to the tremendous impact he had on the imagination of the world, during a reign briefer than Adolf Hitler's. To the people they attacked, the Huns became synonymous with catastrophe, invasion, and darkness. The Hun legend remained powerful for century after century: so much so that Allied propagandists in World Wars I and II could invent no greater insult than to call the Germans "the Huns." Never mind that it was the ancient Germanic nations who were in the forefront of resistance to the steppe nomads! Just as Nazism as a potent movement disappeared with the death of Hitler, the Hun empire crumbled with the death of Attila. His end meant the end of the Huns as a threat to Europe.

We have no reliable portrait of Attila. The medallion on the jacket of this novel is a gripping portrait, but it was drawn centuries later and only loosely fits the verbal descriptions we have of the great king. The addition of devil like goat horns in the hair suggests that the artist exercised considerable freedom of expression. Attila's exact birth date, early life, rise to power, detailed military tactics, and precise methods of administration are mostly unknown. His burial place has never been found, and the circumstances of his death remain a mystery. Some contend that he indeed drowned in his blood after a drunken stupor, but others have theorized that he must have been murdered. In terms of empire, it could be argued he had no lasting influence on the politics of Europe. Yet Attila is the one barbarian we remember. Why?

The only parallel to this irony that I can think of is Jesus of Nazareth, another for whom we have no likeness and who seemed to die ignominiously, only to become the source of one of the world's great religions. While opposites in their careers and purpose, both men obviously had a charisma that left a permanent impression, and a legend and legacy far greater than the immediate facts of their own brief lives.

In Attila's case, the reason he is remembered, I believe, is because of the threat he represented and the immense sacrifice that was required to stop him. Simply put, if Attila had not been defeated at the Battle of Châlons (also known as Maurica, for a Roman crossroads, or the Battle of Nations or the Battle of the Catalaunian Fields) the remnants of Roman civilization preserved by the Christian Church would have been extinguished. The rise of Western Europe would have taken far longer, or it might have been simply absorbed by Islamic or Byzantine civilization, and the planet's history of exploration, conquest, and development would have played out far differently. The fact that Pope Leo helped persuade Attila to retreat from Italy in 452, which was trumpeted by the Church as a miracle, obviously added to the barbarian's legend. The more menacing Attila seems, the more miraculous the pope's success appears. Similarly, in the Nordic and German legend the *Nibelungenlied*, Attila is the basis for the character of Etzel, evidence of how he passed from history into song. In that saga, Etzel is the King of the Huns who the vengeful widow Kriemhild marries and who murders on her behalf: playing a role in story not too different, perhaps, from his role in life. The story of great Eastern invasion echoes and reechoes in Western literature, down to Tolkien's use of it in *The Lord of the Rings*. The Avars would come in the seventh century, the Magyars in the tenth, the Mongols in the thirteenth century, the Turks would besiege the gates of Vienna in the seventeenth century, and the Soviets would conquer in the twentieth. Attila's story resonates so strongly because it is, in part, Europe's story.

This opinion of the importance of Attila, argued by Gibbon in his classic *Decline and Fall of the Roman Empire* and in the nineteenth century by historians such as Edward Creasy in his book *Fifteen Decisive Battles of the World*, is not as popular among modern historians today. Scholars make their reputation by debunking the theories of their predecessors, and some argue that, unlike Genghis Khan, Attila essentially failed as both conqueror and empire maker. To them, Châlons was but an episode in a long saga of Roman decay and the Huns a people who vanished like smoke. All that Flavius Aetius, "the Last of the Romans," achieved at the battle, they contend, was brief continuation of a dying status quo. That Aetius let Attila survive and retreat would seem to make the campaign of 451 even less significant.

Added to this dismissal is disbelief that the Battle of Châlons-sur-Marne (which actually is believed to have occurred closer to present-day Troyes, France) was anything near the titanic struggle portrayed by ancient and medieval historians. These chroniclers suggest numbers engaged of five hundred thousand to a million men, and a death count of one hundred sixty thousand to three hundred thousand soldiers. Such estimates indeed seem fantastic, prone to the hyperbolic exaggeration of the early Dark Ages. Modern scholars routinely cut estimates of the numbers engaged and casualties inflicted in some ancient battles (but not others, for reasons never clear to this author) to a tenth or less, simply out of disbelief in such staggering figures.

I endorse a view somewhere between these ancients and moderns. Just as believers in Christianity argue that *something* happened after Jesus' death to spark a new religion, however improbable the Resurrection is for some to swallow, so I suggest that *something* so set Attila's campaign in Gaul apart from the ordinary barbarian invasion that the memory of it reverberates to the present day. "The fight grew fierce, confused, monstrous, unrelenting—a fight whose like no ancient time has ever recorded," wrote the late ancient chronicler Jordanes. "In this most famous war of the bravest tribes, one hundred sixty thousand men are said to have been slain on both sides." The writer Idiatus puts the number killed at three hundred thousand.

Given that the total casualties of the American Civil War's bloodiest single day, at Antietam, were twenty-three thousand, such a number seems improbable in the extreme. How could the armies of late antiquity supply, move, and command such numbers? And yet something extraordinary happened at Châlons. Ancient armies, particularly barbarian ones, required none of the complex supply we take for granted today: Great numbers might indeed have been assembled for a season's campaigning. What American would believe in the days before Pearl Harbor that by 1945, the United States—with half its present population—could afford to have enlisted sixteen million men and women under arms? Or that the Soviet Union could absorb twenty million dead in that war and still be counted one of the winners? Or that at Woodstock, New York, half a million young people would assemble for an outdoor rock concert in the rain? People do extraordinary things. Attila's greatest battle was probably one of them, though its precise details will never be known. Even its location is vague. Personal inspection of the beautifully rolling countryside between Châlons and Troyes showed a hundred places that fit the vague details of hill and stream described by Jordanes. French military officers have made a hobby of looking for the battlefield, without success. This imprecision is not unusual. The exact site of many decisive ancient battles such as Cannae, Plataea, Issus, and Zama are not known. The ancients didn't make battlefields into parks.

We are hampered because our primary sources about the Huns are so meager. There are three that seem primary. One is the Roman historian Ammianus Marcellinus, who wrote of the early Huns. Another is Olympiodorus of Thebes, whose account of a visit to the Huns was lost but who was used as a source in the surviving accounts by other ancient historians. A third is Priscus of Panium, who accompanied the ill-fated embassy, with its assassination plot, to Attila. He is the inspiration (though the real historian was older and better connected) for Jonas. It is probably a lost fragment of Priscus that provides the later Jordanes with a vivid word picture of Attila: "Haughty in his carriage, casting his eyes about him on all sides so that the proud man's power was to be seen in the very movement of his body . . . He was short of stature with a broad chest, massive head, and small eyes. His beard was thin and sprinkled with gray, his nose flat, and his complexion swarthy, showing thus the signs of his origins."

What *was* the Hun homeland? We don't know. Some scholars put

their starting point as far east as Mongolia, others on the steppes of Rus-
sia. Their origin was a mystery to the Romans, but legend has them appearing on the world stage after following a white deer across the
marshes at the Straits of Kerch into the Crimea.

So, what in this novel is "true"? All the principal characters, with
the exception of Jonas, Ilana, and Skilla, are real-life historical figures.
I've invented details of their lives and words to fit my story, but their
general role is fairly accurate. My depiction of the embassy to Attila and
the campaign of 451 roughly follows the occasionally confusing account
we have from Priscus and other historians. The "facts" include a possible conspiracy by the Huns and King Sangibanus to betray Aurelia (Orléans), and Attila's desperate construction of a funeral pyre after the
awful battle. Yet even the most basic points, such as whether Orléans
was *really* besieged, or whether Attila *really* built the pyre, are recorded in
some accounts but not in others. Such are the problems of the history of
late antiquity.

To research this book I've not only read what accounts we have but
also retraced Attila's likely invasion route in Europe. I visited museums,
looked at surviving artifacts, and did my best to bring back to life a period of extremely complex politics and culture. The task is not easy because no nation wants to claim the Huns. Even the Hungarian National
Museum, while it does have a single room briefly discussing this mysterious people, declines to point out that its nation's name stems from
them. While Attila is still a popular name in Hungary and Budapest
even premiered a rock opera about the famed king in 1993, the country
prefers to date its origin from the Magyars.

Yet what a pity that records are not more complete! Recent studies
have tended to cast "barbarians" in a more favorable light. Perhaps the
Huns deserve better. And my suspicion is that the reality of that tumul-
tuous time was far stranger than what I have imagined. It must have produced true stories, now lost, of conflict and heroism as fascinating as
those in the Wild West. How people must have struggled to keep their
footing on the cracking ice of the Roman Empire!

I have invented a great deal in my plot, of course. There is no
recorded theft of the great sword; all we have is mention of its existence.

(Hungarian royalty actually claimed to have rediscovered the sword six centuries later.) As far as we know, Zerco was merely an unfortunate jester, not an imperial spy, though he was married as described and traded back and forth between Aetius and Attila. While Eudoxius did lead an unsuccessful revolt against Rome and fled to Attila, there is no record of his being an envoy to the Vandals—even though the threat that Gaiseric represented to Rome did enter into Attila's strategic thinking. Bishop Anianus did rally troops on the walls of Aurelia, and a hermit did call Attila "the Scourge of God," but my suggestion that the two are the same person is fictional. There is no report of a fire at Attila's palace set by a woman named Ilana, and Jonas's pivotal role in great events is, alas, made up. In short, I freely embroidered already fascinating history to tell a good yarn.

I must also apologize for inflicting on the reader a vast and confusing geography of world war at a time when names were in flux. Caesar's Gaul, for example, was actually by this time known more by the names of its Roman provinces, such as Aquitania. The Frankish triumph that would give it the name France was still in the future. The Celtic city of Cenabum had become the Roman city of Aurelia or Aurelionum, evolving into the French city of Orléans. To help orient modern readers, Constantinople is today's Istanbul, the ruined city of Naissus is the Balkan city of Niš, the abandoned fort of Aquincum is in the suburbs of Budapest, the Roman tower that Skilla attacks is southeast of Austria's Salzburg, the "wasps" of Sumelocenna are in modern-day Rottenburg, Augusta Treverorum is Germany's Trier, and Tolosa became France's Toulouse.

Who was Attila? What did he mean to history? In many ways his story is as foggy, and fascinating, as that of King Arthur. One thing we do know. The kingdoms that survived the assault of the Huns and the collapse of the Romans, evolved into Western Europe—and thus the civilization that still dominates the world today. When those ancient and doughty warriors beat back the Huns, they laid the foundation for our modern security. To go to the farmland around Troyes and imagine the ghosts of tens of thousands of charging cavalrymen, deciding the fate of the world is a moving experience.

A reader can also visit the island on which Jonas and Ilana finally settled. It's in the Loire River at the town of Amboise in the heart of French château country, the only island high enough in that region to escape frequent flooding. Near where the couple's home stood there is a splendid view westward of the river and its gentle valley.

There is also a sad war memorial, partially sunken into the earth, recording the names of local men killed in recent wars. Unsurprisingly, a section on that memorial has been left blank, providing room for future inscriptions.

So does history march on.